WILLIAM WASSERSTROM
is the author of

Heiress of All the Ages
The Time of *The Dial*

a DIAL
miscellany

Edited with an
Introduction by

WILLIAM
WASSERSTROM

SYRACUSE UNIVERSITY PRESS   1963

810.82
D 54 d
72817
January, 1971

SU
PRESS

Set in Linotype Old Style No. 7, with
display in Monotype Deepdene. Designed
by Freeman Champney. Jacket design by
Freeman Champney and Frank Mahood.

*Manufactured in the United States of America
by Vail-Ballou Press, Inc., Binghamton, New York*

to my son, Robert

ACKNOWLEDGMENTS

It is a pleasure to thank those persons whose generosity has enabled me to complete this work. I am particularly grateful to Miss Louisa Dresser and Mr. Daniel Catton Rich of the Worcester Art Museum for advice in the selection of pictures for reproduction in this anthology. They have provided, too, the use of plates and cuts taken from their own collection. Dr. Nicholas Joost of Southern Illinois University, himself a serious student of *The Dial,* has given up, in behalf of this project, certain claims to material that interested us both. Mr. Walter A. Edwards and Mr. Hermann Riccius have maintained interests of another kind which I have sought to honor. And Dr. J. S. Watson, Jr., *The Dial's* publisher, has managed somehow to concern himself with the fate of my effort and simultaneously to furnish me with as much freedom as I required. Finally, Dean Frank Piskor, Vice-President for Academic Affairs at Syracuse University, provided a grant-in-aid which eliminated the problem of money and allowed me to concentrate on the magazine itself.

WILLIAM WASSERSTROM

Briant's Neck
Mashpee, Massachusetts
June, 1963

CONTENTS

ACKNOWLEDGMENTS vi

INTRODUCTION xi

PROSE FROM *THE DIAL*

James Oppenheim, *Poetry—Our First National Art* 1

John Gould Fletcher, *The Spirit of the Old Hotel* 7

Albert C. Barnes, *Renoir: An Appreciation* 11

John Dewey, *Americanism and Localism* 14

Kenneth Burke, *Mrs. Maecenas* 20

Jean Cocteau, *Cock and Harlequin* (translated by Rollo H. Myers) 35

Louis Aragon, *"Madame a sa Tour Monte . . ."*
(translated by Gilbert Seldes) 57

D. H. Lawrence, *An Episode* 69

Amy Lowell, *A Bird's-Eye View of E. A. Robinson* 75

A. L. Kroeber, *A Study of Language* (review of
Language, by Edward Sapir) 88

John Dos Passos, *Off the Shoals* (review of
The Enormous Room, by E. E. Cummings) 106

Luigi Pirandello, *The Man with the Flower in His Mouth*
(translated by Arthur Livingston) 133

D. H. Lawrence, *Model Americans* (review of
Americans, by Stuart P. Sherman) 147

G. Santayana, *A Long Way Round to Nirvana* 165

Miguel de Unamuno, *The Cavern of Silence*
(translated by Louis How) 176

Marianne Moore, *Well Moused, Lion* (review of
Harmonium, by Wallace Stevens) 196

Padraic Colum, *A Note on Hawaiian Poetry* 213

Glenway Wescott, *In a Thicket* 220

Clive Bell, *Dr Freud on Art* 227

William Carlos Williams, *Marianne Moore* (review of
Observations, by Marianne Moore) 232

Feodor Dostoevsky, *A Christmas Story*
    (translated by C. M. Grand) 243
Gilbert Seldes, *Spring Flight* (review of
    The Great Gatsby, by F. Scott Fitzgerald) 255
Yvor Winters, *Mina Loy* 273
Bertrand Russell, *The Meaning of Meaning* (review of
    The Meaning of Meaning, by Ogden and Richards) 277
Seán O'Faoláin, *Under the Roof* 285
Kenneth Burke, *A "Logic" of History* (review of
    The Decline of the West, by Oswald Spengler) 289
I. A. Richards, *Gerard Hopkins* 296
T. S. Eliot, *Literature, Science, and Dogma* (review of
    Science and Poetry, by I. A. Richards) 305
Robert Hillyer, *Apparition in Early Autumn* 315
Paul Claudel, *A Glance at the Soul of Japan*
    (translated by Lillian Chamberlain) 334
Albert Halper, *On the Shore* 346
Conrad Aiken, *Retreat* (review of *For Lancelot Andrewes,*
    Essays on Style and Order, by T. S. Eliot) 355

VERSE FROM *THE DIAL*

Carl Sandburg, *The Lawyers Know Too Much* 6
Edna St. Vincent Millay, *To Love Impuissant* 10
James Joyce, *A Memory of the Players in a*
    Mirror at Midnight 19
Marianne Moore, *Picking and Choosing* 33
Ezra Pound, *The Fifth Canto* 43
Maxwell Bodenheim, *Instructions for a Ballet* 73
Wallace Stevens, *Revue* 92
Mina Loy, *Apology of Genius* 104
Babette Deutsch, *Hibernal* 112
E. E. Cummings, *Poem* 120
Djuna Barnes, *First Communion* 124
William Carlos Williams, *Full Moon* 183
Lola Ridge, *Mo-Ti* 204
Padraic Colum, *Three Hawaiian Poems* 217
Genevieve Taggard, *Storm Centre* 231
T. S. Eliot, *The Hollow Men* 241

Malcolm Cowley, *Those of Lucifer* 261
Archibald MacLeish, *Nocturne* 269
Hart Crane, *To Brooklyn Bridge* 313
William Butler Yeats, *Among Schoolchildren* 319
Louis Zukofsky, *Four Poems* 332
Stanley J. Kunitz, *Death in Moonlight* 350

DEPARTMENTS OF *THE DIAL*

T. S. Eliot, London Letter (October, 1921) 47
Henry McBride, Modern Art (December, 1921) 51
Editors' Comment, on a letter from
     Vernon Squires, University of North Dakota 54
Paul Rosenfeld, Musical Chronicle (January, 1922) 66
Ezra Pound, Paris Letter (June, 1922) 97
John Eglinton, Dublin Letter (October, 1922) 113
Editors' Comment, on *The Dial*'s
     award to T. S. Eliot 117
Edmund Wilson, Jr., The Theatre (May, 1923) 121
Raffaello Piccoli, Italian Letter (May, 1923) 125
Editors' Comment, on *The Literary Review* 143
Thomas Mann, German Letter (October, 1923) 155
Henry McBride, Modern Art (November, 1923) 162
Paul Rosenfeld, Musical Chronicle (November, 1923) 173
Alexander Eliasberg, Russian Letter (February, 1924) 184
José Ortega y Gasset, Spanish Letter (October, 1924) 206
Editors' Comment, "THE DIAL is an intellectual sewer." . . . 250
Briefer Mention, book reviews 258
Paul Morand, Paris Letter (June, 1926) 262
Henry McBride, Modern Art (May, 1926) 270
Paul Rosenfeld, Musical Chronicle (April, 1927) 310
Gilbert Seldes, The Theatre (January, 1928) 322
Raymond Mortimer, London Letter (March, 1928) 328
Paul Morand, Paris Letter (April, 1929) 351

NOTES ON CONTRIBUTORS 359

INTRODUCTION

IN COMPOSING this anthology, I have not planned to present merely a collection of pieces from an old journal, once famous but now scarcely known, a collection which might help to restore *The Dial* to its special place in the modern history of American letters. Nor do I aim simply to reproduce individual items of prose and verse, still fresh despite a forty-year burial in the library stacks. Rather I have sought primarily to dramatize habits of thought and events of history unknown among younger writers and readers who are informed about only those segments of life in the 1920's which are transmitted in a tidy cluster of clichés and legends. Accustomed to hearing echoes of scandal and vice (the Fatty Arbuckle Case, Sacco and Vanzetti), of scandal and virtue (the *Ulysses* Case and the heroism of Margaret Anderson's *Little Review*), and of scandal and wit (Scott Fitzgerald and *Vanity Fair*), members of the newest generation are taught either to glamorize or derogate life in the 1920's. If they are serious students of modern opinion, they are expected to assume fixed views on the presiding figures of our time. Today, they are enjoined to despise Eliot and idolize William Carlos Williams, relish E. E. Cummings and reject Marianne Moore, marvel at Wallace Stevens, abominate or glorify Ezra Pound, worship Joyce and disregard Mann, mourn Kafka and revere Rilke, recall Gide, neglect Van Wyck Brooks and Lewis Mumford, dismiss Kenneth Burke, admire Aaron Copland, honor Stravinsky, attend Arnold Schoenberg, revive Edgar Varèse, enjoy Gertrude Stein, forget Alfred Stieglitz and John Marin, celebrate Freud and Picasso.

My list of figures is of course carefully made: it includes leading contributors both to modern culture and, in one way or another, to *The Dial*. How extraordinary it is, therefore, that no critic or historian of letters, no art critic or historian of art, and no editor-in-chief or editor by choice has until now issued a volume of selections from the one magazine which represented to people everywhere high art and deep thought in the America of the 1920's. This lapse of interest is the more striking because lesser journals of the day (*The Double-Dealer*, the *Little Review*, *Midland*) as well as reviews closer to our own time (*Partisan, The*

American Scholar, Scrutiny, Horizon, Hudson, Chicago) have been monumentalized in this customary way. Until recently there was neither monument nor mention, and all reference to *The Dial* of the 1920's either evoked its historic coup, publication of "The Waste Land," or stressed Marianne Moore's role as editor. Not until recently, when two magazines, a quarterly of fiction and a quarterly of verse, decided to adopt the same title, was any substantial notice taken of *The Dial's* range and influence. The fiction *Dial* has been suspended.

With this new interest there is suddenly a new and growing sense of an authority and ambience evoked by the title itself. This is evident in a brochure written during 1961 by J. Wm. Myers, editor of the latest *Dial*: "POETRY DIAL is a magazine of new verse bearing a distinguished old name—one that from 1840 to the present has been synonymous with works of unique literary significance. It was founded as THE DIAL in New England by Ralph Waldo Emerson and Margaret Fuller but was to reach its poetic summit during the 1920's under the editorship of Marianne Moore. . . . It is in this tradition of 'the father of the American little magazine' that POETRY DIAL continues to publish the work of the new poets. Therefore, the editorial attitude once expressed by Miss Moore shall be our touchstone, 'if a magazine isn't to be simply a waste of good white paper, it ought to print with some regularity, either such work as would otherwise have to wait years for publication, or such as would not be acceptable elsewhere.' "

But even now there is no general awareness of the originality of its taste or the authority of its style in our letters. Almost no one seems to recall that this magazine established the principle of an annual award, giving "$2000 for service to American literature." Yet it was *The Dial* Award that introduced our current modes of celebration, those annual rites with which magazines, publishers, foundations, and academies now honor new work. From 1921 until 1929, *The Dial* Award, conferred not only to celebrate work accomplished but also to support genius not yet fulfilled, went to the most daring and durable of our writers: Sherwood Anderson, Eliot, Brooks, Marianne Moore, Cummings, Williams, Pound, Kenneth Burke.[1] Of this group, the editors claimed only Cummings as their discovery. They claimed too that they did not specialize

[1] In 1929 the editors considered giving the award to Wallace Stevens but decided on Burke mainly because they admired his techniques and goals but in part, too, because they were unable to pry poems in any number and with any regularity from Stevens.

in first publication and, as we shall see, that they avoided specialization of any kind. From then until now, *The Dial's* critics, having decided to take its editors at their word, have disregarded its prodigious number of firsts and have complained of its use of seconds—of Schnitzler and Von Hofmannsthal and several Georges: Moore, Saintsbury, Santayana.

As a result, almost nobody remembers that J. S. Watson, Jr., the publisher, translated for and printed in his magazine the first English rendition of Rimbaud's *A Season in Hell*. No one recalls that Eliot, deciding to permit this journal to publish "The Waste Land," chose a paper which had already promoted a considerable number of earlier novelties in verse, drama, criticism, and fiction—works by Giraudoux ("Wreck"), Andreyev ("He, the One who Gets Slapped"), Lawrence ("Snake"), Ivan Bunin ("The Gentleman from San Francisco"), Yeats ("Michael Robartes and the Dancer" and "The Second Coming"), and Pound ("Hugh Selwyn Mauberly"). After 1922, *The Dial* would offer Sherwood Anderson's "I'm a Fool," Julien Benda's "Belphégor," Cummings' "Him," Mann's "Disorder and Early Sorrow" and "Death in Venice," Proust's "Saint Loup," Gertrude Stein's "A Long Gay Book," Paul Valéry's "Introduction to the Method of Leonardo da Vinci." In its pages, too, we find the first extended mention or treatment in America of Brecht, Kafka, Pasternak, and Rilke, and the first acceptance or appearance of Georgia O'Keeffe, Glenway Wescott, and Stanley J. Kunitz. Although this list of names and titles contains some that everyone will recognize and some that specialists alone are likely to know, the remarkable thing about it is not its length but—for both the general reader and the special student—its distinction. Realizing, finally, that even Hart Crane was paid his "first literary money" by *The Dial*, it is surprising to hear Ezra Pound say, in summary of nearly ten years of monthly publication, "*The Dial* might fool the casual observer; but its policy was *not* to get the best work or best writers. It got some. But Thayer . . . aimed at names, wanted European celebrities and spent vast sums getting their left-overs." [2]

The particular value of Pound's remark is not the precision of its judgment but the cogency of its confusion in judging *The Dial's* policy and accomplishment. His comment joins two states of mind—disrespect and bewilderment—which until recently underlay virtually every criticism of this magazine's aims and methods. William Carlos Williams,

[2] *The Letters of Ezra Pound 1907–1941*, edited by D. D. Paige (New York 1950), 346.

for example, tore from a 1921 copy a reproduction of Chagall's "On Dit" and wrote in the margin: "If there is a loonier pack of nit wits in the world than you fellows who are making The Dial, they are not advertising it to the world as you are. This is the brazenest kind of prostitution, because it is colossal affectation. The Greenwich Village brand of moral and spiritual and artistic degeneracy. You are not discovering new worlds, but only helping to ruin the beauty in this. You ought to be suppressed—and shamed." [3] Williams' fury was the more heartfelt because he was a leading spokesman for one of the leading principles of art in his time, the doctrine that men and civilization could in fact be reformed and redeemed, that our world could be rediscovered, by imagination. He lambasted *The Dial* for neglect of this first duty of men of letters in America. Furthermore, he was convinced that *The Dial* was criminal in the related matter of payment to contributors, for he was certain that the editor maintained two scales of pay, one for notables abroad and another for hired hands at home. He wrote to the editors wondering how such a procedure would help to inspire native writers to create stories and poems of the highest order. However trivial this complaint sounds now, it pervaded the entire literary community in America forty years ago despite the fact that *The Dial,* as the managing editor Gilbert Seldes explained to Williams, adhered to one pay scale: two cents a word for prose and twenty dollars a page for verse. Although there were occasional demands for more money by one or another noted European, *The Dial's* records show no exceptions.

Paying as much as they could afford for the best work they could find, domestic and foreign, blending economic and literary policy, the editor and publisher undertook to fulfill the very program on which Williams took his stand. Unlike Pound or Williams or any other savior, however, they decided that their journal would proclaim no dogmas and embrace no causes. Instead, they sought to make *The Dial* a perfect model, in quintessence, of its own subject. And although the magazine was called a "Miscellany," Scofield Thayer, the founding editor, did not permit his staff to put together, slapdash, a monthly book of miscellaneous pretty poems and pictures. On the contrary, Thayer insisted that each issue, ninety-six pages long, must be no less carefully made than the best of its pieces. In creating his journal, Thayer introduced an idea new to the history of literary journalism: *The Dial* is unique in letters because it was designed to serve not merely as a vehicle but mainly as a symbol of the highest imaginable art.

[3] Williams' comment is found in *The Dial* papers, Yale University Library.

This credo is most clearly seen in an undated office memorandum, "General Instructions," itself auspicious because it was composed in order to furnish Thayer's successor Marianne Moore with a series of directives which would fix the form and guarantee the quality of the magazine. And from 1925 until 1929, Miss Moore, who shared Thayer's fervor for form, was inflexible in applying the rules he had placed in her trust. "Verse like illustrations should be used to break up long prose stretches," she was told. Not because he was fussy but because he insisted that each item be properly displayed, he required that "two pieces of fiction, like two pieces of verse by different poets, should not be juxtaposed." "Some illustration . . . should if possible immediately precede the foreign Letter or precede whatever precedes the foreign Letter, thus not having all illustrations together in the front of the magazine. No pictures should appear later in the magazine than the heading Book Reviews. . . . Sculpture should be set against black or white background; bronze against white; marble against solid black. Never gray background." *"Look up carefully all information."* "Look up all quotations, *verify everything.*" "Impressionistic figures should follow realistic, and landscape follow figures." Today, reflecting on the whole effect of Thayer's scruple and solicitude, generosity and wit, Malcolm Cowley, a man once unfriendly to *The Dial* but devoted to Harold Loeb's *Broom,* says he is now convinced, "It was the best magazine of the arts that we have had in this country." [4]

This is sudden, this current habit of acclaim which our key men of the 1920's assume in place of their earlier habit, obloquy. Despite acclaim, no one seems to recognize how many new works and writers *The Dial* sponsored, how luminously its shape manifested its design, how exemplary was its conduct of literary affairs, and how consistent, indeed traditional, was its idea of mission. No longer is *The Dial's* quality at issue, nor the value of the enterprise itself. But as Williams' note shows, bewilderment continues to be a main motif of thought whenever anyone refers to this murky matter of *The Dial's* program for culture and art in America. "Whatever Scofield Thayer's interest in publishing that periodical may have been it certainly was an original effort geared to the times. My receipt of The Dial's Award was an epoch making event for me, it put me on my feet." [5]

Although nobody any longer questions its influence or value or service, what remains unclarified still is specified in another note, this time from

[4] Letter, Cowley to Wasserstrom, November 29, 1958.
[5] Letter, Williams to Wasserstrom, November 13, 1958.

Lincoln Kirstein, who says that Eliot's *Criterion* and *The Dial* were the "two dominant influences" on his journal, *Hound & Horn*. "However, the Criterion was, to me, by far the more massive influence, due to our devotion to Eliot at that time; his mind was a great focus for good and bad, but it was focussed and his eye and ear were one person's; one never felt that the Dial had such a concentration of personal authority. . . . Eliot was an Editor . . . a Voice" whereas *The Dial* was filled each month with "goodies." [6] Associating Kirstein's view with Pound's and Williams' and Cowley's, we recognize why *The Dial* confused its most responsive readers and why, too, no one hitherto has offered an anthology drawn from its pages. All literary reviews in England and on the Continent, those that precede *The Dial* and those that follow, represent the eye and ear and voice of a single editor. *The Dial* built its reputation on the quality of its reproductions, the elegance of its format, the weight of its paper, and the acuteness of its judgment. But it refused to echo any one man's voice. As a result it seemed to lack identity and conviction in an age when literary magazines were identified with this or that program for the reform of one or another abuse in the national republic and in the republic of letters. Now, today, it is time to determine what in fact *The Dial* did stand for. And in order to resolve this classic problem in the history of modern thought, we must return to 1919. In that year two young men, just out of Harvard, together bought a magazine which had been published more or less regularly since 1840 when Emerson and Margaret Fuller introduced their *Dial* in order to draw from the whole sphere of imagination in America, as Emerson said, those "thoughts and feelings which can impart life." [7]

2

The year 1919 was the year of catastrophe among intellectuals in America. It was then that the first group of expatriates left the United States and turned up in Paris, where most of them headed for the new bookshop opened by the young woman who was soon to publish *Ulysses*, Sylvia Beach. There the 1855 edition of *Leaves of Grass* was displayed in a kind of shrine. In this way Miss Beach dramatized the literary situ-

[6] Letter, Kirstein to Wasserstrom, November 20, 1958.
[7] In a review-essay on the transcendentalist *Dial*, Henry Steele Commager cites this comment taken from Emerson's "Address to the Readers." *Herald Tribune Books*, December 31, 1961, 3.

ation of the day, a time when Whitman was no longer the guiding genius of national life and when young men of American genius preferred exile abroad to displacement at home.

Just three years earlier, when most of these men had been still in college, Whitman's spirit had been visible everywhere. Most notably it had enlivened a journal called *The Seven Arts,* in which a group of writers (James Oppenheim, Paul Rosenfeld, Waldo Frank, Van Wyck Brooks, and, *ex officio,* Randolph Bourne) had hoped to accomplish what the politics of Herbert Croly's and Theodore Roosevelt's progressivism and the rhetoric and rectitude of Woodrow Wilson had failed to achieve. *The Seven Arts* itself had represented all the leading strains of thought with which, during the preceding ten years, a young generation of messianic bohemians had labored to create new forms of art, new theories of form designed to serve as emblems of virtue both in letters and in society. Their program had been coherent and portentous: because the arts incarnate the best creative energies of man, they argued, Americans must be induced to absorb high art not into a community chest but into the very heart of national culture. When the arts of this nation, supported by new movements in journalism, were properly reformed, this society would in the course of time reform itself. And at last it would be equipped to reassume its historic role as the chief instrument of reform among all nations in this world.

Years earlier, in 1904, this scheme for art and civilization had been offered by Alfred Stieglitz's *Camera Work* to a very small avant-garde audience of disciples. A dozen years later the same scheme in a different format, still avant-garde, was revived by Robert Coady for his journal *Soil* and designed for a public no larger than Stieglitz's. In 1916 Coady, like Stieglitz, spoke for a small group of close friends; fourteen years later, as William Troy remarked, Coady himself was "little remembered." Scarcely anyone recalled Coady's name because the man himself had been "too preoccupied with the future"; in 1930, however, Troy says, "his future has become our present." [8] Although Mr. Troy hoped to reclaim Coady's reputation, neither he nor anyone else has recorded the process by which novelties of thought in 1904 had become stock in trade in 1930. This process had been impelled a considerable distance forward by Randolph Bourne, who in 1917 assumed the office of prophet of American apocalypse in *The Seven Arts.* Leader of a "new fellowship,"

[8] William Troy, "The Story of the Little Magazines," *The Bookman,* LXX (February, 1930), 657–63.

no longer avant-garde, Bourne translated Stieglitz's and Coady's thought into a new vocabulary which dramatized his discontent with the "blind chaos" of American society, his will to create a "fine, free, articulate cultural order." Unlike *Camera Work* and *Soil, The Seven Arts* received general support from American audiences and acquired too an international following. "I rejoice," Romain Rolland told the editors, seeing a magazine in which "the American spirit may seek to achieve consciousness of its nature and its goal." Advising members of *The Seven Arts* group to seek out their "people's dreams," Rolland congratulated them for realizing that Americans compose the community of men "called to recreate the world."

It is a familiar story how this magazine, which flourished at first, soon began to flounder. When President Wilson adopted the course of war, Bourne decided that American entry represented a loss of national virtue, a perversion of the American idea, a failure of apocalypse. Despair replaced delight as the mood of Bourne's mind, for he and other American liberals, pacifists almost to a man, at first had believed that Wilson was truly neutralist. After the declaration of war, they had taken him at his word, trusting him to use "American participation as an instrument in liberalizing the war aims of all the Allied governments," Bourne said. They had hoped that the president would remain unaligned in spirit though committed in battle. Adopting this spirit, he would be qualified to serve in the councils of war; he alone would speak as a disinterested man of reason. But when in 1918 Wilson chose to support vested autocracy in Italy and France and England, *The Seven Arts* group decided America was itself no longer fit to assume extraordinary duties in the affairs of the world.

By 1919 Bourne was dead and *The Seven Arts* was discontinued. In its place were *Smart Set* and *Vanity Fair*. That year, amused but displeased by the condition of letters, distressed by the transfer abroad of Whitman's spirit, Scofield Thayer and James Sibley Watson, Jr. bought a magazine which had been in existence off and on since the Emerson-Margaret Fuller *Dial* of 1840. This original version was published in Boston until 1844. After sixteen years of silence, it reappeared in Cincinnati in 1860, edited by Moncure Daniel Conway. This version was short-lived, and in 1880 another *Dial* was introduced in Chicago, edited until 1916 by Francis F. Browne. During this period this serious but uninspired literary paper absorbed a little magazine of advanced thought, *The Chap-Book*, recalled today as the journal which serialized Henry

James' *What Maisie Knew* and published criticism by Yeats and poetry
by Stephen Crane. Despite this infusion, Browne's *Dial* languished, and
in 1916 Martyn Johnson took over and moved it to New York. Once
sprightly but now stuffy, said Harriet Monroe, editor of *Poetry, The
Dial* by 1918 had been reorganized as a fortnightly journal of social
criticism. Its board of editors included John Dewey, Randolph Bourne,
Thorstein Veblen, Lewis Mumford, and Thayer, its patron. In this form,
it embodied what we can label the "new journalism" in an age marked
by movements in those fields of social science such as the new sociology,
the new anthropology, the new philosophy, jurisprudence, and history
which had shaped what Morton G. White calls the revolt against
formalism, against dogma and delusion in American thought. Acquiring
this form, the journal sustained its fourth transformation since the
Emerson-Margaret Fuller *Dial*, first conceived as a journal which would
attend all spheres of imagination but specialize in none. At the time
when Thayer and Watson bought *The Dial*, therefore, this magazine
had managed to implicate its life in the new thought of each generation
for nearly eighty years.

In 1918 this historic journal seemed to have come to the end of its
life, in part because it lacked funds and in part because Dewey and
Bourne continued to bicker on the very issues, militarism and pacifism,
which had destroyed *The Seven Arts*. Dewey, Bourne's teacher at Columbia, had been a pacifist until 1916 when he shifted his ground. Bourne,
infuriated by the way a frenzy for war had unsettled the minds of our
best men, was convinced that Dewey had sold out to the worst of men,
to Columbia's President Nicholas Murray Butler. He decided too that
Dewey's philosophy was itself pernicious because the system, instru-
mentalism, permitted its creator to justify any act however immoral.
Dewey was of course outraged by Bourne's accusations; he believed
that Germany must be stopped and that the Allies required American
aid. Their debate, a clash of character as well as of opinion, involved all
leading artists and intellectuals in the two centers of culture, New York
and Chicago. And because both men were members of *The Dial's* board
of editors, this clash all but immobilized that magazine.

Thayer, who supported Johnson's paper chiefly as an act of friendship
for Bourne, had hoped to turn this *Dial* into a "vehicle for Bourne's
writing." [9] Because of Dewey's opposition, however, Johnson was compelled to remove Bourne's name from the masthead. Robert Morss

[9] Robert Morss Lovett, *All Our Years* (New York, 1948), 151-52.

Lovett, appointed as an arbiter, was assigned the task of finding a way which would enable both Dewey and Bourne to remain with the magazine. Although Bourne's death in 1918 solved Lovett's problem, this event did not distract Thayer from the pursuit of his plan. Toward the end of that year Thayer came to Watson, with whom he had edited *The Harvard Monthly,* with a new idea for a magazine. Watson agreed to Thayer's plan and proposed that they buy *The Dial.* Together, in 1919, they assumed the liabilities and direction of Johnson's journal.

In January, 1920, the first number of their *Dial* seemed to dramatize a striking discontinuity of ideas, an abyss between generations. Thayer and Watson seemed to speak for a new generation of intellectuals who, disenchanted by dreams of utopia, preferred to substitute the values of art for the values of politics. This view of the new magazine was supported by Thayer's pronouncements of policy, statements which appeared to stress leading issues in the life of art and to disregard troublesome and abiding issues in the life of society. Proposing to include "the best of Europe and the best of America—without any intention of making money, of compromising with popular prejudice, or of undertaking propaganda for any school of art," Watson and Thayer decided that *The Dial* would depend on "no aesthetic system" and embrace no "detailed aesthetic code." In 1920, at a time when *The Seven Arts* group, dispersed, was replaced by "smartly dressed young women from Vassar, Smith and Bryn Mawr and young men from Princeton or Yale" who gamboled, according to Horace Gregory, among the "latest fashions in dress, painting and literature," [10] and when *Century* or *Scribner's* or the *Literary Digest* presented William Lyon Phelps and Brander Matthews as men of authority, Thayer and Watson introduced their *Dial* as the only "complete magazine of the creative and critical arts" in America. Because they wanted to make available "the sort of writing we liked to read and the sort of pictures we liked to see," and because they wished to publish writers "whose work we thought the public should at least have a chance at" they were willing to invest $25,000 each, annually, in this "experiment." By 1922 the experiment had become a triumph: Thayer claimed that it was recognized "here and abroad as the leading review in the English language." By the middle of 1925, as Thayer prepared to turn over his duties to Marianne Moore, *The Dial* claimed the support of 30,000 readers.

The choice of Miss Moore as editor is worth special mention. In the

[10] Horace Gregory, *Amy Lowell* (New York, 1958), 183.

June, 1925 issue, Thayer suddenly announced his decision to leave America, ostensibly to "seek out a little leisure to try to write" but actually to seek Freud's help in Vienna. Although he admired Miss Moore, Thayer first chose Van Wyck Brooks to serve as editor. Brooks refused the offer and, in accord with Thayer's wishes, kept the exchange secret until 1958, when he related it to Gilbert Seldes, who told me. Publicly the first signs of Thayer's special interest in Marianne Moore appear in the announcement that she was to be given *The Dial* Award for 1924 and in an accompanying essay by Glenway Wescott on her new book of poems, *Observations*. Both award and essay record attentions considerably more grand than Marianne Moore had till then encountered in America and, taking her by surprise, affected her deeply. In an unpublished letter to the editor she expressed her feelings [11] and concluded, "I wish that if ever I may serve The Dial I may do it well." Within six months she was absorbed in full-time and single-minded service.

During his term as editor, Thayer had been obsessed by great ambitions, ambitions not measurable by statistics of size or number of readers. Although his obsession was implicit in advertising copy ("Every new subscriber [is] . . . a participant in the success of The Dial—a success which is making artistic history."), it is explicit in a debate between Miss Moore and *The New Republic* during 1927. Reading an editorial in *The New Republic* which stated that *The Dial* had not encouraged a single new writer since 1920, Miss Moore bridled. "Whatever character The Dial may have," she explained, "is the result of a selection not of writers but of writing." Thus she justified her way, inherited from Thayer, of "running a magazine which pretends to general interest—a way which is apt to prove more encouraging to the reader than to the writer." In this subdued fashion Miss Moore defined aims to which Watson and Thayer had agreed in 1919 when together they decided to publish a magazine of art in which the national welfare would constitute their prime concern.

Their journal was to be based on the thinking of Randolph Bourne

[11] On December 23, 1924, she wrote thanking the editor for an "advance copy of The Dial" and saying that she was "deeply moved by that for which I have no adequate expression—your treatment of those whom you choose to champion." Chastened by the "beauty of Mr. Wescott's article," Miss Moore said that she "did not know how to receive so much." She contrasted *Poetry*'s "designation of me as a fanciful acrobat" with Thayer's remark associating her with "Emily Dickinson's rigorous splendor," and felt the latter to be "rare and humbling praise."

and, when Thayer and Watson decided to go ahead, despite Bourne's death, with their plan for a magazine, they reconstituted *The Dial* according to a sequence of ideas derived from Bourne during the last year of his life. Thayer saw himself as the chief heir of Bourne's thought, saw his own image described in Bourne's "Traps for the Unwary": "Do we not want minds with a touch of the apostolic about them," with a "certain edge . . . a little surly" but suffused by an "intellectual as well as an artistic conscience?" Agreeing with Bourne that politics must invariably pervert the American idea, that "the world will never understand our spirit except in terms of art," Thayer realized that his magazine could practice what this prophet preached only if it nurtured the spirit of art, not, in the fashion of *The Seven* Arts, the spirit of utopia. Furthermore, he realized that magazines published in the habitual way, the way of *Masses* or *The Little Review* or the fortnightly *Dial*, were doomed to short life. Such magazines, Miss Moore explained to the editors of *The New Republic*, were usually edited by contributors who were given "the run of the place." And because this was an exciting thing for writers, "magazines of this type" were often "more immediately encouraging to interesting new writers, not to mention movements, than magazines like The Dial."

   The Dial was a bewildering experiment in American journalism, therefore, because its publishers chose to echo no man's voice, to give no one movement the run of the place. By selecting Gilbert Seldes as their specialist in drama and popular culture; Paul Rosenfeld, a disciple of Stieglitz, as their music critic; and Henry McBride, an admirer of Coady, as their art critic,[12] Thayer and Watson presented a synthesis of voices and movements in the arts of the nation. Favoring a balance of excitements, they labored to confront society at large with a literary magazine which was itself an incarnation of the creative life. Out of materials as yet inchoate in the American imagination, Thayer and Watson undertook to fashion a permanent, not short-lived, "free, articulate cultural order" in which men of art and ordinary men shared common bonds of community. Introducing their society to those images of order available only in the most intense works of imagination, their *Dial* would become the first magazine in America which merged its subject and its

[12] "Coady died without much recognition from the public. He did not die without vividly impressing his ideas upon a few of his contemporaries and ideas as potent as his were to have a vitality of their own." Henry McBride, "Modern Art," *The Dial*, LXX (March, 1921), 356–58.

form, the arts of salvation, in order to serve as a mediator between the avant-garde and the general reader. In this way, it would accomplish Emerson's goal, would "impart" true life to a disillusioned people; in this way, too, Watson and Thayer would, in memory of Randolph Bourne, suffuse the nation with Whitman's spirit.

3

The Dial of the 1920's fused image and idea, subject and form. I hope here to recreate its idea, transmit its creed. This task became mine through a sequence of accidents which in turn help to explain why a *Dial* anthology appears almost thirty-five years late. Had the editors undertaken to print a conventional literary paper they would have fashioned a conventional literary group, some member of which at one time or other would have urged someone to publish this book. Or if the editors themselves after 1929 had engaged in the business of literature, had turned to the production or promotion of books, reputations, reviews, careers, a volume of this kind might long ago have seemed natural. But Miss Moore's vocation is of course poetry, and her closest associate during the last years of *The Dial*, Kenneth Burke, has been long engrossed by an attempt to fashion a comprehensive theory of language and culture.

The origins of neglect occur actually in 1925 when Thayer resigned as editor and left for Vienna, for a psychoanalysis with Freud. Thayer himself is a figure of abiding interest among men and women of the 1920's and is mentioned in nearly everyone's reminiscence or correspondence—Padraic and Mary Colum's, Llewellyn Powys' and Alyse Gregory's, Hart Crane's, Miss Moore's, Cummings', Williams'—where he is portrayed as a person of strange mood but compelling mind. Although he is not quite so glamourous a man as he is made to seem in the F. J. Hoffman, C. Allen, and C. F. Ulrich volume, *The Little Magazine,* nevertheless his life and fate have special fascination. His own fascination with Freud dates from the days of boyhood in Worcester, Massachusetts, during Freud's visit to Clark University in that city. Thayer's family lived across the street from Jonas Clark, from the house where G. Stanley Hall, founding president of the university, maintained rooms. Hall was a frequent visitor in the Thayer household; indeed Scofield Thayer's oldest friend today thinks that Freud may well have dined there in 1909. In any event, Freud's treatment was unsuccessful and

Thayer arrived home to live withdrawn from affairs. He continues to live so despite a flurry of attention in 1959 when the Worcester Art Museum presented mainly in his honor a display of paintings and prints called The Dial Collection. This collection, on permanent loan to that museum, is built around pictures Thayer bought for reproduction both in *The Dial* and in his portfolio, *Living Art*.

Watson's life is notable in other ways, but it too is marked by removal from the scenes of literature. During his time with the journal he took a degree in medicine. When in 1927 he returned to his home in Rochester, New York, he turned from the practice of medicine and letters to a wholly different kind of work, converting stables into a studio where he could experiment with the art of film. By 1937 he had made three films (*The Fall of the House of Usher, Lot in Sodom, Highlights and Shadows*) which are still shown and admired. Then in 1941 at the University of Rochester he began the serious study of a problem in radiology on which there had been nearly fifty years of almost fruitless inquiry. According to the former chairman of that department, George H. S. Ramsey, radiologists had long hoped to make a machine which would take X-ray motion pictures of internal organs but would limit exposure to radiation and furnish films of good quality. Watson was asked to help and before long "became a prime mover in the development of suitable apparatus and technics. . . . Mr. Sydney Weinberg, who had previously worked with Dr. Watson as an engineer, photographer, and scientific instrument maker, was brought into the project in 1947." By 1958 Watson and Weinberg had developed not only machines and techniques but also had organized the first national meeting of specialists in a field of study which now bears the name they invented: cinefluorography.

Because Watson preserves a passion for simplicity and anonymity I have resisted the allure of adornment and offered straight fact. But Watson's passion, Thayer's illness, Miss Moore's absorption in verse, and Burke's involvement in criticism, taken together, help to clarify some reasons why *The Dial* has remained till now uncelebrated. No member of that extraordinary group has lobbied for its recognition as a major event of modern American thought. Both the magazine and the 1920's represent a period of work which led to other acts and times no less stirring. Although all the members of the group are, I think, pleased to see this anthology, they may not agree without dissent to arguments and items in the volume itself.

A few observations justifying my decision to reprint one or another piece will, I trust, stand for a general statement on the miscellany as a whole. My choice of James Oppenheim's article on the ways American poetry might address and mold its public, for example, is grounded in *The Dial's* origins. After selecting "Poetry—Our First National Art," I was led to include Dewey's "Americanism and Localism," itself written after all in response to Oppenheim. In this way my anthology not only evokes the presiding mood of literary men in that day but also, within its own pages, illustrates the history of a magazine which began its career by sponsoring "the sort of criticism that was advanced by *The Seven Arts* group."[13] Within a few years we find Eliot, Pound, Burke, and Richards maintaining Watson's view of criticism, a view first uttered by J. E. Spingarn in 1910 in a historic essay, "The New Criticism." Spingarn claimed that a critic's job is to concentrate on the work of art, the object itself, and not to concern himself with the utility of its politics or sociology or morality. Before long New Criticism and nationalist criticism fused in *The Dial,* and we find the management concerned to publish works and studies of literature, painting, music, and popular culture which display the American and the human spirit at the top of its form. From Aragon to Zukofsky, Amy Lowell to Albert Halper, Cocteau and Pirandello to Mann and Rilke, in all departments *The Dial* sought to animate what Thayer called, in outrageous locution, the "Western-Civilized-Christian-European-American-tradition." This tradition, Thayer's desire to support collaboration among leading members of the republic of letters, is most succinctly shown in the conjunction of Burke's "Mrs. Maecenas" with Miss Moore's "Picking and Choosing." The poem, which treats art and criticism, includes reference to the writer within its statement and structure.

But because men fallible in prose style are fallible in other acts of judgment too, I have included certain quirks or lapses of taste which reveal some half-forgotten tendencies of modern thought. We discover a preference for plotlessness in fiction (Fletcher and Hillyer), for romantic lushness of imagery in prose (Rosenfeld) and in verse (Miss Millay). We find too a dated delight in the low blow of argument, the kind of cleverness which joins acerbity and urbanity in comment directed at a man rather than at his ideas (Bell). Above all, we hear in *The*

[13] F. J. Hoffman, C. Allen, C. F. Ulrich, *The Little Magazine, A History and a Bibliography* (Princeton, 1946), 196. This book, the standard work on American literary reviews, offers a blurred but useful short history of *The Dial.*

Dial's tone a fusion of jocularity and piety (Seldes, McBride, Thayer himself) treating the big subject, Art. To our ear this sounds neither knowing nor chic but only self-conscious, as if in the 1920's young men felt that the vocation of letters was unseemly or unmanly, however virile.

Thayer's likes and dislikes too, because they often set the pattern for *The Dial*, have been taken into account either directly or indirectly in this collection. His taste in painting was doctrinaire, and it was he who decided, until 1925, which styles would be represented in the magazine. He regarded Picasso as the chief ornament of our time, rejecting his cubism and cherishing the work of his blue and rose periods. Because Thayer was uninterested in primitivism and abstractionism, in architecture and photography, *The Dial* seldom offered a work or a discussion of techniques or subjects which enlivened the arts of the 1920's. Thayer's enthusiasms were by no means dull, however, and led to special display of Lachaise, Marin, and Demuth. Although he printed an excessive number of stylized sketches, drawings, and caricatures, he was also responsible for introducing expressionist painters who had received little attention and no reputation in America: Kokoschka, Munch, Shiele, Masereel, Barlach, and Chagall. If, then, *The Dial* took few risks of taste, it did fortify and sanction the principle of innovation and experiment and seek to claim for art the same virtue it found in verse and fiction and criticism.[14]

Although I have included nearly all the famous names, I have tried to select materials which have not yet been reprinted elsewhere or have been reproduced in unfamiliar, unremembered, or untranslated books. Had I chosen only the most noted works, the anthology would have been impressive but superfluous. For this reason Eliot's "Literature, Science and Dogma" is offered instead of "Ulysses, Order and Myth," and an unfinished version of "The Hollow Men" is presented rather than "The

[14] Its claims, its creed, and its policy were brought together on one occasion in a unique essay by Paul Rosenfeld. This piece is the more striking in that it represents the sole occasion when Thayer recognized photography as a legitimate mode of imagination and, too, recognized Alfred Stieglitz as one "of the great affirmers of life." His "photographs are the justification of today," Rosenfeld said, because these provide "a perennial means by which all others of his time, who so desire, can help free themselves for the life of the spirit, the life of art." Paul Rosenfeld, "Stieglitz," *The Dial*, LXX (April, 1921), 397–409. For an extensive discussion of the visual arts, see Daniel Catton Rich, "Dial M for Modern," *The Dial and The Dial Collection* (Worcester, 1959), 7–24.

Waste Land." The same reason justifies the use of Mann's Letter and not, say, "Tristan"; one Picasso in place of the forty-seven (paintings, drawings, prints) which appeared from 1921 till 1929. Other figures (Yeats, Hart Crane, Stevens, Pound, Richards, Russell, Claudel, Miss Moore, Williams, Aiken) are presented at the zenith of achievement. Balancing brilliance with lapse of judgment, reprinting novel items by half-anonymous men alongside discarded items by our most famous men, I have intended both to evoke the 1920's *Dial* and to provide this volume with its own sanctions and value.

Despite substantial labor, I have been unable to trace the history of each piece. Poetry, of course, presents no special problems, but prose is customarily hard to track down. So far as I can tell, Oppenheim, Fletcher, Barnes, Dewey, Eliot, McBride, Aragon, Rosenfeld, Lawrence's "Episode," Eglinton, Piccoli, Mann, Santayana, Unamuno, Williams' "Marianne Moore," Eliasberg, Ortega, Winters, Russell, Richards,[15] Hillyer, and Mortimer are reprinted for the first time. Burke's "Mrs. Maecenas" was included in *White Oxen* (1924). Pound's Paris Letter, retitled "Ulysses," occurs in the *Literary Essays of Ezra Pound*, edited by T. S. Eliot (1954). Miss Lowell's study of Robinson, first presented as a lecture in the Brooklyn Institute of Arts and Sciences (January 4, 1917), later discussed in detail with Robinson himself, is found in her *Poetry and Poets* (1930). The Dos Passos review of Cummings is one of the few contemporary essays in *The Shock of Recognition*, edited by Edmund Wilson (1943). Pirandello's play is contained in *The One Act Plays of Pirandello*, edited by Arthur Livingston (1928). Wescott's story is in *Good-Bye Wisconsin* (1928). Some of Seldes' pieces on popular culture were shaped for *The Seven Lively Arts* (1924). Aiken's review of Eliot is part of *A Reviewer's ABC: Collected Criticism of Conrad Aiken*, edited by Rufus Blanchard (1959). A small section of Claudel's essay on Japan appears untranslated in *Pages de Prose*, edited by André Blanchet (1944); Cocteau, also untranslated, appears in *Poésie Critique*, edited by Henri Parisot (1945).

Surely the most notable items are the unique things, poems or essays essential to the careers of major writers but little known or as yet unstudied. Unamuno's "Cavern of Silence" and Ortega's Letter are among these, as is Santayana's essay on Freud, an essay which affirms and con-

---

[15] Reference to I. A. Richards' essay on Gerard M. Hopkins is, strangely, missing from the collective study of Hopkins' poetry by the *Kenyon* critics, 1945, where it is incorrectly listed as "The Windhover."

tradicts views expressed in a letter written that same year: "I have been reading a new book of Freud's and other things by his disciples. They are settling down to a steadier pace and reducing their paradoxes to very much what everybody has always known." Eliot's early, foreshortened version of "The Hollow Men" offers some clues both to the development of his art and to the creative process itself. For similar reasons Pound's fifth canto is remarkable. Eliot's poem in its final form offers whole new sections, becomes a *tour de force* of revision. In Pound's canto a few lines are moved up or down, one line is deleted altogether, and some spelling and punctuation are changed. Aside from a shift of "at" to "and," only one alteration seems to modify meaning—"Good Varchi" becomes "Our Benedetto." The striking thing in this show of method is Pound's control of his mind and its purposes, and this is of course a fact crucial to the biography of that notorious but eminent man.

Yeats' "Among School Children" records another extraordinary series of changes which date from the period between its appearance in *The Dial* (1927) and in *The Tower* (1928). Some changes at first seem minor, quibbles of a fussy mind, but are in fact substantial. The even rhythms of 1927 retain resonance in 1928 but grow jagged and acute. Instead of

> "That changed some childish day to tragedy—"
> "And wonder if she stood so at that age—"
> "Something of every paddler's heritage—"

we see

> "That changed some childish day to
>   tragedy—"
> "And wonder if she stood so at that
>   age—"
> "Something of every paddler's heri-
>   tage—"

"What quinto-cento finger" in *The Dial* turns up in *The Tower* as "What quattrocento finger" and leads toward another group of changes which alter sound and sense in radical ways.

> "And I though never of Ledean kind
> Have wrong to brood upon—enough of that,"

"And I though never of Ledean kind
Had pretty plumage once—enough of that,"

This prepares us for the act of genius inherent in a climactic change of phrase.

"Plato thought nature but a spume that plays
Upon the ghastly images of things"

"Plato thought nature but a spume that plays
Upon the ghastly paradigm of things"

The original line is interesting but the other is miraculous, and the two together offer a new enticement for scholars to brood. A similar invitation is offered by D. H. Lawrence's review of Stuart Pratt Sherman's *Americans*. Published in 1923, Lawrence's essay, "Model Americans," offers a minuscule version of the style and matter of that amazing book, *Studies in Classic American Literature* (1924). Not only Lawrentians but also those American critics who take these *Studies* as a point of departure in recent theories of American literature—Lionel Trilling, Leslie Fiedler, Ihab Hassan—will discover in this review-essay a prime source of new thought in modern criticism.[16]

Describing these few unique pieces I have not exhausted *The Dial*'s fascination or annotated all its rarities. But I come now to what is for me a final statement on a subject which has engaged my attention since April, 1957, when I introduced E. E. Cummings to an undergraduate audience at the University of Rochester. During the preceding weeks, trying to renew my sense of literary conditions in America when Cummings' work first appeared, I browsed in *The Dial*. Until then its title was all I had known. Thereafter, it furnished matter not only for repeated conversations with Dr. Watson, but also for lecture, essay, and book. Despite my effort to avoid saying again what is already in print, these remarks do repeat words and phrases available elsewhere. This summary essay, however, stresses an issue I have not until now developed

[16] I have come upon only one mention of this review in a note so misleading that it dispels any possible interest: "As a reviewer Lawrence was occasionally very amusing. Witness his analysis of Stuart P. Sherman's *Americans*." D. H. Lawrence, *Phoenix: The Posthumous Papers of D. H. Lawrence*, edited by Edward D. McDonald (New York, 1936), xix.

in any detail. Preparing this volume, I realized that *The Dial* is unique among little magazines not simply because it printed more original and influential work than any other journal in America or England, but mainly because, like Cummings that April evening in Rochester, it brought its audience to life. What had begun in 1919 as a form of art for art's sake had merged, by 1925, with the American messianic idea and at the end, in 1929, revealed, both to readers and writers, the most persuasive and intense way of conducting life and letters in our time.

a DIAL
miscellany

POETRY—OUR FIRST NATIONAL ART

By James Oppenheim

Russia first found herself as a people, that is, as a self-conscious nation, through prose fiction; Germany and England through the poetic play; Greece, Rome, and Italy through epics. It begins to appear as if the United States (what a name for a nation, and yet how apt!) is finding herself through a rather loosened-up lyric poetry.

Our land's name reveals our dilemma in art. A society of states, in which each state is a society of races, is not a nation in the Old World sense; it is not an organic fusion, but a collection, in which the differences are more marked than the likenesses. France, we say, has a soul, meaning that Frenchmen, to use James's phrase, "dip their roots in the same pool of consciousness," or more accurately, sub-consciousness; but Americans are held together not by unconscious identity, but by conscious ideals and interests. Americanism is not so much an impulse as a set of ready-made attitudes. Since these can be learned in a short time, the Americanization of immigrants goes on with rapidity.

One might expect then that an American national art would be an impossibility. The national novel, play, or epic requires typic characters, heroes who are the reflection of a people; but where is our typical American? And by typical I do not mean the conscious attitudes and manners of a man, but his essential character; for great art does not so much reveal the garb, speech, and habits, as those deep unconscious forces which differentiate one people from another. If, for instance, I see a certain kinship between J. J. Hill, Daniel Boone, Billy Sunday, and Theodore Roosevelt, or between Emerson, Dr. Eliot, John Dewey, and Woodrow Wilson, or between Lincoln, Gene Debs, John Brown, Mark Twain, and Jane Addams, I also find that, tested by the acid of art, they fail as national symbols. For not one of these is the national character *heightened and intensified,* but rather a sport, a divergence, a personal success. We must not be fooled by the fact that each group held certain ideas, attitudes, and manners in common; these are environmental and not hereditary; and the very fact that there is such a startling sameness in American exteriors argues that there is a corresponding diversity in the unconscious. We wear the same feathers but underneath we are immigrants from many lands.

This explains why our novelists never rise beyond a depiction of manners to a revealing of character. To begin with, only a few of the men mentioned could be subjected to deep treatment. Most of them are stiff fronts, behind which vacancy takes the place of the passions, tumults, *Weltanschauung,* and mystic grandeur which belong to the unconscious. Imagine Woodrow Wilson or Billy Sunday or T. R. as the hero of a great novel! How quickly each would become wooden and unconvincing! The trouble is that they are too typically American; the trouble is that a people united only by conscious bonds, have, for the sake of unity, denied their unconscious and alien character; and behind the striking samenesses gapes a void.

What then of such genuine and deep men as Lincoln and Gene Debs? At first glance we seem to have found what we are seeking. But alas, at second glance we see that their very depth differentiates them from the American people, and that when they are taken over into art they are like foreign particles, austerely and terribly separated from their social environment. Our nationalism screamed in the late war: where did it hold "malice toward none, and mercy for all," to say nothing of democracy? Where was "a race of Lincolns"?

Is the case then hopeless? Possibly yes for any art that requires typic characters; and curiously not so for semi-lyrical poetry. Mark Twain came the nearest to writing a national novel in Huckleberry Finn; and this for the excellent reason that taking a boy as his hero, he could approximate the psychic development of the nation. But we cannot have great national art so long as boys are the measure of our value.

In poetry, however, the case is different. Poetry is an excellent medium for giving environmental colour, snap-shots, ideals and abstract tendencies; it can give the vague flavour of a mixed society; and best of all it can reveal, not through a symbol, but directly, the unconscious of the poet. Now this unconscious is something passed on to the poet through a long descent; it is the common racial inheritance, and differs only according to the stock of the individual. Since he does not have to gather his expression round a typic character, that is, be concrete, he can vaguely allow that mystic depth which is common to all men. And since he strains this, as it were, through the sieve of the American environment, the American ideals, manners, scenery, and chaos, he gets a product which is universal on the one hand but on the other with what might be called the American flavour.

If we examine Walt Whitman we find that the surface or exterior is an arrangement of American facts and creeds, lifeless and discrete in themselves, but become vital because they are fused with the revelation of his own unconscious. In short, we have something universal, or say, human in the broadest sense—something equally the property of every race—camouflaged by American paint. That this is not America is obvious. Yet " 'tis enough, 'twill serve"—for it is indubitably American. We are all this universal masked by Americanism. Hence, its truly national character. Walt was Dutch, yet Carl Sandburg who is Swedish can prance his soul out to the same tunes and get a national expression with only a slightly different tinge. For, as I said before, this universal in us is conditioned by the stock we come from. Whitman and Sandburg differ from each other only in so far as the Dutch and Swedish differ.

Walt Whitman then gave us our first national art. How did he turn the trick? We had several other excellent poets, yet they never found the key which to-day unlocks American expression. I think it was because he realized that he must take a bold, conscious plunge, and not be afraid of creating art deliberately. Our poetry had been Colonial—whether English or European. Hence, the first task was to throw overboard those traditions; and the second was to find an expression more native to ourselves. But where find this? We have no folk, no soil song or literature: we have only our American speech, the resultant of new environment, mixture of races and new experience. This American speech is decidedly different in flavour and construction from English speech. It is not Colonial, but native, that is, environmental. It is a speech, however, which is not strictly polite. I think of Dante deciding to write in Italian vernacular instead of in Latin. Our Latin was our literary English. Whitman decided along Dante's line; namely, to write in American. The meaning of this is that he decided to take the only native expression we have, our conversation, and intensify it.

The result is curious. Without the rootage of folk-song and folk-art there is a certain thinness, a loss of overtones. But there are real compensations—the work is, as I said, indubitably American, fresh, spacious, and free. Perhaps also it might be said that Whitman raises American conversation to oratory; that he carries the common speech into the speaker's stand, and attempts thus to give it a less personal, a more collective fibre.

Our new generation of poets has been unable to ignore Whitman. The strange service he performed for us was to give us a substitute for folk-song. That is to say, we can't go back to folk-art, but can go back to Whitman and thus catch for our own work the overtones of an American past. That the result need not be strictly Whitmanic is obvious. Masters in Spoon River has used conversation and discarded oratory; Frost, Untermeyer, and Lindsay have done the same and discarded free verse; Amy Lowell has developed the form and wherever advisable discarded conversation.

It is necessary to note here that the Whitmanic attempt has appeared in our fiction and essay. Parallel with Whitman came Emerson, and out of Emerson, William James, and writers like Dewey, Veblen, and Randolph Bourne, save that James and Bourne, more than the others, incorporate the conversational in the Whitman manner. Dreiser and Anderson in fiction also spring from Whitman, though here we have the forerunner, Mark Twain; but their success I think is limited by the reasons given above. The result of all this many-stranded development, as well as an inner evolution, is a marked change in American conversation. At Whitman's time there was a choice between Colonial and popular. The choice is different to-day. Popular expression is not the only kind that is American; we have the beginning of an intelligentsia, and this younger world has a conversation of its own. That this conversation bears resemblance to the speech of H. G. Wells and Masefield is not surprising—for these two writers, as well as Rolland, have been under American influence. Wells owes much to William James, Rolland exceedingly much to Whitman. No better proof of the vitality of American style could be produced than this influence abroad.

I should say that our new poetry leans either to the conversation of our intelligentsia or to that of the mass and that its form is divided between the Whitmanic and the traditional. Perhaps more purely than the rest it is Sandburg who carries on the strict Whitman tradition, and takes the common speech, with its slang, as his basis. And it is quite possible that he is the most vital singer of us all. At any rate it would seem as if he, Frost, and Masters wrote most directly out of themselves, putting the accent on expression and giving second place to so-called style.

Recently, in one of our book stores, I went through a bundle of insurgent English poetry. I was shocked into the realization that the art-centre of English poetic expression has shifted from England to the United States: against the stale music, phonographic repetition, and forced freshness of the Englishmen I heard the prairie-breezes of Sandburg, the poignant deep cry of Masters, the colourful tumult of Amy Lowell, and other voices in our masterful chorus, behind which the sea of Whitman forever thunders. And this, I thought, is America. Have we great poetry, barring our one Homer? We do not know; but we do know that we have a genuine living art. An art, I should say, that will grow just in so far as our poets, after having assimilated them, learn to overcome the great masters—just in so far as they release themselves from the dominant influence of every tradition, including the Whitmanic, and trust to their deepest impulse. It is not by saying, "Go to, I will be American," but by allowing the direct impact of environment and the direct response, that they will produce a truer and more American art.

[FEBRUARY, 1920]

THE LAWYERS KNOW TOO MUCH

By Carl Sandburg

The lawyers, Bob, know too much.
They are chums of the books of old John Marshall.
They know it all, what a dead hand wrote,
A stiff dead hand and its knuckles crumbling,
The bones of the fingers a thin white ash.
> The lawyers know
> a dead man's thoughts too well.

In the heels of the higgling lawyers, Bob,
Too many slippery ifs and buts and howevers,
Too much hereinbefore provided whereas,
Too many doors to go in and out of.

> When the lawyers are through
> What is there left, Bob?
> Can a mouse nibble at it
> And find enough to fasten a tooth in?

> Why is there always a secret singing
> When a lawyer cashes in?
> Why does a hearse horse snicker
> Hauling a lawyer away?

The work of a bricklayer goes to the blue.
The knack of a mason outlasts a moon.
The hands of a plasterer hold a room together.
The land of a farmer wishes him back again.
> Singers of songs and dreamers of plays
> Build a house no wind blows over.
The lawyers—tell me why a hearse horse snickers
> hauling a lawyer's bones.

[JANUARY, 1920]

THE SPIRIT OF THE OLD HOTEL
To Edward

By John Gould Fletcher

The dining-room was very old. Nothing, one felt, had been altered in it for a century. From the massive silver candelabrum standing exactly in the middle of the buffet with console legs at one end of the room and seeming to overawe the entire space with its gleaming majesty, to the tall Etruscan Wedgwood vases in the lofty window embrasures, all was exactly the same as when old gentlemen in grey beaver hats and black stocks lifted tired, perspiring children out of postchaises, and the mail-coaches for Holyhead rolled past its open door. Nothing had changed, not even the position of the tables. The meals were still punctually ten minutes late, as they had always been; for however near the twentieth century might creep, there was a spirit which guarded the old hotel.

The mail-coaches for Holyhead no longer rolled by the door, and around the corner there was the desolation of empty yawning stables of granite to witness the fact. But the stables had never been torn down, and if any traveller had deliberately entered the hotel to ask "when the 'bus started for Bangor," no one would have known. That was what the old hotel was like! With the movements of such new-fangled matters as 'buses, it naturally had nothing to do; and through-out the green-walled dining-room the meals were conducted with the stately ceremonial of the past. One felt that the same spirit must be brooding over the bedrooms upstairs, for nothing—nothing what-ever—had been permitted to disturb it. True, there were waitresses now in the dining-room, but the youngest of these was silver-haired. And they said "good afternoon" in such a manner that one felt certain that they, too, had somehow been trained, cherished, protected by the hotel itself since babyhood.

We had walked into the hotel casually, my companion and I, im-pelled by curiosity to take lunch in this huge rambling structure with the grey stone columns in the style of the classic revival, facing its entrance. We had been admitted into the "coffee-room" without realizing the magnitude of our trespass. But the spirit of the hotel was not long in putting us into our proper places. As we did not realize

7

the rule about meals' starting late, we were the first to enter the precincts of the great silver candelabrum, where stood the Wedgwood vases, the silver pitchers and sugar-bowls, polished anew every day. We were soon made aware of the fact that taking a meal here was no ordinary matter. Two minutes after our entry a gong sounded, and five minutes later the first of the other guests swept in—a spare, white-haired lady bearing in one hand a dish with a china cover, presumably containing butter, and with the other her bottle of medicine. She took no more notice of us than if we were non-existent; but her companion, a younger woman, similarly equipped with a medicine bottle, cast in our direction a scowl of contempt. The other guests entered later, each making us feel in some subtle way what utter aliens we were.

Among the guests were a number of young children. At a table over to my right, a girl of about three entered, and striving to climb to her place at the table, upset herself, and emitted a strangled howl. I was unable to see exactly what had occurred, but one of the guests near me remarked placidly: "It would have been better to have kept them in the nursery." The tears of the young offender were soon quenched by the father, who carried her instantly out of the room. At another table, a second girl entered, aged about five, bearing a small Union Jack. The flag was carefully arranged in the midst of the flowers on the table, and the child sat bolt upright during the rest of the meal, eating and drinking and making faces over her food with the air of one who was at least forty. It became a theme of fascination to me to note how all the guests grew middle-aged as soon as they entered the room. The spirit of the hotel was at work amongst us, holding us all with easy mastery, subduing us all into the colours of its faded tradition, weaving us all into the same pattern, its unbroken magic tapestry stretching back to the days when men spoke with veiled awe of Nelson and Waterloo.

At the centre table, reserved for special guests, sat a heavy-built muddy-faced young man in sporting tweeds, whom we readily placed, thanks to the eagerness with which two waitresses fluttered about him, as being the baronet, heir to the great estates on the hill, which comprised also the hotel. He was entertaining two guests, a man and woman similarly attired, who bore the unmistakable signs of not belonging to the landed classes. One of these ventured to ask him a question which I innocently overheard. She said: "What do you think of the League of Nations?" And the heavy-built young man, with the puzzled, half-frightened eyes, replied: "I don't know—it seems mostly upon p-p-paper, doesn't it?"

Even after the other diners had departed, following, as they came, in the silent wake of the spare lady who was dieting, we stayed on, held despite our will by the strange mystic force that had reduced our voices to a whisper and dazzled our eyes. We ordered coffee, to provide ourselves with an excuse for lingering as long as possible; and when the coffee came, after long delay, we sipped the beverage, with its faint taste of burnt grains, with relish, forgetting utterly that a few hunderd yards further on lay a thirteenth-century castle, while not many miles away we might penetrate, if we would, into the baptistery of a tenth-century priory. We lingered as long over our coffee as we reasonably could, but our stay was cut short by the watchful waitress, who feared possibly that we might light our cigarettes, and who therefore hurriedly slipped us our bill. So we bade her farewell, with a feeling as if we should like to incline our heads to the great silver candlestick in the shadows of the dark green wall with its slender Grecian colonnade. We left the hotel, and a few hours later found ourselves again, transported as by magic, back to the too familiar surroundings of the twentieth century.

But the sense of the hotel persisted, and that night I had a strange dream. I seemed to be sitting in the same dining-room, still more brilliant with candles, silver, glass, flowers, and flags. The waitresses were gone, and old men in mutton-chop whiskers, knee-breeches and blue tail-coats with brass buttons moved from table to table, noiselessly. Here was sitting a red-faced Marquess with one leg, the star of some unknown Russian order on his breast; over yonder was Castlereagh; at the centre table was the great Duke of Wellington himself. The glasses winked and bubbled with wine, and I watched the diners, rooted to my seat, unable to utter a sound. I knew that this banquet had been arranged somehow for my benefit, though I had not sought to take part in it. Suddenly Wellington rose to his feet. Glaring at me with intense hatred, he lifted his glass. "Drink," thundered his voice—"drink to the salvation of Europe, our Holy Alliance!" I rose—the dream faded away. Outside in the darkness I heard the shriek of the midnight train.

[JANUARY, 1920]

TO LOVE IMPUISSANT

By Edna St. Vincent Millay

Love, though for this you riddle me with darts,
    And drag me at your chariot till I die—
Oh, heavy prince! oh, panderer of hearts!—
    Yet hear me tell how in their throats they lie
Who shout you mighty: thick about my hair,
    Day in, day out, your ominous arrows purr,
Who still am free, unto no querulous care
    A fool, and in no temple worshipper.

I, that have bared me to your quiver's fire,
    Lifted my face into its puny rain,
Do wreathe you Impotent to Evoke Desire
    As you are Powerless to Elicit Pain!
(Now will the god, for blasphemy so brave,
Punish me, surely, with the shaft I crave!)

[MARCH, 1920]

RENOIR: AN APPRECIATION

By Albert C. Barnes

THE death of Renoir on December the third is so recent that a detached estimate of his place among the great artists of the past is hardly possible. It may be that even expressions of appreciation from those who believe that they know his work, may savour so much of individual bias that they serve chiefly as evidence of the artist's power to generate love and reverence. If, however, there be stated the criteria by which Renoir is judged, the question of mere liking may sink into its deservedly unimportant place. Let us assume the validity of the orthodox statement that all art is automatic, a spontaneous expression of feeling which the artist can neither summon by effort of will nor repress with impunity to his own well-being. If the creative impulse leaves its mark in a material that generates similar feelings in other people, the work of art is a human document of permanent worth. Its degree of worth is determined by the extent to which the artist has enriched, improved, humanized, the common experience of man in the world in which he lives. The manner in which the enrichment occurs is largely by recalling memories and feelings originally associated with perceptions sometimes so nearly forgotten as to have left only the cumulative residue, the "hushed reverberations," which we know as "forms"; and these "forms" necessarily constitute the totals and essence of experience, education and culture. For that reason, art is practical, never exotic, in that it deals with ideas that have served some purpose in human life.

If these axioms of the psychology of aesthetics be accepted, Renoir takes high rank as an artist, because he dealt with the world as it appears to rational beings, he interpreted it in terms of sense and feeling, and his paintings register an enriched record of what humanity sees and feels. He preached nothing but beauty in the world and the joy of living: life is supreme, irresponsible, full of movement, colour, drama, rhythm, music, poetry, and mystic charm. To live for the moment with Renoir's paintings is to be in a haven free from the ravages of one's own troubled spirit and from the vexations of a stupid external world. With him one may live vicariously the whole stream of the free spirit not dulled and depressed by the drab mo-

notony of everyday affairs. The other world he takes us into is *this*
world enriched by his vision. We see the aesthetic strand in all its
fabrics, that runs through all experience, that we ignore in the real
world. He shows us that there is an ideal world in which we would
thrive in peace did we but see it aright. The residuum of our stay
in his world is the conviction of the intrinsic justification of life itself:
a moral value the legitimate offspring of an aesthetic one. If the day-
dream is short-lived, it is none the less real and vital and is capable
of infinite and amplified repetitions; he continues to make good.

Renoir proves that life is fundamentally and chiefly a matter of
feeling. He painted everything in life as we live it; he was preoccupied
with the homely, everyday things, and he made them momentous, as
they really are. Every subject is impregnated with its own essential
and delightful feeling; his flowers are voluptuous, his fruit glows as
in nature, his people at work or play are intent, his nudes are suffused with a high beauty which bars even the suggestion of sensuality.
By his magic he endows every subject with its specific chacteristics,
vitalizes their associations, gives the feeling of delight that we experience when we know that life is good. No painter ever more successfully converted material reality into what it is in its essence, the
expression of the ideal. His perceptions instinctively adjust that
proper amount of emotion to each object, which the fine intelligence demands: he is never literal or prosaic and never sentimental.
He makes the non-material side of the subject the most momentous
part of it.

Renoir's work was the reconstruction of the objects of sense, and
that makes it *per se* of universal interest, with an intrinsic aesthetic
appeal. There can be no beauty except that objectified and no aesthetic interest that is not based upon a taste for existing things
in the real world: mere emotion is the nature in a vacuum which
calls for the psychiatrist. Renoir's creative genius reveals itself in
the penetrating eye that sees to the core of the structure of things
and in the skilled hand that reproduces them so that they reawaken
the intellectual content of the perceptions and bring to life their
exciting associations which we call feeling. It is because "to poets
and philosophers, real things are themselves symbols" that we lose
interest in the merely representative character of Renoir's work and
wander with him into the rich garden of experience where imagination and beauty rule over matter. Renoir is a master precisely be-

cause he stamped the meanings—truth, rationality, humanity, beauty —upon his works, upon the world, and upon us. Not the least of the charm is the simple, direct way he does it: he never defrauds us of our right to intelligence and to a richer vicarious life by either overwhelming the senses, or by bewildering, or by a mystic, irrational sentimentalism. We feel that the paintings are more important than the things he painted.

By what technical means Renoir wrought his magic is a question of no great moment to the appreciator, of but secondary interest to the connoisseur, and the cause of much literary effort and loose thinking on the part of professional critics. Renoir as a free spirit, responsible only to his vision, intelligence and sincerity, has been the target for the fierce opprobrium of those for whom congealed memories and outworn traditions—the academicians—serve as substitutes for thinking and feeling. These, the "vested interests" of art, argue that Renoir's drawing is wrong, his colour raucous, his composition bad. The artists and connoisseurs in whom ideas function in the place of the debris of the academicians, see in Renoir's drawing accurate expressiveness, in his colour a harmony and a structural value in the creation of forms, and in his composition an exquisite sense of the fitness of things. The amateur with even a moderate acquaintance with Renoir's work is very sure that the drawing, made up as it is of convincing colour, iridescent light, parts of form, and loose indeterminate line, constitutes one of the many rhythmic, musical paths into an altogether delightful poetic realm. He feels that the colour sings harmoniously and richly but never stridently; that the composition is made up of charming sensuous elements dramatically meaningful; that the picture soon ceases to be drawing, colour, composition; that it becomes a repose saturated with the spirit of place, where self is no more, where all is peace and harmony and music and poetry. Awakened from the dream, he goes back to life with a conviction and a memory that Renoir breathes the spirit of perpetual youth in a garden of perennial June loveliness.

[FEBRUARY, 1920]

AMERICANISM AND LOCALISM

By John Dewey

When one is living quite on the other side of the world, the United States tend to merge into a unit. One thinks largely in terms of national integers, of which the United States is one. Like a historian of the old school or a writer of diplomatic notes, one conceives of what the United States is doing about this or that. It is taken, as schoolmen say, as an entity. Then one happens to receive a newspaper from one of the smaller towns, from any town, that is, smaller than New York—and sometimes Chicago. Then one gets a momentary shock. One is brought back to earth. And the earth is just what it used to be. It is a loose collection of houses, of streets, of neighbourhoods, villages, farms, towns. Each of these has an intense consciousness of what is going on within itself in the way of fires, burglaries, murders, family jars, weddings, and banquets to esteemed fellow citizens, and a languid drooping interest in the rest of the spacious land.

Very provincial? No, not at all. Just local, just human, just at home, just where they live. Of course, the paper has the Associated Press service or some other service of which it brags. As a newspaper which knows its business, it prints "national" news, and strives assiduously for "national" advertisements, making much on provocation of its "national" circulation. But somehow all this wears a thin and apologetic air. The very style of the national news reminds one of his childhood text-book in history, or of the cyclopaedia that he is sometimes regretfully obliged to consult. Let us have this over as soon as possible and get to something interesting, it all seems to say. How different the local news. Even in the most woodenly treated item there is flavour, even if only of the desire to say something and still avoid a libel suit.

Yet there is a strange phenomenon noted. These same papers that fairly shriek with localisms devote a discreet amount of space to the activities of various Americanization agencies. From time to time, with a marked air of doing their duty, there are earnest editorials on the importance of Americanization and the wickedness of those who decline to be either Americanized or to go back where they came from.

But these weighty and conscientious articles lack the chuckle and relish one finds in the report of the increase of the population of the town and of its crime wave.

One vaguely wonders whether perhaps the recalcitrants who are denounced may not also be infected by the pervading spirit of localism. They decline to get Americanized for the same reason they put up with considerable annoyance rather than go back. They are chiefly concerned with what goes on in their tenement house, their alley, their factory, their street. If a "trained mind"—like the writer's, for example—can't tell very well from these articles just what Americanization is, probably the absorbed denizens of the locality are excusable for not trying to find out more about it. One gathers of course that Americanization consists in learning a language strangely known as English. But perhaps they are too busy making the American language to devote much time to studying the English.

In any case, the editorial emphasis on Americanism stands in extraordinarily vivid contrast to the emphasis in the news columns on local interests. The only things that seem to be "nation-wide" are the high cost of living, prohibition, and devotion to localisms. A Pacific Coast newspaper just reaching Peking contains on its front page the correspondence between President Wilson and Secretary Lansing about the latter's resignation. Doubtless in London the news was of the first importance. The San Francisco editor was too good a journalist not to print the entire correspondence faithfully. But it was entirely overshadowed by a local graft case as to head-lines, space given, and editorial comment.

This remark is not a complaint. It is merely a record of a fact easily verified in almost any city in the United States. The editor doubtless sympathized with the feeling of the mass of the readers that a civic reformation at home was more important than a cabinet revolution in Washington; certainly more important for the "home town," and quite likely for the country—the country, mind you, not the nation, much less the state. For the country is a spread of localities, while the nation is something that exists in Washington and other seats of government.

Henry Adams somewhere remarks in effect that history is a record of victories for the principle of unity in form and of plurality in effect. The wider the formal, the legal unity, the more intense becomes the local life. The defeat of secession diversified the South even more than the North, and the extension of the United States westward to the ocean rendered New England less exclusively a New Englandish homogeneity and created a unique New York, a New York clustering about Wall Street. When we have a United States of the World, doubtless localism will receive its last release —until we federate with the other planets. And yet there are those who fear internationalism as a menace to local independence and variety!

I am not, however, essaying a political treatise. The bearing of these remarks is upon the literary career of our country. They perhaps explain why the newspaper is the only genuinely popular form of literature we have achieved. The newspaper hasn't been ashamed of localism. It has revelled in it, perhaps wallowed is the word. I am not arguing that it is high-class literature, or for the most part good literature, even from its own standpoint. But it is permanently successful romance and drama, and that much can hardly be said for anything else in our literary lines.

The exception, as usual, proves the fact. There are journals of hundreds of thousands—nay, millions of circulation, which claim to be national, and which certainly are not local, even when they locate their stories in New York. This seeming exception is accounted for by the simple fact that localities in the United States are connected by railways and roads upon which a large number of passenger trains and motor cars are moving from one place to another. There is an immense population constantly in transit. For the time being they are not localists. But neither are they nationalists. They are just what they are—passengers. Hence the S—— E—— P—— and other journals expressly designed for this intermediate state of existence. Besides, the motor car fugitives must have advertisements and pictures of their cars. What becomes of all these periodicals? The man who answered this question would be the final authority on literature in America. Pending investigation, my hypothesis is that the brakeman, the Pullman porter, and those who clean out the street-cars inherit them.

Now the thing that makes these periodicals somewhat thin as literature (even if they provide exciting reading matter for those in a state of passage from one locality to another) is that they have to eliminate the local. They subsist for those who are going from one place and haven't as yet arrived at another. They cannot have depth or thickness—nothing but movement. Take all the localities of the United States and extract their greatest common divisor, and the result is of necessity a crackling surface. The bigger and more diversified the country, the thinner the net product.

Isn't this the explanation also of the "serious" novel, of its comparative absence and its comparative failure when it does come into existence? It aims at universality and attains technique. Walt Whitman exhausted the cataloguing of localities, and it hasn't occurred to the novel writer to dig down in some locality mentioned in the gazetteer till he strikes something. The writers of short stories have done something but they have hardly got beyond what is termed local colour. But a locality exists in three dimensions. It has a background and also extensions. I haven't read Mary Wilkins' stories of New England life for many years, but I have only to think of them to recover the whole feel of the life. They are local with a faithfulness that is beyond admiration. But they lack background.

To invert a sentence of Mr. Oppenheim's: The persons in them are characters but they have no manners. For manners are a product of the interaction of characters and social environment, a social environment of which the background, the tradition, the descent of forces, is a part. And in Mary Wilkins' stories, as in the New England she depicts, the traditions are the characters. They have become engrained. There is no background with which they may interact. There are only other characters and the bleak hills and the woods and fields. All, people and nature alike, exist, as the philosophers say, under the form of eternity. Like Melchisedek, they have no ancestry or descent—save from God and the Devil. Bret Harte and Mark Twain have dimensions as well as colour. But the former never attained adequate momentum for lack of a suitable audience. The latter had an audience when he came East but it was an alien one. He tamed himself lest he should shock it too much. His own, his real, locality could not be projected on the Eastern locality without reserve. He believed in his locality, but he believed in his audience more.

We are discovering that the locality is the only universal. Even the suns and stars have their own times as well as their own places. This truth is first discovered in abstract form, or as an idea. Then, as Mr. Oppenheim points out in the February DIAL, its discovery creates a new poetry—at least so I venture to paraphrase him. When the discovery sinks a little deeper, the novelist and dramatist will discover the localities of America as they are, and no one will need to worry about the future of American art. We have been too anxious to get away from home. Naturally that took us to Europe even though we fancied we were going around America. When we explore our neighbourhood, its forces and not just its characters and colour, we shall find what we sought. The beginning of the exploring spirit is in the awakening of criticism and of sympathy. Heaven knows there is enough to criticize. The desired art is not likely to linger long, for the sympathy will come as soon as we stay at home for a while. And in spite of the motor car, moving about is getting difficult. Things are getting filled up—and anyway we only move to another locality.

[JUNE, 1920]

A MEMORY OF THE PLAYERS IN A MIRROR AT MIDNIGHT

By James Joyce

They mouth love's language. Gnash
The thirteen teeth
Your lean jaws grin with. Lash
Your itch and quailing, nude greed of the flesh.
Love's breath in you is stale, worded or sung,
As sour as cat's breath,
Harsh of tongue.

This grey that stares
Lies not, stark skin and bone.
Leave greasy lips their kissing. None
Will choose her what you see to mouth upon.
Dire hunger holds his hour.
Pluck forth your heart, saltblood, a fruit of tears:
Pluck and devour.

[JULY, 1920]

MRS. MAECENAS

By Kenneth Burke

I

Ego vox clamantis in deserto.
Words of St. John.

After many years of faithful service, the professor had become president of the university, taken him a somewhat scandalously younger wife, and died, leaving a string of pompous titles to the wind, and a flourishing widow over thirty to the world. The wife of the head of the physics department, who was usually well up on such things, had prophesied that the president's widow would soon quit the little town for ever, but contrary to expert opinion, she continued living in the same house, nay, even maintained her former connections with the university. The unexpressed consensus of opinion was that this woman was too charming to be beyond suspicion, but yet her scutcheon was radiant with blotlessness. Propriety had been observed with a rigidity that was perhaps even a bit dogmatic, as in the case of her dismissing the chauffeur. And besides, she was left with a little girl, which was even more reassuring.

After the fitting period of black, and another fitting period of subdued colours, she gradually drifted into a superbness of attire which was perhaps not quite so fitting, but was still within the code. For she never appeared again in *smart* clothes; in fact, even the most unfriendly had to admit that she was almost matronly. A big-busted woman, she carried herself with firm dignity, and talked with a Southern accent in a voice that was rich and deep, and might even indicate that she had once been an instructress in elocution.

Within two years after her husband's death, she had acquired a unique position in the life of the university. There were fussy young girls who, as the expression goes, just idolized her. She was the unfailing chaperon at all school functions, since she had succeeded in the difficult task of both entering in with the feelings of the students and yet making them remember that she was not one of them. If she appeared at any of the games, the students, at a sign from their

20

cheer-leader, would doff their caps, and cheer for her. There is no greater tribute to her tact than the fact that she was honorary head of both the Athenian Literary Society and the Society of Fine Arts, two organizations which were always facing each other with backs hunched and teeth bared. It was as patroness of these two organizations that she acquired the flattering nickname of "Mrs. Maecenas." For of all her interests in student activities, her guidance of "the arts" had been most faithful.

In the course of her five years at the university Mrs. Maecenas had judged twelve debates on the single tax, fifteen on the inferiority of women to men, and nine on various phases of prohibition, state, national, and locally optional; and to her credit be it said that her verdicts were not always the same on the same subjects. Mrs. Maecenas had read a gross of horror stories that had received good grades in English Composition 22, and were written after the manner of Edgar Allan Poe; and another gross or two that had been cribbed from O. Henry. Mrs. Maecenas had gone through thousands of rhymed documents on pubescent and adolescent affections, still in her capacity as a protectrice of the arts. And when the war started, and a big man in the German department had called the French a degenerate nation, Mrs. Maecenas had written a charming letter to the school paper in which she denounced the Huns and spoke very beautifully of modern French poetry.

But the truth is that Mrs. Maecenas was getting weary. She had seen ten semesters of the university, and her hopes of mothering a little renaissance out here in the wilderness had gradually pined away as the engineering and agricultural schools grew steadily more vigorous. Everywhere, everywhere, typical young Americans were springing up, sturdy tough daisy-minds that were cheerful, healthy, and banal. How could art thrive here, she asked herself, in a land so unfavourable to the artist's temper! These lusty young throats that cheered her at the football games, they were miserably sane and normal. And Mrs. Maecenas found herself entertaining uncharitable feelings towards these fine young men and women who thought so much of her.

Under the plea of ill health, she began to appear less at school festivities. Also, her child was getting older now, and the need of giving it more attention added motivation to her retirement. She became less kindly in her opinions of the stories and verses she was given to criticize, until this burden had decreased almost to a total nullity. As a consequence, within another year Mrs. Maecenas was hardly more than a widow with a little daughter. An occasional attack of her old weakness for genius-hunting would lure her now and then to one of the literary clubs, but she usually returned from them with such a feeling of exhaustion and disgust that she wondered how she ever could have stood it.

Mrs. Maecenas settled down to be the voice of one whispering very quietly in the wilderness. The great machine of the university could dump its annual output of standardized "leaders of America," could ship them off every commencement day labelled "with all the advantages of a college education"; the alumni could put up a sundial or a gate, or an iron railing, every year in sacred memory of their dear Alma Mater; the great auditorium could tremble with cheering and shouting when big Dick Halloway, handsome blond-haired Dick, the hero of the university, shot the winning goal; all this could go on if it would—but Mrs. Maecenas got farther away from it all, and nearer to her books and her piano. The university became healthier, and she quietly blushed for the future of America. . . .

And then it was that her genius came. By the purest chance she had gone to the Athenian meeting. She found the room peculiarly astir. Little groups were talking quite low together, glancing now and then towards one corner of the room. In this corner, with his back turned towards the members of the Athenian, a rather gawkily formed young man was reading a yellow paper-covered volume which Mrs. Maecenas recognized to be a French novel. There was a slight smell of whiskey in the room.

Mrs. Maecenas knew she had found her genius. Yet at this time Siegfried was barely seventeen.

II

*Ecce quam bonum et quam jucundum
habitare fratres in unum!*

PSALM 132.

Siegfried presented himself at the home of Mrs. Maecenas late the following afternoon. He was just as gawkily formed as the night before, and another yellow-covered book was in his hand, but his breath this time smelled strongly of coffee-beans. In spite of the coffee-beans, however, Siegried had had no more whiskey; with peculiar astuteness in these matters, he had realized that it would probably be a false step to exhale the same shocking odour of the previous night, but on the other hand, to exhale the standard de-stroyer of this odour might give the precisely proper variation. Sieg-fried selected his breath with as much care as less imaginative souls give to their neckties. The door was opened by the widow herself.

"Mrs. Maecenas, I believe?"

"Oh, Siegfried, won't you come in?" She had always insisted on calling the students by their first names.

He stepped into a dark reception hall, and then followed her to the left into her library, Mrs. Maecenas having dispensed with the small-town parlour. "I am very glad you came to see me, although . . ." and here she laughed with her widow roguishness, "although I'm not so sure that I ought to be."

Siegfried was startled. He had not hoped to be taken so freely. But he skimmed the cream of the occasion, and cast away the yoke of his youth in the quality of his equals-to-equals answer, "Throw all caution, etc., I implore you, Mrs. Maecenas, and be less churchly and more Christian. I have come to you as a last hope; deliver me from this American captivity." He began looking over her books without further formality. Mrs. Maecenas sat down tentatively on the piano stool, facing away from the piano, and her two arms stretched back on the key-board.

"Your remarks might lead me to conclude that you are not an American yourself, my dear boy, but nevertheless I'll risk my life that you, like me, were raised under the tutelage of the chopped-down cherry tree." At this Siegfried turned suddenly, like an ill-tempered dog.

"Ugh! My father was an alumnus of this university. Is that credentials enough?" And then just as suddenly cherubic again: "But you have them all, every one! I might think I was by the Pont Neuf."

"The books? Yes, and I should be pleased to lend them to you, if you should ever want any of them."

"And no George Sand! And no Sandeau! And no Bourget! Why, Mrs. Maecenas, I am in the library that *I* shall own some day. Oh, please let me come here, in this modern *thébaïde,* in this elevation above the chewing-gum and sarsaparilla of our beloved countrymen. God bless them, they have carried their Monroe Doctrine into culture. And what a beautiful set of Flaubert!"

"Shhh! *Et les bouquins! Viens!*" With mock caution she led him by the hand to a corner where something square was standing, covered with a drapery of dark purple. She lifted this slowly, disclosing another bookcase. "Popery!" And she slipped out two heavy breviaries, with black leather bindings, and rich gilt edges. She opened one of them at random, and displayed a beautiful front of red and black, with illuminated capitals. Then she pointed to a Dutch edition of Boethius's De Consolatione Philosophiae, in the russet-leather of the seventeenth century. There was the Vulgate in five volumes, the Peristephanon and Psychomachia of Prudentius; Siegfried's eyes followed her hand as it brushed along the books. "I must admit," she said, "*I* did not collect these. They were my husband's. We spoke of them in secret, as though they were the limbs of a child we had pulled apart and stuffed up the chimney." There was also a copy of Huysmans's Sainte Lydwine de Schiedam in Gothic type, Remy de Gourmont's critical anthology of mystic Latin verse, and Saint François de Sales's Introduction à la Vie Dévote in a paper cover of ludicrously innocent blue.

"Popery, bah!" Siegfried exclaimed. "The de Gourmont gives you away. And that, down in the corner, that Petronius! Madam, you are a pagan, for who but a pagan would own such lovely tomes? Nay, you are worse than a pagan; you are a lover of art. I am scandalized. I shall expose you before the world!"

Mrs. Maecenas laughed. "Art was once loved; then it was tolerated; and now it will soon be prohibited, so that we must express our devotion to it in secret, deep in the catacombs. Those are, more or less, the words of de Gourmont. And so you must come here often, Siegfried, and we shall kneel together before the clandestine altar."

After this, they knelt together no less than twice a week. Although Siegfried was more cautious, Mrs. Maecenas plunged headlong into her epithets, and described their evenings as "something rare and wonderful." Love, art, death, renunciation, the beautiful—the two of them drank long draughts of these deep-red vintages, for they each loved art eloquently. Huddled darkly in the crypt, they would discuss all eternal and universal things, and he would read her his prose and verses. She didn't write herself, but what a tender critic!

Perhaps no evening was more wonderful than that sleety night before the holidays. Siegfried had struggled against a persistently vindictive slashing of hail, and arrived with his overcoat feeling like a hulk of iron. As he turned from the street towards the widow's home, he saw the subdued red of the drop-light, "their light," glowing in the window. He felt so deliciously conscious of his health, of his strength, as he stamped on to the porch. Mrs. Maecenas opened the door before he could ring.

"Whew!" he exclaimed, "how many enemies I have out in this night!" He knocked the drippings from his hat, and shook his coat, then stepped into the warm hallway. "I was hardly more than a primitive out in that storm, battling savagely with all the little gods."

She took his coat. "Ah, you have noticed that? It is so easy to understand, when one is fighting a storm, just how the original man had to imagine the world peopled with demons. A cutting wind in your face soon seems like a challenge aimed at you personally, just as a fist in the face might. And you can't walk against it five minutes without squaring your jaw, or even shouting as though you were a fiend yourself."

Thus was the platter handed to Siegfriend. He returned it graciously as they stepped into the library: "And then, to continue the same viewpoint, think how extraordinarily secure this original man must have felt when he had gained his cave, where there was fire, and light, and warmth to reassure him that he had outstrided the demon. . . . Perhaps that is why I feel so peculiarly comfortable now as I see those logs where I can warm my hands." He laughed. "Congratulate me; I feel that I unwound a pretty statement there. . . . But as to the warming of hands, it is a pleasure to warm them before a log fire even when they are not cold."

"Once the hands are warmed before the fire of logs, we can then warm them before the fire of life," and the widow had acquitted herself.

"Ah!" After which, for no defined reason, he thought this a time to summon all his boyishness in a toss of the head, and a patent care-free laugh. "How fortunate it is that Landor is not popular."

"Yes, if I were deprived of that lovely quatrain! How *right* a thing to compose on one's seventy-fifth birthday!"

"Isn't it? It must gratify a man to evolve so perfectly concomitantly with his years, to write patriarchally when he is old, to be so completely an entelechy."

"The entelechy, I always felt, was one of Aristotle's most valuable conceptions," Mrs. Maecenas fell in, thereby advancing the conversation another stage. They were gratified with the way they were talking this evening; already they had, by logical steps, moved from the storm to Aristotelianism, and Siegfried's feet were hardly warm yet. And this in the light of the fact that they had begun with the most deadly of conversations, the weather. Nor had either of them failed to note that the weather itself had been done satisfactorily.

Siegfried was worthy of his task. "Aristotle came centuries too soon. If the divine chronology were in perfect ordination he should have come now, after man had flopped and floundered for so long and so distractedly. For if he came *now,* and offered his massive sanity to the world, men would open their eyes with wonder. But as it is, this astonishing cure for dark thinking was propounded before we began to think darkly, so that we are still *waiting* for someone. If the world should—"

"Pardon me for interrupting you, Siegfried, but I have been watching you. I have been watching your eyes. Siegfried, do you suffer from headaches?"

Siegfried was content; the interruption was significant. Remarks like this had been an ever-swelling note in their song of late. But one must be cautious. "My eyes—yes—Aristotle . . . oh! Do I suffer from headaches? Why, I suppose they are headaches. I had an aunt who went mad, but I don't suppose . . ."

"No, no, no—nothing like that. Don't say it, Siegried!" And Mrs. Maecenas stopped her ears, so that Siegfried noticed her full white arms. . . . There was a lull in the conversation, as was fitting. The big clock in the hall suddenly became important, and flooded the library with its ticking. Siegfried looked lugubriously into the fire, religiously observing the ceremonies of the situation. After a time, the widow ventured a timid triad. It was delicious to be pampered this way! Siegfried was basking in the warm sun of sentiment. Then, as if putting aside a great burden, she broke the silence: "Did you bring anything to read to me this evening, my boy?"

"Some more of my Bible. I did good work on Chapter 37 of the Second Epistle of Josephat. And I have the Forty-first and Forty-third Psalms of Obad. But the latter are too rough yet. You would accuse me of excessive youth. I brought only the Josephat."

"You have been working hard, Siegfried." And she closed her eyes in voluptuous expectation as Siegfried opened his brief-case.

Siegfried returned and sat down by the fire. He prepared to read, then put down the paper again to clear his throat. He cast a quick glance in the direction of the window; she was ready:

"Second Epistle of Josephat.
Chapter 37, Verses 9–17.

9 And the prophet Mehovah, when he was come out of the dry places of Arabia, lifted his voice before the multitude assembled, saying:

10 Many are the sorrows that beset the ways of sinners and those that trespass against the Lord, for His eyes of vengeance are manifold, and His wrath endureth forever.

11 He shall slake their thirst with salt, and feed their hunger with the dry bones of His laughter; their bellies shall be empty, and the tongues parched of those that have sinned against Him.

12 He shall smite them until they cry out with madness, and gape and blubber at the sight of seven moons.

13 And they shall be made to run naked in fields of thistle, where the thistle barbs shall prick them, and strike out at them like hissing snakes.

14 And they shall wander in night as black as their iniquity; in the blackness of night, beasts shall brush against them, and unknown things, and voices shall whine out of the funnel of darkness.

15 And they shall wend from the valleys up into the mountains, and from the tops of the mountains back into the valleys, and find not what they seek; no, not even shall they know the things they are seeking.

16 All these evils and many others shall visit the sons of Belial, and Belial's daughters, but for those blessed with righteousness there shall be playing of harps and dulcimers, and an abundance of honey.

17 And when Mehovah had said these things, he turned again into the desert."

"Excellong!" the widow cried out immediately. "Let me have them. And you recited so beautifully!" Siegfried handed her the manuscript. Glancing through it, she made her criticisms. "The delicate irony of the prophet coming up out of the desert just to deliver a speech of about a hundred words, and then going back again, is the kind of thing we love to find out for ourselves. France would have loved to do it. And how much more capable your prophet was of imagining tortures than bliss; the point is ferociously well made. But, Siegfried, I am afraid of you, with your eager *sadisme littéraire*. Your mind is so gloriously unhealthy, so à la Baudelaire. If Le Mauvais Vitrier were not already written, I am sure you would do it sooner or later. Or some of de Gourmont's Oraisons Mauvaises. You are an incipient Giles de Retz. And—pardon me—so young! But why aren't you younger still, Siegfried, so young that I could throw my arms around you and kiss you for this magnificent performance? Siegfried, you are going to redeem America in the eyes of the world."

Siegfried nursed the moment in silence. Mrs. Maecenas went on. "But there are things lacking yet, Siegfried, *big* things." Thoughtfully: "If you can do this much without experience, on air, as it were, great Heavens, what will you come to when you have lived! Sometimes I feel it is my duty to—to—*aid* you, Siegfried, to be a—a *real* Maecenas, or a real *Mrs.* Maecenas rather." Then explosively: "Oh, Siegfried, my poor, dear boy, the wonderful things you are still to learn." Abruptly: "Think, Siegfried, you haven't even been in love yet!" He said nothing. "Have you?"

"I'm not sure, but there's a charming little prissy in one of my classes whose delicate-pink cheeks I should love to slap."

"Faugh! How young you can be at times! To know no more

about oneself than that! You will begin by loving an older woman."
With a laugh: "But we both know that you must find out all
these things for yourself." And with the echo of this interlude
still rumbling in the far valleys, the conversation turned again to
art.

As he ploughed back through the slush that night Siegfried attempted to place his relationship with Mrs. Maecenas, and finally
contented himself with the conclusion that the general was leading
to the specific. Or there might be room for some sort of a syllogism
somewhere: he needed *Experience;* Mrs. Maecenas wanted him to
have *Experience;* ergo . . . but that didn't quite fit together. In
any case, on the whole the thing had a slight savour of the Aphro-
dite-and-Adonis, with him playing Adonis merely because he didn't
know how to play any one else. He hated to be so frank about the
thing, but it *did* look as though the day was approaching when he
could face the sun stolidly, and proclaim with firmness, "I have become a man." But the important thing was that these evenings were
excellent, and it was delightful to be so worried over.

III

*Nemo mundus a sorde, nec si unius
diei vita ejus sit in terra.*
                              BOOK OF JOB.

A week later. The dim red drop-light was burning in the window,
which might have told the world that this was one of Siegfried's
nights. Outside, a soft snow was sifting quietly, making a mystic
haze about the street-lamps. Siegfried had just finished playing the
Moonlight.

For a moment he sat motionless, still facing the piano. The big
clock in the hall, ever on the alert for such times, promptly loomed
up again. The flames of the gas-fire climbed noisily over the asbes-
tos. He turned slowly towards the widow. "And just think, Mrs.
Maecenas, one isn't allowed to like the Sonata Quasi una Fantasia
any more! . . . But who knows? Perhaps I shouldn't either if it
were literature and not music. . . ." She was looking out the window, and made no answer. He let a few moments more go by, then

instinctively, he plunged into another direction. "You are looking out into the night? . . . It meant a lot to me to come to you through a night like that. It felt as though I were stealing to you. Or as though I were here by the special dispensation of a good fairy who had warned me that I must be home again by the stroke of twelve. . . . The night is full of whisperings about Cinderella. . . . I had to play the Moonlight, you see. But I am silly? Yes?"

"A little, Siegfried—but pleasantly so." They both thought her answer had a sweetly Shakespearean flavour.

"But you should forgive me. We who have not had the big things of life yet, you will find that at bottom we have a horrible amount of silliness; silly little dreams, silly little expectations, silly little longings. Perhaps we are not so pure as the little girls in a convent, but we are every bit as silly.

> 'Little Doris of twelve, what is sillier, Dorrie?
> Is it you, or is it I,
> Or the silly little morning-glory?'

Yes, they are mine; but I never brought them around. I never dared to."

She turned and faced him, having contrived dexterously to keep the divan from creaking. "You should have, Siegfried. I was coming to think of you as a monster. And after all, are we not peculiarly close in our present predicaments? You have not had the things of life, and I . . ." with an uncertain sigh, then explosively, "I have passed them by, I suppose."

Siegfried was sure the flower was in full bloom, but in spite of him, Adonis answered: "Yet we always hold back. There is some sickly longing in man to deprive himself of those things which mean most to him. We are proud, not when we have been happy, but when we have wallowed in misery. *If any one have anything of which he is especially fond, let it be taken from him.* That was, I believe, one of the rules of the Benedictines. It is a sentence that is very beautiful to me, and yet there is no sweeping simile, no brilliance of epithet, nothing but bare bleached bones. It is its sheer austerity which makes it alluring, the mere conception of these self-flagellating temperaments so eager in harvesting their tortures. . . . We no longer have religion, if by religion one means the hierarchy of the angels, and a *Janitor Coeli,* and a God to sit massively on his throne, but ah! . . . how appealing the *instincts* of religion still are to us! I could take the vows of an anchorite, not to attain some ultimate Kingdom of the Blessed thereby, but merely through a vague urge towards asceticism, even though I have nothing for which to be ascetic. For we are all tinged a bit by the stench of holiness, *sanctitatis odore*. . . . Perhaps I might be ascetic for my art, but you tell me that the artist must *live*, not *flee from life*. Blind mouths, as Milton has put it. Blind mouths! We are like frail little kittens hardly a day old, nosing around for the mother's teat." Siegfried was dissatisfied for once, even though his rhetoric had been faultless. Still, he had ended the flight happily enough, it might prove.

There was a long silence. Then the widow began speaking very slowly. "My eloquent child, my baby Nestor, have you ever seen Thackeray's cartoon of Louis XIV? You remember the one drawing of the little runt of a king, old, sallow, dried, hideously devoid of kingliness. Then steps forth Louis the Great, the official Louis, Louis the Emperor Augustus of France, Louis the State, the King of Corneille, of Racine, of Molière. He is stilted, and bejeweled, and sumptuously robed. He is draped and decorated. He is magnified with scaffolds. And behold, he is Regal! In the same way, Siegfried, I should love to make a cartoon of what you have just said. For you have done nothing other than Thackeray says was done to Louis. You have taken a condition that is devoid of interest and value, and you have decked it with royal purples. . . . No, Siegfried, you can say what you like about the beauty of asceticism; but after you have perverted and twisted and beautified to your heart's content, at bottom the original thing remains. . . . For your art's sake, for *America's* sake, you get up and move. . . . The Muse is a woman, Siegfried, and the formula is that the worse you treat a woman the more she loves you. You may find that if you forget art long enough to live, your art may be all the stronger for it afterwards."

Siegfried was content. He found it pleasant to be exhorted, and pled with. But he wished for a way to get off this Adonis strain. He cursed himself for his praise of asceticism; it might have been too discouraging. But while she was making cartoons, why didn't she make another, showing his true attitude towards Experience? Taking the royal purples off his "urge to asceticism" might reveal an urge of an entirely different sort. Siegfried had no essential objection to being Experienced. But, hell . . . there was plenty of time. Yet it was disagreeable to think so practically about these things.

"But the play, Siegfried! We have wasted all this time, and I am determined to hear the entire play this evening. The little snatches you have told me of it . . . I am mad to hear it all. Begin it immediately."

Siegfried rose from the piano, and went out into the hallway for his brief-case. Mrs. Maecenas pulled a chair up to the light for him, and fixed herself on the sofa, with eyes closed. Siegfried returned and took his seat by the light. He paused. Mrs. Maecenas readjusted her pillow, glanced down at the white of her exposed neck, and then over at Siegfried.

"But, Siegfried," she cried out in sudden horror, "what is the matter with your face?"

He looked up in astonishment. Then he thought he understood; she was pampering him, no doubt. "The paleness? Am I unusually pale to-night? I was smoking a lot to-day."

"Uh . . . y-yes. Why, yes, the pallor." Then she seemed to recover. "But that is not unusual, I suppose. The artist's temper . . . nervosity . . . pallor would be natural."

Siegfried understood now. It was not the *pallor*, then, but the *redness. Nemo mundus a sorde;* nature is *such* a tyrant. Yesterday they had broken out, and to-day they were all over his chin. But how annoying that she should react so to pimples!

A few more sentences were offered. She seemed very tired. Siegfried decided tentatively to remember an engagement. "Oh, I am awfully sorry, Siegfried." She would let him go so easily, then? . . .

A few months later they passed on the street, and she nodded to him very sweetly. They even exchanged a couple of words.

She hoped he was getting on well, she said.

[MARCH, 1920]

PICKING AND CHOOSING

BY MARIANNE MOORE

Literature is a phase of life: if
   one is afraid of it, the situation is irremediable; if
one approaches it familiarly,
   what one says of it is worthless. Words are constructive
when they are true; the opaque allusion—the simulated flight

upward—accomplishes nothing. Why cloud the fact
   that Shaw is self-conscious in the field of sentiment but is
      otherwise re-
warding? that James is all that has been
   said of him but is not profound? It is not Hardy
the distinguished novelist and Hardy the poet, but one man

"interpreting life through the medium of the
   emotions." If he must give an opinion, it is permissible that the
critic should know what he likes. Gordon
   Craig with his "this is I" and "this is mine," with his three
wise men, his "sad French greens" and his Chinese cherries—
      Gordon Craig, so

inclinational and unashamed—has carried
   the precept of being a good critic, to the last extreme. And
      Burke is a
psychologist—of acute, raccoon-
   like curiosity. Summa diligentia;
to the humbug whose name is so amusing—very young and very rushed, Caesar crossed the Alps on the "top of a
   diligence." We are not daft about the meaning but this
      familiarity
with wrong meanings puzzles one. Humming-
   bug, the candles are not wired for electricity.
Small dog, going over the lawn, nipping the linen and saying

33

that you have a badger—remember Xenophon;

only the most rudimentary sort of behavior is necessary to put us on the scent; a "right good

salvo of barks," a few "strong wrinkles" puckering the skin between the ears, are all we ask.

[APRIL, 1920]

COCK AND HARLEQUIN

Notes Concerning Music

By Jean Cocteau

Translated from the French by Rollo H. Myers

Art is science in the flesh.

The musician opens the cage-door to arithmetic; the draughtsman gives geometry its freedom.

A work of art must satisfy all the Muses—that is what I call "Proof by nine."

A masterpiece is a game of chess won "check-mate."

A Young Man Must Not Invest In Safe Securities.

Royal families.—Only a sense of hierarchy permits of sound judgement. Amongst works of art which leave us unmoved, there are works which count; one may smile at Gounod's Faust—but it is a masterpiece; one may revolt against Picasso's aesthetic, but recognize its intrinsic value. It is this sense of quality which relates artists belonging to absolutely opposite schools.

Emotion resulting from a work of art is only of value when it is not obtained by sentimental blackmail.

In art every value which can be proved is vulgar.

Truth is too naked; she does not inflame men.

A sentimental scruple which prevents us from speaking the whole truth makes us represent Venus hiding her sex with her hand. But truth points to her sex with her hand.

Every "Long live So-and-So" involves a "Down with So-and-So." One must have the courage to say this "Down with So-and-So" or be convinced of eclecticism.

Eclecticism is fatal to admiration as well as to injustice. But in art, it is a kind of injustice to be just.

It is hard to deny anything, above all a noble work of art. But every sincere affirmation involves a sincere negation.

35

Beethoven is irksome in his developments, but not Bach, because Beethoven develops the form and Bach the idea.

Beethoven says: "This pen-holder contains a new pen; there is a new pen in this pen-holder; the pen in this pen-holder is new"—or *"Marquise, vos beaux yeux, et cetera."*

Bach says: "This pen-holder contains a new pen in order that I may dip it in the ink and write, et cetera," or *"Marquise, vos beaux yeux me font mourir d'amour, et cet amour, et cetera."*

There lies the difference.

There is a moment when every work in the process of being created benefits from the glamour attaching to uncompleted sketches. "Don't touch it any more!" cries the amateur. IT IS THEN THAT THE TRUE ARTIST TAKES HIS CHANCE.

SENSES. The ear repudiates but can tolerate certain kinds of music which, if transferred to the sphere of the nose, would oblige us to run away.

The bad music which superior folk despise is agreeable enough. What is disagreeable is their good music.

Sculpture, so neglected on account of the current contempt for form and mass in favour of the shapeless, is undoubtedly one of the noblest arts. To begin with, it is the only one which obliges us to move round it.

That bird-catcher and scare-crow over there is a conductor.

The creative artist must always be partly man and partly woman, and the woman part is almost always unbearable.

The public asks questions. They ought to be answered by works, not manifestos.

The beautiful looks easy. That is what the public scorns.

Even when you blame, only be concerned with what is first-class.

Impressionist music is outdone by a certain American dance which I saw at the Casino de Paris.

This is what the dance was like. The American band accompanied it on banjos and thick nickel tubes. On the right of the little black-coated group there was a barman of noises under a gilt pergola loaded with bells, triangles, boards, and motorcycle horns. With these he fabricated cocktails, adding from time to time a dash of cymbals, all the while rising from his seat, posturing, and smiling vacuously.

Mr Pilcer in evening dress, thin and rouged, and Mlle Gaby Deslys, like a big ventriloquist's doll, with a china complexion, flaxen hair, and a gown of ostrich feathers, danced to this hurricane of rhythm and beating of drums a sort of tame catastrophe which left them quite intoxicated and blinded under the glare of six anti-aircraft search-lights. The house was on its feet to applaud, roused from its inertia by this extraordinary turn which, compared to the madness of Offenbach, is what a tank would be by the side of an 1870 state-carriage.

To defend Wagner because Saint-Saëns attacks him is too simple. We must cry "Down with Wagner!" together with Saint-Saëns. That requires real courage.

I am not attacking modern German music. Schoenberg is a master; all our musicians as well as Stravinsky owe something to him, but Schoenberg is essentially a blackboard musician.

The German public has a strong stomach which it stuffs with heterogeneous nourishment which is respectfully absorbed but not digested.

In France this nourishment is refused; but there are four or five stomachs which select and digest better than anywhere else in the world.

Germany is the type of an intellectual democracy, France of an intellectual monarchy.

With us a young musician from the beginning meets with opposition, in other words, a stimulant. In Germany he finds ears. The longer they are the more they listen. He is taken up, and academized, and that is the end of him.

We must be clear about that misunderstood phrase, "German

influence." France had her pockets full of seeds and, carelessly, spilt them all about her; the German picked up the seeds, carried them off to Germany and planted them in a chemically-prepared soil from whence there grew a monstrous flower without scent. It is not surprising that the maternal instinct made us recognize the poor spoilt flower and prompted us to restore to it its true shape and smell.

Satie acquired a distaste for Wagner in Wagnerian circles, in the very heart of the Rose-Croix. He warned Debussy against Wagner. "Be on your guard," he said. "A 'property' tree is not convulsed because somebody comes on to the stage." That is the whole aesthetic of Pelléas.

Satie does not pay much attention to painters, and does not read the poets, but he likes to live where life ferments; he has a flair for good inns.

Debussy established once for all the Debussy atmosphere. Satie evolves. Each of his works, intimately connected with its predecessor, is nevertheless distinct and lives a life of its own. They are like a new kind of pudding—a surprise—and a deception for those who expect one always to tread the same piece of ground.

The impressionists feared bareness, emptiness, silence. Silence is not necessarily a hole; you must use silence, instead of using a stop-gap of vague noises.

Black Shadow.—Black silence. Not violet silence, interspersed with violet shadows.

We may soon hope for an orchestra where there will be no caressing strings. Only a rich choir of wood, brass, and percussion.

I should not be averse from substituting for the cult of St Cecilia that of St Polycarpe.

It would be a fine thing for a musician to compose for a mechanical organ, a veritable sound-machine. We should then hear properly employed the rich resources of this apparatus which are now lavished, haphazard, upon hackneyed tunes.

The public, accustomed to redundancy, disregards works that are terse.

To the musical public terseness signifies emptiness, and stuffing prodigality.

The public only takes up yesterday as a weapon with which to castigate to-day.

The indolence of the public: its armchair and its stomach. The public is ready to take up no matter what new game so long as you don't change it, when once it has learned the rules. Hatred of the creator is hatred of him who alters the rules of the game.

PUBLICS. Those who defend to-day by making use of yesterday, and who anticipate to-morrow (one per cent).

Those who defend to-day by destroying yesterday, and who will deny to-morrow (four per cent).

Those who imagine that to-day is a mistake, and make an appointment for the day-after-to-morrow (twelve per cent).

Those of the day-before-yesterday who defend yesterday in order to prove that today exceeds legitimate bounds (twenty per cent).

Those who have not yet learnt that art is continuous and believe that art stopped yesterday in order to go on again, perhaps, to-morrow (sixty per cent).

Those who are equally oblivious of the Day-before-Yesterday, Yesterday, and To-day (one hundred per cent).

To Please, and to Retain One's Merit.—If an artist yields to the public's overtures of peace, he is beaten.

A favourite phrase of the public is: "I don't see what that's meant to be."

The public wants to understand first and feel afterwards.

A fall makes peoples laugh. The mechanism of falling plays an important part in causing the laughter which greets a new work. The public, not having followed the curve which leads up to this work, stumbles suddenly from where it was standing down on to the work which it is now seeing or hearing. Consequently a fall takes place, and laughter.

Music is the only art which the masses will allow not to be like something else. And yet good music is music which has some resemblance.

One does not blame an epoch; one congratulates oneself on not having belonged to it.

Of course Wagner is "good" and Debussy is "good"—we are only discussing what is "good." Needless to say that Saint-Saëns, Bruneau, and Charpentier are very bad.

Pelléas is another example of music to be listened to with one's face in one's hands. All music which has to be listened to through the hands is suspect. Wagner is typically music which is listened to through the hands.

One cannot get lost in a Debussy mist as one can in a Wagner fog, but it is not good for one.

Too many miracles are expected of us; I consider myself very fortunate if I have been able to make a blind man hear.

FRAGMENTS OF IGOR STRAVINSKY AND THE RUSSIAN
BALLET

And the flower-Maidens! Amongst the most recent flower-Maidens, the most maidenly and the most flowery, I class the Russian Ballet.

I had a presentiment that I should have to find an excuse for my enthusiasm for this Barnum, a last scruple before clearing out "on the quiet."

It was in 1910. Nijinsky was dancing the Spectre de la Rose. Instead of going to see the piece, I went to wait for him in the wings. There it was really very good. After embracing the young girl the spectre of the rose hurls himself out of the window . . . . and comes to earth amongst the stage-hands who throw water in his face and rub him down like a boxer. What a combination of grace and brutality! I shall always hear that thunder of applause; I shall always see that young man, smeared with grease-paint, gasping and sweating, pressing his heart with one hand and holding on with the other to the scenery, or else fainting on a chair. Afterwards, having been smacked and douched and shaken he would return to the stage, and smile his acknowledgements.

LE SACRE DU PRINTEMPS

The Sacre du Printemps was given in May 1913 in a new theatre, untarnished by time, too comfortable and too cold for a public used to emotions at close quarters in the warmth of red velvet and gold. I do not for a moment think that the Sacre would have met with a more polite reception on a less pretentious stage; but this luxurious theatre seemed, at first glance, symbolic of the misunderstanding which was confronting a decadent public with a work full of strength and youth. A tired public reposing amidst Louis XVI garlands, Venetian gondolas, luxurious divans, and cushions of an orientalism for which the Russian Ballet must be held responsible. Under such conditions one digests, as it were, in a hammock, dozing; the really New is driven away like a fly; it is disturbing.

Let us recall the theme of the Sacre.

FIRST TABLEAU. The prehistoric youth of Russia are engaged in springtide games and dances; they worship the earth and the wise elder reminds them of the sacred rites.

SECOND TABLEAU. These simple men believe that the sacrifice of a young girl, chosen from amongst all her peers, is necessary in order that Spring may recommence. She is left alone in the forest; the ancestors come out of the shadows like bears, and form a circle. They inspire the chosen one with the rhythm of a long drawn-out convulsion. When she falls dead, the ancestors draw near, receive her body and raise it towards heaven. This theme, so simple, so devoid of symbolism, to-day seems to hold a symbol. I see in it the prelude to the war.

Let us now return to the theatre in the Avenue Montaigne, while we wait for the conductor to rap his desk and the curtain to go up on one of the noblest events in the annals of art. The audience behaved as it ought to; it revolted straight away. People laughed, boo-ed, hissed, imitated animal noises, and possibly would have tired themselves out before long, had not the crowd of aesthetes and a handful of musicians, carried away by their excessive zeal, insulted and even roughly handled the public in the *loges*. The uproar degenerated into a free fight. Standing up in her *loge,* her diadem awry, the old Countess de P. flourished her fan and shouted, scarlet in the face, "It's the first time for sixty years that anyone's dared to make a fool of me." The good lady was sincere; she thought there was some mystification.

At two o'clock in the morning Stravinsky, Nijinsky, Diaghilev, and I piled into a taxi and drove to the Bois de Boulogne. No one spoke; the night was fresh and agreeable. We recognized the first trees by the smell of the acacias. When we had reached the Lakes, Diaghilev, enveloped in opossum furs, began to mutter in Russian; I felt Stravinsky and Nijinsky listening, and when the driver lit the lamps I saw that there were tears on the impresario's face. He went on muttering, slowly and indefatigably. "What is it?" I asked. "Pushkin." Again there was a long silence; then Diaghilev stammered out a short sentence, and the emotion of my two companions seemed so acute that I could not refrain from interrupting in order to know the reason. "It is hard to translate," said Stravinsky, "really very hard; too Russian . . . too Russian. It means, roughly, *Veux-tu faire un tour aux îles*. Yes, that's it; it is a very Russian expression, because, you know, in our country one goes to the islands in the same way as we are going to the Bois de Boulogne to-night, and it was in going to the islands that we conceived the Sacre du Printemps."

It was the first time the scandal had been alluded to. We came back at dawn. You cannot imagine the state of softness and nostalgia of these men, and whatever Diaghilev may have done since, I shall never forget his great wet face, in the cab, reciting Pushkin in the Bois de Boulogne.

[JANUARY, 1921]

THE FIFTH CANTO

By Ezra Pound

Great bulk, huge mass, thesaurus;
Ecbatan, the clock ticks and fades out;
The bride awaiting the god's touch; Ecbatan,
City of patterned streets; again the vision:
Down in the viae stradae, toga'd the crowd, and arm'd,
Rushing on populous business, and from parapets
Looked down—at North
Was Egypt, and the celestial Nile, blue-deep
          cutting low barren land,
Old men and camels working the water-wheels;
          Measureless seas and stars,
Iamblichus' light, the souls ascending,
Sparks like a partridge covey,
          Like the "ciocco," brand struck in the game.
"Et omniformis":
          Air, fire, the pale soft light.
Topaz, I manage, and three sorts of blue;
          but on the barb of time.
The fire? always, and the vision always,
Ear dull, perhaps, with the vision, flitting
And fading at will. Weaving with points of gold,
Gold-yellow, saffron . . .
          The roman shoe, Aurunculeia's,
And come shuffling feet, and cries "Da nuces!
"Nuces!" praise and Hymenaeus "brings the girl to her man."
Titter of sound about me, always,
          and from "Hesperus . . ."
Hush of the older song: "Fades light from seacrest,
"And in Lydia walks with pair'd women
"Peerless among the pairs, and that once in Sardis
"In satieties . . .
          "Fades the light from the sea, and many things
"Are set abroad and brought to mind of thee,"
And the vinestocks lie untended, new leaves come to the shoots,

North wind nips on the bough, and seas in heart
Toss up chill crests,
            And the vine stocks lie untended
And many things are set abroad and brought to mind
Of thee, Atthis, unfruitful.
            The talks ran long in the night.
And from Mauleon, fresh with a new earned grade,
In maze of approaching rain-steps, Poicebot—
The air was full of women.
            And Savairic Mauleon
Gave him his land and knight's fee, and he wed the woman.
Came lust of travel on him, of *romerya;*
And out of England a knight with slow-lifting eyelids
Lei fassar furar a del, put glamour upon her . . .
And left her an eight months gone.
            "Came lust of woman upon him,"
Poicebot, now on North road from Spain
(Sea-change, a grey in the water)
            And in small house by town's edge
Found a woman, changed and familiar face;
Hard night, and parting at morning.

And Pieire won the singing, Pieire de Maensac,
Song or land on the throw, and was *dreitz hom*
And had De Tierci's wife and with the war they made:
            Troy in Auvergnat
While Menelaus piled up the church at port
He kept Tyndarida. Dauphin stood with de Maensac.

John Borgia is bathed at last.
            (Clock-tick pierces the vision)
Tiber, dark with the cloak, wet cat gleaming in patches.
Click of the hooves, through garbage,
Clutching the greasy stone. "And the cloak floated"
Slander is up betimes.
            But Varchi of Florence,
Steeped in a different year, and pondering Brutus,
Then
            "SIGA MAL AUTHIS DEUTERON!

"Dog-eye!!" (to Alessandro)
          "Whether for Love of Florence," Varchi leaves it,
Saying, "I saw the man, came up with him at Venice,
"I, one wanting the facts,
"And no mean labour.
                    "Or for a privy spite?"
          Good Varchi leaves it,
But: "I saw the man. *Se pia?*
"*O impia?* For Lorenzaccio had thought of stroke in the open
"But uncertain (for the Duke went never unguarded) . . .
"And would have thrown him from wall
"Yet feared this might not end him," or lest Alessandro
Know not by whom death came,
                    O si credesse
"If when the foot slipped, when death came upon him,
"Lest cousin Duke Alessandro think he'd fallen alone
"No friend to aid him in falling."
                    Caina attende.
As beneath my feet a lake, was ice in seeming.
And all of this, runs Varchi, dreamed out beforehand
In Perugia, caught in the star-maze by Del Carmine,
Cast on a natal paper, set with an exegesis, told,
All told to Alessandro, told thrice over,
Who held his death for a doom.
In abuleia.
          But Don Lorenzino
"Whether for love of Florence . . . but
          "O si morisse, credesse caduto da se."

SIGA, SIGA!

The wet cloak floats on the surface,
Schiavoni, caught on the wood-barge,
Gives out the afterbirth, Giovanni Borgia,
Trails out no more at nights, where Barabello
Prods the Pope's elephant, and gets no crown, where Mozarello
Takes the Calabrian roadway, and for ending
Is smothered beneath a mule,
                    a poet's ending,
Down a stale well-hole, oh a poet's ending. "Sanazarro

"Alone out of all the court was faithful to him"
For the gossip of Naples' trouble drifts to North,
Fracastor (lightning was midwife) Cotta, and Ser D'Alviano,
Al poco giorno ed al gran cerchio d'ombra,
Talk the talks out with Navighero,
Burner of yearly Martials,
                    (The slavelet is mourned in vain)
And the next comer
                    says "were nine wounds,
"Four men, white horse with a double rider,"
The hooves clink and slick on the cobbles . . .
Schiavoni . . . the cloak floats on the water,
"Sink the thing," splash wakes Schiavoni;
Tiber catching the nap, the moonlit velvet,
A wet cat gleaming in patches.
                              "Se pia," Varchi,
"O empia, ma risoluto
"E terribile deliberazione"
                    Both sayings run in the wind,
Ma si morisse!

[August, 1921]

LONDON LETTER

September, 1921

LOOKING back upon the past season in London—for no new season has yet begun—it remains certain that Strawinsky was our two months' lion. He has been the greatest success since Picasso. In London all the stars obey their seasons, though these seasons no more conform to the almanac than those which concern the weather. A mysterious law of appearance and disappearance governs everybody—or at least everybody who is wise enough to obey it. Who is Mr Rubenstein? The brilliant pianist. This summer he was everywhere; at every dinner, every party, every week-end; in the evening crisp and curled in a box; sometimes apparently in several boxes at once. He was prominent enough to have several doubles; numbers of men vaguely resembled him. Why this should have happened this year rather than last year, perhaps rather than next year, I for one cannot tell. Even very insignificant people feel the occult influence; one knows, oneself, that there are times when it is desirable to be seen and times when it is felicitous to vanish.

But Strawinsky, Lucifer of the season, brightest in the firmament, took the call many times, small and correctly neat in pince-nez. His advent was well prepared by Mr Eugene Goossens—also rather conspicuous this year—who conducted two Sacre du Printemps concerts, and other Strawinsky concerts were given before his arrival. The music was certainly too new and strange to please very many people; it is true that on the first night it was received with wild applause, and it is to be regretted that only three performances were given. If the ballet was not perfect, the fault does not lie either in the music, or in the choreography—which was admirable, or in the dancing—where Madame Sokolova distinguished herself. To me the music seemed very remarkable—but at all events struck me as possessing a quality of modernity which I missed from the ballet which accompanied it. The effect was like Ulysses with illustrations by the best contemporary illustrator.

Strawinsky, that is to say, had done his job in the music. But music that is to be taken like operatic music, music accompanying and explained by an action, must have a drama which has been put

47

through the same process of development as the music itself. The spirit of the music was modern, and the spirit of the ballet was primitive ceremony. The Vegetation Rite upon which the ballet is founded remained, in spite of the music, a pageant of primitive culture. It was interesting to any one who had read The Golden Bough and similar works, but hardly more than interesting. In art there should be interpenetration and metamorphosis. Even The Golden Bough can be read in two ways: as a collection of entertaining myths, or as a revelation of that vanished mind of which our mind is a continuation. In everything in the Sacre du Printemps, except in the music, one missed the sense of the present. Whether Strawinsky's music be permanent or ephemeral I do not know; but it did seem to transform the rhythm of the steppes into the scream of the motor horn, the rattle of machinery, the grind of wheels, the beating of iron and steel, the roar of the underground railway, and the other barbaric cries of modern life; and to transform these despairing noises into music.

MR BERNARD SHAW

It is not within my province to discuss Back to Methuselah, but the appearance of the book may make some observations on Mr Shaw not impertinent, and it is an advantage for my purpose that the book is as well known in America as it is here. A valedictory tone in this book (already noticed by Mr Seldes) is not inapposite to a successful season of his plays by Mr Macdermott's company. Blanco Posnet is now running at the Court Theatre. The recognition indicated by this success implies perhaps that Mr Shaw has attained, in the most eulogistic sense of his own term, the position of an Ancient.

Seven years ago, in 1914, when Mr Shaw came out with his thoughts about the War, the situation was very different. It might have been predicted that what he said then would not seem subversive or blasphemous now. The public has accepted Mr Shaw, not by recognizing the intelligence of what he said then, but by forgetting it; but we must not forget that at one time Mr Shaw was a very unpopular man. He is no longer the gadfly of the commonwealth; but even if he has never been appreciated, it is something that he should be respected. To-day he is perhaps an im-

portant elder man of letters in a sense in which Mr Hardy is not.
Hardy represents to us a still earlier generation not by his date of
birth but by his type of mind. He is of the day before yesterday,
whilst Shaw is of a to-day that is only this evening. Hardy is
Victorian, Shaw is Edwardian. Shaw is therefore more interesting to us, for by reflecting on his mind we may form some plausible
conjecture about the mind of the next age—about what, in retro-
spect, the "present" generation will be found to have been. Shaw
belongs to a fluid world, he is an insular Diderot, but more serious.
I should say—for it is amusing, if unsafe, to prophesy—that we
shall demand from our next leaders a purer intellect, more scientific, more logical, more rigorous. Shaw's mind is a free and easy
mind: every idea, no matter how irrelevant, is welcome. Twenty
years ago, even ten years ago, the Preface to Methuselah would
have seemed a cogent synthesis of thought instead of a delightful
farrago of Mr Shaw's conversation about economics, politics, biology, dramatic and art criticism. It is not merely that Mr Shaw is
wilful; it is also that he lacks the interest in, and capacity for, continuous reasoning.

Mr Shaw has never cajoled the public; it is no fault of his that
he has been taken for a joker, a cleverer Oscar Wilde, when his intention was always austerely serious. It is his seriousness which
has made him unpopular, which made Oscar Wilde appear, in comparison, dull enough to be a safe and respectable playwright. But
Shaw has perhaps suffered in a more vital way from the public
denseness; a more appreciative audience might have prevented
him from being satisfied with an epigram instead of a demonstration. On the other hand Mr Shaw himself has hardly understood
his own seriousness, or known where it might lead him: he is somehow amazingly innocent. The explanation is that Mr Shaw never
was really interested in life. Had he been more curious about the
actual and abiding human being, he might have been less clever
and less surprising. He was interested in the comparatively tran-
sient things, in anything that can or should be changed; but he was
not interested in, was rather impatient of, the things which always
have been and always will be the same. Now the fact which makes
Methuselah impressive is that the nature of the subject, the attempt
to expose a panorama of human history "as far as thought can
reach" almost compels Mr Shaw to face ultimate questions. His crea-

tive evolution proceeds so far that the process ceases to be progress, and progress ceases to have any meaning. Even the author appears to be conscious of the question whether the beginning and the end are not the same, and whether, as Mr Bradley says, "whatever you know, it is all one." (Certainly, the way of life of the younger generation, in his glimpse of life in the most remote future, is unpleasantly like a Raymond Duncan or Margaret-Morris school of dancing in the present.)

There is evidence that Mr Shaw has many thoughts by the way; as a rule he welcomes them and seldom dismisses them as irrelevant. The pessimism of the conclusion of his last book is a thought which he has neither welcomed nor dismissed; and it is pessimism only because he has not realized that at the end he has only approached a beginning, that his end is only the starting point towards the knowledge of life.

The book may for a moment be taken as the last word of a century, perhaps of two centuries. The eighteenth and nineteenth centuries were the ages of logical science: not in the sense that this science actually made more progress than the others, but in the sense that it was biology that influenced the imagination of non-scientific people. Darwin is the representative of those years, as Newton of the seventeenth, and Einstein perhaps of ours. Creative evolution is a phrase that has lost both its stimulant and sedative virtues. It is possible that an exasperated generation may find comfort in admiring, even if without understanding, mathematics, may suspect that precision and profundity are not incompatible, may find maturity as interesting as adolescence, and permanence more interesting than change. It must at all events be either much more demoralized intellectually than the last age, or very much more disciplined.

T. S. ELIOT

[OCTOBER, 1921]

MODERN ART

NOT because I was there but because everybody else was there does it seem necessary to make of the Paris scene a little prelude for the history of the New York winter.

Apparently Greenwich Village had emigrated *en masse* to the Latin Quarter and like a flock of birds in process of migration was agitatedly fluttering about the Café de la Rotonde as though fully convinced that that was to be the final resting place but finding it nervously impossible after the long flight from the land of dollars to settle into position at once. Some of the hardier birds such as Marsden Hartley and Edna St Vincent Millay rooted themselves instantly and with decision to the wicker chairs of the terrasse. Marsden told me himself that most of his first week in Paris was devoted exclusively to the Café de la Rotonde. He went early in the afternoon that he might certainly have a chair for the evening. The method did appear to be the swiftest one for getting in touch with all Paris. If there were any new heroes bulking large they weighed in at the Rotonde. If they weren't there in person then the news of them was. Scouts from the various camps were continually arriving. John Storrs there for a night on his way back from Rome where he had been arrested for speaking awkwardly the Italian to an official; Marcel Duchamp, pale ascetic, with the tolerant faint grin upon his face of the elderly man who has been through it all before but relishes the smell of the sawdust *quand même;* Man Ray just landing and being whisked off instanter to the secret little café in a passage from the great boulevard where Tzara and the other Dadaists meet every night at six o'clock; and Lipchitz the sculptor who had just finished a remarkable bust of Gertrude Stein; and Braque who had just punched Leonce Rosenberg the dealer upon the jaw at the sale of the Kahnweiller Collection, all, All were there, and all bore the look of exaltation and solid satisfaction that had seemed so significant upon the faces of Hartley and Miss Millay.

The mob that made seats difficult and generally impossible to obtain was composed of the usual picturesque pre-war elements. On the night of quatorze juillet Waldo Pierce pointed out a young man at one of the neighbouring tables and explained that it was a young woman. I asked with much virtuous indignation how on earth he knew but Pierce had turned indifferently away and some one else gave the answer, "Why, don't we see her here every night in skirts!" The young lady certainly was an excellent imitation of a young man, and my informant went on to say that she was very well known in the quarter due to a proclivity she had for appearing on her balcony in a state of nature at odd moments during the middle of the night—a proclivity, it must be said for the vindication of the French, that had brought out loud protests from the neighbours. And there was the tall young fellow in evening dress and a monocle, a Chilian, who never took a seat but moved about chatting from group to group, and who, Charley Demuth told me, had established a record of staying thirty-six consecutive hours at the Rotonde, evening dress, monocle, and all. And there were the two identical coloured lady models who used to flaunt so haughtily in and out of the Rotonde in 1914 and who survived the great war unscathed. And there were, of course, innumerable young things, here, there, and everywhere. It was, in fact, very like the *vie de bohème* of ten years ago, twenty years ago, of the memoirs of Benvenuto Cellini.

Of actual news there was little. The gossip centred for a while upon the Braque-Rosenberg encounter which was the first little affair of the kind since the war and had the effect of making everyone feel that real life had begun again. Part of its success was due to the known good-nature and quietness of Braque which made it the more surprising that he of all those who were disgruntled with Leonce Rosenberg should lead the attack. Braque and his friends not only accused the dealer of having been the reverse of generous during the difficult period of the war, but of being actually against Braque's interests, in his quality as expert, in the Kahnweiller sale. The Henry Kahnweiller Collection, the property of a Viennese, had been confiscated by the French Government and was now to be sold for the public benefit, and as it was rich in productions by the modernists, the entire group were intensely interested in an outcome that it was felt would go a great way towards definitely placing these much debated men. Whatever the rights and wrongs of Braque and his circle may have been—and it is unbecoming for a foreigner to take sides in family disputes—there can be no doubt but that the blow that was struck in the presence of Miss Stein, Matisse, and the assembled multitude, let loose a great wave of sympathy for the artist, a sympathy no doubt that helped the subsequent prices. The Braque prices compared favourably with the Picasso prices, his top price being thirty-two hundred francs, a respectable enough auction figure considering the despicable leanness of everyone's pocketbook. Two Picassos fetched thirty-one hundred francs each, but prices having been mentioned, it is only fair to add that Derain eclipsed all, selling several for over ten thousands francs and selling one for eighteen thousand. Derain, it seems, has a vogue in England, which is clever of England; hence his prices.

No great new giants have appeared. The advanced guard still considers Braque, Derain, Picasso, Lipchitz, Gris, and Matisse sufficiently in advance of the public taste for its purposes although Matisse is dangerously near to becoming fashionable. He is in every show and usually dominates it, painting joyously in the now familiar manner. Lipchitz and Braque, with whom I dined at Miss Stein's, are still deploring the passing of Guillaume Apollinaire, and insist that what the new movement chiefly lacks is an adequate spokesman. It may be, however, that Jean Cocteau, whose Nouveaux Mariées sur le Tour Eiffel at the Ballet Suédois was an immense success, is he whom Providence designs for this rôle. It should be added, too, that Miss Stein takes the new café exhibitions in the Boulevard Montparnasse and in Montmartre seriously, believing they will replace the Independents whose spirit has been crushed by the deadly atmosphere of the Grand Palais.

So, on the whole, it may be seen that Paris is again Paris, the city of light, but this wholesale sweeping towards it of the American moths is something I regard with misgiving. Our Greenwich Village which had assumed respectable proportions during the war, will drift again, with its chief characters gone, into a mere waystation on the route to the Latin Quarter. I never obtained much soul food myself in Greenwich Village—the place meant almost nothing to me—but I am loth to lose a shred of such atmosphere as we had managed to accumulate. I hate, in fact, to see my countrymen accept provincialism as their portion. I cheer myself with the reflection that we are very rich, that we have all the gold that there is, and that where the gold is there comes that ease of living that flowers into artistic expression, but apparently we are in for a dull year or two until all our pig-headed geniuses realize that New York is, after all, the centre of the universe and return to it. I like Paris, too, you understand . . . but I think the time has come when it is no longer necessary for a first-rate American to go there.   HENRY McBRIDE

[DECEMBER, 1921]

COMMENT

ANATOLE FRANCE has, on the day we write, been named for the Nobel Prize in literature by the Swedish Academy, and although it may seem a trivial thing for us to say we confess to an especial feeling of happiness. We are publishing in this issue the end of M France's memories of his childhood and, as far as we know, this is the first time that any work of M France has appeared simultaneously in English and in French. That the work of an acknowledged master in the ordinary course of events waits many years before its introduction to America confirms in us our belief that THE DIAL, by bringing European work immediately to America, fulfils a highly necessary function.

The Nobel Prize to M France affects us in another way. Within a few weeks we shall announce through the newspapers the name of the recipient of THE DIAL's award. According to the original statement the award will go to a young American writer, one of our contributors, in recognition of his service to American letters. These are, to be sure, limitations forced upon us by lack of those millions which enable the Swedish Academy to range the world for their prizemen. But the distinction of THE DIAL's award, in our own eyes, is that it is to be given annually to one who has already accomplished a service, yet has not completed his work. The money we pay to the recipient will give him leisure for a year, if leisure is what he wants most; it will in any case afford him an opportunity to do what he wishes to do and out of that to enrich and develop his work. The Nobel Prize (particularly in literature) is the bestowal of an honour, and with that we cannot quarrel; our own small award is intended for encouragement and opportunity.

THE present number of THE DIAL completes our second year as a journal of art and letters. The Dean of the College of Liberal Arts at the University of North Dakota makes the occasion felicitous by the following letter:

". . . I have been following THE DIAL for some time with considerable curiosity. I can remember when THE DIAL was a distinct credit to American letters, but that day has certainly gone by. Indeed, I am at a loss to know its reason for existence. Perhaps it is to be regarded as a humorous publication. If so, its humor is too dull and gross to merit any attention. It is equally a failure if one attempts to take it seriously. Its ethics are rotten, its style is often loose and inartistic, its illustrations are disgusting. *It represents nothing but degeneracy*.[1] I shall certainly not recommend it to any of my students. In fact, I have given orders to have it stopped at the library as soon as our present subscription expires.

Yours, with scant respect,

Vernon P. Squires"

Tros, runs a line in Virgil, the motto of The North American Review, *Tros Tyriusve mihi nullo discrimine agetur*. Our modernist Trojan, our classic Tyrian, are treated thus; but for the first time we understand *nullo discrimine*.

Dean Squires cannot know. Even the most degenerate of us have our moments, our moments of longing for "ancient beauty and austere control." At times it has seemed to us that we have floundered out of the morass, have published one picture, one poem, one line even of prose, which represented something not degenerate. We had thought that with the spread of culture, which means the capacity to make distinctions, our readers had recognized our tragic efforts. We have been mistaken. We represent nothing but.

An eminent English critic has written us that alone among magazines we stand without respect of persons for the honour of letters and we have tried to believe him. Now we cannot. But faithful always to our duty we make the following report to our readers:

Their number is increasing. More important, the rate of increase is going up, so that each month shows a gain over the preceding. The comparatively profitless sales at newsstands has improved for us, since we have been able to distribute more copies to the stands and have virtually no returns. What we want is subscriptions. Shortly it will become necessary to print more copies; and if our casual readers will subscribe (the business department assuring us that subscriptions are now offered on most favourable terms) they will help us to decide how much larger to make our coming editions.

To those who subscribe we can promise a few things. We have so far not been persuaded to abandon the greatest of our projects, to serve American letters by publishing the best work of known and un-

---

[1] The italics are ours.

known Americans, expressed in new or traditional forms, together with the best work of the same type produced in Europe. We have been called to account for not excluding established writers and for admitting Europeans; we have undoubtedly lost readers because of our refusal to omit work unsanctified by time. But nothing has yet been said to convince us that legitimate change in the form of artistic expression came to an end in the reign of the good Queen Anne; nor have we any reason to believe that the perfection of a traditional form is an effort unworthy of the encouragement of publication. We are aware (and think it natural) that some of the work we publish should seem eccentric to some of our readers and we appreciate their criticism; what makes us understand the rack and the wheel is the assurance from our friends that if we dropped everything modern we should have a great magazine. Possibly they are right. We will not say that in that case we should have a great dead magazine; but we are certain that we should be doing exactly half our job and no more.

WE want more and better work from American artists. We have no closed list of regular contributors. One thing only we cannot see: the advisability of publishing second-rate work in order to encourage other Americans. We have noted at the Metropolitan and at the Theatre Guild that the supposed necessity of producing an American work (*pour encourager les autres*) has often resulted in the production of a bad American work; and we have always felt that the real encouragement (to the others, of course) came from the hard-hearted and totally unpatriotic critics who damned the venture out of hand. Fortunately there are in the fields we cultivate Americans who refuse to do the cheap and scamped and meretricious thing; if they are not Titans they are artistically honest men and women. On them our case, and our success, stands.

[DECEMBER, 1921]

"MADAME A SA TOUR MONTE . . ."

By Louis Aragon

Translated from the French by Gilbert Seldes

"La froide majesté
de la femme sterile."
C. B.

For the first time in literature, Matisse is not a Russian princess but a girl with red hair who was born in the Batignolles—more than twenty years ago, however. Her arms are the longest arms in the world, ending in rough sketches of hands so large that you fancy they were made to support a pensive brow. Hers, low and fretted at the top by a meagre bang, would hardly justify the adjective; her eyes devour it, diminish it excessively, seem to refuse to take any account of anatomy. As she does not wish to be conspicuous and wants you to believe that the immensity of her eyes comes from make-up, Matisse lengthens her palpebral slits with a stroke of black and extends the arches of her eyebrows to the roots of her hair; to acquit them of devouring her cheeks she underlines her eyes with soft shadows. By nature her transparent skin shows the blood underneath, but out of modesty Matisse conceals her circulation under a metallic iridescent paste over which she powders green, so that her cheeks harmonize agreeably. Her well-cut, slightly aquiline nose gives a touch of architectural firmness to this countenance. The thin long lips are carmined at the centre only and so gain an ambiguous effect, for you think you are seeing two mouths, one little, the other endless, neither of which ever sings the same tune as the other. Matisse has a horror of symmetry and therefore has but one ear, protected, shaded, without a pendant; but on the other side her hair discloses an emerald buckle by way of compensation. Her strongly modelled jaw grows more delicate towards the chin. Her body remembers that it was for her that the expression *fausse maigre* was invented. Her left hip, more prominent than the other as a resting place for her fist, no doubt, gives a roll to her gait which alone betrays the sensuality of this reserved creature so little disposed to reveal her solid temperament. The exiguity of her feet is astonishing, until you recall in time to which sex Matisse belongs.

57

She is fond of strong common perfumes, patchoulis of low degree, like masks which bring a hundred contemptuous thoughts in her direction. In this taste, however complicated by modern intentions, you recognize the atavisms of the eastern or western harems in which her forbears used to pass their lives watching the sunlight through the shutters. Emancipated, she still speaks in a soft artificial voice which contrasts oddly with the freedom of her manner. She pronounces with great distinction the vulgar phrases of fashionable young girls, an outmoded slang which sounds as false as the dry laugh with which she accompanies the worn out puns she makes now and then like little social formulas. Nothing in her conversation would lead you to believe that she has read all the good authors, nor, for that matter, that in private she prefers the bad ones. A graduate violinist, she now plays nothing but ragtime and two-steps; classical music makes her yawn. She is generally supposed to be rich because she has no lover and yet does not get the consideration due to a woman of social standing. As the source of her income is unknown she excites curiosity, but only for a very little while since she offers no food for evil tongues. Furthermore, she does not appear strange except by comparison. Alone, in the street, she does not attract a second glance; but in a crowd she monopolizes attention.

Her clothes are less indecent than eccentric; Matisse does not dress in the latest fashion but in the one after that. Three months from now her frock will be worn by all the *petites bourgeoises* whom it now disturbs. However, no matter what the rage of the day may be, two elements in her costume are constant; always light colours and always long wide gloves caught at the wrist. For Matisse believes that a woman's clothes must be adapted to her body; she knows that she has wretched arms and hides them, too brilliant hair and tones it down. At least she acts as if she thought and knew these things. She adores lace trimmings and is lavish with them, especially when they are least in fashion. So that other women often seem undressed beside her. She speaks with a certain repugnance of a bodice through which you can see the ribbons of corset-covers or chemises. Lacking information I fancy that under her dress she wears only a combination in green silk. I can say of her stockings that they are uninteresting, but of her boots that

> Always Matisse's boots,
> Coloured with life and fashion,

Cheerfully equivocate
Between the arts and passion.

In addition to the emerald which is nothing but green as the blinds
of a house with a tiled roof, Matisse wears two jewels, one a golden
tooth mounted in a pendant, to which she attaches no symbolic meaning, the other a pretty Browning automatic in Toledo steel which
she carries in her muff in winter, in her handbag in summer, and which
synthesizes for her the devastating action of the past. Her handbag
contains, besides, the necessary arsenal for make-up. Also to be
found there are a pocket-level, a compass, a kaleidoscope for her
hours of ennui, some red pimentos to deceive her hunger, and a little
scalpel with no other purpose than to make you think of James Feni-
more Cooper.

Matisse's apartment is almost entirely furnished with kitchen
chairs, drawing-tables, and arm-chairs which have the theoretical
form of arm-chairs. You have to look closely to see that they aren't
of white wood at all, but of the most precious materials. Matisse
hates style. "Style," she says, "is only a convenient method of
getting someone else to judge of the beauty of a piece of furniture."
Some of her chairs are only intersections of feet, backs, and bars;
others affect the linear aspect of furniture which is always seen in
profile by school children. If Matisse uses electric light she is not
ashamed of it and does not try to hide the bulbs in the cornices as
do all American millionaires in elaborately mounted films and in
the descriptions in Nick Carter. She leaves to milliners and ro-
manticists the ridiculous mania for justifying their presence by
making them come out of a flower or assigning them a hazardous
rôle in a scene from mythology. The electric light seems to her to
be an accessory to the furniture endowed with a personal beauty
which must not be spoiled by a useless fixture. For the rooms where
the light must be dimmed, Matisse chooses glazed bulbs and dresses
them in those shades, white inside and green outside, which are
used in business offices. She also possesses a lot of coloured bulbs
to replace the usual lights in accordance with the whim of the
moment. In the same spirit, instead of hiding the radiators in a
box or behind the woodwork, Matisse has placed them in the open,
and in her study they run all around the walls like bookshelves in
other houses. She loves these great immobile and sinuous serpents

whose humour, reserved and cold, or communicative and ardent, can be regulated by a wooden wheel. In place of wall-paper she has covered her walls with posters which cut into one another so that you cannot read a single one through, so your curiosity is primed and uncertainty lets you dream. Under the glass table-top she has pretty sketches overlaid with inscriptions in honour of a storage warehouse, a trunk factory, and the spring mattresses made by S. & Co. The fan lying on the table sings the praises of some little Breton village, the drinking cup looks exactly like those you find in the Paris post office stations. Around the neck of the carafe, over the matchbox, on the calendar, you can read business addresses. Finally, at night, electric lettering announces the week's sales in the big department stores.

In this little *salon* Matisse feels vividly excited by the manifestations of human activity about her and her own inactivity weighs upon her deliciously. She feels the charm of being an expensive animal and like a cat she closes her eyes and purrs. At other times she sets herself in harmony with her furnishings, fights for life, suffers from the advantage which the lighting gives to one poster on the wall to the prejudice of another; she owns stock in the enterprise thus compromised; she grows desperate, cries out that this Mene Tekel Upharsin of a pharmacist is a lie, extinguishes the lamp, lights another, puts in a bulb which makes the invading poster turn grey, and triumphs like a captain of industry in the success of her preferred product. Again, at times, she sticks letters to the partitions until they seem to dance about her in a fantastic round. On days when her *boudoir* seems too populous, Matisse goes into her studio to rest.

The studio is formed by two superimposed suites which Matisse has united by having the ceiling broken through. You would fancy yourself in a demolished house; the marks left by the flooring remain on the walls and you can see the torn wall-paper of the different rooms. The six windows in two ranks like soldiers look down with an air of reproachful melancholy on this interior. On the upper floor the doors seem absolutely silly opening on a void. A corner of the lower room is still fitted out like a bar, a shelf for bottles, adjustable chairs, a counter painted to imitate pink marble with a zinc top to which counterfeit coins are nailed. Here Matisse receives the importunate; they are soon unable to bear the desolate atmosphere of the place any longer and find an excuse to flee. At night Matisse lights up her demolitions with a single lamp hung from the beam, immense shadows are projected upon the ceiling, and Matisse plans novels.

She comes an orphan from the village where her parents were solid farming folk to the bar in Paris kept by her uncle, her last living relative, her last hope. Here she is, naïve and pure, helpless before the desires of wheelwrights and men with terrifying faces. What will become of her? She reads her fate in the eyes of a poor girl being bullied by her lover. Her uncle arranges to turn her over to a Russian prince; it is done, but behold The Unknown who appears and saves her! This mysterious personage, strong, rich, and handsome, has a secret in his life. When it is known the novel will be finished. Or perhaps Matisse is a light woman who has ruined grandees of Spain, driven children to suicide, hurried bankers into bankruptcy, clerks to theft, students to assassination. Dressed as a street-walker she comes to seduce the innocent bottle-washer at a *café de barrière*. Here the scene becomes realistic and Matisse suddenly perceives a medal round the young man's neck, or a birthmark, or some indelible tattooing; it is her son whom she abandoned one snowy night at the door of a church. After such an adventure she becomes a nun or more likely goes into the bedroom.

The bedroom is for rest only; daylight comes in through the shutters whose slats turn according to the time of day and replace ungracious blinds which Matisse has had taken down. In this striped ambiance nothing can disorder the imagination or trouble the senses, lest the slightest over-excitement should banish that sleep of which it is the shrine. Nothing more intimate, nothing more secret than this room; you dare speak only in whispers. The modest chairs hide their skeletons under sombre draperies of red-brown or garnet; not a chair, not a stool, shows its wood. Everything breathes softness and abandon; the skins thrown on the floor deaden your footfall; no mirror in these arcana reflects a luxurious object which might trouble Matisse in her sleep like an eye or might introduce into her dreams the last vision, before she drowses off, of her too lovely nakedness. The immense bed occupies the centre of this room like a ship. A calm sea carries it on; when Matisse lies down she is tempted to recall Morpheus and his myths (her eyelids are the poppies) and this resting place becomes the fulfilment of the world. To make the silence more palpable, near the window, catching the light, a violin lies silent in its mahogany coffin lined with blue plush, and the bow which shares its resting place becomes the bond between this lifeless universe and the world of reality.

You catch sight of the world by leaning out of the window: roofs of Paris like grey linoleum, irregular chimneys the beauty of which Matisse could only describe with the Latin word "formosa," more sensuous than any praise of ours; studios whose windows let you guess the play of dust within; bevelled faces of apartment houses beside which others will be built later; vague lots; in a courtyard the glass shows a servants' stairway mounting like a prayer or like a snail; the vast garages where automobiles come and go, attracted by the capital letters on the façade. The sudden cry of a train comments on the scene and one learns the name of the quarter: Rome, which links the idea of ancient civilization with the magic of modern cities.

The bath-room surprises you as you come out of the torpor of the bedroom. You would think you were coming into an operating room; everything is neat, shining, geometric, brilliant, incisive. The visitor's first thought is to estimate the cubic feet of air in the space. The walls in white enamel, innocent of all covering, cruelly reflect a light which would neither help a wrinkle to deceive nor save a grey hair from being pulled out. Admirably glazed, the apparatus for hydrotherapy and electric massage make you think of the torture chambers of the Middle Ages. On the dressing table there is an army of files, orange-sticks, polishers, scissors, curling-irons, battalions of jars of paint, of colgate, of cold cream, carmine for the finger nails, phalanxes of rouge-sticks, rabbits' feet, hair combs, of all sizes and for all purposes, awaiting the daily combat without any visible impatience. Rubber sponges, the triumph of man, are enthroned on the toilet table. The smell of toothpaste completes the scene.

If by carelessness you accidentally turn the tap handle in the toilet the wrong way, a trap opens in the ceiling and an iron ladder descends. Matisse could not bear to have an apartment in which she could not hide a criminal, conspire against the safety of the state, or dispose of a corpse. That is why she established this clandestine communication with the next floor, rented as constituting the upper part of the studio; the other rooms are a hiding place which need envy nothing in detective stories. The one you come into first is empty, as if abandoned, in order to throw visitors off the scent; on the unpainted, unpapered walls workmen have written their names, done sums, set down reflections on life, and outlined their ideal woman; on the windows the masons have scratched in white the symbol of infinity. But the rest of the apartment is a complete arsenal of detective's accessories; microphones which let you hear conversations on the floor below; dictaphones concealed in the desks; photographic apparatus in the chiffoniers, chairs which fold their arms over any one imprudent enough to sit down in them; safes in the shape of beds and imitation safes which ring an alarm when opened or catch the thief in a trap; sliding panels so you can see what is happening in the next room, periscopes to watch the actions and gestures of slaters on the roof (you never can tell when they will try to come down the chimney like telephone repairmen). There Matisse has gathered the latest mechanisms for silent killing, swiftly or slowly. She is particularly fond of those which look innocent; there is the curare-ring, the bearer of which can kill any one whose hand he shakes; there are the silent compressed-air-pistol, the boomerang which does its destructive duty and returns intelligently to its master, the vulgar sandbag, the carbon dioxide apparatus which asphyxiates the patient in his sleep; the book with poisoned pages which punishes ill-mannered people for moistening their finger to turn the leaves; the liquid-air bomb for blowing up safes, electric contrivances which forbid entrance to the room on pain of death, radium tubes, tubes with infrared or ultra-violet rays destroying those on whom they are played; tubes with coloured rays producing madness, co-aenesthetic, or febrile states; there is finally and above all the great revolver clock which at the appointed hour kills the detective tied to the chair in front of it, or rather which does not kill him because his cousin arrives disguised as a telegraph operator or because the criminal's daughter falls in love with the fair face of the condemned (it is not so astonishing when you realize that her mother was a good woman) or again because at one minute of three, the very last second, the house, mined by a devoted assistant or by fire-worshippers, blows up and hurls into the Hudson, which flows right below, the interesting hero of these modern epics.

Wrongly would one conclude from the peculiarities of her habitation that Matisse is a romantic; like a good stay-at-home woman all she wants is that her home should be ready for all eventualities. In her house you can choke your neighbour, arrange a combine for the Bourse, negotiate a treaty, read a play, or undermine the ministry; nothing will seem out of place, nothing shocking. However, the mistress of the house has made no provision for amorous adventures. Just as she does not conceive of eating at home, so she does not allow any abandon there to too tender sentiments; it is not only in restaurants that she has her habits. According to her notions, one possesses a residence to receive friends, to think alone, to sleep, or again, for she is afflicted with no prejudice, to display accomplishments. She does not object to having people read at home, but for herself reserves this occupation for her trips in the Metro. Matisse formulates her tastes neatly because she practises them. She never fails to answer the questionnaires which appear in the magazines: Which are your favourite books? What was your strongest emotion? and a thousand other questions, the puerility of which does not escape her, but which she prides herself on being the only one to take seriously. She answers them with the fervour of a penitent at confession, and this systematic exploration of herself fills her with comfort. Each time she discovers a new corner of her thoughts which had remained unknown to her she laughs like a child looking at herself in the mirror for the first time and registering her discovery. Hereafter she will be able to say when any one tells her about herself, "Well, what do you want? That's how I am." For she fears lest someone else should know her better than herself.

One day Matisse went to the country; the trees, the ditches, the roads, the meadows, bored her; she followed a little stream to keep herself in countenance, but she yawned.

Suddenly she saw a factory rising before her; quickly she ran to this Paradise Regained and as soon as she got into the yard she sniffed the good smell of smoke and coal, listened to the whistling, the grinding of machinery, let herself be elbowed about by the workmen, closed her eyes and fancied herself back in Paris.

A presumptuous but very rich young man who wanted to inspire Matisse with a passion for himself, gave her, in the belief that a woman of taste must dote on the fine arts, a genuine Rembrandt and a bust by Houdon. She gave the painting to her concièrge without telling her its value so that several years later a fortunate expert discovered it and bought it for a song. As for the bust, she painted it black because she found that, stained, it resembled one of her negro grooms.

If Matisse were not so coldly reasonable she would soon dominate the city, as Ninon once upon a time or Sorel to-day; she is satisfied to live in it.

[JANUARY, 1922]

MUSICAL CHRONICLE

Schoenberg's Five Orchestral Pieces, presented in New York for the first time nine years since their publication and nine years since Sir Henry Wood performed them in London, modelled the sketchy portrait of the enigmatical and piercing singer left long in us by the inertia of conductors. The bizarre and elusive music brought it in upon us with new vehemence that when the uncouth and wondrous pierrot leaves off theorizing and utters the rustle and tumult in his choked breast, he becomes as troubling, capricious, and seraphic an artist as any the world holds to-day. It was the part ultra-Tristanish, part grotesque, lyricism announced by the Kammersymphonie and the Quartet Op. 7 that, sharpened, clarified, and given diaphanous pinions, was shaken loose by the Philadelphia Orchestra the night late in November. Not that traces of the grating, wingless, Schoenberg of the nine piano pieces were entirely obliterated. The fifth of the orchestral pieces, like its brethren of Op. 11 and Op. 17, remained heavily aground, an unfriendly, leaden, post-Brahmsian mass. One was minded of the theorizing, insensitive state always ready pitfall-like to swallow the Viennese musician. But, fantastically and abruptly in the first and fourth numbers, Vorgefühle and Péripétie; ecstatically and with almost painful tenderness in Vergangenes and Der Wechselnde Akkord, the instruments gave forth quivering modern life, and made Schoenberg the penetrating, the subtle, the clairvoyant creator vivid as never before over us.

Two facets of Schoenberg's originality stand out from the many fleeting impressions left by the performance. The one remains as a memory of grotesque starts, abrupt sudden flights of sound, trilling of brasses in their lower register, fluttering of woodwind, sudden roaring climaxes of sound, followed by equally sudden silences. They recall the silent and atrocious music that goes on in the body during bad quarter hours. A sudden twinge of fear. Another, more piercing quirk. Then, the dead weight plunged suddenly into the entrails. The heart jumps a beat, commences pounding. The Schoenberg orchestra meshed in the nerves begins a clamour, a mad fiddling, shrilling, and blasting. It was as an image of those states of sick presentiment that the first of the five pieces became reality. The fourth, Pérepétie, seemed to imagine another such iron livid hell,

one of those that are about us in the hours when we suddenly find
ourselves caught in an inevitable catastrophe of life; when some
unexpected crushing news is brutally transmitted; when the ruthless
decision of some needed creature strikes us to the earth. Savage
tearing arpeggios of brass and woodwind in contrary motion. In
the interstices of the grinding storm, the muted horns sing a voice-
less, broken song; speak some nightmare consciousness of the cruelty of fortune; make a moment of aching relief in the lashing whirlwind. Again a blow; a flight of clarinets; and the world topples in.

The other facet that remained underscored was Schoenberg's almost ecstatic voluptuousness. The swooning sensuousness was always evident in him, even when he used an idiom not yet wholly personal. It gives the sextet its mordant, soprano-like delicacy, its
moonlit texture. One hears it, grown graver, more biting, in the
penultimate section of the quartet Op. 7. But in the second and third
of the five orchestral pieces, it utters itself with a poignancy grown almost insupportable. Schoenberg appears to have inherited all of the
refined burning sensuousness of Wagner, of Debussy, of Scriabine, and
to have expressed it anew. His orchestration has a softness, an aerial
dreaminess of harps, celesta, muted strings that remind one of the
first encounters with the second act of Tristan, with the tower and
murder scenes of Pelléas. A terrific tension expresses itself in him in
slow, overlapping phrases, in almost imperceptible changes of harmony, in immense, far-flung chords, that reach far out into overtones.
The celesta murmurs against solo strings; the chord of the won-
drously still, ecstatic third piece twitches rathermore than changes;
the orchestra sings with a strange, contained, many-voiced passion.
The music seems to lead us back into some moment when tenderness
became almost a searing flame, an agony; when the whispering voice
became laden with glamour; when the touch of a hand thanked as
no words can. With Schoenberg, it is either ecstasy of pain, or ecstasy of pleasure; and the two become wellnigh one.

What in others remains half-conscious, moving like a dim silent
sea, breaking only at moments into definite perceptions, that in
Schoenberg's mind becomes tone. He has some contact; for the
quivering of his fine modern nerves, the delicate perceptions, intima-
tions, the atrocious contractions and stoppage of breath, the singing
of the past in him are issued again into the world as life. What he has
experienced suddenly becomes the playing of the instruments of the

band, a new melody, rhythm, tone-colour. Gestures appear, that make him feel certain curves, certain combinations of instruments, and set him categorically the task of realizing them. It is this imperative he is seeking to explain when he says *"Der Künstler tut nichts, was andere fur schön halten, sondern nur, was ihm notwendig ist."* He hears in almost epigrammatic rapidity; jumps processes of relation which to others appear necessary, feels a dominant pitch in what to others may seem a succession of dissonances. He hears, it would seem, primarily tone-colour; his instruments play in families; he has increased the number of clarinets, say, in order to be able to retain whole passages in a precise timbre. The fragmentariness of his early work, Verklärte Nacht and Gurrelieder, is transcended.

The life communicated by the music was in every one of the auditors in Carnegie Hall that Tuesday evening. And still, the assemblage sat like patients in dentist chairs, submitting resignedly to a disagreeable operation. What probably deterred from a more positive expression of distaste was a memory of certain hasty and mistaken prejudices, entertained in the same place. None of the auditors was old enough in the flesh to remember the days when the terrible Dr Hanslick of Vienna had found Wagner's music like the screeching of tomcats. But everyone there doubtlessly remembered the days when a certain Richard Strauss, who has since been discovered the tamest of domestic animals, an old dog who likes to lie in the sun sleepily, blinking, wrote "crazy-music" and was "an anarch of art." Still, at the conclusion of the Schoenberg, the entire assemblage almost to a man fell into trap neatly laid for them by Dr Stokowski. As the bugle call of Wotan's Abschied sounded, a storm of clapping arose. Fools! they did not perceive that they were applauding the very man whose music sounded just as dull and cacophonous to their grandparents as that of the Viennese had but an instant before sounded to them.

It was the old inability to receive the new at the moment when reception is a creative act that was evidenced. The newspaper critics showed it most. They were like a crowd of morons forced to act, say, to take a bath. The older ones fell to quoting the Bible. The younger accused their Mercury of unmentionable things.

Meanwhile, one begins to entertain respect again for Dr Stokowski. If only he would repeat the splendid dose! One might find oneself admiring him as of yore. PAUL ROSENFELD [JANUARY, 1922]

AN EPISODE

By D. H. Lawrence

As he lay thinking of nothing and feeling nothing except a certain weariness, or dreariness, or tension, or God-knows-what, he heard a loud hoarse noise of humanity in the distance, something frightening. Rising, he went on to his little balcony. It was a sort of procession, or march of men, here and there a red flag fluttering from a man's fist. There had been a big meeting, and this was the issue. The procession was irregular, but powerful, men four abreast. They emerged irregularly from the small piazza into the street, calling and vociferating. They stopped before a shop and clotted into a crowd, shouting, becoming vicious. Over the shop-door hung a tricolour, a national flag. The shop was closed, but the men began to knock at the door. They were all workmen, some in railwaymen's caps, mostly in black felt hats. Some wore red cotton neck-ties. They lifted their faces to the national flag, and as they shouted and gesticulated Aaron could see their strong teeth in their jaws. There was something frightening in their lean, strong Italian jaws, something inhuman and possessed-looking in their foreign, southern-shaped faces, so much more formed and demon-looking than northern faces. They had a demon-like set purpose, and the noise of their voices was like a jarring of steel weapons. Aaron wondered what they wanted. There were no women —all men—a strange male, slashing sound. Vicious it was—the head of the procession swirling like a little pool, the thick wedge of the procession beyond, flecked with red flags.

A window opened above the shop, and a frowsty-looking man, yellow-pale, was quickly and nervously hauling in the national flag. There were shouts of derision and mockery—a great overtone of acrid derision—the flag and its owner ignominiously disappeared. And the procession moved on. Almost every shop had a flag flying. And every one of these flags now disappeared, quickly or slowly, sooner or later, in obedience to the command of the vicious, derisive crowd, that marched and clotted slowly down the street, having its own way.

Only one flag remained flying—the big tricolour that floated from the top storey of the house opposite Aaron's hotel. The ground floor of this house consisted of shop-premises—now closed. There was no sign of any occupant. The flag floated inert aloft.

The whole crowd had come to a stop immediately below the hotel, and all were now looking up at the green and white and red tricolour which stirred damply in the early evening light, from under the broad eaves of the house opposite. Aaron looked at the long flag, which drooped almost unmoved from the eaves-shadow, and he half expected it to furl itself up of its own accord, in obedience to the will of the masses. Then he looked down at the packed black shoulders of the mob below, and at the curious clustering pattern of a sea of black hats. He could hardly see anything but hats and shoulders, uneasily moving like boiling pitch away beneath him. But the shouts began to come up hotter and hotter. There had been a great ringing of a door-bell and battering on the shop-door. The crowd—the swollen head of the procession—talked and shouted, occupying the centre of the street, but leaving the pavement clear. A woman in a white blouse appeared in the shop-door. She came out and looked up at the flag and shook her head and gesticulated with her hands. It was evidently not her flag—she had nothing to do with it. The leaders again turned to the large house-door, and began to ring all the bells and to knock with their knuckles. But no good—there was no answer. They looked up again at the flag. Voices rose ragged and ironical. The woman explained something again. Apparently there was nobody at home in the upper floors—all entrance was locked—there was no caretaker. Nobody owned the flag. There it hung under the broad eaves of the strong stone house, and didn't even know that it was guilty. The woman went back into her shop and drew down the iron shutter from inside.

The crowd, nonplussed, now began to argue and shout and whistle. The voices rose in pitch and derision. Steam was getting up. There hung the flag. The procession crowded forward and filled the street in a mass below. All the rest of the street was empty and shut up. And still hung the showy rag, red and white and green, up aloft.

Suddenly there was a lull—then shouts, half-encouraging, half derisive. And Aaron saw a smallish black figure of a youth, fair-haired, not more than seventeen years old, clinging like a monkey to the front of the house, and by the help of the heavy drain-pipe and the stone-work ornamentation climbing up to the stone ledge that ran under ground-floor windows, up like a sudden cat on to the projecting footing. He did not stop there, but continued his race like some frantic lizard running up the great wall-front, working away from the noise below, as if in sheer fright. It was one unending wriggling movement, sheer up the front of the impassive, heavy stone house.

The flag hung from a pole under one of the windows of the top storey—the third floor. Up went the wriggling figure of the possessed youth. The cries of the crowd below were now wild, ragged ejaculations of excitement and encouragement. The youth seemed to be lifted up, almost magically on the intense upreaching excitement of the massed men below. He passed the ledge of the first floor, like a lizard he wriggled up and passed the ledge or coping of the second floor, and there he was, like an upward-climbing shadow, scrambling on to the coping of the third floor. The crowd was for a second electrically still as the boy rose there erect, cleaving to the wall with the tips of his fingers.

But he did not hesitate for one breath. He was on his feet and running along the narrow coping that went across the house under the third-floor windows, running there on that narrow footing away above the street, straight to the flag. He had got it—he had clutched it in his hand, a handful of it. Exactly like a great flame rose the simultaneous yell of the crowd as the boy jerked and got the flag loose. He had torn it down. A tremendous prolonged yell, touched with a snarl of triumph, and searing like a puff of flame, sounded as the boy remained for one moment with the flag in his hand looking down at the crowd below. His face was odd and elated and still. Then with the slightest gesture he threw the flag from him, and Aaron watched the gaudy remnant falling towards the many faces, whilst the noise of yelling rose up unheard.

There was a great clutch and hiss in the crowd. The boy stood still unmoved, holding by one hand behind him, looking down from above, from his dangerous elevation, in a sort of abstraction.

And the next thing Aaron was conscious of was the sound of trumpets. A sudden startling challenge of trumpets, and out of nowhere a sudden rush of grey-green carabinieri battering the crowd wildly with truncheons. It was so sudden that Aaron *heard* nothing any more. He only saw.

In utmost amazement he saw the greeny-grey uniformed carabinieri rushing thick and wild and indiscriminate on the crowd: a sudden new excited crowd in uniforms attacking the black crowd, beating them wildly with truncheons. There was a seething moment in the street below. And almost instantaneously the original crowd burst in a terror of frenzy. The mob broke as if something had exploded inside it. A few black-hatted men fought furiously to get themselves free of the hated soldiers; in the confusion bunches of men staggered, reeled, fell, and were struggling among the legs of their comrades and of the carabinieri. But the bulk of the crowd just burst and fled—in every direction. Like drops of water they seemed to fly up at the very walls themselves. They darted into any entry, any doorway. They sprang up the walls and clambered into the ground-floor windows. They sprang up the walls on to window-ledges, and then jumped down again, and ran—clambering, wriggling, darting, running in every direction; some cut, blood on their faces, terror or frenzy of flight in their hearts. Not so much terror as the frenzy of running away. In a breath the street was empty.

And all the time, there above on the stone coping stood the long-faced, fair-haired boy, while four stout carabinieri in the street below stood with uplifted revolvers and covered him, shouting that if he moved they would shoot. So there he stood, still looking down, still holding with his left hand behind him, covered by the four revolvers. He was not so much afraid as twitchily self-conscious because of his false position.

Meanwhile, down below the crowd had dispersed—melted momentaneously. The carabinieri were busy arresting the men who had fallen and been trodden underfoot, or who had foolishly let themselves be taken: perhaps half a dozen men, half a dozen prisoners; less rather than more. The sergeant ordered these to be secured between soldiers. And last of all the youth up above, still covered by the revolvers, was ordered to come down. He turned quite quietly, and quite humbly, cautiously picked his way along the coping towards the drain-pipe. He reached this pipe and began, in humiliation, to climb down. It was a real climb down.

Once in the street he was surrounded by the grey uniforms. The soldiers formed up. The sergeant gave the order. And away they marched, the dejected youth a prisoner between them. . . . The scene was ended.

[FEBRUARY, 1922]

INSTRUCTIONS FOR A BALLET

By Maxwell Bodenheim

Raise the right foot—bound in sheer
Reasons of white and gold—
One inch from the black stage-floor.
Then perform these torpid words:
"Money is dangerous to men:
It shames the clearness of their thoughts."
After thus accounting
For the loquacious smallness
Of those rare gifts that come from doubting men,
Tear the left foot vigorously
From the black grip of the floor,
And attend its nakedness
With this coronation of words:
"Money is emptiness
Curiously violated by colour.
Crown it with originality
That burns with careless discernment,
And amaze the limpid
Familiarity of Time."
After thus accounting
For an improbable situation,
Abandon the farce and shrewdly
Tiptoe across the stage,
Peering down at your feet
And mistaking their lean mysteries
For possibilities in syncopation.
Having thus emulated
The tension of a psycho-analyst
Who confuses routines with causes,
Suddenly kneel upon the floor,
Limp with the collapse of sightless longing,
And raise one hand to the sky
While clenching the other hand at your audience,
Thus expressing the thoughtful perturbations

Of Occidental religions.
Then dance across the stage,
Giving complex decisions to your legs
And interrupting the dance with a pause
In which you question its cumbersome cause.
Having thus defended.
The broken rhythm of Western philosophers—
Sprinkled with a carnival of details—
Change the dance to a borrowed waltz,
Picking suave tricks from a harp
That lacks an ascending scale of notes,
And insisting that the result is music.
The end of the ballet should portray
A gradual sinking to the floor,
With plentiful whispers resenting
The final intrusion of Buddha.

[MARCH, 1922]

A BIRD'S-EYE VIEW OF E. A. ROBINSON

By Amy Lowell

Why does any one want a "collected edition" of anything? That is a question I often ask myself when I turn from the shelves in my library where the collected editions, each in the full panoply and monotony of its uniform binding, stand in august and unsympathetic splendour, to those other shelves, crowded with faded and alluringly well-read volumes, the first, or at least the early, unpretentious editions before the halo of "collected" was wrapped about the author's head. And yet, even as I leave the half-calf, seventeen volume Browning for Paracelsus in boards and Men and Women in faded green cloth, I know full well the answer; for all of us are not sentimental book-collectors or connoisseurs of literary vintages, and even those of us who are, at times, these reprehensible things, may be, at other times, critics and students, and to critics and students the "collected edition" is a handy tool. Still, if a critic wish to run his author to ground, he can by no means ignore the earlier issues of his author's books. So book-collectors are of some use other than the sentimental, after all.

Lazy readers like collected editions because, in buying them, they are sure of getting all of an author's books without the trouble of knowing their titles beforehand. Impecunious readers (by far the largest class everywhere at all times) get much for little, and this last is reason enough to account for the fondness of publishers for this particular article. Yet I can never help feeling that a "collected edition" is something like a tombstone set at the head of its author's "six feet of earth." Of course, there is really nothing to prevent an author's adding new books to those already collected, nothing at all. But the very fact of their being a collection proclaims to the world not only that a man has done something, but that that something will, in all probability, be the major part of his production. If to call the "collected" a tombstone already in place is going a bit far, we can at least consider that with it the "six feet" are at any rate pre-empted, and the tombstone designed, with nothing lacking but the inscription.

Mr Robinson's Collected Poems does not intimidate by its volu-

minousness as Browning's seventeen volumes certainly do. But, as
I heave its weight off the table beside me and strain my eyes over its
narrow-spaced type, I sigh for the charming little volumes in which
I am wont to read him; and, having collated the contents of this big
book with the eight little ones, I put it down and read the poems for
their poetry in the smaller volumes.

This Collected Poems is valuable only for its cheapness, it costs
less than the eight separate volumes put together, but there its value
stops, unless we take it in some measure as accolade—an accolade by
no means needed by the poet—and it is a little jarring to find a tombstone preparing for so very much alive and active a person as Mr
Robinson. Not only is he not written out, he is producing more rapidly every year. As to accolade, is it possible for any man to receive
a greater tribute from his contemporaries than the spontaneous appreciations printed by the New York Times on the occasion of his
fiftieth birthday, two years ago?

Mr Robinson has always been extremely reticent in, what I may
call, *propria persona*. He writes poems for publication, never prose.
He has given us no hint in any paper or review of his opinions of his
fellow poets or himself, he has never put on record in ordinary speech
his reactions to the literature of the past. He places no prefaces before his books; he and his poetry are indivisible, what we make of
him is what we make of that, if we are the public. But it is just because of this that the collected edition becomes of real value to the
student, for his exclusions and inclusions in the matter of poems do
open up a certain insight into his mind. And what we chiefly make
out is that Mr Robinson started fully-fledged and fully armed, that,
to continue my extremely mixed metaphor, he has grown very few
new feathers in the course of years, and that his sword has not only
not been stropped since the beginning, it has not needed stropping.

There are various ways of collecting poems. The horrible way of
the Browning editors has been to group together poems of a species,
thus losing all the aesthetic value of the juxtaposition of a poem of
one type with a poem of another type. Wise authors compose their
books to obviate weariness. In a grouping by types there is no escape for a reader but to close the book. Another way of collecting is
the quasi-chronological, followed by Buxton-Forman in his Keats
editions—the early poems come first and each book is given intact in
the order of its first appearance. Still another way is the strictly

chronological, in which separate books are entirely ignored and the poems are placed in the order in which they were written.

Mr Robinson's plan has been none of these exactly, and, for a collection published in the poet's lifetime, the method he has adopted is excellent. He has kept his books intact throughout, but he begins with The Man Against the Sky and follows it with his first volume, The Children of the Night. After this, the books succeed one another in the sequence of their publications, except that Merlin is interpolated between Captain Craig and The Town Down the River, for no reason that I can see unless to separate it from Lancelot.

Here we are at once at a bit of personal criticism. For it is evident that Mr Robinson agrees with the majority of his critics in considering The Man Against the Sky his best book. He has made no changes in it, no changes in the order of the poems, that is. I have not sought for textual changes in many of the poems, but in those I have examined minutely there are none. In fact, the only volumes he has felt called upon to edit are The Children of the Night and The Town Down the River, and it is significant that he has dropped thirteen of the original poems from The Children of the Night and only one from The Town Down the River. A man who shows himself not averse to excisions on occasion, and yet who finds all he wishes to make (with one exception) in his earliest published work, proves his artistic career to have been singularly of a piece. This fact is evidence that if he and his creative faculty started together, his power of self-criticism has grown, for he has made no mistake in his excisions. The poems he has left out need cause no reader regret, except possibly the title poem of The Children of the Night, and that is not so important as poetry as it is as revelation. Without it, the critic must begin with Mr Robinson in mid-air.

Four years ago, I wrote an article on Mr Robinson which was afterwards reprinted as the first chapter of my Tendencies in Modern American Poetry, and nothing since has caused me to alter the opinions I there expressed. I have no space here to recapitulate the steps by which I reached my conclusions, but I can write nothing on Mr Robinson without stating as a point of departure the main theme of my argument.

Let us begin at once by acknowledging that Mr Robinson is the most finished and settled of the poets alive in America to-day. By "finished," I mean accomplished, polished, master of his medium;

by "settled," I mean fixed and oriented in his own point of view and expression. If a contemporary dare to say that any living writer is sure to rank among the most important poets of his nation, I dare to say this of Mr Robinson. Granting that, then, and admitting that contemporary judgement is a hazardous undertaking, let us see how and why he is what he is, and briefly consider that he is—what?

The main theme by which I set such store is that Mr Robinson is a sort of temporal Colossus of Rhodes; he straddles a period. It seems to me almost impossible to understand Mr Robinson without some knowledge of the society into which he was born. Recollect what Puritanism has meant to America, the good and the bad. Remember how long it held sway, and realize that this sway persisted much longer in the small towns and country districts than it did in the large cities. Mr Robinson grew up in the 'seventies and 'eighties, and if any reader can recall from personal experience country New England in the 'seventies and 'eighties, no more need be said. This growing up of Mr Robinson's took place in Gardiner, a most charming little town on the Kennebec River in Maine. I love Gardiner myself, but I can imagine what it must have been like in the 'seventies and 'eighties. How Mr Robinson could have started, as he did, in the heart of Gardiner, we cannot even conceive until we know more of him and his antecedents than we know now. From Gardiner he went to Harvard, and Harvard in the early 'nineties I do remember. Need I say that no one would have picked it for a forcing bed for Mr Robinson's genius, but still it must have been an improvement on Gardiner.

Now Mr Robinson is a dyed-in-the-wool New Englander, and that must never be forgotten. His tenacity of purpose is thoroughly New England, so is his austerity and his horror of exuberance of expression. His insight into people is pure Yankee shrewdness, as is also his violent and controlled passion. He is absolutely a native of his place, the trouble was that he was not a native of his time. He was twenty years ahead of his time, and that advance has set the seal of melancholy upon him; or, to speak in the cant of the day, it has wound him in inhibitions which he has been unable to shake off.

This is why The Children of the Night (the poem, not the book) is so important. It shows Mr Robinson avowing a creedless religion. I say a creedless religion advisedly, for I do not imagine Mr Robinson to be either an agnostic or an atheist. But a creedless religion in

Gardiner must have made the holder of it feel as though branded with the mark of Cain. Now evolution, in religion as in other things, is a sane and salutary process which leads to no bitterness and is merely the door to freedom. Revolution, on the other hand, is the bread of sorrow and the wine of despair. To be called upon to do in oneself in a few years what nations take centuries in bringing about, means a severe wrenching of intellect and emotion. Read Matthew Arnold's Dover Beach and see what the admitting of a creedless religion means to a man brought up to a formal order, or, indeed, read The Children of the Night. There is gain, of course, but that is dim; there is loss, and that is present and overwhelming.

Mr Robinson could by no means be Gardiner, he could by no means be America at that moment. He began to see life with a touch of irony because it was not his life. His life was nowhere, he withdrew mentally within himself; he withdrew more and more, but he would not compromise. He would be himself regardless of consequences, but that self was an outsider. And, all the time, the old order was holding him, shackling him; again and again he escaped, but it was one continuous fight between himself and himself, between the old Puritan atavism and the new, free spirit. Every poem that Mr Robinson writes is his dual self personified. If he thought his own thoughts, he could in no wise control the form in which he set them; if he spoke his own direct speech, he could put it to no unrestrained or novel music. The luxuriance he innately feared, he drove away; to him, it was an intellectual scarlet woman. He could not be happy, but he could be strong. He could mutter "Courage!" and nerve himself to endurance. He looked to no future, he had no time to build a new order and never guessed that he was building it, he strove to keep himself, his point of view, above water, and he strove magnificently. This is what we read in The Children of the Night, Captain Craig, and The Town Down the River. He raised for himself an altar—the success of failure—and at this he warmed his heart. It is a meagre flame, but it has sufficed him, and we must not quarrel that the pedestal is gaunt and severe.

Then, suddenly, in 1912, a new interest in poetry began to manifest itself. Mr Robinson very likely did not think of himself as a part of it, at first; and I am sure that with much that has come to pass since he has been heartily out of sympathy. But, whatever he may have thought, he was its forerunner; he was even more than that, he was its oldest and most respected exemplar. And however the "new poetry" may have affected Mr Robinson, it brought his audience in its train. He had always been admired by a few, now that few widened to many. It is good for an artist to be admired, and The Man Against the Sky, published six years after its predecessor, The Town Down the River, shows a heightening of power in every direction. Before, he had written almost defiantly, now he is satisfied to write, now he has the contact of an audience to spur him on.

There is no new departure in The Man Against the Sky—Mr Robinson struck his gait in The Children of the Night and he has scarcely varied it since—but there is a greater ease and abundance. Flammonde is one of the most beautiful poems in stanza form that Mr Robinson has done, Ben Jonson Entertains a Man from Stratford probably the best of his monologues. The Man Against the Sky itself, an advance over The Children of the Night. That poem was a cry, this is a question. The excellence of his early vignettes, John Evereldown, Cliff Klingenhagen, Richard Cory, could hardly be surpassed, but there is a greater delicacy in Fragment, a deeper tenderness in The Poor Relation, an extraordinary weirdness and horror in Stafford's Cabin. Captain Craig contained Isaac and Archibald and Aunt Imogen, and nothing could be better in their kinds than these, but John Gorham far outdoes The Woman and the Wife and The Book of Annandale.

Mr Robinson is always at his best in contemporary scenes, and among contemporary people, with the brilliant exception of Ben Jonson. His historical monologues are seldom apt as portraiture. An Island, in which the dying Napoleon is the speaker, is false to its original in every line. Saint Paul addressing the Romans in The Three Taverns is a daring attempt which utterly fails. Lazarus lacks everything except its excellent execution. In Rahel to Varnhagen, Mr Robinson has been able to feel that his characters are contemporary, and to deal with them as though he had created them, and the result is a triumph of two people and an atmosphere.

Two people and an atmosphere is Mr Robinson's forte. Crowd his stage as in Captain Craig, or parts of Merlin and of Lancelot, and his edge becomes blunted. It may be objected that Captain Craig is virtually a monologue, but we can never forget the chorus of young men who are talked at, and the shadowy recorder who is occasionally permitted to speak. Mr Robinson needs to feel his characters in intimate contact, which is very natural. Emotions run deeper and higher between two people who are in close relations with each other than they do in any other sort of grouping except that of a mob swayed by some over-mastering impulse. Mr Robinson is too selective and secret to find inspiration in a mob. We cannot imagine his poems become the marching cry of a multitude. He builds his poetic world out of a series of poignant incidents, and by the deftest of little touches. The crumbling of Merlin's world is shown more vividly in the old man's appreciative dalliance with Vivian than in his weary reception of the king's agonized questions. In Lancelot, the hopeless fate of King Arthur's realm does not lie for us on the battle-fields strewn with dead knights; it is not in the king's chamber at dawn, where Arthur, Gawaine, and Bedivere await the first stroke of what all are aware is doom; it is not even in the conversation between Lancelot and the dying Gawaine. It is in the meeting of Lancelot and Guinevere in the garden, in their terrible interview by fire-light with the rain streaming over the deserted battlefields outside. It should be also in the final parting of Lancelot and Guinevere in the convent parlour, but it is not, for the single reason that the poem is already spent emotionally before the end is reached. This chill finale Mr Robinson surely expected to be an epitome of the whole tragic tale, but the parting of the lovers is too cool in its outward aspect to rouse his invention, and the final scene is a succinct, but rather stereotyped, winding up.

In spite of Mr Robinson's fine gift of irony, he has a real liking for the melodramatic. Where the human element is very powerful, this urge towards melodrama is not too evident, it merely mutters like a coming storm outside the scene on which the event is staged; but where the human element is, for any reason, weakened to the poet's mind, melodrama runs foaming over the story. The worst example of this is Avon's Harvest, but there are many other cases in which the same thing happens in a greater or lesser degree: London Bridge, for example, or The Valley of the Shadow, or The Return of Morgan and Fingal. There is not the slightest objection to melodrama as such, but when Mr Robinson can skate the edge of it so successfully as he often does, to plunge in seems a lowering of technique. I believe that the reason for this sensation of lowering is because the poet's peculiar tenderness and pity are drowned out when mere event becomes too strenuous. For melodrama is circumstance due to external happening; tragedy is circumstance due to human emotion. A melodramatic occurrence such as Macbeth's murder of Banquo may rise to tragedy through its result upon human character. Shakespeare is for ever using melodrama as the spark to light his tragedy, but with Mr Robinson melodrama, when he indulges in it, is itself alone. Perhaps I should qualify this, as Stafford's Cabin, Richard Cory, and many other poems skirt melodrama all the time by virtue of their subjects, but in these cases it is so obviously subordinate to the human scheme as scarcely to deserve its name.

I have spoken of Mr. Robinson's feeling for atmosphere. Never were pictures drawn with more economy than those he gives us, but they are unforgettable. Since the first day I read it, I have never forgotten how

> "The cottage of old Archibald appeared.
> Little and white and high on a smooth round hill
> It stood, with hackmatacks and apple-trees
> Before it, and a big barn-roof beyond;
> And over the place—trees, house, fields and all—
> Hovered an air of still simplicity
> And a fragrance of old summers."

Again, take the house in Fragment:

> "Faint white pillars that seem to fade
> As you look from here are the first one sees
> Of his house where it hides and dies in a shade
> Of beeches and oaks and hickory trees."

Merlin is full of pictures, and they are no longer of New England; we feel the difference at once, not only in the scenes themselves, but in the more elaborate wording with which they are presented:

> "Gay birds
> Were singing high to greet him all along
> A broad and sanded woodland avenue
> That led him on forever, so he thought,
> Until at last there was an end of it;
> And at the end there was a gate of iron,

Wrought heavily and invidiously barred.
He pulled a cord that rang somewhere a bell
Of many echoes, and sat down to rest,
Outside the keeper's house, upon a bench
Of carven stone that might for centuries
Have waited there in silence to receive him.
The birds were singing still; leaves flashed and swung
Before him in the sunlight; a soft breeze
Made intermittent whisperings around him
Of love and fate and danger, and faint waves
Of many sweetly-stinging fragile odours
Broke lightly as they touched him."

People are sketched quite as briefly and inevitably as places. Mr Robinson has the gift of epigrammatic expression. Flammonde comes from

" . . . God knows where,
With firm address and foreign air,
With news of nations in his talk
And something royal in his walk."

Richard Cory "glittered when he walked." Aaron Stark's

" . . . thin, pinched mouth was nothing but a mark;
And when he spoke there came like sullen blows
Through scattered fangs a few snarled words and close,
As if a cur were chary of its bark."

Mr Robinson is a master of brevity and exact, straight-forward speech in his poems, and that makes his frequent habit of circumlocution appear not a little odd and contradictory. It almost seems as though Mr Robinson were, at times, afraid of his own theory of straight-forward speech. He refers to the characteristics of a certain gentleman as "his index of adagios," he speaks of billiard balls as "three spheres of insidious ivory," and calls a hypodermic syringe "a slight kind of engine." I believe this sort of verbal juggling is an atavistic impulse; the same fear of the commonplace which produced the old poetical jargon which Mr Robinson has done so much to banish from present-day poetry.

Allied to this tendency is the cryptic quality of much of his work. Although I do not believe for a moment that he realizes it, this cryptic quality is merely a poetic trick. All poets have their technical tricks, and all good poets make use of suggestion, but suggestion which has to be worked out like a puzzle, and half-statements confused in their own windings, are tricks carried a little too far. Browning was obscure because of a certain difficulty of expression; he triumphed in spite of it, not because of it. But Browning was crystal clear compared to Mr Robinson in these cases. And Mr Robinson has never the slightest difficulty in expressing himself. No, this is a poetic manner due to atavism, it is an evidence of the "shackling" of which I have already spoken.

Edwin Arlington Robinson is a man of stark and sheer vision. He found his voice at a time when America was given over to pretty-prettinesses of all kinds. Some curious instinct for a harsher diet turned him to Crabbe. That alone would show how solitary a thing his development has been, for few poets have been more persistently neglected than George Crabbe. Mr Robinson's sonnet on him begins by admitting the neglect:

> "Give him the darkest inch your shelf allows,
> Hide him in lonely garrets, if you will,—
> But his hard, human pulse is throbbing still."

It is just the "hard, human pulse" that Mr Robinson craved for his own work. He is a far better poet than ever Crabbe was, because Crabbe saw only what is, while Mr Robinson has a deep insight into why it is. In this, he is more akin to Thomas Hardy, whom he has celebrated in another poem in The Children of the Night, omitted in this collected edition. In this poem, he speaks of himself as longing "to feel once more a human atmosphere" and this he finds in the "grand sad song" which is Hardy's, given under the figure of a river. The poem ends:

> "Across the music of its onward flow
> I saw the cottage lights of Wessex gleam."

The hard, human pulse in Thomas Hardy is mellowed and deepened by a poetry of soul which Crabbe had not. Mr Robinson has this poetry of soul to a far greater extent than Crabbe, but he has not yet attained to the reach of Thomas Hardy. Hardy is no such poetical technician as Mr Robinson, but he has a more probing understanding. Hardy touches his characters reverently, even as he dissects them; Mr Robinson is not reverent, his nearest approach to it is a dry-eyed pity. Mr Robinson has resisted life; Hardy has submitted to life as to a beloved master. Hardy is a great architect of tales and poems, The Dynasts is monumental in conception and arrangement, but the details are inadequate; Mr Robinson is a rare craftsman of detail, but his vision is pointillistic.

I have dwelt so long upon the juxtaposition of these two poets because such a juxtaposition makes clear what Mr Robinson has and what he lacks. Thomas Hardy is a product of evolution, Mr Robinson of revolution. His own lines in Lancelot sum up his position not too badly:

> "God, what a rain of ashes falls on him
> Who sees the new but cannot leave the old."

Mr Robinson has left the old, but the dust of it on his shoes still impedes him at times; and he has struggled laboriously out of the rain of ashes, although the white powder lingers on his coat.

Some critics have professed to find in Mr Robinson's work the beating of the knell of doom. I think that is to mistake his attitude and the subtlety of his thought. Doom there may be, but it is an adjunct, not a preoccupation. His preoccupation is with the unanswered question: Is the Light real or imagined, is man dupe or prophet, is faith unbolstered by logic an act of cowardice or an expression of unconscious, pondering intellectuality? There are poems of his to illustrate all these angles of vision. He doubts himself into cynicism, and rises from it through the conception of unexplained beauty. He seeks below life for the undercurrents by which he may discover its meaning. Sometimes he finds one thing, sometimes another; but, whatever he finds, the innate Puritan fortitude and spirituality keep him to his quest. He has not reached his goal nor found his Grail, but he never turns aside from the search, continuing it always with a wistful nobility of purpose which our literature has not seen before.

The arrival of a belated admiration has had a twofold effect upon the poet. It has induced a more abundant creation, and it has urged his ambition to attempt things of larger scope. Here I think we can say that Mr Robinson has possibly not been wise. The technique of the short or semi-long poem, he has mastered completely; for the long poem, he has been obliged to seek models. Merlin as a series of intervals (particularly lyric intervals) is excellent. As a whole long poem, it is inchoate and without direction or climax. These faults do not appear in Lancelot, but something else does. Mr Robinson himself abdicates in favour of many masters of the past. The poem is built, not after a pattern, but to a pattern. It is fine, moving, dramatic, but it is so in just the manner hallowed by time. Mr Robinson does manage to creep in here and there, but, as a rule, some one else takes his place, not any particular person, Mr Robinson does not plagiarize, but a fusion of dramatic poets all speaking at once.

Mr Robinson's old gospel of failure serves him again in Lancelot. The "Light" he has always believed in shines somberly across the poem, but, more than in Merlin, it seems a will-o'-the-wisp gleam. The only hint of poignance in the end of the poem is the very failure of the "Light" to emit any warm glow. Lancelot riding away, seeking to comfort himself by this wan flame, is a pathetic figure.

Mr Robinson's poetry is pathetic, even when it is most vigorous. There is infinite pathos in the lot of the pioneer. Mr Robinson is rather more an outcast from an old order than an enthusiastic adherent of a new. He is preoccupied with the effort and pain of escape. Recognition has come too late for him to experience the sharp joy which lies in conscious upbuilding. It is almost as though he regarded his achieved position with something akin to wonder. He has always believed in his work, but it is a new sensation to believe in the public, and he seems scarcely to dare to surrender himself to the thought of success. Success is a heady wine. In Mr Robinson's case, fearful as he is to find himself sipping it, it has induced both a greater desire to write and a greater self-consciousness, but it has also lulled his critical faculty somewhat, a not uncommon result of the beverage. Would he have written Avon's Harvest ten years ago?

Avon's Harvest appears to be a mere tale. A "detective story," as Mr Robinson has called it, told for the pleasure of the telling. In many other poets, this would be enough, but it is not enough where Mr Robinson is concerned. If the poem could be taken as a psychological study of fear, it might justify its existence—as far as theme is concerned, its execution is, of course, admirable—but the evidence of the very tangible dagger on the dictionary, and the presence of the man passing before the house, are too obviously real to leave the fear in the realm of psychology. No, Mr Robinson's bugbear has fairly got him in this book. It is melodrama pure and simple, and, no matter how well it is done, melodrama shorn of suggestion is not worthy of Mr Robinson. I may point out what melodrama can do when used as the veneer for ethical and psychological truth in even so recent a book as Mr Aiken's Punch. I have already cited Macbeth as an example, Faust is another, but there are so many examples they have only to be thought of.

I believe that Avon's Harvest is the direct result of Mr Robinson's deserved success. Some poets thrive best on lack of recognition; let us hope that Mr Robinson is not one of these, for of all living poets he is the one most assured of his future. He can never again compose in a sympathetic seclusion, but he must shut his ears to plaudits and censures, he must forget his assured public and seek again the silence of his own personality which seems the only condition under which his genius can freely create.

Mr Robinson's is not a wide or inclusive art; it is narrow and deep. He has almost no early failures to look back upon with regret. His later work shows no marked advance over his earlier, even in the matter of technique. More than any other poet I can think of, he gained his full stature remarkably young, and we can scarcely expect any considerable increase of cubits to come. Mr Robinson is a poet of extraordinary, if restricted, achievement, he is at the fulness of his power, and that he will add many more to these collected poems is certain, but, more or not, he has won a high and permanent place in American literature.

[FEBRUARY, 1922]

A STUDY OF LANGUAGE

LANGUAGE. *By Edward Sapir. 12mo. 258 pages.*
Harcourt, Brace and Company. $1.75.

ONE result of the peculiar separateness from general intelligence
of linguistic, mathematical, and musical faculty is that the higher
branches of learning built upon these faculties seem to the average man distressingly remote and difficult. We have only to hear
the stimulus word "dry-as-dust" to react at once with "grammarian." The whirling solar system, the mysteries of space, the wonders of electricity, the fossils in the earth's bowels excite a natural
interest; but we wonder that any one should by choice devote his
life to the dative and the gerund—or for that matter, to calculus or
counterpoint.

It is not strange, then, that of all departments of scholarship, philology has been the most sharply defined and rigorous, the most
critical, the one approaching nearest to the methods of exact science.
It could attain these qualities precisely because of its aloofness from
the give and take of life; because, in spite of its professions to be
the very foundation stone of the humanities, it was essentially un-
human. The technique of modern philology has something superb
about it. It is as austere as anything in the world. The work of an
accepted leader like Brugmann is of an order unsurpassed in any
branch of learning. But it cannot be popularized. No one has tried
any Easy Lessons in Brugmann. And when professional philologists
have left their unsparingly exact *minutiae* in order to broaden out
they have regularly swerved straight into the abstractions of con-
ceptual logic and philosophy. Paul's Principles is a beautifully
done book; but it is written for University professors and those who
aspire to be such. Whitney's Life and Growth of Language starts
out promisingly, yet nine-tenths of it presupposes a cultivated philological interest.

Here is where Edward Sapir's work, appropriately entitled simple
Language, is new. It comes from the pen of a philologist for those
who are not; is scholarly throughout, never approaching the primer
and yet intelligible to any one of intellectual interests whether or not
he knows anything about language; in short, is broad in its grasp and
approach. Sapir has brought to this work a truly unusual combina-

tion. It is clear that he is natively endowed with linguistic faculty to a remarkable degree. He gives evidence of being thoroughly trained in the orthodox philology—that is, the technical study of the Indo-European and Semitic languages. And as chief of the ethnological research which the Canadian Government has carried on for the past ten years, he has been thrown into first-hand contact with the manifold forms of speech of unlettered, primitive peoples, the native tribes of America. Add aesthetic interests and some literary experience to this philological background, and it is apparent that there might well come a book combining range with concreteness, scholarship with humanity, as sound professionally as it is untechnical and free from metaphysical leanings or logical formalism. This is precisely what Language is.

For instance, in the chapter on Drift—the irresistible tendency of all languages to change—Sapir takes a phrase like *Who did you see?* and shows why in spite of its "incorrectness" we all at times slip into it. *Whom* has become isolated, the only word of its class, the only emphatic and interrogative word normally at the head of its sentence, that maintains the objective ending. Unconsciously, the "m" makes us uncomfortable. The rules teach it, but the rules are no longer living; they are in conflict with the irrational but psychologically valid drift of modern English, and we feel happier with *who* than with *whom* in our mouths. The uneducated abandon themselves unrestrainedly. The sophisticated and timid vacillate between the discomfort of breaking with the authority of tradition and the irritation of a usage that has slipped into silent contradiction with the real forces that make English a living tongue. But all alike we edge ever farther away from the *whom* because of the "hesitation values" which are hooking themselves to it. These hesitation values are due to several factors. Consequently the hidden repugnance that is slowly strangling *whom* is stronger in some phrases than in others. We feel it most mildly in *The man whom I referred to;* few educated people would say *who I referred to.* The resistance to *whom* is slightly greater in *The man whom they referred to;* still stronger in *Whom are you looking at?* and at its height in *Whom did you see?* —in which the impulse to say *Who* raises its head most vigorously.

Try them for yourself; you will agree. The reader who is not interested in why he does things or in the motives of his fellow-men will stop there, content with the sanction of one learned authority for his lapses. The one who is, can follow the causes farther as the author develops that the dying of *whom* is but one of many symptoms of the larger tendencies at work in English and all other languages. The whole chapter is a masterpiece of refined psychological penetration. "We do not object to nuances as such; we object to having them formally earmarked for us." Nothing of the conventional grammarian here; but much for the grammarian to bite on.

And so there is much in the chapter on Types of Linguistic Structure, a subject in which philologists have for a century been at their most logical, prejudiced, hard and fast, ineffective, and worst, with a classification into isolating, agglutinative, and inflective types—compartments that accommodate perhaps thirty per cent of the languages of mankind. "There is something irresistible"—to an unimaginative mind, Sapir might have added—"about a method of classification that starts with two poles, exemplified, say, by Chinese and Latin, clusters what it conveniently can about these poles, and throws everything else into a 'transitional type.' " Or again, as to sentimental satisfactions in science: "Champions of the 'inflective' languages are wont to glory in the very irrationalities of Latin and Greek except when it suits them to emphasize their profoundly 'logical' character. Yet the sober logic of Turkish or Chinese leaves them cold."

Sapir's own classification, which follows these thrusts, is too finely integrated a conception to be mutilated in abbreviation here. One does not pack the delicate structure of an organism into a sentence, nor try to convey the quality of a great painting in a twenty-stroke sketch. The professionals will have their reaction to this new approach—unless they find it most convenient to ignore altogether. How far Sapir's scheme will stand permanently, only time can tell. But if courage, freshness, range of exact knowledge and especially of insight, amount to anything, its ultimate influence will be revolutionizing. It is stimulating to hear the dry bones rattle in the box; and, to one who is a bit of philologist himself, a thrill to see them rearticulate with originality.

The general reader will be even more interested in the chapter on Language, Race and Culture; and writers, in the final one on Language and Literature. This last starts off with a fascinating search for the causes that make one piece of literature reasonably translatable, and another—a ballad of Swinburne, for instance—so hopelessly baffling in any but its original medium. Sapir finds the reason in two levels of which speech is composed: a generalized, latent layer, and an upper one in which the particular conformation of each language inheres. Literature that moves chiefly in the upper stratum is as good as untranslatable. Yet every language, being a medium of its own, exacts in some measure a style peculiar to it. Latin—and Eskimo—lend themselves to an elaborately periodic structure that would be boring in English, which in turn demands a looseness that would be insipid in Chinese. And this has "a compactness of phrase, a terse parallelism, and a silent suggestiveness that would be too tart, too mathematical, for the English genius." Verse depends more specifically still on the unconscious dynamic habits of language—on inherent sense of contrasting syllable weight in Greek, number and echo in French, the same plus alternating pitches in Chinese, contrast of stresses primarily in English. Where no poet appears, it is not from weakness of his mother tongue as an instrument, but because the culture of the nation is not favourable.

There is not a diacritical mark in the book, yet its philology is sound; not a foot-note reference, yet it is scholarly; not a page that is difficult for an interested layman, yet it opens new paths of thought. A rare felicity pervades it, a freedom from the hackneyed; and its balance equals its spontaneity. It is unique in its field, and is likely to become and long remain standard.

A. L. KROEBER

[MARCH, 1922]

REVUE

By Wallace Stevens

BANTAMS IN PINE-WOODS

Chieftain Iffucan of Azcan in caftan
Of tan with henna hackles, halt!

Damned universal cock, as if the sun
Was blackamoor to bear your blazing tail.

Fat! Fat! Fat! Fat! I am the personal.
Your world is you. I am my world.

You ten-foot poet among inchlings. Fat!
Begone! An inchling bristles in these pines,

Bristles, and points their Appalachian tangs,
And fears not portly Azcan nor his hoos.

THE ORDINARY WOMEN

Then from their poverty they rose,
From dry catarrhs, and to guitars
They flitted
Through the palace walls.

They flung monotony behind,
Turned from their want, and, nonchalant,
They crowded
The nocturnal halls.

The lacquered loges huddled there
Mumbled zay-zay and a-zay, a-zay.
The moonlight
Fubbed the girandoles.

And the cold dresses that they wore,
In the vapid haze of the window-bays,
Were tranquil
As they leaned and looked

From the window-sills at the alphabets,
At beta b and gamma g,
To study
The canting curlicues

Of heaven and of the heavenly script.
And there they read of marriage-bed.
Ti-lill-o!
And they read right long.

The gaunt guitarists on the strings
Rumbled a-day and a-day, a-day.
The moonlight
Rose on the beachy floors.

How explicit the coiffures became,
The diamond point, the sapphire point,
The sequins
Of the civil fans!

Insinuations of desire,
Puissant speech, alike in each,
Cried quittance
To the wickless halls.

Then from their poverty they rose,
From dry guitars, and to catarrhs
They flitted
Through the palace walls.

FROGS EAT BUTTERFLIES. SNAKES EAT FROGS. HOGS EAT SNAKES. MEN EAT HOGS.

It is true that the rivers went nosing like swine,
Tugging at banks, until they seemed
Bland belly-sounds in somnolent troughs,

That the air was heavy with the breath of these swine,
The breath of turgid summer, and
Heavy with thunder's rattapallax,

That the man who erected this cabin, planted
This field, and tended it awhile,
Knew not the quirks of imagery,

That the hours of his indolent, arid days,
Grotesque with this nosing in banks,
This somnolence and rattapallax,

Seemed to suckle themselves on his arid being,
As the swine-like rivers suckled themselves
While they went seaward to the sea-mouths.

A HIGH-TONED OLD CHRISTIAN WOMAN

Poetry is the supreme fiction, madame.
Take the moral law and make a nave of it
And from the nave build haunted heaven. Thus,
The conscience is converted into palms,
Like windy citherns hankering for hymns.
We agree in principle. That's clear. But take
The opposing law and make a peristyle,
And from the peristyle project a masque
Beyond the planets. Thus, our bawdiness,
Unpurged by epitaph, indulged at last,
Is equally converted into palms,

Squiggling like saxophones. And palm for palm,
Madame, we are where we began. Allow,
Therefore, that in the planetary scene
Your disaffected flagellants, well-stuffed,
Smacking their muzzy bellies in parade,
Proud of such novelties of the sublime,
Such tink and tank and tunk-a-tunk-tunk,
May, merely may, madame, whip from themselves
A jovial hullabaloo among the spheres.
This will make widows wince. But fictive things
Wink as they will. Wink most when widows wince.

O, FLORIDA, VENEREAL SOIL

A few things for themselves,
Convolvulus and coral,
Buzzards and live-moss,
Tiestas from the keys,
A few things for themselves,
Florida, venereal soil,
Disclose to the lover.

The dreadful sundry of this world,
The Cuban, Polodowsky,
The Mexican women,
The negro undertaker
Killing the time between corpses
Fishing for crawfish . . .
Virgin of boorish births,

Swiftly in the nights,
In the porches of Key West,
Behind the bougainvilleas,
After the guitar is asleep,
Lasciviously as the wind,
You come tormenting,
Insatiable,

When you might sit,
A scholar of darkness,
Sequestered over the sea,
Wearing a clear tiara
Of red and blue and red,
Sparkling, solitary, still,
In the high sea-shadow.

Donna, donna, dark,
Stooping in indigo gown
And cloudy constellations,
Conceal yourself or disclose
Fewest things to the lover—
A hand that bears a thick-leaved fruit,
A pungent bloom against your shade.

THE EMPEROR OF ICE-CREAM

Call the roller of big cigars,
The muscular one, and bid him whip
In kitchen cups concupiscent curds.
Let the wenches dawdle in such dress
As they are used to wear, and let the boys
Bring flowers in last month's newspapers.
Let be be finale of seem.
The only emperor is the emperor of ice-cream.

Take from the dresser of deal,
Lacking the three glass knobs, that sheet
On which she embroidered fantails once
And spread it so as to cover her face.
If her horny feet protrude, they come
To show how cold she is, and dumb.
Let the lamp affix its beam.
The only emperor is the emperor of ice-cream.

[JULY, 1922]

PARIS LETTER

May, 1922

ULYSSES

Πολλῶν δ' ἀνθρώπων ἴδεν ἄστεα, καὶ νόον ἔγνω· All men should "Unite to give praise to Ulysses"; those who will not, may content themselves with a place in the lower intellectual orders; I do not mean that they should all praise it from the same viewpoint; but all serious men of letters, whether they write out a critique or not, will certainly have to make one for their own use. To begin with matters lying outside dispute I should say that Joyce has taken up the art of writing where Flaubert left it. In Dubliners and The Portrait he had not exceeded the Trois Contes or L'Education; in Ulysses he has carried on a process begun in Bouvard et Pécuchet; he has brought it to a degree of greater efficiency, of greater compactness; he has swallowed the Tentation de St Antoine whole, it serves as comparison for a single episode in Ulysses. Ulysses has more form than any novel of Flaubert's. Cervantes had parodied his predecessors and might be taken as basis of comparison for another of Joyce's modes of concision, but where Cervantes satirized one manner of folly and one sort of highfalutin' expression, Joyce satirizes at least seventy, and includes a whole history of English prose, by implication.

Messrs Bouvard and Pécuchet are the basis of democracy; Bloom also is the basis of democracy; he is the man in the street, the next man, the public, not our public, but Mr Wells' public; for Mr Wells he is Hocking's public, he is *l'homme moyen sensuel;* he is also Shakespeare, Ulysses, The Wandering Jew, the Daily Mail reader, the man who believes what he sees in the papers, Everyman, and "the goat" . . . πολλὰ πάθεν . . . κατα θυμὸν.

Flaubert having recorded provincial customs in Bovary and city habits in L'Education, set out to complete his record of nineteenth century life by presenting all sorts of things that the average man of the period would have had in his head; Joyce has found a more expeditious method of summary and analysis. After Bouvard and his friend have retired to the country Flaubert's incompleted narrative drags; in Ulysses anything may occur at any moment; Bloom

97

suffers *kata thumon;* "every fellow mousing round for his liver and his lights": he is *polumetis* and a receiver of all things.

Joyce's characters not only speak their own language, but they think their own language. Thus Master Dignam stood looking at the poster: "two puckers stripped to their pelts and putting up their props. . . .

"Gob that'd be a good pucking match to see, Myler Keogh, that's the chap sparring out to him with the green sash. Two bob entrance, soldiers half price. I could easy do a bunk on ma. When is it? May the twenty second. Sure, the blooming thing is all over."

But Father Conmee was wonderfully well indeed: "And her boys, were they getting on well at Belvedere? Was that so? Father Conmee was very glad to hear that. And Mr Sheehy himself? Still in London. The House was still sitting, to be sure it was. Beautiful weather it was, delightful indeed. Yes, it was very probable that Father Bernard Vaughn would come again to preach. O, yes, a very great success. A wonderful man really."

Father Conmee later "reflected on the providence of the Creator who had made turf to be in bogs where men might dig it out and bring it to town and hamlet to make fires in the houses of poor people."

The dialects are not all local, on page 406 we hear that:

"Elijah is coming. Washed in the Blood of the Lamb. Come on, you winefizzling ginsizzling, booseguzzling existences! Come on, you dog-gone, bullnecked, beetlebrowed, hogjowled, peanut-brained, weaseleyed fourflushers, false alarms and excess baggage! Come on, you triple extract of infamy! Alexander J. Christ Dowie, that's yanked to glory most half this planet from 'Frisco Beach to Vladivostok. The Deity ain't no nickel dime bumshow. I put it to you that he's on the square and a corking fine business proposition. He's the grandest thing yet, and don't you forget it. Shout salvation in King Jesus. You'll need to rise precious early, you sinner there, if you want to diddle Almighty God. . . . Not half. He's got a coughmixture with a punch in it for you, my friend, in his backpocket. Just you try it on."

This varigation of dialects allows Joyce to present his matter, his tones of mind, very rapidly; it is no more succinct than Flaubert's exhaustion of the relation of Emma and her mother-in-law; or of Père Rouault's character, as epitomized in his last letter to Emma; but it is more rapid than the record of "received ideas" in Bouvard et Pécuchet.

Ulysses is, presumably, as unrepeatable as Tristram Shandy; I mean you cannot duplicate it; you can't take it as a "model," as you could Bovary; but it does complete something begun in Bouvard; and it does add definitely to the international store of literary technique.

Stock novels, even excellent stock novels, seem infinitely long, and infinitely encumbered, after one has watched Joyce squeeze the last drop out of a situation, a science, a state of mind, in half a page, in a catechismic question and answer, in a tirade à la *Rabelais*.

Rabelais himself rests, he remains, he is too solid to be diminished by any pursuer; he was a rock against the follies of his age; against ecclesiastic theology, and more remarkably, against the blind idolatry of the classics just coming into fashion. He refused the lot, lock, stock, and barrel, with a greater heave than Joyce has yet exhibited; but I can think of no other prose author whose proportional status in pan-literature is not modified by the advent of Ulysses.

James (H.) speaks with his own so beautiful voice, even sometimes when his creations should be using *their* own; Joyce speaks if not with the tongue of men and angels, at least with a many-tongued and multiple language, of small boys, street preachers, of genteel and ungenteel, of bowsers and undertakers, of Gertie McDowell and Mr Deasey.

One reads Proust and thinks him very accomplished; one reads H. J. and knows that he is very accomplished; one begins Ulysses and thinks, perhaps rightly, that Joyce is less so; that he is at any rate less gracile; and one considers how excellently both James and Proust "convey their atmospheres"; yet the atmosphere of the Gerty-Nausika episode with its echoes of vesper service is certainly "conveyed," and conveyed with a certitude and efficiency that neither James nor Proust have excelled.

And on the home stretch, when our present author is feeling more or less relieved that the weight of the book is off his shoulders, we find if not gracile accomplishments, at any rate such acrobatics, such sheer whoops and hoop-las and trapeze turns of technique that it would seem rash to dogmatize concerning his limitations. The whole of him, on the other hand, lock, stock, and gunny-sacks is wholly outside H. J.'s compass and orbit, outside Proust's circuit and orbit.

If it be charged that he shows "that provincialism which must be forever dragging in allusions to some book or local custom," it must also be admitted that no author is more lucid or more explicit in presenting things in such a way that the imaginary Chinaman or denizen of the forty-first century could without works of reference gain a very good idea of the scene and habits portrayed.

Poynton with its spoils forms a less vivid image than Bloom's desired two story dwelling house and appurtenances. The recollections of In Old Madrid are not at any rate highbrow; the "low back car" is I think local. But in the main, I doubt if the local allusions interfere with a *general* comprehension. Local details exist everywhere; one understands them *mutatis mutandis,* and any picture would be perhaps faulty without them. One must balance obscurity against brevity. Concision itself is an obscurity for the dullard.

In this super-novel our author has also poached on the epic, and has, for the first time since 1321, resurrected the infernal figures; his furies are not stage figures; he has, by simple reversal, caught back the furies, his flaggellant Castle ladies. Telemachus, Circe, the rest of the Odyssean company, the noisy cave of Aeolus gradually place themselves in the mind of the reader, rapidly or less rapidly according as he is familiar or unfamiliar with Homer. These correspondences are part of Joyce's mediaevalism and are chiefly his own affair, a scaffold, a means of construction, justified by the result, and justifiable by it only. The result is a triumph in form, in balance, a main schema, with continuous inweaving and arabesque.

The best criticism of any work, to my mind the only criticism of any work of art that is of any permanent or even moderately durable value, comes from the creative writer or artist who does the next job; and *not,* not ever from the young gentlemen who make generalities about the creator. Laforgue's Salomé is the real criticism of Salammbô; Joyce and perhaps Henry James are critics of Flaubert. To me, as poet, the Tentation is *jettatura,* it is the

effect of Flaubert's time on Flaubert; I mean he was interested in
certain questions now dead as mutton, because he lived in a certain
period; fortunately he managed to bundle these matters into one or
two books and keep them out of his work on contemporary subjects; I set it aside as one sets aside Dante's treatise De Aqua et
Terra, as something which matters now only as archaeology. Joyce,
working in the same medium as Flaubert, makes the intelligent
criticism: "We might believe in it if Flaubert had first shown us St
Antoine in Alexandria looking at women and jewellers' windows."

Ulysses contains 732 double sized pages, that is to say it is about
the size of four ordinary novels, and even a list of its various points
of interest would probably exceed my alloted space; in the Cyclops
episode we have a measuring of the difference between reality, and
reality as represented in various lofty forms of expression; the
satire on the various dead manners of language culminates in the
execution scene, blood and sugar stewed into clichés and rhetoric;
just what the public deserves, and just what the public gets every
morning with its porridge, in the Daily Mail and in sentimento-
rhetorical journalism; it is perhaps the most savage bit of satire
we have had since Swift suggested a cure for famine in Ireland.
Henry James complained of Baudelaire, "Le Mal, you do yourself
too much honour . . . our impatience is of the same order as . . .
if for the 'Flowers of Good' one should present us with a rhapsody
on plum-cake and eau de cologne." Joyce has set out to do an inferno, and he has done an inferno.

He has presented Ireland under British domination a picture so
veridic that a ninth rate coward like Shaw (Geo. B.) dare not even
look it in the face. By extension he has presented the whole occident
under the domination of capital. The details of the street map are
local but Leopold Bloom (*né Virag*) is ubiquitous. His spouse
Gea-Tellus the earth symbol is the soil from which the intelligence
strives to leap, and to which it subsides *in saeculum saeculorum*.
As Molly she is a coarse-grained bitch, not a whore, an adulteress,
il y en a. Her ultimate meditations are uncensored (bow to psychoanalysis required at this point). The "censor" in the Freudian
sense is removed, Molly's night-thoughts differing from those versified in Mr Young's once ubiquitous poem are unfolded, she says
ultimately that her body is a flower; her last word is affirmative.
The manners of the genteel society she inhabits have failed to get

under her crust, she exists presumably in Patagonia as she exists in Jersey City or Camden.

And the book is banned in America, where every child of seven has ample opportunity to drink in the details of the Arbuckle case, or two hundred other equodorous affairs from the 270,000,000 copies of the 300,000 daily papers which enlighten us. One returns to the Goncourt's question, "Ought the people to remain under a literary edict? Are there classes unworthy, misfortunes too low, dramas too ill set, catastrophies, horrors too devoid of nobility? Now that the novel is augmented, now that it is the great literary form . . . the social inquest, for psychological research and analysis, demanding the studies and imposing on its creator the duties of science . . . seeking the facts . . . whether or no the novelist is to write with the accuracy, and thence with the freedom of the savant, the historian, the physician?"

Whether the only class in America that tries to think is to be hindered by a few cranks, who cannot, and dare not interfere with the leg shows on Broadway? Is any one, for the sake of two or three words which every small boy has seen written on the walls of a privy, going to wade through two hundred pages on consubstantiation or the biographic bearing of Hamlet? And ought an epoch-making report on the state of the human mind in the twentieth century (first of the new era) be falsified by the omission of these half dozen words, or by a pretended ignorance of extremely simple acts. Bloom's day is uncensored, very well. The foecal analysis, in the hospital around the corner, is uncensored. No one but a Presbyterian would contest the utility of the latter exactitude. *A great literary masterwork is made for minds quite as serious as those engaged in the science of medicine.* The anthropologist and sociologist have a right to equally accurate documents, to equally succinct reports and generalizations, which they seldom get, considering the complexity of the matter in hand, and the idiocy of current superstitions.

A Fabian milk report is of less use to a legislator than the knowledge contained in L'Education Sentimentale, or in Bovary. The legislator is supposed to manage human affairs, to arrange for comity of human agglomerations. *Le beau monde gouverne*—or did once—because it had access to condensed knowledge, the middle ages were ruled by those who could read, an aristocracy received

Macchiavelli's treatise before the serfs. A very limited plutocracy now gets the news, of which a fraction (not likely to throw too much light upon proximate markets) is later printed in newspapers. Jefferson was perhaps the last American official to have any general sense of civilization. Molly Bloom judges Griffith derisively by "the sincerity of his trousers," and the Paris edition of the Tribune tells us that the tailors' congress has declared Pres. Harding to be our best dressed Chief Magistrate.

Be it far from me to depreciate the advantages of having a president who can meet on equal trouserial terms such sartorial paragons as Mr Balfour and Lord (late Mr) Lee of Fareham (and Checquers) but be it equidistant also from me to disparage the public utility of accurate language which can be attained only from literature, and which the succinct J. Caesar, or the lucid Macchia-velli, or the author of the Code Napoléon, or Thos. Jefferson, to cite a local example, would have in no ways despised. Of course it is too soon to know whether our present ruler takes an interest in these matters; we know only that the late pseudo-intellectual Wilson did not, and that the late bombastic Teddy did not, and Taft, McKinley, Cleveland, did not, and that, as far back as memory serves us no American president has ever uttered one solitary word implying the slightest interest in, or consciousness of, the need for an intellectual or literary vitality in America. A sense of style could have saved America and Europe from Wilson; it would have been useful to our diplomats. The *mot juste* is of public utility. I can't help it. I am not offering this fact as a sop to aesthetes who want all authors to be fundamentally useless. We are governed by words, the laws are graven in words, and literature is the sole means of keeping these words living and accurate. The specimen of fungus given in my February letter shows what happens to language when it gets into the hands of illiterate specialists.

Ulysses furnishes matter for a symposium rather than for a single letter, essay, or review.

Ezra Pound

[June, 1922]

APOLOGY OF GENIUS

By Mina Loy

Ostracized as we are with God—
    The watchers of the civilized wastes
    reverse their signals on our track

    Lepers of the moon
    all magically diseased
    we come among you
    innocent
    of our luminous sores

    unknowing
    how perturbing lights
    our spirit
    on the passion of Man
    until you turn on us your smooth fool's faces
    like buttocks bared in aboriginal mockeries

    We are the sacerdotal clowns
    who feed upon the wind and stars
    and pulverous pastures of poverty

    Our wills are formed
    by curious disciplines
    beyond your laws

    You may give birth to us
    or marry us
    the chances of your flesh
    are not our destiny—

    The cuirass of the soul
    still shines—

And we are unaware
if you confuse
such brief
corrosion with possession

In the raw caverns of the Increate
we forge the dusk of Chaos
to that imperious jewellery of the Universe
      —the Beautiful—

While to your eyes
      A delicate crop
of criminal mystic immortels
stands to the censor's scythe.

[JULY, 1922]

OFF THE SHOALS

THE ENORMOUS ROOM, *By E. E. Cummings, 12mo.*
271 pages. Boni and Liveright. $2.

WHEN the American Chicle Company brings out gum of a new shape
and unfamiliar flavour gumchewers are delighted and miss their subway trains in rush hour and step on each other's heels crowding
round slot machines in their haste to submit to a new sensation.
Frequenters of cabarets and jazzpalaces shimmy themselves into
St. Vitus dance with delight over a new noise in the band or a novel
squirm in the rhythm. People mortgage their houses to be seen in the
newest and most bizarre models of autos. Women hock their jewels
and their husbands' insurance policies to acquire an unaccustomed
shade in hair or *crêpe de chine*. Why then is it that when any one
commits anything novel in the arts he should be always greeted by
this same peevish howl of pain and surprise? One is led to suspect
that the interest people show in these much talked of commodities,
painting, music, and writing, cannot be very deep or very genuine
when they wince so under any unexpected impact.

The man who invented Eskimo Pie made a million dollars, so one
is told, but E. E. Cummings, whose verse has been appearing off and
on for three years now, and whose experiments should not be more
appalling to those interested in poetry than the experiment of surrounding ice-cream with a layer of chocolate was to those interested
in soda fountains, has hardly made a dent in the doughy minds of
our so-called poetry-lovers. Yet one might have thought that the
cadences of

> "Or with thy mind against my mind, to hear
> nearing our hearts' irrevocable play—
> through the mysterious high futile day
> an enormous stride
>   (and drawing thy mouth toward
>
> my mouth, steer our lost bodies carefully downward)"

would have melted with as brittle freshness on the senses of the readers
of THE DIAL as melted the brown-encrusted oblongs of ice-cream in

the mouths of tired stenographers and their beaux. Can it be that people like ice-cream and only pretend to like poetry?

Therefore it is very fortunate that this book of E. E. Cummings' has come out under the disguise of prose. The average reader is less self-conscious and more open to direct impressions when reading prose than verse; the idea that prose is ART will have closed the minds of only a few over-educated people. Here at last is an opportunity to taste without overmuch prejudice a form, an individual's focus on existence, a gesture unforeseen in American writing. The attempt to obscure the issue, on the paper cover blurb and in the preface, will fool no one who reads beyond the first page. It's not as an account of a war atrocity or as an attack on France or the holy Allies timely to the Genoa Conference that The Enormous Room is important, but as a distinct conscious creation separate from anything else under heaven.

Here's a book that has been conceived unashamedly and directly without a thought either of the columnists or the book trade or Mr Sumner, or of fitting into any one of the neatly labelled pigeonholes of novel, play, essay, history, travel book, a book that exists because the author was so moved, excited, amused by a certain slice of his existence that things happened freely and cantankerously on paper. And he had the nerve to let things happen. In this pattern-cut generation, most writers are too afraid of losing their private reputations as red-blooded clear-eyed hundred-percenters, well-dressed, well-mannered and thoroughly disinfected fashion plates, to make any attempt to feel and express directly the life about them and in them. They walk in daily fear that someone will call them morbid, and insulate themselves from their work with the rubber raincoat of fiction. The Enormous Room seems to me to be the book that has nearest approached the mood of reckless adventure in which men will reach the white heat of imagination needed to fuse the soggy disjointed complexity of the industrial life about us into seething fluid of creation. There can be no more playing safe. Like the old steamboat captains on the Mississippi we'll have to forget the hissing of the safety-valve and stoke like beavers if we are to get off the sticky shoals into the deeper reaches beyond. And many an old tub will blow sky high with all hands before someone makes the course. The Enormous Room for one seems to me at least to have cleared the shoals.

Along with Sandburg and Sherwood Anderson, E. E. Cummings

takes the rhythms of our American speech as the material of his prose as of his verse. It is writing created in the ear and lips and jotted down. For accuracy in noting the halting cadences of talk and making music of it, I don't know anything that comes up to these two passages. This is a poem that came out in THE DIAL:

"Buffalo Bill's
  defunct
     who used to
     ride a watersmooth-silver
                stallion
and break onetwothreefourfive pigeonsjustlikethat
                                  Jesus

  he was a handsome man
               and what i want to know is
  how do you like your blueeyed boy
  Mister Death"

This from The Enormous Room:

"Sunday: green murmurs in coldness. Surplice fiercely fearful, praying on his bony both knees, crossing himself. . . . The Fake French Soldier, alias Garibaldi, beside him, a little face filled with terror . . . the Bell cranks the sharp-nosed priest on his knees . . . titter from bench of whores—

"And that reminds me of a Sunday afternoon on our backs spent with the wholeness of a hill in Chevancourt, discovering a great apple pie, B. and Jean Stahl and Maurice le Menusier and myself; and the sun falling roundly before us.

"—And then one *Dimanche* a new high old man with a sharp violet face and green hair—'You are free my children, to achieve immortality —*Songez, songez, donc—L'Eternité est une existence sans durée— Toujours le Paradis, toujours l'Enfer*' (to the silently roaring whores) 'Heaven is made for you'—and the Belgian ten-foot farmer spat three times and wiped them with his foot, his nose dripping; and the nigger shot a white oyster into a far-off scarlet handkerchief—and the priest's strings came untied and he sidled crablike down the steps—the two candles wiggle a strenuous softness . . .

"In another chapter I will tell you about the nigger.

"And another Sunday I saw three tiny old females stumble forward, three very formerly and even once bonnets perched upon three wizened skulls, and flop clumsily before the priest, and take the wafer hungrily into their leathery faces."

This sort of thing knocks literature into a cocked hat. It has the raucous directness of a song and dance act in cheap vaudeville, the willingness to go the limit in expression and emotion of a negro dancing. And in this mode, nearer the conventions of speech than those of books, in a style infinitely swift and crisply flexible, an individual not ashamed of his loves and hates, great or trivial, has expressed a bit of the underside of History with indelible vividness.

The material itself, of course, is superb. The Concentration Camp at La Ferté-Macé was one of those many fantastic crossroads of men's lives where one lingered for unforgetable moments, reaching them one hardly knew how, shoved away from them as mysteriously by some movement of the pawns on the chessboard, during the fearfully actual nightmare of war. A desperate recklessness in the air made every moment, every intonation snatched from the fates of absolute importance. In The Wanderer and Jean le Negre and Surplice and Mexique and Apollyon and the Machine Fixer and in those grotesque incidents of the fight with the stovepipes and Celina's defiance we have that intense momentary flare in which lifetimes, generations are made manifest. To have made those moments permanent on a printed page is no common achievement.

For some reason there is a crispness and accuracy about these transcripts of the smell and taste and shiver of that great room full of huddled prisoners that makes me think of Defoe. In the Journal of the Plague Year or in the description of a night spent among enormous bones and skeletons in the desert journey in Captain Singleton one finds passages of a dry definiteness that somehow give the sort of impression that gives this hotly imaged picture of a roadside crucifix:

"I banged forward with bigger and bigger feet. A bird, scared, swooped almost into my face. Occasionally some night-noise pricked a futile, minute hole in the enormous curtain of soggy darkness. Uphill now. Every muscle thoroughly aching, head spinning, I half-straight-ened my no longer obedient body; and jumped: face to face with a little wooden man hanging all by itself in a grove of low trees.

"—The wooden body, clumsy with pain, burst into fragile legs with absurdly large feet and funny writhing toes; its little stiff arms made abrupt cruel equal angles with the road. About its stunted loins clung a ponderous and jocular fragment of drapery. On one terribly brittle shoulder the droll lump of its neckless head ridiculously lived. There was in this complete silent doll a gruesome truth of instinct, a success of uncanny poignancy, an unearthly ferocity of rectangular emotion.

"For perhaps a minute the almost obliterated face and mine eyed one another in the silence of intolerable autumn."

Perhaps one thinks of Defoe because of the unashamed directness with which every twitch of the individual's fibres, stung or caressed by the world's flowing past outside, is noted down. There is no strain-ing through the standard literary sieve.

Of the English eighteenth century too is the fine tang of high ad-venture along roads among grotesque companions that comes to the surface in passages like this:

"The highroad won, all of us relaxed considerably. The *sac* full of suspicious letters which I bore on my shoulder was not so light as I had thought, but the kick of the Briouse *pinard* thrust me forward at a good clip. The road was absolutely deserted; the night hung loosely around it, here and there tattered by attempting moonbeams. I was somewhat sorry to find the way hilly, and in places bad underfoot; yet the unknown adventure lying before me, and the delicious silence of the night (in which our words rattled queerly like tin soldiers in a plush-lined box) boosted me into a condition of mysterious happiness. We talked, the older and I, of strange subjects. As I suspected he had not always been a *gendarme*. He had seen service among the Arabs."

and the first description of The Wanderer:

"B. called my attention to a figure squatting in the middle of the cour with his broad back against one of the more miserable trees. This figure was clothed in a remarkably picturesque manner; it wore a dark sombrero-like hat with a large drooping brim, a bright red gipsy shirt of some remarkably fine material with huge sleeves loosely falling, and baggy corduroy trousers whence escaped two brown, shapely, naked feet. On moving a little I discovered a face—perhaps the handsomest face that I have ever seen, of a gold brown color, framed in an amazingly large and beautiful black beard. The features were finely formed and almost fluent, the eyes soft and extraordinarily sensitive, the mouth delicate and firm beneath a black moustache which fused with the silky and wonderful darkness falling upon the breast. The face contained a beauty and dignity which, as I first saw it, annihilated the surrounding tumult without an effort. Around the carefully formed nostrils there was something almost of contempt. The cheeks had known suns of which I might not think. The feet had travelled nakedly in countries not easily imagined. Seated gravely in the mud and noise of the *cour* under the pitiful and scraggly *pommier* . . . behind the eyes lived a world of complete strangeness and silence. The composure of the body was graceful and Jovelike. This being might have been a prophet come out of a country nearer to the sun. Perhaps a god who had lost his road and allowed himself to be taken prisoner by *le gouvernement français*. At least a prince of a dark and desirable country, a king over a gold-skinned people who would return when he wished to his fountains and his houris. I learned upon inquiry that he travelled in various countries with a horse and cart and his wife and children, selling bright colors to the women and men of these countries. As it turned out he was one of the Delectable Mountains; to discover which I had come a long and difficult way. Wherefore I shall tell you no more about him for the present, except that his name was Joseph Demestre.

"We called him The Wanderer."

There is about this sort of writing a gusto, an intense sensitiveness to men and women and colours and stenches and anger and love that, like the face of Joseph Demestre, "annihilates the surrounding tumult without an effort." When a book like The Enormous Room manages to emerge from the morass of print that we flounder in, it is time to take off your new straw hat and jump on it.

JOHN DOS PASSOS

[JULY, 1922]

HIBERNAL

BY BABETTE DEUTSCH

The park is winter-plucked. The sky
and the grey pavement show a sheeted face:
the covered stare of one who had to die.
Now, when men sweat,
shovelling muddy snow or heaving ice,
they know the helpless sweat that will not wet them twice,
they know the staggering heart, the smothered breath
that stand between this knowing and the end.
Though they must drag a net of heavy hours
about their straining limbs,
though they behold
love like a pillar of cloud, a pillar of fire—
this net will break before they tire,
this cloud, this flame will vanish and be cold.
Men think of this who limp against the wind
that freezes hate and sucks at their desire.
Winter is on us now, and will return:
soiled snows will choke the city streets again,
bleak twilights dull the windows as before,
dark hurrying crowds push towards lit rooms in vain.
One day we shall not kiss or quarrel any more.

[SEPTEMBER, 1922]

DUBLIN LETTER

September, 1922

ALTHOUGH Dublin has never inspired in any of its poets quite the feelings with which Sir Walter Scott apostrophized Edinburgh—"piled close and high, mine own romantic town!"—it has not lacked honour in literature. Without reckoning two conspicuous works produced within the last dozen years, enormous in volume and unique in form and design, one might make a considerable list of novels and social studies of life in Dublin, historic or domestic; and of recent years there has been evident in our poets a desire to see Dublin in the light of romance, to name its streets in verse (with something of the defiant spirit of Walt Whitman) in a word, by means of art, to create a spiritual Dublin, not built with hands. The Anglo-Irish, however, it must be owned, have never evolved a local sentiment for "dear dirty Dublin" comparable with that of the Lowland Scotch for "Auld Reekie." Its squares and streets, named hitherto mostly after members of the English nobility, are paced by its citizens with little glow of communal feeling. "Sydney Parade!" I once exclaimed to A. E., "Could Villon himself have brought that name into a poem?" His reply was that there was no locality in Dublin which he would shrink from naming proudly in verse; and when next I met him he had, in fact, produced some resounding verses in which he had not hesitated to mention Rathgar Road in the same breath with Nineveh and Babylon. His poem was a noble one; but I had been thinking less of such daring poetic *coups* as Francis Thompson's stanza about Charing Cross, or Walt Whitman's occidental orientalism in Broadway, than of such simple things as "Within a mile of Edinboro' town," or "The boat rocks at the pier o' Leith," or even, "The Lord in his mercy be kind to Belfast!" A folk-spirit flowering spontaneously and cordially into local references of this kind, the poets of Dublin do not inherit. And the reason is that Dublin, for all its antiquity and romance (it is mentioned, as is well known, on Ptolemy's map of about 150 A. D.) and its beauty of hills and waters, possesses only a vague historic individuality. It wears its metropolitan crown with a rakish and seedy air. There exists in Dublin no corporate sentiment such as belongs, I fancy, only to places which retain the memory of some good cause which has triumphed there, or of some phase of moral enthusiasm

113

which has been the sanction of subsequent well-being and prosperity. If any place in Dublin was sacrosanct it should have been, one would have thought, the chamber in which its ancient archives were stored. And yet, not many weeks ago, about noon, when we Dublin citizens were at our work, we were shaken by a monstrous explosion, and rushing out of doors soon perceived, under black volumes of smoke rolling seaward, gleaming objects which we rightly surmised to be the shreds of the intimate records of Dublin's life for many hundreds of years, the documents over which Sir Samuel Ferguson had labored. And this was the deed of no Caliph Omar, but of a patriot who bore the name of Ireland's last monarch, Mr Roderick O'Connor.

Thus it will be understood by the reader who may wish to learn what kind of reception Mr Joyce's Ulysses has found in Dublin, that there is here, as I say, no corporate sentiment likely to take offence at his cruel realism. The book has, in fact, been received with enthusiasm by those who provisionally determine literary fame in Ireland. "A marvellous book—it has broken up English literature!"—"it puts Ireland at the head of European literature!"—these are some of the phrases in circulation; chiefly among the newly emancipated youth of the National University colleges, who disparage the Protestant-minded Shaw with a whole-heartedness which would satisfy even Mr Ezra Pound, and turn to the pure diabolism of Mr Joyce as to the living waters of a new art. The first was the phrase of a Dublin book-seller who was pleased by the number of orders he had booked. I have heard a highly intelligent Catholic admirer of Mr Joyce express a doubt as to whether any one but a Catholic could really understand the book, and perhaps to savour it perfectly the reader should be a Catholic born and bred in Dublin. Mr. Pound however makes light of its difficulties, and several non-Catholics of my acquaintance recognize it as an epoch-making achievement—being chiefly, I must own, of a somewhat malicious turn of mind. For Dublin, I must repeat, is not a nurse of moral enthusiasms. Dublin produces the scholar and the mocker: the scholar, chiefly I think among the descendants of the old Protestant ascendancy, who in these changed times bury themselves in their books; the mocker, chiefly among those Catholic youths whom Mr. Joyce presents to us in this work and in his Portrait of the Artist as a Young Man.

Mr. Joyce is both a scholar and a mocker. But his standing as a philosophical humorist must be determined by the answer to the question, whether he universalizes the objects of his mockery, or is in the main merely a local satirist. It has been maintained by a recent critic of Swift that the caricature of humanity in Gulliver was suggested by Swift's observation of the "Wild Irish." Swift however bore the Teagues of his time no ill will; but Mr Joyce is so minutely personal in his mockery that the doubt arises whether his original intention— to catch in a work of art the whole phantasmagoria of a day of life in Dublin—has not been prejudiced by something short of good humour. Thus A. E. passes by, and Mr Joyce sets us all cachinnating. It is extremely well done, and we cannot help joining in, but it is not—shall I say, very high class. I except all that relates to Bloom in this epic work. In the philosophic Bloom Mr Joyce has added a new character to that company of real-imaginary personalities whom we know better than our nearest acquaintances, perhaps better than ourselves.

I see that it is in debate among those who have received Ulysses as a great event in literature, whether the work has artistic unity. Of unity in one sense Mr Joyce is always sure; for though, Heaven knows! there is enough variety in his book, everything in it is atoned to one mood, the only mood, in fact, which he appears to have at his command. In a normal work of art (if one may use the expression) certain incidents would be discordant and would shake our faith in the moral and intelligent governor of the little world to which we are admitted, to wit, the artist; but in the world of mockery which Mr Joyce has brought into being, anything may drop into its place as easily as a paragraph in a newspaper. In a normal work of art—I will say it, in a true work of art, this faith in a moral and intelligent creator is stirred in proportion to its manifestation of the author's artistic power. I do not say this in order to accuse Mr Joyce of atheism, or of not being a god himself, but to explain what I mean by saying that his work, with its infinite variety, is monotonous, as only the cinema or the hippodrome entertainment is monotonous, and that monotony is not unity. Also, is it not a mistake in construction that this memorable Day has two beginnings: we are well on towards noon with Dedalus when we have to return to the waking-up of Mr Leopold Bloom. I have managed to read one way or the other nearly the whole of this work, but I confess that after a hundred pages or so I read on with an admiration chiefly of the heroic persistence of the author; of the number of things he knows, notices, remembers; of the unfailing vitality and purity of his phrase; of his superb powers of mimicry and literary impersonation; of the half-kindly and painstaking exactness which mitigates his cruelty. Such a display of erudition is only possible where a man has subordinated all his reading and research for a long period to a single purpose. This alone is admirable; and it condones the use (which one suspects) of encyclopaedias and above all of Thom's Dublin Directory.

All the same, I doubt whether this massive work is of good augury for Irish literature. Just as it was a disappointment that Sweden—a land, one fancied, with bones of iron and breath fragrant with the pine—should produce as her literary representative a mere bundle of nerves like Strindberg, such as the exhausted Mediterranean races could so well understand; so it is a little disconcerting to find Ireland —the country where, as the world fancied, Faith still lingered in all its bookless artlessness—breathing out no healing airs from its boglands into European literature, but rather—in this its most important contribution to literature for some time—a particularly strong and composite odour from mean streets and brothels. Mr Joyce's masterpiece is a violent interruption of the movement known as the Irish Literary Renascence, and I shall look forward to the new edition of Mr Ernest Boyd's history of that movement, in which he will study its significance.

JOHN EGLINTON

[OCTOBER, 1922]

COMMENT

THE editors have the pleasure of announcing that for the year 1922 THE DIAL's award goes to Mr T. S. Eliot.

MR ELIOT has himself done so much to make clear the relation of critic to creative artist that we hope not to be asked whether it is his criticism or his poetry which constitutes that service to letters which the award is intended to acknowledge. Indeed it is our fancy that those who know one or the other will recognize the propriety of the occasion; those who know both will recognize further in Mr Eliot an exceedingly active influence on contemporary letters.

Influence in itself, however, is no service, and what makes Mr Eliot a significant artist is that his work, of whatever nature, is an indication of how ineffective the temptation to do bad work can, for at least once, become. Few Americans writers have published so little, and fewer have published so much which was worth publication. We do not for a moment suspect Mr Eliot of unheard-of capacities; it is possible that he neither has been pressed to nor can write a popular novel. But the temptation not to arrive at excellence is very great, and he is one of the rare artists who has resisted it. A service to letters peculiarly acceptable now is the proof that one can arrive at eminence with the help of nothing except genius.

Elsewhere in this issue will be found a discussion of Mr. Eliot's poetry, with special reference to his long work, The Waste Land, which appeared in THE DIAL of a month ago; in reviewing The Sacred Wood, and elsewhere, we have had much to say of his critical work, and may have more. At this moment it pleases us to remember how much at variance Mr Eliot is with those writers who having themselves sacrificed all interest in letters, are calling upon criticism to do likewise in the name of the particular science which they fancy can redeem the world from every ill but themselves. As a critic of letters Mr Eliot has always had preeminently one of the qualifications which he requires of the good critic: "a creative interest, a focus upon the immediate future. The important critic is the person who is absorbed in the present problems of art, and who wishes to bring the forces of the past to bear upon the solution of these problems." This is precisely what Mr Eliot has wished, and accomplished, in his function as critic of criticism. It is impossible to read the opening essays of The Sacred

Wood without recognizing that it is from these pages that the attack upon perverted criticism is rising. The journalists who wish critics to be for ever concerned with social laws, economic fundamentals, and the science of psychoanalysis, and never by any chance with the erection into laws of those personal impressions which are the great pleasure of appreciation, would do well to destroy Mr Eliot first; for it is from him that new critics are learning "that the 'historical' and the 'philosophical' critics had better be called historians and philosophers quite simply" and that criticism has other functions, and other pleasures to give.

There is another, quite different sense, in which Mr Eliot's work is of exceptional service to American letters. He is one of a small number of Americans who can be judged by the standards of the past—including therein the body of Occidental literature. It is a superficial indication of this that Mr Eliot is almost the only young American critic who is neither ignorant of nor terrified by the classics, that he knows them (one includes Massinger as well as Euripides) and understands their relation to the work which went before and came after them. There are in his poems certain characters, certain scenes, and even certain attitudes of mind, which one recognizes as peculiarly American; yet there is nowhere in his work that "localism" which at once takes so much of American writing out of the field of comparison with European letters and (it is often beneficial to their reputations) requires for American writers a special standard of judgment. We feel nothing aggressive and nothing apologetic in his writing; there is the assumption in it that the civilized German can count Shakespeare and even Poe as part of his inheritance.

When Prufrock in paper covers first appeared, to become immediately one of the rarest of rare books (somebody stole ours as early as 1919) Mr Eliot was already redoubtable. Since then, poet with true invention, whom lassitude has not led to repeat himself, critic again with invention and with enough metaphysics to draw the line at the metaphysical, his legend has increased. We do not fancy that we are putting a last touch to this climax; we express gratitude for pleasure received and assured. If pleasure is not sufficiently high-toned a word, you may, in the preceding paragraphs, take your pick.

MR. ELIOT's command of publicity is not exceptional, and we feel it necessary to put down, for those who care for information, these hardily gleaned facts of his biography. In 1888 he was born in St. Louis; in 1909 and 1910 he received, respectively, the degrees of Bachelor and of Master of Arts at Harvard; subsequently he studied at the Sorbonne, the Harvard Graduate School, and Merton College, Oxford. He has been a lecturer under both the Oxford and the London University Extension Systems, and from 1917 to 1919 he was assistant editor of The Egoist. We have heard it rumoured that he is still "A Londres, un peu banquier"; those who can persuade themselves that facts are facts will find much more of importance in the Mélange Adultère de Tout, from which the quotation comes; as that poem was written several years ago it omits the names of Mr Eliot's books: The Sacred Wood, Poems, and The Waste Land (not to speak of the several volumes later incorporated in Poems) and omits also the fact that Mr Eliot is now editor of The Criterion, a quarterly which we (as it were *en passant*) hereby make welcome. The most active and, we are told, the most influential editor-critic in London found nothing to say of one of the contributions to the first number except that it was "an obscure, but amusing poem" by the editor. We should hate to feel that our readers can judge of the state of criticism in England by turning to the first page of our November issue and reading the same poem there.

[DECEMBER, 1922]

E. E. CUMMINGS

suppose
Life is an old man carrying flowers on his head.

young death sits in a café
smiling, a piece of money held between
his thumb and first finger

(i say "will he buy flowers" to you
and "Death is young
life wears velour trousers
life totters, life has a beard" i

say to you who are silent.—"Do you see
Life? he is there and here,
or that, or this
or nothing or an old man 3 thirds
asleep, on his head
flowers, always crying
to nobody something about les
roses les bluets
                    yes,
                        will He buy?
Les belles bottes—oh hear
, pas chères")

and my love slowly answered I think so. But
I think I see someone else

there is a lady, whose name is Afterwards
she is sitting beside young death, is slender;
likes flowers.

[JANUARY, 1923]

THE THEATRE

THE ADDING MACHINE, written by Elmer L. Rice and presented by the Theatre Guild, is, in its first half anyway, absolutely first rate. Though it is in a vein which has already become rather familiar, it brings to its tragic satire of our commercial civilization an energy, an intensity, and a sureness of stroke which we do not often find in this sort of thing. I am not sure that BABBITT, THE HAIRY APE, or FROM MORN TO MIDNIGHT, all of which it touches at some point, achieve the vigour or the accuracy of aim of the first scenes of this play. They are the accuracy and vigour—as well as the cruelty and hardness—of the adding machine itself—of the society of which the adding machine is master. Even the expressionism is used sparely and efficiently for the purpose of driving home the right effects.

And behind the heavy ax-blade of the author Mr Digges puts a force and precision equal to it. He gives his poor henpecked over-worked boob a relentlessly tragic dignity. The difficult scene in the office in which he has to render not only the smarting backfire of his bicker with his fellow clerk, but at the same time the undercurrent of desire and fear which is running in his weary brain; his doglike servility to the boss who has come to lay him off for an adding ma-chine; his dazed return home after the murder and his gentle surrender to the police; and finally the agonizing spectacle of his attempt to justify himself to the jury; were like so many blows stiffly dealt in a war for human dignity and freedom.

But having once made us believe in Mr Zero's dignity, the author proceeds to take it all away from him. Mr Zero ascends to the Elysian Fields only to discover that he is incapable of enjoying them and to learn that he must return to earth and resume his serfdom to eternity. Once a drudge, for ever a drudge. No act of courage can save him.— Now it is obvious that, even apart from the sociological question, there is a strong dramatic objection to such an ending. It seems a mistake to begin a play with revolt and to end it with a dreary subsi-dence. And in THE ADDING MACHINE the climax comes at the begin-ning. Mr Zero is made to burst from the living coffin of his life with an éclat which commands our sympathy and then, during the latter half of the evening, we are obliged to see him slowly nailed back into it.

And is this not something more than a dramatic weakness? Is it

not a psychological mistake as well? Would even a slave object to
Mr Rice's Paradise on the ground that it was not respectable? Surely
this is a caricature even of a man like Mr Zero. It is a mistake to
suppose that the standardized mechanical lives of our commercial-
industrial human beings really represent all the native impulses of
the more primitive grades of humanity. They are not strong enough to
free themselves, it is true; if they were strong enough, they would
do so; they do not even, if you like, want to strongly enough. But it
does not follow that, if you substituted for their present state something easier and more agreeable, they would not much prefer it to the
other. Respectability is more easily shed than Mr. Rice would have us
believe. Other instincts lie deeper and stronger. I used to see Mr Zero
very often with the American army in France and I know that, confronted with feebler temptations than Mr Rice has supplied him in
Paradise and given freedom of stronger codes, he seldom resigned.

I UNFORTUNATELY missed the first act of SANDRO BOTTICELLI, but
from the programme and what I saw afterwards I know it must have
been like this:

LEONARDO DA VINCI: What ails our friend Botticelli? He seems
silent and distracted to-day—this day of all days, the birthday of
Lorenzo the Magnificent, when the people are dancing in the streets
like cicadas after rain.

FRA LIPPO LIPPI: They say he is enamoured of Giuliano's mistress,
the beautiful Simonetta. But look, here comes Lorenzo himself with
Poliziano!

LORENZO DE' MEDICI: Ha, our incomparable Leonardo! How goes
the Mona Lisa and what are your latest experiments in engineering?

POLIZIANO: Gentlemen, I must confess it. I have turned another
little canzone to Simonetta. *Per bacco,* I cannot find it in my heart to
keep away from the subject. (*All laugh.*)

FRA LIPPO LIPPI: No more can our friend Botticelli! (*All laugh.*)

BOTTICELLI (*joining them*): Greeting, good Master Leonardo,
and Your Most Excellent Highness Lord Lorenzo. Is it not a day for
men and for angels, for music, for flowers—

LEONARDO: And for lovers? (*All laugh.*)

POLIZIANO: All Florence is laughing to the sun. Come, let us taste
some of our host's wine. (*Exeunt omnes—except Botticelli, who hides*

behind a potted rose-bush to watch Eva Le Gallienne make her en-trance.)

Mr John Murray Anderson's JACK AND JILL has been produced with infinitely pretty costumes and with a tolerably successful attempt to make it exquisite and well-bred. But in spite of all this—and Ann Pennington—it is the old grind of musical comedy. You recognize The Prince of Pilsen and cannot help being bored.

WITH the publication of his volume of essays, The Flower in Drama,[1] Mr Stark Young establishes himself as one of the few American minds of any distinction who have devoted themselves to dramatic criticism seriously. His book is full of fine taste and sound judgements, and the only possible objection to it would be that it takes the theatre a little *too* seriously. I feel that Mr Young is often writing about the stage in a style which is not proper to it—the style of the aesthetic criticism of the last century and particularly of Walter Pater. Pater was already sufficiently, himself, an offender in this respect. He had a tendency to write about the setting-up exercises of Sparta as if they were the Duncan dancers, and to translate the even prose of Plato into the literary filigree of the time. But Mr Young has sometimes been known to lavish on the commonplaces of current acting language which Ruskin would surely have thought excessive for the glories of the Renaissance. He has a way of describing even things he thinks indifferent in a sort of mood of antique rapture, and he is in the habit of surrounding his nouns with such prismatic clouds of modifiers that we can scarcely catch a glimpse of them at all. I would warn him—in all admiration—to vent his lyric strain on Tintoretto and to leave us for Ben Ami and Charlie Chaplin his native intelligence and taste.

EDMUND WILSON, JR.

[MAY, 1923]

[1] The Flower in Drama, by Stark Young (12mo, 162 pages; Scribner: $1.50).

FIRST COMMUNION

By Djuna Barnes

The mortal fruit upon the bough
Hangs above the nuptial bed.
The cat-bird in the tree returns
The forfeit of his mutual vow.

The hard, untimely apple of
The branch that feeds on watered rain,
Takes the place upon her lips
Of her late lamented love.

Many hands together press,
Shaped within a static prayer
Recall to one the chorister
Docile in his sexless dress.

The temperate winds reclaim the iced
Remorseless vapours of the snow.
The only pattern in the mind
Is the cross behind the Christ.

[August, 1923]

124

ITALIAN LETTER

SINCE my visit to La Verna and to Papini, Italy has gone through a clamorous political upheaval, and many things which at the time were still affecting a semblance of solidity, have now quietly dissolved into thin air. Other shapes, other images, other idols, after a violent incubation, have taken their place, and are bent on sucking the blood of reality with concentrated eagerness. I thank my private, personal God, who has not assigned the lot of a political correspondent to me: I am not thereby forced to cut the Gordian knot of my perplexities, and to anticipate the judgement of posterity on the swift shadows weaving their intricate webs against the walls of my cavern.

But certain aspects of the visible drama, certain words and gestures of the protagonists, seem to point insistently to an inner meaning, to a spiritual design, to a soul within the body. There is a passionate desire to recapture the obsolete forms of religion, to fix one's ideals as permanent values, to crown these forms and these values with a mystical halo, and to employ them in curbing a reluctant history to the will of men. The war, and this stormy peace even more (since the war might still have appeared as a kind of common work) have narrowed the horizon of these men to the nation; a revulsion against the shallow official idealism of the war, and the fear of social dissolution, have made of democracy and humanitarianism the most execrable of taboos. The nation becomes, consciously, a myth, in the pragmatic sense given by Sorel to the word, to be worshipped in thought and action by its adepts, with firm faith, severe discipline, and blind obedience. The "immortal principles" are made fun of, and the Nineteenth Century is dismissed, with Daudet, as a huge and stupid mistake.

Moscow and Rome, Communism and Fascism, are often compared to each other; their striking resemblance (hatred of democracy, and of the *bourgeois* ideology; belief in the power of violence and of myths; voluntarism) and their not less striking opposition (hierarchy against equality; individual against collective economy; the nation against the world) are emphasized and commented upon. And indeed, within Italy herself the struggle has had some of the bitterness and fierceness of a war of religion; and in continental Europe, the two *formae mentis* are undoubtedly the essential spiritual outcome of the war until now. The nations which have not yet reached either the one or the other, are still involved in the meshes of an irrevocable past; but they will come to one of them soon: they will have to go through one of them.

There is not a third horn of the dilemma: these curves will have to be fully described before the dawn of a different day. Of these curves, the immediate and common origin is in that Messianic spirit which filled the European atmosphere at the end of the war so thickly that you could then almost breathe it in the air. Millennium was the name of the only land to which it seemed possible and reasonable to travel, if you were just emerging from the blood-stained mud of a trench. For a short, charmed interval Europe lived in that magic climate out of which great religions are born; but the Procession of the Apocalypse ended in the Pageant at Versailles, and for peace we were given the confusion of tongues, for one beaten enemy, the sword turning against itself and the nations divided.

Yet that Messianic spirit had posited an exigency which can be eluded, but not overcome. Whatever Fascism and Communism may become for the future historian, they must appear to their adepts as religions, that is, as collections of universal principles sufficient to the whole spirit of man. They must affirm themselves as complete answers to that undeniable spiritual need, and deny the validity of that need in relation to those questions which they leave too clearly unanswered. Therefore both their positive and their negative aspects, their fanaticism and their cynicism, must be studied as elements of a coherent faith, as parts of one body of passionate beliefs.

This study would probably be easier for Communism than for Fascism: the former has had more time and greater opportunity, and its failure, in spirit much more than in practice, is apparent. As for Fascism, though the forms and the acts are manifest, the soul which they intend to reveal, the inner meaning, the spiritual design, are still dubious and involved. Within Fascism itself, a strong though not numerous group is now making a valiant effort to interpret these forms and these acts in terms of Gentile's philosophy, or "actual Idealism." If the attempt should succeed, it would result not in a mere interpretation, but in a conquest. A philosophy cannot become a religion unless it has "thought itself out," and is therefore ready to stabilize itself as the substance of faith, and to be told in spontaneous and intelligible mythical terms: has "actual Idealism" reached this stage of maturity, and supposing it had reached it, how is it to be explained that it did not appear as a faith or as a collection of myths before the advent of Fascism, and independently? And again, supposing this philosophy to be truly endowed with the power of blossoming out into a religion, will it succeed in conquering those elements of Fascism which are obviously repugnant to it? Will it produce a schism? Will it end by fighting against that which it is now willing to support? Or, being defeated, will it content itself with becoming the cold, servile theology of a discordant truth?

For the present, "actual Idealism" is not an *actual*, but only a potential factor of the religion of Fascism, towards which an infinitely more powerful and more substantial body of myths and beliefs is now also spreading its tentacles: the Church of Rome. Fascism will be the new Faust in this secular tragedy, the struggle between Catholicism and modern thought, the choice being between a form whose spirit is dead, and a spirit which may not yet be able to fashion its own form. The defeat of "actual Idealism" would only mean that modern thought is still unripe for the function to which it aspires, and that it will have to go back again, for a few years or for a few centuries, to the catacombs of individual experience and culture, before finding its place in the sun. In any case, the outcome of the struggle, in this particular episode, will not seal the fate of either of the antagonists, but of Fascism itself. The saint and the devil fought for the soul of Guido da Montefeltro, as some of Dante's readers may remember; and the devil won it with his logic. In human affairs, it is only after the event that we can tell whether logic was on the saint's or on the devil's side.

It may happen, after all, that both the priests and the philosophers will come out of this struggle empty-handed, the black-shirted Faust deciding to keep his soul as it is, without any infusion of either new or ancient sanctity. This would make things much easier for the spiritual investigator, since it would then be sufficient for him to take those words, those gestures, of which we were speaking before, at their face value, that is, as words, as gestures having a definite and sufficient meaning in themselves, dramatic, political. The philosopher of history and the historian of religions would then be able to point to a continuous process of involution, from the universality of the Mediaeval Mind (and even of the Roman Empire) to the particularity

of modern European nations. Europe would have found its several religions, of the nations, of the *"gentes,"* of the tribes, instead of discovering the religion for which it seemed to be thirsting, of man, human. And for the religion of Italy, of Fascism in its concrete Italian
revelation, *habemus prophetam:* all its elements, and even a few more
which have not yet passed into the heart of the multitude, can be
found in the work of Gabriele d'Annunzio, and especially in this last
book of his, Per l'Italia degli Italiani.

No present-day writer, in any country, holds a position approaching
d'Annunzio's position in Italy. Rudyard Kipling came very near to
being England's d'Annunzio, but the Boer War blasted his chance, and
the Great War found him too old, irreparably out of touch with the
new temper of his countrymen; and besides, d'Annunzio, though lacking some of Kipling's raciness, of his immediacy, of his popular quality, possesses undoubtedly a much vaster personality. Though not
yet over sixty, he has behind himself forty-five years of an immensely
varied literary experience and activity: each of his thirty odd volumes,
incursions, experiments, accomplishments in all the fields of fiction,
poetry, and drama, has been the sensation of its day and, together
with the events and adventures of his private, practical life (his loves,
his finances, his houses, horses, and dogs) a passionate object of wonder, and scorn, of admiration, of scandal, for two generations of Ital-
ians.

All fashions and schools of aesthetic and semi-philosophical thought
in Europe, from the pre-Raphaelite Poets to the Russian novelists,
from Ibsen to Nietzsche, from Wagner to Scriabine, are reflected in
his work: through him, Italian literature (in the narrow meaning of
the word, as contrasted to living, original thought) entered once more
into the circle of European literature, though more passively perhaps
than at any other time in the course of its history. But the high-water
mark of his fortune as a writer falls between 1890 and 1905: his surviving disciples date all from those years. And his place in the general
history of literature remains with the French Parnassians and Decadents, and with their cognate and derived writers abroad, the
Wildes, the Yeatses, the Hofmannsthals: that is, with the last brood
of irreparably "stupid Nineteenth Century" writers. After 1905,
though he has never given up the pretence of being and of looking
"up to date," yet the novel fashions began to be introduced by

younger (and often much lesser) men; and at the same time the temper of Italian culture swerved decidedly from the literary to the philosophical.

But the Wars were far more generous to him than to Kipling: they gave him, in exchange for his lost literary leadership, an indisputable national laureateship. In a time of rapidly deepening and widening patriotic emotions, his truly amazing knowledge and his exclusive love of things Italian—words, works, landscapes, deeds, tempers, traditions—present in every page of his books, marked him out as the true depositary of the nation's spirit. His "moral" ideal, in which Nietzschean phrases and attitudes, literally understood, were adapted as a modern disguise to the Renaissance *principe* and *condottiero,* seemed sufficient to supply with a standard of heroism an age which had lost every perception of the tragic. But it would be unfair to regard either of these aspects of d'Annunzio's personality as superficial and false: they are both true and native, and deep, with all the depth of which he is capable. And their popularity is also deep and genuine: not on account of any aesthetic sympathy (d'Annunzio has never learnt to speak or to write so as to be intelligible to the *non-literati*) but because of a practical, emotional, temperamental affinity with the moods and needs of a new generation.

The Canzoni della Gesta d'Oltremare were the epics of our war with Turkey. Having been sent forth from what d'Annunzio calls his exile in France, their effect was considerably enhanced by a space-perspective, not less favourable than time-perspectives are to the transformation of a man's image in the group's mind: the transformation, in this case, of the Egotist and the Aesthete into the Patriot and the Soldier. And in the Canzoni, written during a crisis of mysticism to which we owe one of d'Annunzio's most subtle prose works, the Considerazione della Morte, as well as the ultradecadent Mystère de Saint Sébastien, the Catholic myths and rites appear as an indispensable element of the national tradition: if not as a religion, at least as a superstition essential to the heroic behaviour of the group.

The Great War put its final seal on the transfiguration. The campaign for the intervention of Italy, four years of strenuous war life (d'Annunzio revealing himself as a born soldier, a true lover of danger and scorner of death, a *principe* and a *condottiero*) and lastly the Fiume expedition, fixed his new image as an incarnate model of his own ideal of Italian *virtù*. To the more precise delineation and fuller adornment of this image, d'Annunzio himself, after having furnished the raw material of action, has also attempted to contribute the poetical and legendary elaboration in a book written during a forced pause in the war, Il Notturno, and in the one which has just been published.

There is a short paragraph in the Notturno in which d'Annunzio defines the nature and the limits of his own personality with a more cruel lucidity than any of his critics ever did: "Life is not an abstraction of aspects and events, but a kind of diffuse sensuousness, a knowledge offered to every sense, a substance good to smell, to feel, to eat." It was with this elementary form of consciousness, with all his animal spirits, as they would have been called in the Middle Ages, wide awake, alert, ready to enjoy and to suffer, and to make of every danger and of every suffering the source of a deeper, intenser joy, that d'Annunzio went so youthfully, so gallantly through the war. Every healthy young soldier has known this exhilaration of the dangerous life: courage is often but the sacrifice of all practical and moral motives to the taste of this depth and intensity of primitive feeling. A beautiful thing in itself, accompanied by an incomparable sense of spiritual freedom, since the spirit, reduced to its simplest functions, is all here, in this body, in this instant, and the body accepts and enjoys the conditions of its instantaneous existence; and a wonderful thing, a prodigy, in a man of d'Annunzio's age.

Even the infirmity which keeps him in his bed, blind and helpless, while he writes, line after line, on narrow strips of paper, this long succession of visions of the war and of his past life, adds new visions, new sensations, to the immense store from which he is drawing. The intention to build up his own legend is unconcealed: in all his novels he always made himself the protagonist, under a mask; here, at last, he drops the mask, and is the hero of his own song. And yet of this book it can be repeated what a brilliant critic said of his novels in general: it is but a collection of lyrical motives and residua. Admirable, in this respect, and the exquisite texture of the phrase, the delicious richness of the language are a continuous joy to the connoisseur. But no human image becomes visible through these fragments; and this is as it should be, since no true humanity can exist in a world of pure sensuousness, in which the aesthetic dimension may counterfeit at times, but never actually generates out of itself, the essential human dimensions, intellectual and moral.

The book has an even, hard, shiny surface, only occasionally and very slightly troubled by the legendary intention. The war decomposes itself into a multitude of intense sensations of which the poet is the subject and the centre. Events materially tragic, being constantly referred to this centre only, are represented as vivid appearances, in their mere materiality; but more than any of them the reader is likely to remember the episode of the death of the horse Aquilino—a recollection from childhood—since a horse's tragedy can hardly make him feel the absence of the human substance of tragedy.

The new book, Per l'Italia degli Italiani, is much more uneven and fragmentary than the Notturno, since the deliberate aim of presenting the ideal image of himself as the model of Italian humanity more frequently interferes with the poet's genuine inspiration. Apart from the pages in which d'Annunzio is still, even here, the naïvely egocentric poet delighting in rare and sometimes fierce, dolorous sensations, the book has no other reality than that which belongs to beautiful words and highly decorative gestures. It is, on the whole, a strange, a pathetic piece of work, in which the author, in his vain attempt to evade the bounds of his purely sensuous and aesthetic world, reminds the reader of a white bear pacing rhythmically the narrow artificial rock which is its prison.

The word Spirit, in its Italian and Latin forms (since this Italian prose is frequently interspersed with Latin mottos and fragments like a sacred oration: one symptom, among many others, of senescence and rhetoric involution)—the word Spirit is everywhere in the book. But the thing is absent: from the first to the last page we are constantly kept in the same tense, oratorical, and oracular atmosphere, looking at a succession of symbols, which not even the amazing mimetic powers of the writer can persuade us to accept as truly significant. There is no movement, no development, no progress; that is, no evidence of a real dialectic, spiritual, moral drama.

But these static symbols which we find here clothed in the most gorgeous verbal forms, are substantially those of which we spoke at the beginning of this letter as the popular symbols of a national, political religion. In d'Annunzio, however, strangely coupled with his innate love of violence, we may discover also a yearning towards something more human and higher: a Franciscan ideal of peace and meekness, which resolves itself, like every other element of the d'Annunzian ideal, in a mere attitude. We can therefore easily disregard the difference, and having dismissed this book as a work of art capable of adding but one leaf to the poet's crown, yet treasure it among the documents of these troubled times, not less important because essentially negative.

RAFFAELLO PICCOLI

[MAY, 1923]

THE MAN WITH THE FLOWER IN HIS MOUTH

A Dialogue

By Luigi Pirandello

Translated From the Italian by Arthur Livingston

CHARACTERS

The Man With the Flower in His Mouth
A Customer (With Time on His Hands)

Twice, during the Dialogue, a melancholy woman, in a black dress, and an old hat with drooping feathers, will appear round the corner.

An avenue, lined with trees; electric lights gleaming through the foliage. On either side, the last houses of a street crossing the avenue. Among the houses to the left, a miserable all-night café, with tables and chairs on the sidewalk. In front of the houses on the right a street-lamp lighted. Astride the angle made by the two walls of the house to the left, which has a front both on the street and on the avenue, a street-lamp, also lighted. It is shortly after midnight. Faintly, from a distance, comes at intervals the thrumming of a mandolin. As the curtain rises, The Man With the Flower in His Mouth is seated at one of the tables, silently observing the Customer, who, at a neighbouring table, is sipping a mint frappée through a straw.

MAN WITH THE FLOWER: Ah!—I was just going to say! . . . So you are a good-natured sort of a fellow. . . . You lost your train?

THE CUSTOMER: By less than a minute. I get to the station—and there it is—just pulling out!

MAN WITH THE FLOWER: You might have caught it by running!

THE CUSTOMER: I suppose I might. It's absurd, I know. If I hadn't been all cluttered up with a dozen packages, more or less —huh! worse than a pack-horse! . . . Oh, these women! . . . One errand after another—world without end! Why, it took me three minutes, after I got out of my taxi, to get my fingers through the strings of all those packages! Two on every finger!

MAN WITH THE FLOWER: I'd like to have seen you! . . . You know what I would have done? I would have left the blamed things in the carriage!

THE CUSTOMER: And when you got home—eh? . . . How about the old woman—and my girls—not to mention those from the neighbourhood!

MAN WITH THE FLOWER: Let 'em shriek! . . . I'd have enjoyed it— I would!

THE CUSTOMER: Guess you don't know what it's like to have a brood of women with you on a vacation in the country!

MAN WITH THE FLOWER: Oh, I guess I do—in fact, I say so because I do. . . . (*A pause.*) They all say they won't need to take a blessed thing!

THE CUSTOMER: And you think they stop there? According to them, they go to the country to save money. . . . Well, the moment they get to some place out there, in the backwoods—the uglier it is, the dirtier it is, the more they insist on dressing up in all their Sunday togs. Oh—women, my dear sir! . . . But, after all, dressing is their profession! . . . "The next time you run into town, dear, I wish you'd stop in at So-and-So's. And then, if you don't mind, dear, on the way back—no trouble, is it, really?—will you stop at my dress-maker's and—" . . . and they're off! . . . "But how am I going to get all that done in three hours?" you say. . . . "Oh, that's easy, take a taxi!" . . . And the worst of it is, that in my hurry to get away, I forgot to take the keys of my house, here in town.

MAN WITH THE FLOWER: Ah—that's a good one! . . . And so—

THE CUSTOMER: I left that pile of bundles in the parcel room at the station. Then I went to dinner in a restaurant. Then, to get my temper back, to the theatre. . . . Hot? . . . Hot was no name for it! On coming out, I say to myself: What next? . . . Midnight. . . . And the next train leaves at 4 a. m. —three hours left for a bit of a nap. . . . Not worth the money. . . . So here I am! . . . This place doesn't shut up, I hope—

MAN WITH THE FLOWER: Never shuts up, this place. (*A pause.*) So you left your bundles in the parcel room—eh?

THE CUSTOMER: Why not? Safe, aren't they? All pretty well tied up!

MAN WITH THE FLOWER: No—no—I didn't mean that. . . . (*A pause.*) Well tied up, eh? Oh, I imagine so. Boys in the shops these days can wrap a bundle up quick as scat. (*A pause.*) What hands they have! . . . Here's a long strip of doubled paper—pink—with wavy lines—Ah! a sight for sore eyes! . . . How smooth it is! You'd almost like to put your face on it to feel the cool! And they roll it out, there on the counter, as nice as you please! And they put your cloth in the middle of it, all neatly folded up. First, they take the back of the hand, and they raise one edge of the paper. Then they bring the other hand down from above, and—how clever and graceful they are! They fold down one strip—a strip they don't really need—just for the art of the thing! Then, first on one side, then on the other, they fold the corners down, to make two triangles. Then they turn the points under. . . . Then they reach for the twine with one hand. . . . They pull out just what they need—to an inch—and they have it tied up for you before you've really had time to admire their skill! . . . And there you have your bundle, with a ring to put your finger through!

THE CUSTOMER: Aha! . . . You seem to have watched clerks in the stores pretty closely!

MAN WITH THE FLOWER: I? . . . Huh! . . . I've watched them whole days at a time. Why, I can spend an hour in front of a store, looking through the show window! Helps me to forget myself. . . . Why—I feel as though . . . oh—I'd like to be that piece of silk in there—that strip of braid—that red or that blue ribbon, which the girls in the dry goods stores after they've measured it with their tape-measure . . . did you ever notice what they do? . . . They make an "8" of it around the thumb and finger of their left hand before they wrap it up. . . . (*A pause.*) And I watch the man or the woman, when they come out of the shop with the bundle either hanging to one of their fingers, or held under one of their arms. And I watch them till they are out of sight . . . imagining—uh-h! . . . all that I imagine! . . . You couldn't guess half of it! (*A pause.—Then gloomily, reflectively, as though speaking to himself.*) But it does me good—some good at least.

THE CUSTOMER: Good? That's interesting. What good does it do you?

MAN WITH THE FLOWER: Oh—it helps to attach me—in my imagination, I mean—attach me to life—much as a vine clings to the bars of an iron gate. (*A pause.*) Oh . . . I never let it rest a moment—my imagination! I cling with it, persistently, to life—to the lives of other people! Not of people I know. No—no. I couldn't—with people I know. That disgusts me, somehow. Sort of sick to your stomach, eh?—No, I cling to the life of other people—of strangers, with whom my imagination can wander freely—But not capriciously, you understand—oh, no! . . . On the contrary—taking careful account of the least things I notice in them! And you have no idea how it works! I get right in on the inside track with some of them. . . . I can see this man's house, for instance. I live in it. I come to feel quite at home there—down to the point of noticing—say, you know, every house has a certain faint odour peculiar to it? There's one in your house—there's one in mine. But in our houses, of course, we don't notice it—because it's the very breath of our lives—understand! Oh—I can see that you agree!

THE CUSTOMER: Yes. Because—well—you must have a good time—just imagining all those things!

MAN WITH THE FLOWER (*wearily, after some reflection*): A good time? I?

THE CUSTOMER: Yes. . . . I suppose—

MAN WITH THE FLOWER: A good time! . . . I should say! . . . Tell me—have you ever been to see a good doctor?

THE CUSTOMER: I? . . . No. Why? . . . I've never been sick.

MAN WITH THE FLOWER: No—no. . . . I meant, have you ever noticed, in a doctor's office, the waiting-room where the patients sit until their turn comes?

THE CUSTOMER: Ah, yes. . . . I once took my daughter to see a doctor. . . . Something wrong with her nerves—

MAN WITH THE FLOWER: Well—I wasn't prying, you know. I meant that those waiting-rooms. . . . (*A pause.*) Did you ever notice?—a black horse-hair sofa in some old-fashioned style . . . upholstered chairs, that hardly ever match . . . an arm-chair or two—huh—second-hand stuff—picked up where they can find it. Put there for the patients. . . . Nothing to do with the house, you see. . . . The doctor—huh! . . . for himself, his wife, and his wife's friends, he has a fine parlour, comfortable, done up in style. . . . And what a noise one of those chairs in the parlour would make if you stuck it in there in the waiting-room! . . . Why—you need things about as they are—good, decent stuff, of course—not too showy—stuff that will wear. Because it'll be used by all sorts of people who come to see the doctor. I wonder. . . . When you went to the doctor's with your daughter that time—did you notice the chairs you sat on while you were waiting?

THE CUSTOMER: To tell the truth, I . . . I didn't!

MAN WITH THE FLOWER: Oh, of course you didn't—because you weren't sick. . . . (*A pause.*) But even sick people don't always notice—all taken up as they are with what's wrong with them. (*A pause.*) And yet, oftentimes some of them sit there, looking so carefully at one of their fingers, which is going round and round, making letters and numbers that have no meaning, on the varnished arm of the chair where they are sitting. They're thinking. They don't really see. (*A pause.*) But what a strange impression it makes on you, when, as you go through the waiting-room again, after you are through with the doctor, you catch a glimpse of that chair where you were sitting just a few moments before—anxious to have some opinion on your mysterious disease. There it is—empty, indifferent, waiting for somebody—anybody at all—to come and sit down in it. (*A pause.*) What were we saying?—Oh, yes. I remember. The pleasures we take in imagination—how do you suppose I came to think of a chair in one of those waiting-rooms in a doctor's office, where the patients sit waiting for their turn?

THE CUSTOMER: Yes—in fact—

MAN WITH THE FLOWER: You don't understand?—Neither do I. (*A pause.*) But the fact is that certain mental associations—oh! between things worlds apart—are so peculiar to each of us, and they are determined by considerations, experiences, habits

of mind, so individual that people would never understand
one another unless they avoided them when they talked. Nothing more illogical, sometimes, than these associations. (*A pause.*)
But the relation, perhaps, may be this—funny, eh? Do you
suppose those chairs get any pleasure out of imagining who
the patient is to be who will next sit down in them, waiting
for his turn to see the doctor?—what disease he will have?—
where he will go?—what he will do after he has been examined?
. . . No pleasure at all! And so it is with me. . . . No pleasure
at all! So many patients come, and they are there, poor chairs,
to be sat on! . . . Well—my job in life is something like theirs.
Now this thing, and now that, occupies me. This moment it
happens to be you, and . . . pleasure?—Believe me, I find no
pleasure at all in thinking of the train you lost—of the family
you have in the country—all the annoyances I can imagine
you have.

THE CUSTOMER: There are a lot of them, I can tell you!

MAN WITH THE FLOWER: Well, you ought to thank God that you've
nothing worse than annoyances!—(*A pause.*) Some of us, you
know, are worse off than that! (*A pause.*) I'm telling you
that I need to attach myself in my imagination to the lives
other people lead. But—in my peculiar way—without pleasure—
without any real interest, even—in such a way, in fact—yes,
just so—in such a way, precisely, as to sense the annoyances
they encounter. . . . In such a way as to be able to understand how stupid and silly life is, so that no one, really, ought
to care a snap about being rid of the thing! (*With sullen rage.*)
And that's a good deal to prove, you know. It takes arguing
and proof—continual examples, which we have to keep impressing upon ourselves—mercilessly—because, my dear sir—
we don't know what it is, exactly—but it's there, just the same
—it's there—and we all feel it, every one of us, catching us—
here—by our throats—a sort of anguish—a thirst for living
that is never satisfied, that is never quenched—that can never be
quenched. Because life, as we live it from moment to moment,
is always such a hurrying—such a stuffy thing—that it never
lets us get the full taste of it. The flavour of life is in the
past, which remains always as something living within us. Our
enjoyment of it comes from back there—from the memories

which hold us bound—but bound to what? Bound to these stupidities, precisely—to these annoyances—to all these silly illusions, all these insipid occupations of ours. Yes—yes—this little bit of foolishness here—this little annoyance . . . little?—why little? Even this great misfortune—a real misfortune—yes, sir—four, five, ten years hence will have, who knows, what flavour for us? Who knows what keen enjoyment, mingled with its tears! And life—God! Life—the moment we think of losing it—especially when it is only a matter of days— (*At this point, a woman, dressed in black, appears around the corner on the right.*) . . . Say—do you see that—I mean, over there—at the corner? You see that woman? Ah! She's gone again.

THE CUSTOMER: A woman?—Where? . . . Who was it?

MAN WITH THE FLOWER: You didn't see her? . . . She has gone now.

THE CUSTOMER: A woman? . . .

MAN WITH THE FLOWER: My wife. . . . Yes. . . .

THE CUSTOMER: Ah! . . . Your wife!

MAN WITH THE FLOWER (*after a pause*): She keeps her eye on me. . . . Sometimes, you know, I feel almost like getting up and giving her a kick! But what good would that do—after all? . . . She's like one of those stray dogs you take into the house. . . . Obstinate! . . . The more you kick them and beat them, the closer they stick to your heels. (*A pause.*) What that woman is going through on my account, you can't imagine, sir! . . . Goes without her meals—rarely ever goes to bed—just follows me around, day and night—that way —at a distance! . . . I wish she would be a little more attentive to her appearance! She might brush her clothes once in a while, at least . . . and that old hat she wears! She looks more like a rag doll than like a woman! . . . Ah!— and the dust!—the white dust has settled on her hair, too, here, around her forehead . . . and barely thirty-four at that! . . . (*A pause.*) I get so mad at her sometimes—you've no idea! . . . And I lose my temper—and I go up to her, and I almost scream in her face—"Idiot!—Idiot!" . . . and I give her a shaking! . . . Nothing—She swallows it all, and just stands there looking at me, with eyes . . . with

eyes . . . Well—I could choke the life out of her, then!
. . . But no—she waits till I am some distance off—and then
she takes up the trail again! . . . (*At this point the woman's head again appears around the corner.*) Look!—Look!
. . . There she is again! . . . See her?—Did you see
her?

THE CUSTOMER: Poor thing!

MAN WITH THE FLOWER: Poor thing! . . . Huh! . . . Do you know
what that woman wants of me? She wants me to stay quiet
—peaceful-like—at home where she can cuddle me and humour
me with her tenderest and most affectionate attentions! . . .
every room in perfect order . . . every piece of furniture in
its place—and the varnish clean and polished. . . . Silence
. . . deadly silence . . . broken only by the tick-tock, tick-
tock of the grandfather's clock in our dining-room. . . . Huh!
. . . That's her notion of life! . . . Well—I'll leave it to you.
Isn't that about the limit of absurdity! . . . Absurdity?—
Ferocity, I would say rather. . . . A kind of ghoulish cruelty!
Do you suppose, sir, that the houses of Avezzano, or the
houses of Messina, knowing that the earthquake was going
to topple them over within a very few days, could have been
persuaded to sit still there, under the moonlight—all in nice
straight lines, radiating from the squares—eh?—the way the
Town Planning Committee decided they ought to be? . . .
No, sir!—Brick and stone though they were, they would have
found legs, somehow, to run away! And the people who lived
in them—do you think that if they had known what was going to happen to them, they would have gone to their bedrooms every night as usual—folded their clothes up nicely,
set their shoes outside their doors, and then crawled com-
fortably into bed between their nice white sheets—knowing
for certain that in a few hours they would be dead? . . . Do
you think they would?

THE CUSTOMER: But, perhaps your Signora. . . .

MAN WITH THE FLOWER: Just a moment. . . . If death, my
dear sir, were like one of those strange, loathsome insects
you sometimes find walking up your coat sleeve. . . . Here
you are, going along the side-walk. . . . A man comes up to
you, all of a sudden—stops you, and then, cautiously, hold-

ing out two fingers of his hand, says to you—"Beg pardon—
may I?" . . . And with those two fingers he skips the insect
off! . . . Ah! . . . That would be fine! . . . But death isn't
like one of those loathsome insects. Many people walk by
you, but no one notices anything. They are all absorbed in
what they are going to do to-morrow or the next day. . . .
Now, I, my dear sir—look! (*He gets up.*) Just step this
way—(*He draws the man aside till they are standing in the
full light of the street-lamp.*) Look! . . . I want to show
you something. . . . See this spot, under my moustache?—
Pretty violet colour, isn't it! . . . Do you know what they call
that?—A pretty name!—like a verse from a poem—E-pi-
the-li-o-ma! . . . Epithelioma! . . . Say it yourself, and
you'll notice how nice it sounds!—Epithelioma! . . . But
death—you understand—death! . . . Death has passed my
way, and put this flower in my mouth—"A souvenir, my dear
sir! Keep it—no charge! . . . I'll be back this way a few
months hence!" (*A pause.*) Now, you tell me, sir—whether,
with a flower like this in my mouth, I can sit quietly at home,
there, as that poor woman would like to have me do! . . .
(*A pause.*) I scream at her—"Yes—Yes! . . . Don't you
want me to kiss you?" . . . "Yes—kiss me!" she says.
. . . And you know what she did, the other day? She took a
pin and scratched her lip, and then seized me by the head
and tried to kiss me—kiss me—here—on my lips—because she
wants to die with me, she says! . . . (*A pause.*) Crazy
woman! (*Then, angrily.*) But I refuse to stay at home! I've
simply got to stand around, looking into the shop windows,
admiring the deftness of the clerks at the counters! . . .
Because, you understand, if I should permit myself one single idle moment—why, I might go mad! . . . I might pull out
a revolver and shoot someone who never did me the least harm
in the world! . . . Why, I might shoot you, for instance—
though all you've done, so far as I can see, is to have lost
your train! . . . (*He laughs.*) Oh, no!—no! . . . Don't be
afraid. . . . I'm only joking! . . . (*A pause.*) Well—I
must be going. . . . (*A pause.*) At the very worst, I might
kill myself some day—(*A pause.*) But, you see, this is the
fruit season, and I like apricots. . . . How do you eat

them?—Skin and all, I suppose. Ah!—that's the way! . . .
You cut them in halves, and you bring your two fingers together, and you suck in the juice, eh?—Ah! that's the way!
. . . How good they are! . . . (*He laughs. A pause.*)
Well—give my regards to your wife and daughters, when you
get back to the country. (*A pause.*) I imagine them dressed
in white and blue, sitting on the green grass in the shade
of some tree. . . . (*A pause.*) Do something for me to-morrow morning, when you get home—will you? . . . I suppose
your villa will be some little distance from the station.
Well—you'll get there about sunrise, won't you? And you'd
enjoy making the trip on foot. Well—the first tuft of grass you
notice on the roadside—just count the blades for me! The
number of those blades of grass will be the number of the
days I still have to live! . . . (*A pause.*) . . . Choose a good-
sized clump, if you please—eh? . . . (*He laughs.*) Well—
good-night! . . . good-night! . . . (*He walks away, humming through his closed lips the movement played by the distant mandolin. He heads at first toward the corner on the
right, but then, reflecting that his wife is probably there waiting for him, he turns around and walks off in the other direction. The Customer sits there, looking after him in amazement.*)

CURTAIN

[OCTOBER, 1923]

COMMENT

IT was precisely in Paris (where we had gone to see a man about a painting) that we read an editorial in The Literary Review which flattered us to the point of bedazzlement and then struck home. Magazines travel more slowly than ideas, so we will reprint the blow (assuming that the bouquets remain fresh in the ever-grateful memories of our readers):

"*The Dial* apparently would have us make the same mistake over again [the mistake of Longfellow]. Here, its editors say—by implication and sometimes directly—here is the way to write; these are the subjects, these the methods of modern European literature; go you and do likewise and we shall have an American literature! . . .

"But we do not want another age of Longfellow. Bring Europe to us by all means and in every measure. Encourage us to experiment, break down the prejudices that withhold us from novelty, fertilize the American soil with ideas from abroad; but don't tell us to write like Schnitzler, D. H. Lawrence, or Paul Fort, or any one else whose environment and tradition are utterly different from our own. Ever since the mid-eighteenth century, when Americans began to feel that they were not Europeans, some worthy missionary or another has been bringing in Europe to civilize us, saying: 'Drink this; then act like little Europeans, and your souls will be saved.' And those who like Hawthorne refused to act, or who, like Walt Whitman and Mark Twain, rejected the cup, have best pleased both the Europeans and ourselves. We thank *The Dial* and *Broom* and the rest for giving us more of Europe, but will not join them in acting Longfellow over again. That play is out of date."

The Literary Review owes a debt to THE DIAL which it proposes to acknowledge later. (We know this from the same article, which uses those words and specifies the indebtedness.) May we suggest that a revision of the statements quoted above would be a fair way to pay off? For they are, as far as they apply to us, sheer nonsense, and if some stupidity of idea or carelessness of phrase has given any one the impression that we want Americans to write like Europeans or like Hindus, we are ready to go into sackcloth and Hergesheimer for six months. Have we really given American writers to believe that we are publishing the work of European writers as an object lesson? The discourtesy to the Europeans would be a little too great, and the insult to Americans too smart. And precisely like what Europeans do we want our Americans to write? Will Cabell be better for imitating Lawrence, or Anderson clear up his style by reading Morand, or Willa Cather gain an intensity by a study of Bunin? And will the result be worth a hang if there is a result? It has been our fear, precisely, that too many young Americans would begin writing like James Joyce; and the manuscripts we have rejected proved that our fear was well-grounded. Writing like anything or anybody is as good a way as any for a writer to get his manuscript back by return mail; and if what we have published in any case bears a resemblance to the work of some vast European genius, it will be found that the resemblance is due to an identity, a necessary and justifiable coincidence, in character or expression.

If we have already history behind us, if American letters owe us something, it is simply because we have never published anything or anybody for any reason but the one natural reason: because the work was good. We have published European work not as exotics and not as exemplars; only because we feel that Americans are at work in the same *milieu* and in the same tradition of letters as the Europeans—that we are all in the Western-civilized-Christian-European-American tradition, and that American letters have their independent existence and their separate, precious character, within that circle, just as German and Italian letters have. It is true that an Italian can say, I shall write in the manner of Petrarch (and as like as not miss the excellence of the tradition he aspires to) and an American, casting about for definite models will find few names to buoy him on. But the American who feels that he has not inherited Dean Swift as surely as he has inherited Mr Dooley, is simply missing half of his heritage and, unless he be a startling individual genius, will not write half so well. We have pointed out, perhaps too often, that the whole sighing for a background in America is due to the false, political feeling that we are cut off from the main stream of European art and letters. There is no evidence of the fact—except for the wailing. Mr Sinclair Lewis has written two American books which owe more to Flaubert than anything Jean Cocteau or Paul Morand has created. And Huck Finn is accepted in Germany exactly as Tom Jones is accepted. Nor were we aware when we published Mr Anderson's I'm a Fool that it was written in the image—of whom? Perhaps The London Mercury which published the same story later thought it an imitation of something, or published it for young English writers to imitate. Perhaps—we offer the suggestion in a spirit of editorial confraternity—they thought it a good story.

But when we consider "implications"—does The Literary Review mean that a number of American writers, accustomed to praise elsewhere, are here treated with scant respect, while a number of European writers are praised in our pages? It has been THE DIAL's habit to find intelligent reviewers and then to let them have as free a hand as any creative artist can have; no one has been instructed to praise or dispraise and delicate hints have generally had results the opposite of what we hoped; and if our reviewers have not been clubby about American books it is because that is how they feel, and it is our fault only because we've chosen the wrong men. A careful reading of our review pages will indicate that European writers have not got off easily; and if in the past two or three years a majority of the books we have praised have come from Europe— we do not know whether this is so or not—it has been their quality and not their provenance which has influenced us. The truth is that a few great Europeans are producing work of exceptional merit; that these books arrive in translation or in American editions; and as long as we believe that the love of letters knows no frontiers we are going to praise them—we, including our reviewers. And the equal truth is that for a long time American writers have not been subjected to serious and severe criticism, that they have lived on "notices" and puffs; and THE DIAL adds itself to the small number of journals which see no reason for praising a book except that the book deserves praise when viewed with the same unsentimental eye as looks out upon the literary scene abroad. It is no use saying that one ought to be more tender to Gertrude Atherton than to May Sinclair, because May Sinclair lives in a literary *milieu;* or that it will not help Anderson to be as severely handled as Schnitzler. We fancy that not a few of the authors who have been mercilessly attacked in these pages prefer that attack to any suggestion that they are only in primary school and are not to be marked on the same scale as the bigger boys abroad. We aren't to be sure marking anybody or setting up prize-boys. We are discussing creative work.

If the work of European artists continues to be nobler in conception and more honest in execution than the work of Americans, we shall undoubtedly print the former in preference to the latter. But we ask The Literary Review to continue to watch what happens. It is barely possible that our greatest service to American letters will turn out to be our refusal to praise or to publish silly and slovenly and nearly-good-enough work. The Americans we publish have at least the certainty that we publish them not because they are Americans, but because they are artists.

[JUNE, 1923]

MODEL AMERICANS

Americans. *By Stuart P. Sherman. 12mo. 336 pages. Charles Scribner's Sons. $2.*

Professor Sherman once more coaxing American criticism the way it should go.

Like Benjamin Franklin, one of his heroes, he attempts the invention of a creed that shall "satisfy the professors of all religions, and offend none."

He smites the marauding Mr Mencken with a velvet glove, and pierces the obstinate Mr More with a reproachful look. Both gentlemen, of course, will purr and feel flattered.

That's how Professor Sherman treats his enemies: buns to his grizzlies.

Well, Professor Sherman, being a professor, has got to be nice to everybody about everybody. What else does a professor sit in a chair of English for, except to dole out sweets.

Awfully nice, rather cloying. But there, men *are* but children of a later growth.

So much for the professor's attitude. As for his "message." He steers his little ship of Criticism most obviously between the Scylla of Mr Mencken and the Charybdis of Mr P. E. More. I'm sorry I never heard before of either gentleman: except that I dimly remember having read, in the lounge of a Naples hotel, a bit of an article by a Mr Mencken, in German, in some German periodical: all amounting to nothing.

But Mr Mencken is the Scylla of American Criticism, and hence, of American Democracy. There is a verb "to menckenise," and a noun "menckenism." Apparently *to menckenise* is to manufacture jeering little gas-bomb phrases against everything deep and earnest, or high and noble, and to paint the face of corruption with phosphorus, so it shall glow. And a *menckenism* is one of the little stink-gas phrases.

Now the *nouveau riche jeune fille* of the *bourgeoisie*, as Professor Sherman puts it; in other words, the profiteers' flappers, all read Mr Mencken and swear by him: swear that they don't give a nickel for any Great Man that ever was or will be. Great Men are all a bombastical swindle. So asserts the *nouveau riche jeune fille*, on whom, apparently, American democracy rests. And Mr Mencken "learnt it her." And Mr Mencken got it in Germany, where all stink-gas comes and came from, according to Professor Sherman. And Mr Mencken does it to poison the noble and great old spirit of American Democracy, which is grandly Anglo-Saxon in origin, but absolutely AMERICAN in fact.

So much for the Scylla of Mr Mencken. It is the first essay in the book. The Charybdis of Mr P. E. More is the last essay: to this monster the professor warbles another tune. Mr More, author of the Shelbourne Essays, is learned, and steeped in tradition, the very antithesis of the nihilistic stink-gassing Mr Mencken. But alas, Mr More is remote: somewhat haughty and supercilious at his study table. And even, alasser! with all his learning and remoteness, he hunts out the risky Restoration wits to hob-nob with on high Parnassus; Wycherley, for example; he likes his wits smutty. He even goes and fetches out Aphra Behn from her disreputable oblivion, to entertain her in public.

And there you have the Charybdis of Mr More: snobbish, distant, exclusive, disdaining even the hero from the Marne who mends the gas bracket: and at the same time absolutely *preferring* the doubtful odour of Wycherley because it is—well, malodorous, says the professor.

Mr Mencken: Great Men and the Great Past are an addled egg full of stink-gas.

Mr P. E. More: Great Men of the Great Past are utterly beyond the *mobile vulgus*. Let the *mobile vulgus* (in other words, the democratic millions of America) be cynically scoffed at by the gentlemen of the Great Past, especially the naughty ones.

To the Menckenites, Professor Sherman says: Jeer not at the Great Past and at the Great Dead. Heroes are heroes still, they do not go addled, as you would try to make out, nor turn into stink-bombs. Tradition is honourable still, and will be honourable for ever, though it may be splashed like a futurist picture with the rotten eggs of menckenism.

To the smaller and more select company of Moreites: Scorn not the horny hand of noble toil; "—the average man is, like (Mr More) himself, at heart a mystic, vaguely hungering for a peace that diplomats cannot give, obscurely seeking the permanent amid the transitory; a poor swimmer struggling for a rock amid the flux of waters, a lonely pilgrim longing for the shadow of a mighty rock in a weary land. And if 'P. E. M.' had a bit more of that natural sympathy of which he is so distrustful, he would have perceived that what more than anything else to-day keeps the average man from lapsing into Yahooism is the religion of democracy, consisting of a little bundle of general principles which make him respect himself and his neighbour; a bundle of principles kindled in crucial times by an intense emotion, in which his self-interest, his petty vices, and his envy are consumed as with fire; and he sees the common weal as the mighty rock in the shadow of which his little life and personality are to be surrendered, if need be, as things negligible and transitory."

All right, Professor Sherman. All the profiteers, and shovers, and place-grabbers, and bullies, especially bullies, male and female, all that sort of gentry of the late war were, of course, outside the average. The supermen of the occasion.

The Babbitts, while they were on the make.

And as for the mighty rocks in weary lands, as far as my experience goes, they have served the pilgrims chiefly as sanitary offices and places in whose shadows men shall leave their offal and tin cans.

But there you have a specimen of Professor Sherman's "style." And the thin ends of his parabola.

The great arch is of course the Religion of Democracy, which the professor italicizes. If you want to trace the curve you must follow the course of the essays.

After Mr Mencken and Tradition comes Franklin. Now Benjamin Franklin is one of the founders of the Religion of Democracy. It was he who invented the creed that should satisfy the professors of all religions, not of universities only, and offend none. With a deity called Providence. Who turns out to be a sort of superlative Mr Wanamaker, running the globe as a revolving dry-goods store, according to a profit-and-loss system; the profit counted in plump citizens whose every want is satisfied: like chickens in an absolutely coyote-proof chicken-run.

In spite of this new attempt to make us like Dr Franklin, the flesh wearies on our bones at the thought of him. The professor hints that the good old gentleman on Quaker Oats was really an old sinner. If it had been proved to us, we *might* have liked him. As it is, he just wearies the flesh on our bones. *Religion civile,* indeed.

Emerson. The next essay is called The Emersonian Liberation. Well, Emerson is a great man still: or a great individual. And heroes are heroes still, though their banners may decay, and stink.

It is true that lilies may fester. And virtues likewise. The great Virtue of one age has a trick of smelling far worse than weeds in the next.

It is a sad but undeniable fact.

Yet why so sad, fond lover, prithee why so sad? Why should Virtue remain incorruptible, any more than anything else? If stars wax and wane, why should Goodness shine for ever unchanged? That too makes one tired. Goodness sweals and gutters, the light of the Good goes out with a stink, and lo, somewhere else a new light, a new Good. Afterwards, it may be shown that it is eternally the same Good. But to us poor mortals at the moment, it emphatically isn't.

And that is the point about Emerson and the Emersonian Liberation—save the word! Heroes are heroes still: safely dead. Heroism is always heroism. But the hero who was heroic one century, uplifting the banner of a creed, is followed the next century by a hero heroically ripping that banner to rags. *Sic transit veritas mundi.*

Emerson was an idealist: a believer in "continuous revelation," continuous inrushes of inspirational energy from the Over-soul. Professor Sherman says: "His message when he leaves us is not, 'Henceforth be masterless,' but, 'Bear thou henceforth the sceptre of thine own control through life and the passion of life.'"

When Emerson says: "I am surrounded by messengers of God who send me credentials day by day," then all right for him. But he cozily forgot that there are many messengers. He knew only a sort of smooth-shaven Gabriel. But as far as we remember, there is Michael too: and a terrible discrepancy between the credentials of the pair of 'em. Then there are other cherubim with outlandish names, bringing very different messages than those Ralph Waldo got: Israfel, and even Mormon. And a whole bunch of others. But Emerson had a stone-deaf ear for all except a nicely aureoled Gabriel *qui n'avait pas de quoi.*

Emerson listened to one sort of message, and only one. To all the rest he was blank. Ashtaroth and Ammon are gods as well, and hand out their own credentials. But Ralph Waldo wasn't having any. They could never ring *him* up. He was only connected on the Ideal 'phone. "We are all aiming to be idealists," says Emerson, "and covet the society of those who make us so, as the sweet singer, the orator, the ideal painter."

Well, we're pretty sick of the ideal painters and the uplifting singers. As a matter of fact we have worked the ideal bit of our nature to death, and we shall go crazy if we can't start working from some other bit. Idealism now is a sick nerve, and the more you rub on it the worse you feel afterwards. Your later reactions aren't pretty at all. Like Dostoevsky's Idiot, and President Wilson sometimes.

Emerson believes in having the courage to treat all men as equals. It takes some courage *not* to treat them so now.

"Shall I not treat all men as gods?" he cries.

If you like, Waldo, but we've got to pay for it, when you've made them *feel* that they're gods. A hundred million American godlets is rather much for the world to deal with.

The fact of the matter is, all those gorgeous inrushes of exaltation and spiritual energy which made Emerson a great man, now make us sick. They are with us a drug habit. So when Professor Sherman urges us in Ralph Waldo's footsteps, he is really driving us nauseously astray. Which perhaps is hard lines on the Professor, and us, and Emerson. But it wasn't I who started the mills of God a-grinding.

I like the essay on Emerson. I like Emerson's real courage. I like his wild and genuine belief in the Over-soul and the inrushes he got from it. But it is a museum-interest. Or else it is a taste of the old drug to the old spiritual drug-fiend in me.

We've got to have a different sort of sardonic courage. And the sort of credentials we are due to receive from the god in the shadow would have been real bones out of hell-broth to Ralph Waldo. *Sic transeunt Dei hominorum.*

So no wonder Professor Sherman sounds a little wistful, and somewhat pathetic, as he begs us to follow Ralph Waldo's trail.

Hawthorne: A Puritan Critic of Puritanism. This essay is concerned chiefly with an analysis and a praise of The Scarlet Letter.

Well, it is a wonderful book. But why does nobody give little Nathaniel a kick for his duplicity. Professor Sherman says there is nothing erotic about The Scarlet Letter. Only neurotic. It wasn't the sensual act itself had any meaning for Hawthorne. Only the Sin. He knows there's nothing deadly in the act itself. But if it is Forbidden, immediately it looms lurid with interest. He is not concerned for a moment with what Hester and Dimmesdale really felt. Only with their situations as Sinners. And Sin looms lurid and thrilling, when after all it is only just a normal sexual passion. This luridness about the book makes one feel like spitting. It is something worked up: invented in the head and grafted on to the lower body, like some serpent of supposition under the fig-leaf. It depends so much on *coverings*. Suppose you took off the fig-leaf, the serpent isn't there. And so the relish is all two-faced and tiresome. The Scarlet Letter is a masterpiece, but in duplicity and half-false excitement.

And when one remembers The Marble Faun, all the parochial priggishness and poor-bloodedness of Hawthorne in Italy, one of the most bloodless books ever written, one feels like giving Nathaniel a kick in the seat of his poor little pants and landing him back in New England again. For the rolling, many-godded mediaeval and pagan world was too big a prey for such a ferret.

Walt Whitman. Walt is the high priest of the Religion of Democracy. Yet "at the first bewildering contact one wonders whether his urgent touch is of lewdness or divinity," says Professor Sherman.

"All I have said concerns you."—But it doesn't. One ceases to care about so many things. One ceases to respond or to react. And at length other things come up, which Walt and Professor Sherman never knew.

"Whatever else it involves, democracy involves at least one grand salutary elementary admission, namely, that the world exists for the benefit and for the improvement of all the decent individuals in it."—O Lord, how long will you submit to this Insurance Policy interpretation of the Universe! How "decent"? Decent in what way? Benefit! Think of the world's existing for people's "benefit and improvement."

So wonderful, says Professor Sherman, the way Whitman identifies himself with everything and everybody: Runaway Slaves and all the rest. But we no longer want to take the whole hullabaloo to our bosom. We no longer want to "identify ourselves" with a lot of other things and other people. It *is* a sort of lewdness. *Noli me tangere,* "you." I don't want "you."

Whitman's "you" doesn't get me.

We don't want to be embracing everything any more. Or to be embraced in one of Waldo's vast promiscuous armfuls. *Merci, monsieur!*

We've had enough democracy.

Professor Sherman says that if Whitman had lived "at the right place in these years of Proletarian Millenium, he would have been hanged as a reactionary member of the *bourgeoise.*" ('Tisn't my spelling.)

And he gives Whitman's own words in proof: "The true gravitation hold of liberalism in the United States will be a more universal ownership of property, general homesteads, general comforts— a vast intertwining reticulation of wealth. . . . She (Democracy) asks for men and women with occupations, well-off, owners of houses and acres, and with cash in the bank and with some craving for literature too"—so that they can buy certain books. Oh, Walt!

Allons! The road is before us.

Joaquin Miller: Poetical Conquistador of the West. A long essay with not much spirit in it, showing that Miller was a true son of the Wild and Woolly West, in so far as he was a very good imitator of other people's poetry (note the Swinburnian bit) and a rather poor assumer of other people's played-out poses. A self-conscious little "wild" man, like the rest of the "wild" men. The Wild West is a pose that pays Zane Grey to-day, as it once paid Miller and Bret Harte and Buffalo Bill.

A Note on Carl Sandburg. That Carl is a super-self-conscious literary gent stampeding around with red-ochre blood on his hands and smeared-on soot darkening his craggy would-be-criminal brow: but that his heart is as tender as an old tomato.

Andrew Carnegie. That Andy was the most perfect American citizen Scotland ever produced, and the sweetest example of how beautifully the *Religion Civile* pays, in cold cash.

Roosevelt and the National Psychology. Theodore didn't have a spark of magnanimity in his great personality, says Professor

Sherman, what a pity! And you see where it lands you, when you play at being pro-German. You go quite out of fashion.

Evolution of the Adams Family. Perfect Pedigree of the most aristocratic Democratic family. Your aristocracy is played out, my dear fellows, but don't cry about it, you've always got your Democracy to fall back on. If you don't like falling back on it of your own free will, you'll be shoved back on it by the Will of the People.

"Man is the animal that destiny cannot break."

But the Will of the People can break Man, and the animal man, and the destined man, all the lot, and grind 'em to democratic powder, Professor Sherman warns us.

Allons! en-masse is before us.

But when Germany is thoroughly broken, Democracy finally collapses. (My own prophecy.)

An Imaginary Conversation With Mr P. E. More: You've had the gist of that already.

Well, there is Professor Sherman's dish of cookies which he bids you eat and have. An awfully sweet book, all about having your cookies and eating 'em. The cookies are Tradition, and Heroes, and Great Men, and $350,000,000 in your pocket. And eating 'em is Democracy, Serving Mankind, piously giving most of the $350,-000,000 back again. "Oh, nobly and heroically get $350,000,000 together," chants Professor Sherman in this litany of having your cookies and eating 'em, "and then piously and munificently give away $349,000,000 again."

D. H. Lawrence

P. S. You can't get past Arithmetic.

[May, 1923]

GERMAN LETTER

September, 1923

OUR theatre . . . oh, do not let me spend many words on our theatre! It is in decay, like our highways, and like the whole martyred nation whose economic and social collapse the world awaits with such astonishing indifference. Christianity! Have you not yet learned that the cry over "Huns and Barbarians" was not seriously meant, that it was an implement of war, a piece of pious lying propaganda? Shall a noble member of the family of white peoples perish and die before the eyes of her phlegmatic cousins through the fault of an effective but stupid advertisement? . . . I beg forgiveness. I am already quiet. I am speaking of our theatre and am announcing that its condition leaves much to be desired. For some time you have known more about the great voices from our operas than we. Our corps of singers is a little like Demeter's daughter, the lovely Persephone, who was stolen by Pluto (the god of wealth, if I am not mistaken) and persuaded to taste the fruits of his realm, whereby she became his for at least the half of each year. Meanwhile the divine mother (the German public) wanders disconsolately through the devastated fields. Not a bad picture, these devastated fields, to give an idea of the German opera in its entirety. It is going downhill. Naturally the national impoverishment shows up first in this *de luxe* article. It is threatened with shabbiness, and of all things that is the last quality which can fit with the notion of the opera, the notion of splendour and material luxury. The leaders of this institution are struggling against this depletion; and so the strongest and the most brilliant of them—who are not compelled to struggle under this depletion and to whom the world stands open—are not to be held at their posts, nor is there any adequate substitution for them.

Such was the case with Bruno Walter, who left the Munich opera-house some time ago amid endless ceremonies of departure, after ten years of the most triumphant guidance there as general music conductor. I name him because a short time ago he visited America, where—unless our papers exaggerated patriotically—he met with extraordinary successes. He is undoubtedly a composer of the first rank, a musical genius of great power and intensity. Trained under Mahler in Vienna—Mahler's bust by Rodin adorns his work-room, and he has made his friendship with Mahler and his recollections of him into a glowing cult—he is certainly a softer, less abrupt and Caesarian nature than the master; but his relationship to his art is just as absolute in earnestness and fervour, and he is an incomparable interpreter of the symphonic struggles which this tragic worshipper had with genius. Walter's services to the art of the Bavarian capital deserved all the honours which were afforded him at his departure. He enlivened the orchestra, dignified the repertoire, and enriched the *ensemble* with distinguished talents, such as Frau Ivogün, Frau Reinhardt, and the baritone Schipper. His restorations, particularly of works from the German romantic sphere, as Undine, Hans Heiling, Oberon, were events. It was he who stood godfather to Pfitzner's Palestrina, a work which, regardless of how one now feels towards its mild melancholy, its unfriendliness to life, stands in any case head and shoulders above all the rest of contemporary opera as an intellectual accomplishment. Walter laid the way for it. Further, he was no less effective in the concert hall than in the conductor's chair at the opera. Many critics felt compelled to insist that there are more rigorous rhythmists; but no one disputed his unparalleled sense of sound-values. He is the most subtle, the most thoroughly musical accompanist at the piano, I have ever seen. No one who has heard Schubert's Winterreise done by him and Van Roy can forget it. In Vienna I saw an audience of two thousand deeply moved at his playing in company with the violinist Arnold Rosé.

Walter's last act as conductor of the Munich state opera was an evening of one-acters which captivated as much by their inherent charm as by their rich significance historically. He played Handel's Acis and Galatea, this tragic pastoral in which more than one accent gives a premonition of Wagner; he followed with Pergolese's charming Serva Padrona, which prepared the way for the opera bouffe and Mozart; and he finished with a German musical comedy of the eighteenth century, Schenk's Dorfbarbier, which leads in a straight line to the Waffenschmid and Nicolai's Lustige Weber. I hardly need to excuse myself for speaking of an opera performance which took place so long back; for the mere fact that I return to this subject after so great a time indicates the unusual pertinacity of the impression which it produced. For the costumes and decorations an artist had been secured who, long known as an original graphic artist, has only recently begun employing his imagination and his taste in the service of the theatre: Emil Preetorius, a native of Darmstadt who is living in Munich. What he gave us to look at was, in its gradation from the idyllic and the heroic through the *bourgeois* and the elegant to the humoristic and the popular, extraordinarily delicate and felicitous. And since Walter had given the whole of his industry and love to the study of the musical part, and furthermore since the best resources of our theatre were brought forward, a truly glorious evening resulted. I should like especially to say something about Acis and Galatea, this splendid work which one hardly ever met with in the theatre, and which Walter has restored to it by this production of his. For all the tenderness and sorrow with which it is filled is aroused in me again as I think back on it; and the tragic humanness which it represents has, in my mind, much to say to our feelings of the present day. But if I am to tell anything at all about our drama this time, I must take account of my space.

The popular power which overshadows and threatens to stifle the theatre of the spoken word is the cinema. With the prodigality of a *parvenu,* it can attract the mimetic talent. It breaks up the *ensembles.* Indeed, art communities such as played Ibsen and Hauptmann twenty years ago in the Berlin Lessingtheater, or even such as I found as a young man in Munich when Possart developed his drastic virtuosity, his highly amusing art of speech, in the Hoftheater—such a stylistically fixed and disciplined body of players really no longer exists in Germany. Berlin, the leading theatrical city of Europe a quarter of a century ago, has suffered great losses; it is not only since Max Reinhardt retired to his castle near Salzburg that it has deteriorated in the attractiveness of its theatre. (I hear that you are receiving a visit from him in America. Oh, he will undoubtedly show you very remarkable things!) The Reinhardt-Theater! I do not forget how I first became acquainted with it. Gorki's Night Lodging, the comedies of Shakespeare, Schiller's Die Räuber! Those were rousing evenings, full of a charm which lost none of its intensity despite a certain intellectual, or shall we say artistic-moralistic, distrust which we brought to them; performances which dealt a radical blow to the Protestant temperance, the strenuous inwardness of Brahmsian naturalism with its poverty of gesture—a blow of the theatre, a breaking through of the wild primitive spirit of comedy, and at the same time a new step in modernity, an irresistibly charming mixture of intellectualism and exaggeration, sensuality and wit. In short, the *most interesting* theatre which had ever existed; a theatre which one might say was executed on the basis of sheer virtuosity; and a theatre which benefited by appealing to the sense of criticism, since one could not help considering as an asset the intellectual pleasure derived from the exercise of the critical faculties. It has been fifteen or sixteen years since Reinhardt was a guest director for two or three summer seasons at the Munich Ausstellungspark. Corruption and decay, the degeneration into the sensational, developed rapidly under the scourge of Wilhelm's turbulent metropolis with its vulgar hunger for excitement. When, some years ago, Reinhardt handed over to his managers and dramaturgists the theatres which he had united under his authority, and withdrew into a private life interspersed with guest plays given abroad, he certainly did not do this through personal weariness, but because he had felt that his contribution to German culture had already been fulfilled.

What one sees to-day in the Berlin Deutsches Theater and the Grosses Schauspielhaus shows occasional remains of the old charm, but it lacks true intellectual scope. For in addition there is the fact that the theatre, in accordance with its adaptive, sympathetic nature, indicates most clearly the lowering of level which our public taste has undergone through war, revolution, and the emerging of new social classes. In the Grosses Schauspielhaus, where the audience sits in a space resembling an enormous cave of stalactites, and where there are accommodations for five thousand people, I recently saw a performance of Shakespeare's Taming of the Shrew which was worth thinking about in this connexion. I confess that I got but slight enjoyment. The talent and the personal appeal of some of the actors was estimable, but the spirit of the organization was thoroughly brutal. Their principal joke consisted in Petruc-chio's continually taking his wild little wife over his knee in front of the footlights, pulling up her skirts, and spanking her black and blue. This amused a public which is filling the seats now that our educated middle class is hungering or has become proletarian. Indeed, after fifty years in Germany, one can no longer feel quite at home there. It has become a country to excite the curiosity, but very foreign.

In any case, in order to be able to discuss the condition of our

theatre, one does not have to reside in the capital. The "provinces"
—I place the word in quotation marks since there has never been a
"province" in our culturally uncentralized country which corresponds to the bleak sense of the word in French—are not seldom to
be taken more seriously in this respect than that gigantic market
place in the North. This fact is also known to our dramatic authors, who are certainly not so keen as formerly on having their
premières in Berlin, but often give preference to one of the smaller
state or even city theatres. As to the South-German *Centrum*, as to
Munich, it really never was, in the truest sense of the word, a theatrical city, any more than it was ever a literary city, or more accurately, any more than it was ever a city in which intellectual concerns could lay claim to any special domestic privileges. Yet is it
an art city? Certainly; or essentially not so much a city of art as
a city of the higher applied arts, of an art which is employed for
festivity and is primarily decorative. The Munich type of artist is
not the intellectual type; rather, he is a cheerful fellow of sensuous culture, with the instincts of a born arranger of feasts and car-
nivals. This trait, it will be objected, should be an asset to the art
of the theatre in Munich. It is an asset. The Munich Künstler-
theater stood for the most complete expression of everything which
is meant here by dramatic art. The designer was absolute master
in the house, the piece an opportunity to display a culture of applied arts, the actor a spot of colour. The scenic artist forbade the
red-robed king in Hamlet from kneeling to make his prayer which
never to heaven went. He had to stand upright, and precisely because the artist, as he declared, "needed the red vertical line."
That is Munich. In As You Like It, Olivia, on whose very antip-
athy for the colour yellow the funniest scene of the play is based,
wears a canary-yellow dress during the entire evening. This had
suited the artist from the colouristic standpoint, and the good man
had quite frankly not read the play. That is Munich.

It is not always so bad as that, but what really interests Munich
in the theatre is neither the word nor the play, nothing intellectual,
that is, but the incidental of the plastic arts. This is even true of
our most literary theatre, the Kammerspiele which, under its artistic director Otto Falkenberg, is often able to captivate powerfully
the theatre lover. I recently saw there a comedy by the lyric writer
Josef von Eichendorff, Die Frier. The evening was stimulating
and highly Munichese. The piece is an amiable nothing made up

of love, vagabondage, and the humour of disguise; but the scenery, which once again Emil Preetorius had undertaken, was rich in funny and delightful inventions. To be sure, on the last evening spent in this theatre all the emphasis was laid on the literary, even the literarily historic. They gave part of Swinburne's Mary Stuart cycle, the Chastelard, and tormented themselves righteously with the hyper-aesthetic pre-Raphaelite style of poetry, in which the confused passion and psychology of chivalry acquired a somewhat aloof sympathy—but this will hardly grace the repertoire for long.

I love Munich too much to risk being the least misunderstood in my judgment of this city which was once so jolly, but which is now saddened by the general fate of Germany and is torn by political hatreds. The "spirit" which I spoke of as not being at home there is really the critico-literary spirit of European democracy which is represented in Germany chiefly by Judaism, although this movement hardly exists in Munich, and so far as it does it is exposed to a popular disfavour which on occasion takes the most drastic forms. Munich is the city of Hitler, the leader of the German *fascisti;* the city of the *Hakenkreuz,* this symbol of popular defiance and of an ethnic aristocracy the aspects of which are genuinely aristocratic and which above all lacks every connexion with the feudalism of Prussia before the war. Bavaria, and Munich in particular, was democratic long before there was any talk in Germany of "democracy" in the revolutionary sense. It was and is democratic in the national, racial sense of the word. That is to say, in its spirit of conservatism; and herein lies its opposition to the socialistic North, its anti-Semitism, its dynastic loyalty, its obstinacy in matters to do with the republic.

Generally speaking, our modern repertoire has undergone slight rejuvenation in recent years. Since Gerhart Hauptmann no new dramatic talent has appeared of sufficient vastness to captivate the nation. For a time Ibsen was completely crowded off the German stage by Strindberg; yet lately there have been signs of something like an Ibsen renaissance—which can be taken as an indication of restorative tendencies, of the longing for set forms. Wedekind is losing in popular interest. Shaw is still a favourite. It is to be regretted that Schnitzler's graceful, melancholy, and technically so perfect masterpieces are not demanded more often. The comedies of Hermann Bahr continue to please.

The new growth, the young school, what is called dramatic expressionism, has as a theory aroused a great deal of discussion or has discussed itself a great deal; from the standpoint of production it has been greatly disappointing. Still a few names from this sphere have gained an international reputation, although without having touched the heart of their own people. In foreign countries one knows of the social theatrics of Georg Kaiser, the penetrating satires of the *bourgeoisie* by Carl Sternheim, whose talent for comedies criticising his times is undeniable, but is absolutely without warmth. There is much more heart and feeling in Ernst Toller who, since he was a leader of the Munich communists of 1919, has been languishing for some years in a Bavarian prison. Yet unfortunately his artistry falls greatly short of his humanity; and his drama, Die Maschinenstürmer, which received demonstrative applause in Berlin, is a very weak imitation of The Weavers.

By a piece of daring—which one may, by the way, construe differently—Arnold Bronnen aroused tremendous respect from the youngest generation with his drama, Vatermord (Patricide) a crass and gloomy work which represents stylistically a kind of neo-naturalism, and in which all offences from incest through homosexuality to the dereliction mentioned in the title keep a solemn tryst. Similarly, there is much storming and stressing in the dramas of young Bert Brecht, whose first play, Trommeln in der Nacht, the bitter story of a soldier returning from the war, has two good acts, but then falls flat. Munich's state theatre, Das Residenztheater, felt called upon to accept his second play, Dickicht, although with all its ability it was inferior to the first from the standpoint of artistic discipline and intellectual fineness. The popular conservativism of Munich was on its guard. It will not stand for any Bolshevist art. At the second or third performance it entered protest, and this in the form of gas bombs. Frightful fumes suddenly filled the theatre. The public wept bitterly; yet not through emotion, but because the expanding gases had a strongly sympathetic effect on their tear ducts. The theatre had to be aired, and ushers appeared with ozone sprayers to purify the atmosphere. It was half an hour before the public could return to their seats in the parquet and the boxes in order to hear the piece to an end, although still crying from purely physical reasons. . . . That also is Munich. And with this cataclysm I shall close my present letter.

THOMAS MANN [OCTOBER, 1923]

MODERN ART

Had I arrived two days sooner in Paris I should have seen the *décor* that Juan Gris made for the Ballet Russe charity performance in the Salle des Glaces at Versailles. Gertrude Stein had a card to see it privately in the afternoon and could have taken me. Gertrude liked it very much. From the description it certainly was new in idea— quantities of tin being used, covering the floor, I believe, and the steps to the platform, and gilt joining in—but startling only to those capable of being startled by ideas, for the passionately fashionable charitable folk who paid immense sums to attend seemed unaware that there was a *décor* there at all, taking the setting casually as a part of the original *salle*. Alice Toklas said it was not objectionable to walk upon—though any one who has ever attempted to walk upon a tin roof would recoil from dancing upon tin. But those Russians really are very expert and recoil from nothing.

That Juan Gris should be known to Diaghilev and that Braque, Picasso, and he should do *décors* for him is merely one hint that the pre-war receptivity is still on. Indeed the receptivity is almost frantic, but beyond the admittance of our own Man Ray to the ranks of the magicians there seems to be no new name to be learned. The Parisians are just dying to have an affair with some new artist, but the boldness of the blandishments they offer seems to frighten rather than attract, and young geniuses, if they exist, are incredibly coy. One does not hear of them even at the Café du Dôme. Speaking of blandishments, the Ballet Russe projects one of Molière's pieces with *musique* by Gounod re-arranged by Erik Satie and with a *décor* by Juan Gris. It is a project and not a certainty, but merely to think of such a combination is going some in the way of liberality; is it not?

Pascin gave me a miniature banquet—*moi qui vous parle*. That is, there were at least twenty at table and that, I think, entitles it to be called a banquet. I had supposed I was dining *seul*, but when I reached the top of the almost endless series of stairs on the Boulevard de Clichy I found ladies, exuberant children, a solid *bourgeois* who had been rendered more *distingué* by the loss of one eye at the front—and a measurable family atmosphere that was a distinct surprise *chez* Pascin. In a minute we all descended to the street made more than usually noisy by the Fêtes de Montmartre then in progress and I did my share in marshalling the exuberant children among whom and the most so, was a young mulatress of about ten. As it couldn't possibly be a French party without somebody getting lost we promptly discovered that three or four of us were missing. But we soon found them. The one-eyed gentleman —whose name I never mastered—and several of the children were discovered astride the shiny fat pigs of the merry-go-round whirling in the air above our heads. Then we were re-united only to be separated again into different taxis for it seemed we were to go to the Café du Dôme for the *apéritifs*. The ride across town was extremely gay, made so by the children who were continually crying and waving to each other from the various vehicles and inciting the chauffeurs to race. Pascin and I had the young mulatress with us and she was enchanted that we won the race. We made a distinct sensation arriving at the Café du Dôme, and without in the least meaning to boast I think I may say that I shared the honours with the young mulatress. People did look at us. If there is receptivity for art in Paris there seems even to be plenty of this commodity for art critics and there was a constant stream of persons coming up to claim acquaintance not only with Pascin, but with me. So much so that we scarcely had a moment actually to sit and Mahonri Young who had thought perhaps he might be of service to a newcomer retired abashed after one curious glance at the young coloured person. The café *terrasse* was crowded with the usual early Saturday evening crowd of students, oh, so much more gaunt and hollow-cheeked than they had been two years before; or so they did seem to me, comfortable in the knowledge that I certainly was to have a dinner. This festivity took place finally in a restaurant over near the Bal Bullier and the eats and the spiritual uplift were quite all right though the one-eyed gentleman took the host to task for allowing the men to be seated at one end of the table solidly and the ladies at the other; "If there is any possible way to bungle it trust Pascin," said he, with affectionate wrath. It was this gentleman who owned the large touring car that awaited without and into which about ten of us were whisked to the Café Suédois later on, standing up or clinging to side-steps as best we could, college boy style. Of the children who had gaily started out from Montmartre with us only the young mulatress was left and she was still maintaining a social status when I retreated from the Café Suédois at the discreet hour of *minuit*. At this party I met among others Mac-Orlan the writer and Laborde the artist, both of them keen and delightful, with worldly success apparently staring them in the face and André Salmon, the critic, equally delightful, but not so certain to get on in this life; and renewed acquaintance with Madame Pascin, one of the most remarkable women in Paris, which is saying much, and Mina Loy, the poetess.

At the banquet I asked Pascin when I could have a second look at his drawings and he suggested coming to lunch the Monday following. Galanis was there when I arrived and two young women who seemed not enthusiastic over my advent. Afterward I learned that Pascin had forgotten having asked them for Monday or had forgotten having asked me and they were promptly chased away. However they said *bon jour* with the calmness of duchesses and will have had it made up to them by Pascin later, doubtless. Then after Galanis left I was allowed to look through piles of drawings, including all the ones made in Tunis and which I like particularly, and the series of mocking allegories in which *"offrandes* to Venus" and hitherto suppressed details in the life of Scheherazade are lightly sketched. From the débris on the table I turned up two books, both of them inscribed. One was Paul Morand's Fermé la Nuit which contained on the fly-leaf the author's wish that Pascin might illustrate the work sometime. Morand is about to have his wish, I understand, Pascin having undertaken to do the drawings. The other book was by Cocteau also with compliments upon the fly-leaf. Then, too, Meier-Graefe is to do a Pascin album; so here is one artist at least who cannot complain of an indifferent press.

We lunched at the Café Manière. At the café we found Mac-Orlan and Laborde, both of whom were charming as usual and full of curiosity in regard to America. When I told MacOrlan that I had dined at Brancusi's and that Brancusi himself had acted as *chef* and had *énormément de talent comme cuisinier,* he said that to cook was quite *à la mode* now.

The dinner was wonderful—but gracious heavens—I see I have not left myself space enough in which to describe it. Believe me it would require space!

HENRY MCBRIDE

[NOVEMBER, 1923]

A LONG WAY ROUND TO NIRVANA

or, Much Ado About Dying

By G. Santayana

THAT the end of life is death may be called a truism, since the various kinds of immortality that might perhaps supervene would none of them abolish death, but at best would weave life and death together into the texture of a more comprehensive destiny. The end of one life might be the beginning of another, if the Creator had composed his great work like a dramatic poet, assigning some lines to one character and some to another. Death would then be merely the cue at the end of each speech, summoning the next personage to break in and keep the ball rolling. Or perhaps, as some suppose, all the characters are assumed in turn by a single supernatural Spirit, who amid his endless improvisations is imagining himself living for the moment in this particular solar and social system. Death in such a universal monologue would be but a change of scene or of metre, while in the scramble of a real comedy it would be a change of actors. In either case every voice would be silenced sooner or later, and death would end each particular life, in spite of all possible sequels.

The relapse of created things into nothing is no violent fatality, but something naturally quite smooth and proper. This has been set forth recently, in a novel way, by a philosopher from whom we hardly expected such a lesson, namely Professor Sigmund Freud. He has now broadened his conception of sexual craving or *libido* into a general principle of attraction or concretion in matter, like the Eros of the ancient poets Hesiod and Empedocles. The windows of that stuffy clinic have been thrown open; that swell of acrid disinfectants, those hysterical shrieks, have escaped into the cold night. The troubles of the sick soul, we are given to understand, as well as their cure, after all flow from the stars.

I am glad that Freud has resisted the tendency to represent this principle of Love as the only principle in nature. Unity somehow exercises an evil spell over metaphysicians. It is admitted that in real life it is not well for One to be alone, and I think pure unity is no less barren and graceless in metaphysics. You must have plurality to start with, or trinity, or at least duality, if you wish to get anywhere, even if you wish to get effectively into the bosom of the One, abandoning your separate existence. Freud, like Empedocles, has prudently introduced a prior principle for Love to play with; not Strife, however (which is only an incident in Love) but Inertia, or the tendency towards peace and death. Let us suppose that matter was originally dead, and perfectly content to be so, and that it still relapses, when it can, into its old equilibrium. But the homogeneous (as Spencer would say) when it is finite is unstable: and matter, presumably not being coextensive with space, necessarily forms aggregates which have an inside and an outside. The parts of such bodies are accordingly differently exposed to external influences and differently related to one another. This inequality, even in what seems most quiescent, is big with changes, destined to produce in time a wonderful complexity. It is the source of all uneasiness, of life, and of love.

"Let us imagine [writes Freud [1]] an undifferentiated vesicle of sensitive substance: then its surface, exposed as it is to the outer world, is by its very position differentiated, and serves as an organ for receiving stimuli. Embryology, repeating as it does the history of evolution, does in fact show that the central nervous system arises from the ectoderm; the grey cortex of the brain remains a derivative of the primitive superficial layer. . . . This morsel of living substance floats about in an outer world which is charged with the most potent energies, and it would be destroyed . . . if it were not furnished with protection against stimulation. It acquires this through . . . a special integument or membrane . . . The outer layer, by its own death, has secured all the deeper layers from a like fate. . . . It must suffice to take little samples of the outer world, to taste it, so to speak, in small quantities. In highly developed organisms the receptive external layer of what was once a vesicle has long been withdrawn into the depths of the body, but portions of it have been left on the surface immediately beneath the common protective barrier. These portions

[1] The following quotations are drawn from Beyond the Pleasure-Principle, by Sigmund Freud; authorized translation by C. J. M. Hubback. The International Psycho-Analytic Press, 1922, pp. 29–48. The italics are in the original.

form the sense-organs. [On the other hand] the sensitive cortical layer has no protective barrier against excitations emanating from within. . . . The most prolific sources of such excitations are the so-called instincts of the organism. . . . The child never gets tired of demanding the repetition of a game. . . . he wants always to hear the same story instead of a new one, insists inexorably on exact repetition, and corrects each deviation which the narrator lets slip by mistake. . . . According to this, *an instinct would be a tendency in living organic matter impelling it towards reinstatement of an earlier condition,* one which it had abandoned under the influence of external disturbing forces—a kind of organic elasticity or, to put it another way, the manifestation of inertia in organic life.

"If, then, all organic instincts are conservative, historically acquired, and directed towards regression, towards reinstatement of something earlier, we are obliged to place all the results of organic development to the credit of external, disturbing, and distracting influences. The rudimentary creature would from its very beginning not have wanted to change, would, if circumstances had remained the same, have always merely repeated the same course of existence. But in the last resort it must have been the evolution of our earth, and its relation to the sun, that has left its imprint on the development of organisms. The conservative organic instincts have absorbed every one of these enforced alterations in the course of life, and have stored them for repetition; they thus present the delusive appearance of forces striving after change and progress, while they are merely endeavouring to reach an old goal by ways both old and new. This final goal of all organic striving can be stated too. It would be counter to the conservative nature of instinct if the goal of life were a state never hitherto reached. It must be rather an ancient starting point, which the living being left long ago, and to which it harks back again by all the circuitous paths of development . . . *The goal of all life is death.* . . .

"Through a long period of time the living substance may have . . . had death within easy reach . . . until decisive external influences altered in such a way as to compel [it] to ever greater deviations from the original path of life, and to ever more complicated and circuitous routes to the attainment of the goal of death. These circuitous ways to death, faithfully retained by the conservative instincts, would be neither more nor less than the phenomena of life as we know it."

Freud puts forth these interesting suggestions with much modesty, admitting that they are vague and uncertain and (what it is even more important to notice) mythical in their terms; but it seems to me that, for all that, they are an admirable counterblast to prevalent follies. When we hear that there is, animating the whole universe, an *élan vital,* or general impulse toward some unknown but single ideal, the terms used are no less uncertain, mythical, and vague, but the suggestion conveyed is false, whereas that conveyed by Freud's speculations is true. In what sense can myths and metaphors be true or false? In the sense that, in terms drawn from moral predicaments or from literary psychology, they may report the general movement and the pertinent issue of material facts, and may inspire us with a wise sentiment in their presence. In this sense I should say that Greek mythology was true and Calvinist theology was false. The chief terms employed in psychoanalysis have always been metaphorical: "unconscious wishes," "the pleasure-principle," "the Oedipus complex," "Narcissism," "the censor"; nevertheless, interesting and profound vistas may be opened up, in such terms, into the tangle of events in a man's life, and a fresh start may be made with fewer encumbrances and less morbid inhibition. "The shortcomings of our description," Freud says, "would probably disappear if for psychological terms we could substitute physiological or chemical ones. These too only constitute a metaphorical language, but one familiar to us for a much longer time, and perhaps also simpler." All human discourse is metaphorical, in that our perceptions and thoughts are adventitious signs for their objects, as names are, and by no means copies of what is going on materially in the depths of nature; but just as the sportsman's eye, which yields but a summary graphic image, can trace the flight of a bird through the air quite well enough to shoot it and bring it down, so the myths of a wise philosopher about the origin of life or of dreams, though expressed symbolically, may reveal the pertinent movement of nature to us, and may kindle in us just sentiments and true expectations in respect to our fate—for his own soul is the bird this sportsman is shooting.

Now I think these new myths of Freud's about life, like his old ones about dreams, are calculated to enlighten and to chasten us enormously about ourselves. The human spirit, when it awakes finds itself in trouble; it is burdened, for no reason it can assign with all sorts of anxieties about food, pressures, pricks, noises, and pains. It is born, as another wise myth has it, in original sin. And the passions and ambitions of life, as they come on, only complicate this burden and make it heavier, without rendering it less incessant or gratuitous. Whence this fatality, and whither does it lead? It comes from heredity, and it leads to propagation. When we ask how heredity could be started or transmitted, our ignorance of nature and of past time reduces us to silence or to wild conjectures. Something—let us call it matter—must always have existed, and some of its parts, under pressure of the others, must have got tied up into knots, like the mainspring of a watch, in such a violent and unhappy manner that when the pressure is relaxed they fly open as fast as they can, and unravel themselves with a vast sense of relief. Hence the longing to satisfy latent passions, with the fugitive pleasure in doing so. But the external agencies that originally wound up that mainspring never cease to operate; every fresh stimulus gives it another turn, until it snaps, or grows flaccid, or is unhinged. Moreover, from time to time, when circumstances change, these external agencies may encrust that primary organ with minor organs attached to it. Every impression, every adventure, leaves a trace or rather a seed behind it. It produces a further complication in the structure of the body, a fresh charge, which tends to repeat the impressed motion in season and out of season. Hence that perpetual docility or ductibility in living substance which enables it to learn tricks, to remember facts, and (when the seeds of past experiences marry and cross in the brain) to imagine new experiences, pleasing or horrible. Every act initiates a new habit and may implant a new instinct. We see people even late in life carried away by political or religious contagions or developing strange vices; there would be no peace in old age, but rather a greater and greater obsession by all sorts of cares, were it not that time, in exposing us to many adventitious influences, weakens or discharges our primitive passions; we are less greedy, less lusty, less hopeful, less generous. But these weakened primitive impulses are naturally by far the strongest and most deeply rooted in the organism: so that although an old man may be converted or may take up some hobby, there is usually something thin in his elderly zeal, compared with the heartiness of youth; nor is it edifying to see a soul in which the plainer human passions are extinct becoming a hot-bed of chance delusions.

In any case each fresh habit taking root in the organism forms a little mainspring or instinct of its own, like a parasite; so that an elaborate mechanism is gradually developed, where each lever and spring holds the other down, and all hold the mainspring down together, allowing it to unwind itself only very gradually, and meantime keeping the whole clock ticking and revolving, and causing the smooth outer face which it turns to the world, so clean and innocent, to mark the time of day amiably for the passer-by. But there is a terribly complicated labour going on beneath, propelled with difficulty, and balanced precariously, with much secret friction and failure. No wonder that the engine often gets visibly out of order, or stops short: the marvel is that it ever manages to go at all. Nor is it satisfied with simply revolving and, when at last dismounted, starting afresh in the person of some seed it has dropped, a portion of its substance with all its concentrated instincts wound up tightly within it, and eager to repeat the ancestral experiment; all this growth is not merely material and vain. Each clock in revolving strikes the hour, even the quarters, and often with lovely chimes. These chimes we call perceptions, feelings, purposes, and dreams; and it is because we are taken up entirely with this pretty music, and perhaps think that it sounds of itself and needs no music-box to make it, that we find such difficulty in conceiving the nature of our own clocks and are compelled to describe them only musically, that is, in myths. But the ineptitude of our æsthetic minds to unravel the nature of mechanism does not deprive these minds of their own clearness and euphony. Besides sounding their various musical notes, they have the cognitive function of indicating the hour and catching the echoes of distant events or of maturing inward dispositions. This information and emotion, added to the incidental pleasures in satisfying our various passions, make up the life of an incarnate spirit. They reconcile it to the external fatality that has wound up the organism, and is breaking it down; and they rescue this organism and all its works from the indignity of being a vain complication and a waste of motion.

That the end of life should be death may sound sad: but what other end can anything have? The end of an evening party is to go to bed; but its use is to gather congenial people together, that they may pass the time pleasantly. An invitation to the dance is not rendered ironical because the dance cannot last for ever; the youngest of us and the most vigorously wound up, after a few hours, has had enough of sinuous stepping and prancing. The transitoriness of things is essential to their physical being, and not at all sad in itself; it becomes sad by virtue of a sentimental illusion, which makes us imagine that they wish to endure, and that their end is always untimely; but in a healthy nature it is not so. What is truly sad is to have some impulse frustrated in the midst of its career, and robbed of its chosen object; and what is painful is to have an organ lacerated or destroyed when it is still vigorous, and not ready for its natural sleep and dissolution. We must not confuse the itch which our unsatisfied instincts continue to cause with the pleasure of satisfying and dismissing each of them in turn. Could they all be satisfied harmoniously we should be satisfied once for all and completely. Then doing and dying would coincide throughout and be a perfect pleasure.

This same insight is contained in another wise myth which has inspired morality and religion in India from time immemorial: I mean the doctrine of Karma. We are born, it says, with a heritage, a character imposed, and a long task assigned, all due to the ignorance which in our past lives has led us into all sorts of commitments. These obligations we must pay off, relieving the pure spirit within us from its accumulated burdens, from debts and assets both equally oppressive. We cannot disentangle ourselves by mere frivolity, nor by suicide: frivolity would only involve us more deeply in the toils of fate, and suicide would but truncate our misery and leave us for ever a confessed failure. When life is understood to be a process of redemption, its various phases are taken up in turn without haste and without undue attachment; their coming and going have all the keenness of pleasure, the holiness of sacrifice, and the beauty of art. The point is to have expressed and discharged all that was latent in us; and to this perfect relief various temperaments and various traditions assign different names, calling it having one's day, or doing one's duty, or realizing one's ideal, or saving one's soul. The task in any case is definite and imposed on us by nature, whether we recognize it or not; therefore we can make true moral progress or fall into real errors.

Wisdom and genius lie in discerning the prescribed task and in doing it readily, cleanly, and without distraction. Folly on the contrary imagines that any scent is worth following, that we have an infinite nature, or no nature in particular, that life begins without obligations and can do business without capital, and that the will is free, instead of being a specific burden and a tight hereditary knot to be unravelled. This romantic folly is defended by some philosophers without self-knowledge, who think that the variations and further entanglements which the future may bring are the manifestation of spirit; but they are, as Freud has indicated, imposed on living beings by external pressure, and take shape in the realm of matter. It is only after the organs of spirit are formed mechanically that spirit can exist, and can distinguish the better from the worse in the fate of those organs, and therefore in its own fate. Spirit has nothing to do with infinity. Infinity is something physical and ambiguous; there is no scale in it and no centre. The depths of the human heart are finite, and they are dark only to ignorance. Deep and dark as a soul may be when you look down into it from outside, it is something perfectly natural; and the same understanding that can unearth our suppressed young passions, and dispel our stubborn bad habits, can show us where our true good lies. Nature has marked out the path for us beforehand; there are snares in it, but also primroses, and it leads to peace.

[NOVEMBER, 1923]

MUSICAL CHRONICLE

JAZZ is a series of jerks. In rhythm, you do not have to be conscious of the one two, one two; or of the one two three, one two three. Not even in Mendelssohn. But in jazz, to get your pleasure, you have to count the beat. Because jazz is every old thing which has ever been, distorted. Anticipated a little; suspended a little. It is the most banal with tobasco sauce; beans with ketchup plentifully. Ten minutes of it used as entertainment, makes a bore. For dance music, it cannot compare with Viennese waltzes. You do not even have to go to Johann Strauss. Waldteufel, flat as he is.

But some people in Paris talk of the rhythms of jazz. Three times in a century, to gratify some vaguest longing—people in Paris have dreamed fantasies, and called them by the name of America. First, nostalgic Chateaubriand and the Natchez. The Apollo in the hide of the *"peau rouge."* Second, Baudelaire and the great pale American Christ. The great pallid American Christ wandering the streets of New York was Edgar Allan Poe. Third, certain fatigued contemporaries who, more or less because Marinetti stood on the prow of a dreadnaught in a Byronic fame of mind, mistake material brutishly used in America for primitive art. A steel-construction with Antwerp plastered over its flanks in architecture. "The Parthenon was built for use." The Parthenon, with the plumb of its columns subtly varied that the eye may be enchanted! Then, Charlot, Fattie, and Mees Pearrrl White. The Saturday Evening insensibility as the American story. And jazz. The rhythms of jazz.

One wonders: have any of these charming dreamers ever seen or heard the objects they mistake for beauty, or clarity, or significance? They have seen Charlot. And, no doubt, his films are much funnier than the shows in Paris, though you do see some very funny ones at the Théâtre Nationale de l'Opéra, and at the Maison de Molière. But what is it they have really seen and heard? Some people opened a little place off the Place de la Madeleine, and Cocteau, who had made quite a success with the pieces of the battery in the performance of Milhaud's Choephores, insisted on playing something which he qualified with the name "Jazz Americain." A great many ladies heard, and seemed greatly edified at having

finally gotten the real right thing. But some friends, American—
persuaded Cocteau to desist. And still, jazz is the American music,
or the chrysalis of American music. And the machine and its products—must be accepted.

This Gerald Stanley Lee, Marinetti categorical imperative, has
no importance for any one doing work either in the field of mechanics or that of art. The creative mechanic no more than the
artist "accepts" the machine. Like his poetical brother, he has in
his mind an ideal objective. And for the purpose of approaching
that objective, he makes friends with his instrument, and drives it
relentlessly to the limit of its capacities. There have always been
machines, since ever the first humanoid took up a club and began
freeing his mind; and between the man who drives the machine
relentlessly to its limit and the man who tells a perfect story, there
is no opposition. Both are driven by the selfsame need, the need
of things of quality enrooted in the living human breast. Both
are moving toward the same ideal goal. Neither is responsible for
the mess rotting modern life. Responsible for that are, far more,
the people moved by no ideal objective. The good-enough people
in the field of machine-work. And the people who sit about, and
talk.

Whether French people wanted us to be savages or no would be
of no matter in the United States; all the talk of skyscraper primitive art would be harmless, were work proceeding here, and voices
calling. The existing machinery, jazz, Charlie Chaplin, would find
the artist, for the artist never has to go find the raw stuff of nature. But there is no faith among the American workers; and in
all ages wanting inner direction, a subjective sense of inferiority
drives men to searching for ready-made formulae before starting
off on their adventures; and to playing up to the eyes of certain
people whom they take pleasure in conceiving as superior to themselves. It is for this reason that the charming fantasies of contemporary France seem to us to contain a principle dangerous to
the young art-men in America. These fantasies are supplying a
number of embryonic artists with cheap formulae, keeping them
from working from their sensibilities. They are also persuading a
number of incipient advertising-men that they have something to
do with art, preventing them using their talents properly in selling
tomato-sauce and soap. No doubt, the will to worship a lot of

quarter-baked material will eventually be discarded by the deter-mined artists, and lead the incipient advertisers to flattering mil-lionaires more directly, and building up circulation for frankly mil-lionaire-flattering journals. But much breath will go lost. And we have so little breath to lose.

PAUL ROSENFELD

[NOVEMBER, 1923]

THE CAVERN OF SILENCE

By Miguel de Unamuno

Translated From the Spanish by Louis How

IN the centre of the kingdom there was a large thick wood. In it every kind of tree with perennial foliage grew luxuriantly. They did not turn yellow in the fall, nor had they need in the spring to clothe themselves again in tender green. The sun did not enter to warm the grass; the foliage was too thick. And divers brooks wandered about in the wood. No wild beasts infested it. Simple paths, traced by the feet of those that came there, and almost always running along the banks of the brooks, following their course, led to an open space that was in the middle of the wood.

Nobody could recall that it had ever rained in that open space; and a very old and rooted tradition held that really it never did rain in that clearing in the wood. Even on stormy days, which were very few, it seemed as if there must be a hole in the clouds, made to prevent that mysterious open space from being wet by the waters of heaven. And in that open space was the cavern.

The cavern consisted of an opening in the rock, a mouth of stone, within which a little pathway ran down, very steep, but easy to follow. The pathway ran into the cave, until at about two hundred steps' distance, it turned abruptly behind a projecting boulder and was lost to sight.

Nobody knew, nobody could know, what there was in the depths of the cavern behind the boulder. None of those that had passed that point had ever returned, or had ever given any sort of sign by which their fate might be guessed. Children had entered there, youths, and full-grown men—women, old men—sane people and mad, unhappy and gay; and not one had given the least hint of what was within there. Once they had rounded the turn, nothing further was known of them: neither the sound of a fall, nor a scream, nor a groan, nor even a sigh. They were swallowed in complete and utter silence.

But this silence of the cavern occurred only when it received its devotees. On certain days, more often in autumn than in the other seasons of the year, and at certain hours—at the drawing in of evening—there came from the depths of the cavern a mysterious music veiled in the mist of an aroma, intoxicating and unearthly. There came the sound as of the song of a numerous procession, a moving, melancholy song as sung by many persons. But the melancholy of that distant and melodious complaint was very sweet and soothing. It was on hearing that, that a great many of all those who continually hovered around the cavern's mouth, hurried into the depths inside.

All kinds of investigations had been made. A man would go in tied with a stout rope, so that he might be pulled out when he sig nalled: and every time this was tried, the rope had finally been pulled out, untied, and without there having been any signal. Once they had welded a metal belt around a man's waist, and welded a chain to that: and they had pulled out belt and chain without the man. How could he have freed himself? . . . Another time a man had gone in carrying the corpse of a friend—they wanted to see whether the cavern received the dead. The next morning the corpse was found in the pathway in front of the turning; but of the living man that had carried it in nothing more was ever known, just as in every other case. And after that there could be no doubt that the cavern admitted only the living.

Another experiment was thought of and several times tried: and that was to drive animals into the cave. These came out shortly afterwards, but they came out frightened and upset; and they never again in their whole lives made any sound. They came out mute. An animal that returned from the cavern did not bark, or mew, or bleat, or low, or roar, or cackle, during the rest of its life. And no one ever saw the cave entered by a toad, a rat, a lizard, a fly, or a gnat.

More than once, too, they had tried having several people go in attached one to another by their hands. And as soon as the first one had reached the turning and gone around, he was loosed from his neighbour, no matter how firmly he might be held, and he was lost in the silence of the cavern's depth; or else the whole string of men was lost there.

Every class of people had been lost in the mysterious and musical cave. Once the father of a family was drawn in by that mystery, and his children gathered at the entrance to call him:

"Father! Father!" and they were drawn in after him. But what alarmed the king and the whole kingdom was the frequency with which pairs of young lovers and young married people let themselves be swallowed up by the cave. It was one of the favourite wedding-journeys: a journey with no return. And despite the prolific habit of that kingdom, where a family with fewer than ten children was rare, the continual loss of young couples disquieted the rulers.

A sacred respect had prevented all the kings of that country from prohibiting access to the cavern. And there had even been one king lost in it: since when no other had ever ventured near. But the fatal enchantment became such that finally it was decided to place sentinels at the mouth of the cave, who by force of arms should prevent any one from entering. But it always ended by the sentinels' going in themselves; and when once the guard had surrendered, all those that had been kept outside followed along in.

Not a little strange was the behaviour of the suicides. It would seem natural that in that country there should not have been any, because whoever was tired of life or disgusted with it, had only to go into the depths of the cavern instead of killing himself: and nevertheless, it was not so. There were a great many cases of suicide in the kingdom of the mysterious cavern, and the greater part of them took place in the very mouth of the cave. And it was observed that those were people who had intended to go in, but who turned back after a few steps, before reaching the fatal turning. Once a poor man that suffered with a chronic disease so painful that he could no longer bear it, committed suicide, and left a letter saying that if he had started into the cave and then come back, it was because he feared that there inside his pains might continue and he be unable to kill himself—it was for fear of an immortal pain.

The government made use of the cavern for capital punishments. Instead of executing the condemned, it made them go into the cavern; and naturally they did so with the greatest pleasure. Not all of them, however. There were some that began to tremble horribly and refused to enter, and this despite the fact that a guard of archers at the cave's mouth threatened to shoot them if they didn't. And more than once the soldiers had to carry out from the entrance, close to the turning, the corpse of some criminal who preferred death to being buried there.

Once there arrived from a far and vague country, from a distant land whose mere existence was known, an old blind beggar, accompanied by a young boy. The old man spoke only his own language, a language completely and totally unintelligible to those of this kingdom. When he addressed the lad that led him, no matter how short were his words, nobody could guess what he was talking about. But the lad could mumble a bit of the language of this kingdom. Sometimes the old man sang; and his singing had a remote resemblance to the far-away and mysterious song that was heard arising from the cavern's depths in the twilights of autumn, and veiled in a mist of intoxicating aromas. It was a song like the song sung over his work by Lazarus, the brother of Martha and Mary, during his second life, after Christ had raised him from the grave. And everyone stopped to listen to the poor blind man; and all who heard him felt moved to go to the wood, and to enter until they reached the open space, and to lose themselves in the cavern.

And it came to pass that the old blind beggar turned his steps, he and the lad, to the wood, and then on into the open space, and to the cavern; and pushing through a thick crowd, went on, guided by the lad, and following the pathway entered into the cave, singing. And the boy that led him did not return; but the old blind man did return—the only person in centuries! Everybody flocked to see him. He came back blind, as he went. And no one understood a word of what he said; nor could they, by his tone, or by his gestures, or by his bearing, guess at anything whatever. He disappeared in the thick woods, and no one heard of him again. But his return from the cavern, that unique return, stamped on that people an irremovable impression.

And in that kingdom the whole of life, absolutely the whole, depended on the secret of the cavern. All art, all science, literature, the government, everything revolved around it. Not but that people died there as they do elsewhere. Oh, yes, the majority of the inhabitants died as one dies in other countries, of the same diseases, and in the same way.

In the vicinity of the cavern's mouth there was always a multitude of fascinated people, who passed hours, days, months, years, in some cases an entire lifetime, gazing at the turning of the path. And when there rose from the depths that suave and melancholy song, sung by a distant chorus, the multitude crowded together to intoxicate itself with the strange music and with the no less strange aroma that veiled it. The greater part of those unfortunates did not dare to go inside, and they perished miserably in the neighbourhood of the cavern's mouth, longing for its depths. The nearby groves of the wood were full of cabins and tents where those unhappy ones bewitched found a shelter. And when some one of them finally decided to enter, the rest stared at him in terror and in envy. And always, always, always, despite their repeated disappointments, they bade him, while they said good-bye: "Let us know what there is inside. Answer when we call to you." And never did any of those that went in answer.

There were a great many people in the kingdom, certainly most people, who had never gone near the cavern or even the wood that enfolded it, but they were not less than others held by the fascination of the cavern's secret. Some, and those not few, were even indignant that such a thing should be talked about; but perhaps they were the ones that thought about it most. And people were not even lacking—though in numbers to be counted on the fingers—who denied that such a cavern really existed.

In that kingdom all philosophy, all science, all literature, was, as we have said, suffused with the secret of the cave; and all the philosophy, all the science, all the art, all the literature that expressly purported to ignore that secret, was most of all suffused with it. The less people spoke about it, the more it was present in their imagination.

There were—and how could it have been otherwise?—there were among the thinkers of that kingdom no end of hypotheses and theories about what the cavern might contain. Somebody suggested penetrating it by another road, having engineers open it up: but it was impossible to find a workman that would dare give the first blow with his pick. Besides, people remembered that one king had wanted to close up the cavern's mouth with a wall, and that those who began to work either left off to go into the cave, or else very soon died. And every morning the work done the day before was always found undone. And for this reason it had to be abandoned.

Among the neighbouring peoples the secret of the cavern was a subject for jests mingled with fear. All the foreigners that had come into the kingdom to investigate the secret, either had not investigated at all, or had not returned home to recount what they saw because being conquered by the strange enchantment they had been lost in the cavern, or they had gone back without having even been able to enter the wood. The foreigner that did enter the wood and penetrate as far as the open space where it never rained, invariably went into the depths of the cavern. To this there was no exception.

Of the foreigners that were unable even to enter the wood—it caused them such repulsion—and who founded all their reports on what they heard said by persons who had never been in either, some pretended to take the whole affair as a joke, others shrugged their shoulders, and still others gave a symbolical explanation of the matter.

These explanations, however, the symbolical and allegorical, were the most discredited of all by those that knew anything whatever about the wood. It was no case of a symbol, but of a very real reality.

It is no case of a symbol, no: and not of an allegory either. It is not a case of abstract thought, of sociological reflections dressed in a concrete and allegorical form. Nothing of all that.

Yesterday, the eighth of this month of September, this month so charming in my Basque mountains, I walked past the castle of Butrón along the banks of the river of the same name; which is the boundary of Gorliz beach. And I afterwards returned to Bilbao, to this Bilbao of mine, and went to bed in the very room I occupied as a boy. And I was slow in going to sleep, turning and turning in my bed, and preparing what I am to say the day after to-morrow in honour of the sculptor of Bilbao, Nemesio Mogrovejo, dead in the flower of his years.

Among Mogrovejo's works there is a relief representing the torment of the Count Ugolino, just as Dante so sculpturally relates it to us in the Divine Comedy. And last night I went to sleep, after turning many times, with the Divine Comedy in my mind.

Toward midnight I was awakened by a loud clap of thunder and a violent downpour. And on waking I discovered that I knew this tale of the secret of the cavern. And I knew it for the first time, without any explanation or symbol, with all its inherent contradictions. And the whole of it, entire, with all the details. I lighted the light and began to write it, to write it to dictation.

To whose dictation? I don't know. Whence came this tale? I don't know that either. The only thing I do know is that it is not a symbol, it is not an allegory, it is not what it is. Somebody told it to me—I don't know who—and I tell it to you as somebody told it to me.

[JANUARY, 1924]

FULL MOON

By William Carlos Williams

Blessed moon
noon
of night

that through the dark
bids Love
stay—

curious shapes
awake
to plague me

Is day near
shining girl?
Yes day!

the warm
the radiant
all fulfilling

day.

[January, 1924]

RUSSIAN LETTER

December, 1923

Two years ago it looked as though all artistic and poetic activity had been stifled beneath the Bolshevik régime, and as though the remaining Russian writers, with a very few exceptions, would go into voluntary exile. But what was true two years ago is true no longer. Conditions are such to-day that one could speak of two Russian literatures, each quite sharply differentiated from the other: one in dispersion abroad, and one in Soviet Russia. The former is represented by the writers who fled to other countries during and after the revolution; the latter—as with many other things among the ruins of the Russian empire—is in the process of becoming.

The difference between these two literatures does not lie, as one might readily assume, in matters of politics: not all the poets active in Soviet Russia are Communists, nor do all those abroad stand in irreconcilable opposition to Bolshevism. The difference is much deeper, and is determined by the difference of the soil out of which each grows and draws its sap. While the literature arising outside of Russia in recent years continues and develops the pre-revolutionary traditions, the literature which has grown on the home soil turned up by the plough of revolution has entirely new characteristics and has hardly anything but the language in common with the other. We shall begin with the former, as it is the older.

The Russian authors and savants who fled from Russia during the terrors of the first years of revolution soon spread over the whole of Europe, and Russian publishing houses and periodicals rapidly arose: in Berlin, Paris, Prague, Stockholm, Sophia, even in America and China. But gradually a new centre of Russia's extra-territorial intellectuals crystallized in Berlin, which is now known even in the mother country as the "third capital of Russia" (along with Petrograd and Moscow). Gradually the representatives of Russian literature, art, and science who were originally scattered throughout Europe have, with a few exceptions, collected in Berlin; and they were automatically joined by those who fled or were turned out of Russia later on. The number of Russian publishing houses in Berlin is already over fifty. Of course, the reasons for the concentration of so many Russian poets and savants in the capital of Germany is partially of an economic nature; but a much greater factor seems to be the present political transitions of both countries. The Russian publishing houses in Paris have dropped to one, and there are only four well-known Russian writers still in France: Merezhkovski, Gippius, Balmont, and Bunin.

Dmitri Merezhkovski, who succeeded in escaping from Petrograd in 1920, settled in Paris with his wife Zinaïda Gippius, and soon began an intensely active campaign of publicity against Bolshevism, to which he is most grimly opposed. In numerous magazine articles and "open letters," and in his polemical work, The Realm of the Antichrist, which he issued in collaboration with Zinaïda Gippius and others, and which is filled with an honest conviction, but contains many deplorable aberrations (as for instance, the unfounded attacks on Gorki) he tried to arouse the people of Europe against the "Antichrist" which is Bolhevism. As he failed in this, he became convinced that the Western Europeans also had lost Christ: the poet and thinker withdrew from the Godless present into the grey, god-filled past, devoting himself to the study of the religions of ancient Egypt, Babylon, Assyria, Canaan, and attempting to trace in them the spirit of Christ which the peoples of antiquity, he claims, had anticipated, but which is obscured in the present. Mysteries of the East, a patient work planned to cover several volumes, is appearing as the fruits of this study. The treatment is not consecutive, systematic, and scholarly, but is a loose array of selections from documents on the history of religion, mingled with quotations from Dostoevsky, Rosanov, and others, and with occasional statements and beliefs of the author himself which are often surprisingly profound. This work, which is engrossing throughout, and is permeated with a deep faith, seems to me the crowning of Merezhkovski's peculiar religious system. Zinaïda Gippius, who took part in her husband's anti-Bolshevik campaigns, has published a new volume of poems some of which, written in voluntary exile, may be said to surpass in beauty even the earlier works of this great lyrist. Konstantin Balmont has issued several new books of verse and his first prose work, a novel. In the poems there are still a few arresting lines but all the rest, including the novel, is insignificant; and the poet who was celebrated twenty years ago as the greatest Russian lyrist cannot even command attention to-day. Ivan Bunin, the outstanding continuator of the classical Russian tradition of story-writing lives like the others in an implacable, if silent, opposition to everything that goes by the name of Russia to-day; he has written only a few new stories and poems, every one of which is a gem.

At this point should be mentioned the name of a new writer who made his first reputation abroad: Georgi Grebenshikov. He is a born story-teller, but is distinguished from the others by a new note: he comes from Siberia, belongs to a hardier and more untouched stock; and every line of his breathes the pure air peculiar to the boundless forests and steppes of Russian Asia. He has written a number of stories, and a novel containing uncommonly interesting material—the Churayevs, a chronicle of a Siberian family.

All the remaining writers who fled or were driven out of Russia have settled in Berlin, the "third capital" of Russia, headed by the Nestor of the Russian moderns, Nikolai Minski, who will soon be in his sixties. Maxim Gorki is also living in Germany now; he produces very little, and only now and then releases bits of his reminiscences and diaries, which are among the most valuable things he has written. Aleksei Remizov is displaying an unusually fertile activity on German soil. Immediately after his flight he published (1921) a little volume, Russia in Flames, which begins with a stirring Elegy on the Russian Land. Of his numerous later works we shall name Russia in Type, a collection of curious glosses to all sorts of printed and manuscript records in the possession of the author—a stylistic masterpiece of the first rank—and delightful paraphrases of Russian tales and legends. With the appearance of his novel, The Road to Calvary, in Berlin in 1922, Alexey Tolstoy steps forth as a mature master. The novel forms the first part of a projected trilogy, in which the author has set himself a vast ambition: just as his great namesake gives in War and Peace a colossal picture of the times of the Napoleonic campaigns, Alexey Tolstoy is attempting to paint a panorama of the recent years of war and revolution in Russia, while this serves also as background for the life history of a Petrograd family—and it must be admitted that he has mastered his task brilliantly. We should not have unmentioned an intimate book which appeared at the same time: Nikita's Childhood, a modern counterpart to the elder Tolstoy's Childhood, Boyhood, Youth. Alexey Tolstoy's newest work is the fantastic novel Aëlita. The plot is laid on the planet Mars and in Bolshevik Petrograd. The distinction from other Mars novels lies in the fact that the heroes are Russians who attempt to start a Bolshevik uprising on Mars, and the legend of sunken Atlantis is brought in with the greatest ingenuity, while the whole is accompanied by a delicate love melody. Andrei Byely, who has also come to Berlin, is at work on an autobiographical "epic," and at the same time he is publishing his extraordinarily important Reminiscences of Blok. This latter work is much more than its title would indicate: although Blok really does form the pivot, it deals with the development of the entire Russian modern movement in the first decade of the twentieth century, and it contains portraits of the first Russian "decadents" (particularly Merezhkovski and his wife) and of other outstanding personalities of the times (for instance, Vladimir Soloviov) which are so life-like that only a great artist and creator could have done them. We shall pass over various second-rate poets who are living in Berlin, and shall give one more name—it was not entirely unknown before the war, but it first became prominent abroad, in Berlin. It is Ilya Ehrenburg.

Ilya Ehrenburg, born at Moscow in 1891, at eighteen came as a political refugee to Paris, where his first volume of poetry appeared. In this there was a note formerly unfamiliar to Russian poetry: Ehrenburg had fallen under the spell of the French poet Francis Jammes, and also took on a bit of his literary Catholicism. His enthusiasm went so far that he, a Jew by birth, was about to become a Catholic and enter a Benedictine monastery. At the start of the last revolution he returned to Russia and joined eagerly in the Communist movement. But as pure Communism began to degenerate into Bolshevism and was leading to the same grotesque results which it had originally combatted in capitalism, Ehrenburg left Russia, where he had previously issued a volume of poetry, and retired in disillusionment to Berlin. Here a list of books by him appeared in quick succession, and he was suddenly famous. His most significant work is the monumental satire, The Unusual Adventures of Julio Jurenito and his Disciples (a Frenchman, a German, an American, a Russian, an Italian, the author Ehrenburg himself, and a little Senegalese negro) in the Days of Peace, War, and Revolution in Paris, Rome, Moscow, et cetera. The hero of this satire on the world events of the last ten years, the Mexican adventurer Jurenito, comes to Europe shortly before the World War, secures his seven disciples, and unfolds a set of feverish and secret activities which lead to the well-known developments following August 1, 1914. With a scepticism surpassing that of an Anatole France, all the blossoms of modern European and American culture—capitalism and Bolshevism, militarism and pacifism, nationalism and socialism, Church and State—are picked apart, and not a single one of the nations is spared. With the exception of the uncorrupted little negro, the German comes out best: he is at least thoroughly and unselfishly devoted to his cause. The work aroused much discussion, and after its appearance was translated into several languages. Besides the Jurenito, Ehrenburg published several volumes of short stories, which are filled with the same spirit of scepticism. As to style and technique, although he lives abroad he belongs to the new school which is active in Soviet Russia and which we shall soon discuss.

Of the more important poets remaining in Russia only Valerii Briussov has officially entered the camp of the Bolsheviks. Before me lies his volume of poems which appeared in 1919 under the modest title, Experiments. It is in reality a text-book of versification, and the poems are invented purely as illustrations for countless rhythmic and metrical possibilities. Some of them are truly astonishing. Sologub, Ivanov, and Kusmin are in Russia involuntarily. Sologub published a new novel, The Snake-Charmer. Here the "snake's nest" is a morally degenerate capitalist family; the charmer is a working girl Vera, trained in the principles of Marxism. Artistically this novel signals the end of the great poet Sologub. I have read some touching and melancholy Winter Sonnets by Vyacheslav Ivanov, who is living in ill health somewhere in the Caucasus. During the war Kusmin produced an enormous number of short stories and novels which showed a falling off in quality; later, like all the others, he was condemned to silence during the first years of Communism, but he has recently begun publishing verses of great dexterity. Here and there he sounds futurist notes which are not meant in complete seriousness, but which form a piquant accompaniment to his former consciously old-fashioned music (Mozart, Rossini).

In the first years of the strict Communist régime all poets remaining in Russia (with the exception of the officially recognized futurists, whom we are still to discuss) were condemned to silence. All literary reviews were suspended, all publishing houses and presses "socialized" and for the most part also suspended; and the censorship, which far surpassed that of the Czarist times in stringency, would not let anything pass through the press which did not directly serve as Bolshevik propaganda. The lot of the poets in these hard times is told with beautiful humour by Mikhail Kusmin in a poem (1922) called The Commission, in which he asks a "wanderer" who is going to Berlin to tell a certain blonde Tamara:

> ". . . that we are not yet dead but hardened rather
> And soon will turn to saints;
> We have neither food nor drink nor shoes
> And are living on spiritual nourishment.
> That we are doing a wonderful business;
> Selling everything and buying nothing,
> Looking up into the cheerful spring sky
> And thinking of our distant friends.
> Whether our hearts are weary,
> Whether our hands are lamed,
> These things shall be learned from our new books,
> If ever they appear. . . ."

In the meantime conditions have changed after the failure of Communism and the return to so-called free trade, that is, the return to the capitalist order; a great number of public enterprises began again, and the appearance of works of a purely literary nature serving the needs of the *bourgeoisie* was gradually permitted. And now it became evident that not only had the poets already mentioned written new works in the meantime which were simply waiting for publication, but also a whole array of previously unknown or little known poets had matured. These young people, who had come through all the horrors of war, revolution, and the first period of Bolshevism, and whose talents had developed under the most unfavourable conditions, represent the newest Russian literature grown on Russian soil; it is as strongly differentiated from the previous literature as new Russia is from the old. The most prominent earmarks of this new literature rest in part on purely exterior circumstances; the following probably figure among the most important. When the publications of all works of *belles-lettres* was permitted again, paper was at first very rare (as was previously manuscript paper) and the space in the few periodicals was limited; this forced the writers into the most extreme brevity, and resulted in the peculiar telegraphic style of the newest narrative art. Everything which was in the least dispensable was left out; every word had to be clear and essential in the way that a steel beam is essential in the construction of a building. Among other things all psychology was looked upon as dispensable; and so this most important property of classical Russian literature suddenly dropped away. In the barest and most precise words only the naked facts are detailed; everything is as hard and ascetic as all of life in a Communist state; and the construction of the story, unobscured by psychological refinements and detail-painting, stands out as bare as the steel frame-work in a modern factory building. It can even be said that between present-day Russian literature and that of yesterday the same external difference exists as between a modern American railroad bridge and a baroque palace.

Along with economy in the use of means of expression and the renouncing of the psychological, there is a third prominent element in the newest Russian literature: the strong emphasis on subject-matter. The poet creates exclusively out of the reality that surrounds him, and consequently the content of his stories is just as unusual and enormous as this: cannibalism, murder, violation, fear of hell, and blood, whole seas of blood. The dry circumstantiality and the laconic style make the horrible seem even more horrible, and lend the sketches an unusual power of conviction. It is to be emphasized that this whole literature lacks every tendency to complain or to justify; a poet describes reality as it presents itself to him, without any additional purpose, and is concerned only with giving as perfect and as terse a construction as is possible to the whole.

This is the new realism; it shows signs of breaking out in the modern plastic arts also; and it has an element of strangeness.

In Petrograd the new story writers have organized a group and call themselves the Serapionovy Brothers. Yet with E. T. W. Hoffman they have only strangeness in common, although with them this is not dreamed, but looked upon with calm eyes. The most significant of the Serapionovy Brothers, Vsevolod Ivanov, usually describes the terrors of the civil war in Siberia, as in his story Armoured Train No. 14-69. Another short story, Empty Arabia, deals with peasants who, driven by the famine of the year 1922, and led by an insane old man, are moving to a fantastic promised land and are dying on the way like flies. There is a peasant among them who is so strong and fat in spite of hunger that he arouses suspicion that he has concealed provisions somewhere. In the night the others steal up to him, and while he sleeps they feel him as they would a fattened animal to see if it were ready for slaughter. In the story The Child, he tells how Bolshevist insurgents in Siberia clubbed a White officer and his wife and appropriated their child. In order to keep this child alive on the way they steal a Kirghiz woman with a nursing baby and make her wet-nurse for the officer's child. After some time they become suspicious that the Kirghiz woman is giving her own child preference; they find out by weighing that the White child is really lighter, and they take the Kirghiz child in a sack into the steppes. The White child flourishes, and the people now have their untroubled joy in it and its wet-nurse. All of Ivanov's other works are just as dismal—which is also true of another brother, Nikolai Nikitin, who is identical with him and who describes by preference the terrors of the revolution in the provinces and in the country. Among the members of this circle Konstantin Fedin and Mikhail Sostchenko should also be mentioned. They too are hard to distinguish from the ones already named, as the Serapionovy Brothers form a kind of academy with established traditions.

Of the many new prose writers belonging to no school or academy we shall name only the most interesting of all, Boris Pilnyak. His development is not yet quite determined, but it justifies our highest expectations. Like the other young Russian story writers, he describes reality; yet without the dry circumstantiality of the Serapionovy Brothers, as he sees with an expressionistic eye. At times his style is reminiscent of Remizov, although it is of great originality; and one can readily say that of all the poets of this generation Pilnyak's work is the most personal. He also lacks the cool objectivity of the Serapionovy Brothers, being completely permeated with the spirit of Soviet Russia; although it should not be said that he writes problem stories. His palette is richer in colours; and in the steel framework of his constructions there are many scattered elements of the baroque. But first of all he is, in opposition to the new Petrograd "academy," a man who is searching and is in ferment. He also likes to describe revolution and civil war in the villages and the provinces; and one has the impression that he has touched on the peculiar tone and rhythm of the Russian revolution better than any one else. In his best work, The Naked Year, he places the old crumbling passive Russia over against the new young active and unsentimental Russia, and his sympathies belong to the latter, although he is certainly not a Communist. It is not necessary to be one in order to prefer the living to the dead. We shall also mention that in all his works the erotic plays a great *rôle:* naturally, it is not the tender love-hunger of Turgenev's heroes, but the sinister and strongly animal eroticism of the new men, whom he characterizes in the following passage:

"Men hard as leather, in leather jackets, all of the same stature, all powerful, all handsome devils with curly hair tumbling from under their caps and about their necks. Each has a maximum of will—will and daring—in his hide-bound jawbone, in the creases about the corners of his mouth, in the movements of his arms, which are nearly always swinging. The pick of the free and easy Russian people. That they wear leather jackets is good: thus they are protected against the lemonade of psychology. We have foreseen that, we know it, we want it, and so! Further, not a one of them has read Marx."

The lyric has held the same important place in modern Russia which it always held in Russian literature. Several years before the war futurist influences had already become noticeable; and among the futurists there was one not insignificant lyrist—Igor

Severyanin. He called himself Ego-Futurist; and, departing from Balmont, he wrote very musical and relatively tame verses. The only "futuristic" elements in them were new word-formations which were quite tame and generally understandable. But as they were not constructed in the spirit of the Russian language, they are completely unfitted for life, and signify a vitiation rather than a perfecting of the language. Others wrote poems consisting of senseless words, syllables, and even letters, and having not the least to do with art. As far back as that, Merezhkovski had seen in futurism a menace, or rather the symptoms of an approaching catastrophe. And when this catastrophe broke, futurists supported by the Bolshevik authorities in power enjoyed for some time unrestricted control. The best known representatives of this official poetry are Valdimir Mayakovski, Anatolii Mariengof, and Wadim Shershenevich. Mayakovski, who by now passes as the "classicist" of futurism, is the only really gifted writer among them. Their poetry, in both form and content, signifies the end of *all* art. Every law of prosody is dispensed with as a matter of course. A rhythm, even a free one, is no longer considered. The vocabulary (as these poets themselves boast) is derived from the street, and even from articles on abortion. The content is blasphemy. Streams of stinking hogwash are poured not only over the political opponents of the Soviet state, but also over the *bourgeoisie* and the priests, and even the Saviour and His Mother. Pushkin and Raphael are stood up to the wall and shot. All attempts to enforce Futurist literature upon the subjects of the Soviet government proved just as ineffectual as many other Bolshevist experiments. The proletarian masses who were to be inoculated with this kind of art were the first to protest against it, and to demand a more digestible fare. To-day the futurist lyric is cultivated only in a few clubs and cafés in Moscow and Petrograd.

Besides the futurists, writers of peasant and proletarian origin were also protected by the Soviet authorities, and among these there are a few real talents. We shall mention first Sergei Yesenin, who was born in Central Russia in 1895. The son of a peasant, he spent his boyhood as a true country-boy in a village. Yet it was not intended that he should become a peasant, but a village school teacher; he was sent to a religious school. Instead of becoming a teacher, he very rapidly grew famous as a poet. His uncommonly powerful and picturesque poems have an outward resemblance to the visions of Ezekiel or the Revelations of John. But the content is blasphemous, or at least heretical. The prophet (who is doubtless meant for Yesenin) promises the Russ Land a new heaven and a new God. In places he reaches the persuasion and the impetus of the Old Testament writers. Nikolai Klyuyev also comes from the peasantry. He is famous and over-rated in Soviet Russia for his Cabin Songs, but his poems which were published before the war (with their suggestion of Nekrassov) seem to me much more significant. As to the so-called "proletarian" poets, several of them are said not to be genuine proletarians, but intellectuals of college training who opportunistically mask as proletarians. Vassilii Kasin is of genuine proletarian origin (by trade a roofer); he is one of the most interesting young Russian lyrists. His poems are unusually interesting rhythmically, and while they betray a thorough study of classical models, they are entirely original, and modern in the best sense of the word.

Boris Pasternak holds the leading place among the young non-proletarian Russian lyrists. We see in him the most fitting continuator of the great line of Russian verse descending from Pushkin. He was also known before the war, but it is only in recent years that he became prominent. Pasternak uses classical forms and meters, preferably iambs, but the inner dynamics of his verses, the sentence structure and the images, are frequently of such an unusual and yet quite spontaneous peculiarity that he can often be recognized in a single one of his lines. This is especially true of the images, which are so simple and so near at hand, that his predecessors had overlooked them precisely on account of their simplicity. Pasternak's best volume of poems is called My Sister, Life.

Of the remaining modern lyrists let us mention the following: Ossip Mandelstamm was very highly thought of by connoisseurs before the war. Like Pasternak, he is a Jew, and the two have much in common. He is more pathetic than Pasternak, and shows the influence of Briussov and Vyacheslav Ivanov. Nikolai Tichonov belongs to the circle of the Petrograd Serapionovy Brothers, and tries to utilize the peculiarities of this school in the lyric. Vladislav Khodasevich is somewhat cool, yet profound; he sings of death in verses as finished as Sologub's.

In closing let us mention two lyric poetesses who stand up favourably with the others I have named. Anna Achmatova has been known for some time, and is a genuine follower of Blok. All her poems are formally perfect; there is really nothing feminine about them. They are filled with a quiet sorrow, and their theme is eternally old and eternally new: unhappy love. In the most striking possible contrast to her is Marina Zvetayeva, whose reputation is quite recent. She is completely a woman, with a wild gipsy-like passionateness, free as the wind, as untamed as the South Russian steppes. Her verses sound like gipsy music and robber songs, and are as unrestricted in form as these. In lyric poetry the divergence between the Russians abroad and those under the Soviet cannot be followed so clearly as in prose. But if the spirit of liberated Russia has its expression anywhere in the lyric, it is first of all in the work of Marina Zvetayeva, although the poetess lives abroad and is opposed to Bolshevism.

From the preceding sketch it is to be seen that literature in Russia is by no means dead, as seemed to be the case two years ago. It is flourishing with undiminished vigour, and is an indication and a pledge that this country will not go to ruin.

ALEXANDER ELIASBERG

[FEBRUARY, 1924]

WELL MOUSED, LION

HARMONIUM. *By Wallace Stevens. 12mo. 140
pages. Alfred A. Knopf. $2.*

IT is not too much to say that some writers are entirely without
imagination—without that associative kind of imagination certainly,
of which the final tests are said to be simplicity, harmony, and truth.
In Mr Stevens' work, however, imagination precludes banality and
order prevails. In his book, he calls imagination "the will of things,"
"the magnificent cause of being," and demonstrates how imagination may evade "the world without imagination"; effecting an escape
which, in certain manifestations of *bravura,* is uneasy rather than
bold. One feels, however, an achieved remoteness as in Tu Muh's
lyric criticism: "Powerful is the painting . . . and high is it hung
on the spotless wall in the lofty hall of your mansion." There is the
love of magnificence and the effect of it in these sharp, solemn,
rhapsodic elegant pieces of eloquence; one assents to the view taken
by the author, of Crispin whose

> ". . . mind was free
> And more than free, elate, intent, profound."

The riot of gorgeousness in which Mr Stevens' imagination takes
refuge, recalls Balzac's reputed attitude to money, to which he was
indifferent unless he could have it "in heaps or by the ton." It is "a
flourishing tropic he requires"; so wakeful is he in his appetite for
colour and in perceiving what is needed to meet the requirements of
a new tone key, that Oscar Wilde, Frank Alvah Parsons, Tappé,
and John Murray Anderson seem children asleep in comparison with
him. One is met in these poems by some such clash of pigment as
where in a showman's display of orchids or gladiolas, one receives
the effect of vials of picracarmine, magenta, gamboge, and violet
mingled each at the highest point of intensity:

> "In Yucatan, the Maya sonneteers
> Of the Caribbean amphitheatre
> In spite of hawk and falcon, green toucan
> And jay, still to the nightbird made their plea,

As if raspberry tanagers in palms,
High up in orange air, were barbarous."

One is excited by the sense of proximity to Java peacocks, golden pheasants, South American macaw feather capes, Chilcat blankets, hair seal needlework, Singalese masks, and Rousseau's paintings of banana leaves and alligators. We have the hydrangeas and dogwood, the "blue, gold, pink, and green" of the temperate zone, the hibiscus, "red as red" of the tropics.

> ". . . moonlight on the thick, cadaverous bloom
> That yuccas breed . . ."

> ". . . with serpent-kin encoiled
> Among the purple tufts, the scarlet crowns."

and as in a shot spun fabric, the infinitude of variation of the colours of the ocean:

> ". . . the blue
> And the colored purple of the lazy sea,"

the emerald, indigos, and mauves of disturbed water, the azure and basalt of lakes; we have Venus "the centre of sea-green pomp" and America "polar purple." Mr Stevens' exact demand, moreover, projects itself from nature to human nature. It is the eye of no "maidenly greenhorn" which has differentiated Crispin's daughters; which characterizes "the ordinary women" as "gaunt guitarists" and issues the junior-to-senior mandate in Floral Decorations for Bananas:

> "Pile the bananas on planks.
> The women will be all shanks
> And bangles and slatted eyes."

He is a student of "the flambeaued manner,"

> ". . . not indifferent to smart detail . . .
> . . . hang of coat, degree
> Of buttons" . . .

One resents the temper of certain of these poems. Mr Stevens is never inadvertently crude; one is conscious, however, of a deliberate bearishness—a shadow of acrimonious, unprovoked contumely. Despite the sweet-Clementine-will-you-be-mine nonchalance of the Apostrophe to Vincentine, one feels oneself to be in danger of unearthing the ogre and in Last Looks at the Lilacs, a pride in unserviceableness is suggested which makes it a microcosm of cannibalism.

Occasionally the possession of one good is remedy for not possessing another as when Mr Stevens speaks of "the young emerald, evening star," "tranquillizing . . . the torments of confusion." Sunday Morning on the other hand—a poem so suggestive of a masterly equipoise—gives ultimately the effect of the mind disturbed by the intangible; of a mind oppressed by the properties of the world which it is expert in manipulating. And proportionately; aware as one is of the author's susceptibility to the fever of actuality, one notes the accurate gusto with which he discovers the negro, that veritable "medicine of cherries" to the badgered analyst. In their resilence and certitude, the Hymn From a Watermelon Pavilion and the commemorating of a negress who

> "Took seven white dogs
> To ride in a cab,"

are proud harmonies.

One's humour is based upon the most serious part of one's nature. Le Monocle De Mon Oncle; A Nice Shady Home; and Daughters With Curls: the capacity for self-mockery in these titles illustrates the author's disgust with mere vocativeness.

Instinct for words is well determined by the nature of the liberties taken with them, some writers giving the effect merely of presumptuous egotism—an unavoided outlandishness; others, not: Shakespeare arresting one continually with nutritious permutations as when he apostrophizes the lion in A Midsummer Night's Dream—"Well moused, lion." Mr Stevens' "junipers shagged with ice," is properly courageous as are certain of his adjectives which have the force of verbs: "the spick torrent," "tidal skies," "loquacious columns"; there is the immunity to fear, of the good artist, in "the blather that the water made." His precise diction and verve are grateful as contrasts to the current vulgarizations of "gesture," "dimensions," and "intrigue." He is able not only to express an idea with mere perspicuity; he is able to do it by implication as in Thirteen Ways of Looking at a Blackbird in which the glass coach evolved from icicles; the shadow, from birds; it becomes a kind of aristocratic cipher. The Emperor of Icecream, moreover, despite its not especially original theme of poverty enriched by death, is a triumph of explicit ambiguity. He gets a special effect with those adjectives which often weaken as in the lines:

> . . . "That all beasts should . . .
> . . . be beautiful
> As large, ferocious tigers are"

and in the phrase, "the eye of the young alligator," the adjective as it is perhaps superfluous to point out, makes for activity. There is a certain bellicose sensitiveness in

> "I do not know which to prefer . . .
> The blackbird whistling
> Or just after,"

and in the characterization of the snow man who

> ". . . nothing himself, beholds
> The nothing that is not there and the nothing that is."

In its nimbleness *con brio* with seriousness, moreover, Nomad Exquisite is a piece of that ferocity for which one values Mr Stevens most:

> "As the immense dew of Florida
> Brings forth
> The big-finned palm
> And green vine angering for life."

Poetic virtuosities are allied—especially those of diction, imagery, and cadence. In no writer's work are metaphors less "winter starved." In Architecture Mr Stevens asks:

"How shall we hew the sun, . . .
How carve the violet moon
To set in nicks?

Pierce, too, with buttresses of coral air
And purple timbers,
Various argentines"

and The Comedian as the Letter C, as the account of the craftsman's
un "simple jaunt," is an expanded metaphor which becomes as one
contemplates it, hypnotically incandescent like the rose tinged fringe
of the night blooming cereus. One applauds those analogies derived
from an enthusiasm for the sea:

"She scuds the glitters,
Noiselessly, like one more wave."

"The salt hung on his spirit like a frost,
The dead brine melted in him like a dew."

In his positiveness, aplomb, and verbal security, he has the mind and
the method of China; in such conversational effects as:

"Of what was it I was thinking?
So the meaning escapes,"

and certainly in dogged craftsmanship. Infinitely conscious in his
processes, he says

"Speak even as if I did not hear you speaking
But spoke for you perfectly in my thoughts."

One is not subject in reading him, to the disillusionment experienced in reading novices and charlatans who achieve flashes of beauty
and immediately contradict the pleasure afforded by offending in
precisely those respects in which they have pleased—showing that
they are deficient in conscious artistry.

Imagination implies energy and imagination of the finest type involves an energy which results in order "as the motion of a snake's
body goes through all parts at once, and its volition acts at the same

instant in coils that go contrary ways." There is the sense of the architectural diagram in the disjoined titles of poems with related themes. Refraining for fear of impairing its litheness of contour, from overelaborating felicities inherent in a subject, Mr Stevens uses only such elements as the theme demands; for example, his delineation of the peacock in Domination of Black, is austerely restricted, splendour being achieved cumulatively in Bantams in Pine-Woods, The Load of Sugar-Cane, The Palace of the Babies, and The Bird With the Coppery Keen Claws.

That "there have been many most excellent poets that never versified, and now swarm many versifiers that need never answer to the name of poets," needs no demonstration. The following lines as poetry independent of rhyme, beg the question as to whether rhyme is indispensably contributory to poetic enjoyment:

> "There is not nothing, no, no, never nothing,
> Like the clashed edges of two words that kill"

and

> "The clambering wings of black revolved,
> Making harsh torment of the solitude."

It is of course evident that subsidiary to beauty of thought, rhyme is powerful in so far as it never appears to be invented for its own sake. In this matter of apparent naturalness, Mr Stevens is faultless—as in correctness of assonance:

> "Chieftan Iffucan of Ascan in caftan
> Of tan with henna hackles, halt!"

The better the artist, moreover, the more determined he will be to set down words in such a way as to admit of no interpretation of the accent but the one intended, his ultimate power appearing in a selfsufficing, willowy, firmly contrived cadence such as we have in Peter Quince at the Clavier and in Cortège for Rosenbloom:

> ". . . That tread
> The wooden ascents
> Of the ascending of the dead."

One has the effect of poised uninterrupted harmony, a simple appearing, complicated phase of symmetry of movements as in figure skating, tight-rope dancing, in the kaleidoscopically centrifugal circular motion of certain mediaeval dances. It recalls the snake in Far Away and Long Ago, "moving like quicksilver in a rope-like stream" or the conflict at sea when after a storm, the wind shifts and waves are formed counter to those still running. These expertnesses of concept with their nicely luted edges and effect of flowing continuity of motion, are indeed

> ". . . pomps
> Of speech which are like music so profound
> They seem an exaltation without sound."

One further notes accomplishment in the use of reiteration—that pitfall of half-poets:

> "Death is absolute and without memorial,
> As in a season of autumn,
> When the wind stops. . . .
> When the wind stops."

In brilliance gained by accelerated tempo in accordance with a fixed melodic design, the precise patterns of many of these poems are interesting.

> "It was snowing
> And it was going to snow"

and the parallelism in Domination of Black suggest the Hebrew idea of something added although there is, one admits, more the suggestion of mannerism than in Hebrew poetry. Tea takes precedence of other experiments with which one is familiar, in emotional shorthand of this unwestern type, and in Earthy Anecdote and the Invective Against Swans, symmetry of design is brought to a high degree of perfection.

It is rude perhaps after attributing conscious artistry and a severely intentional method of procedure to an artist, to cite work that he has been careful to omit from his collected work. One regrets, however, the omission by Mr Stevens of The Indigo Glass In The Grass, The Man Whose Pharynx Was Bad, La Mort du Soldat Est Près des Choses Naturelles (5 Mars) and Comme Dieu Dispense de Graces:

> "Here I keep thinking of the primitives—
> The sensitive and conscientious themes
> Of mountain pallors ebbing into air."

However, in this collection one has eloquence. "The author's violence is for aggrandizement and not for stupor"; one consents therefore, to the suggestion that when the book of moonlight is written, we leave room for Crispin. In the event of moonlight and a veil to be made gory, he would, one feels, be appropriate in this legitimately sensational act of a ferocious jungle animal.

MARIANNE MOORE

[JANUARY, 1924]

MO-TI

By Lola Ridge

You talked in mellow day-ends
as the rallying sun
spread quivering spokes of gold
like an iridescent fan behind the pagodas,
and smells of bamboo shoots cooked in spices
drifted out of the blown fires.

You pitted your words against the words of princes . . .
but softly . . . in even tones . . . and few listened . . .
so that you were not nailed on four boards
or smeared with honey and left naked where sands crawl
        living under the sun.

Perhaps only a few boys listened
while the rice was cooling in the bowls
and auburn sunsets
changing into lavender and jade
shuffled into the lilac dusks.
A few boys listen always when one gives out of his silence.

I do not think there were girls who listened . . .
girls . . . whose lustrous pale skins
threw back in dusky echoes
the faint gold light of evenings
that loitered with silken slippers upon the pinnacles.

Not your speech could have touched their deep quietness. . . .
Incomprehensible . . . moving darkly under the froth of little
words and the soft purling of their blood that perhaps
sang to meet your blood . . . you passing them all unknowing
while the light on the horizon was like a topaz wine.

Did women . . . scattering dry words
as trees dead leaves

The Mountain. By Gaston Lachaise

Landscape: Camiers. By Andre Derain

Tightrope. By William Gropper

Goldfish. By Henri Matisse

Two Nudes and One Draped Figure by the Sea. By Pablo Picasso

Landscape: Kragerö. By Edvard Munch

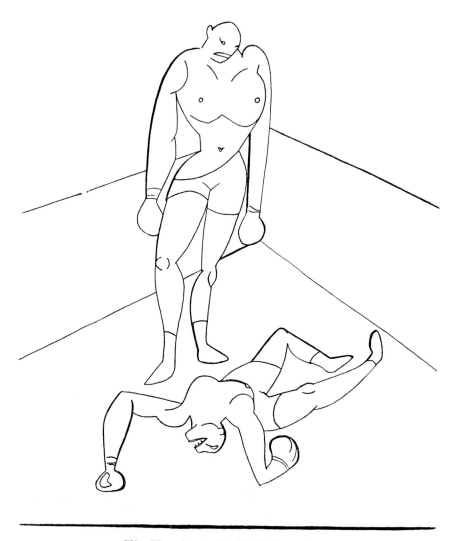

The Knockout. By E. E. Cummings

Trees, Rocks, Sea: Maine. By John Marin

Poet Marianne Moore, editor of *The Dial* from 1925 to 1929, as sketched by Hildegarde Watson (Mrs. James Sibley Watson, Jr.)

All other illustrations reproduced here are from The Dial Collection, on loan at the Worcester Art Museum, Worcester, Mass.

that are no more communicants of the green sap . . .
women with shining secrets in their eyes . . .
alertly curious eyes,
not baffled because not wondering . . .
catch a garbled word or so
and mutely
quiver along the margins of their silences?

Not again, Mo-Ti,
when heated days turn yellow at the edges,
and the sun comes down like a peacock to drink out of the rivers,
will lemon-pale boys,
pressed against the narrow darkness of their eyes,
bring to you their spindling hungers . . .
(what becomes of all the boys that have touched silence for a white
        shaken moment . . .
does the shy wild light that comes into their eyes
there beat itself out like a too long shut-in thing?)

I do not know if they talked with you in those gone saffron twilights.
Only your
words have floated out of the night, enfolding them and you in its
        seamless shadow . . .
words still seeking in vain noise
for some green hush to rest upon . . .
words carrying light like sunsets upon wings.

[AUGUST, 1924]

SPANISH LETTER

July, 1924

IN a view of the countryside of the Escorial, the monastery is merely the largest of many rocks, distinguished by a greater firmness and finish of line from the surrounding masses of stone. In these days of spring there is an hour at which the sun, like a golden bubble, is shattered upon the peaks, and a soft light, tinged with blue, violet, and carmine, floods the mountainsides and valleys, gently obliterating all contours. The builded stone then mocks the plans of the builder and, in obedience to a mightier will, reverts to an identity with the quarries that gave it birth.

Francisco Alcàntara, who knows so many things about Spain, is wont to say that this light of central Castile is a quintessence of the lights of the provinces, just as the Castillian tongue integrates in a way the dialects and languages of the surrounding regions of Spain.

It is this light of Castile that a little before the coming of night—like a cow, slow-moving over the heavens—transfigures the Escorial into a gigantic mass of flint awaiting the impact, the decisive shock that will open the veins of fire that furrow its strong entrails. Sullen and silent the granite group with its great lyric stone in the centre awaits a generation worthy of wresting from it the spark of spiritual fire.

To whom did Philip II dedicate this enormous profession of faith which, after St. Peter's at Rome, weighs more heavily upon the earth than any other credo in Europe? One answer to the question may be found in the king's own words in the charter of foundation: "This monastery we dedicate to the name of blessed Saint Lorenzo because of the particular devotion which, as aforesaid, we feel toward that glorious saint and in memory of the grace and victory that God has granted us on and since Saint Lorenzo's day." This grace of God was the victory of Saint Quentin. But, after all, the patience of Saint Lorenzo, admirable as it is, will not suffice to explain these colossal walls.

There can be no doubt that Philip II chose from among the various plans laid before him the one in which he found expressed his interpretation of the divine.

206

All temples, obviously, are erected *ad majoram Dei gloriam* but God is an idea and no authentic temple has ever been dedicated to anything so abstract as an idea. The apostle who, while wandering about in Athens, came upon an altar bearing, as he thought the inscription "To the unknown God" suffered from an illusion; no such altar has ever existed. Religion is not content with an abstract God, with a mere idea; it must have a concrete God who can be actually felt and experienced. Hence it is that there are as many images of God as there are men; each man in the seething of his innermost soul fashions his God from whatever material he finds at hand. The rigour of Catholic dogmatisms confines itself to exacting that the faithful shall admit the canonical definition of God and leaves the individual free to imagine and feel his God as he chooses. Taine tells of a girl who, on being taught that God is in the heavens, exclaimed "In the heavens like the birds? Then he must have a beak." That child might well be Catholic; the definition of the catechism does not exclude the beak of God. Looking about within us we search out what seems most worthy in the seething mass, and of that we fashion our God. Divinity is idealization of the nobler parts of man and religion is the devotion that half of every individual yields to his other half, the worship of his more vigorous and heroic by his more abject and inert aspects.

The monastery is a voluminous commentary on the God of Philip II or, in other words, on his ideal. What is the meaning of this massive structure? If every monument is an effort devoted to the expression of an ideal, what may be the ideal affirmed and deified by this ostentatious sacrifice of effort?

There is a moment in the evolution of the European mind that although it is of the greatest interest, has as yet been very little studied. It is a time at which the soul of the Continent suffered one of those appalling intimate crises which, despite their gravity and the acute pain that they cause, are manifested only by indirect means. It is at this hour that the Escorial was built.

The most mature fruits of the Renaissance are products of the middle of the sixteenth century. The Renaissance stands for a fulness of life and the joy of living. Once again men feel that the earth is a paradise. Aspiration and reality perfectly coincide. Bitterness, let us observe, is always born of the disparity between desire and attainment. *"Chi non può quel che vuol, quel che può voglia,"* said Leonardo da

Vinci. The men of the Renaissance desire only what they can attain and attain all that they desire. If at times restlessness and discontent do appear in their works, they appear with a beauty that makes them totally unlike this thing that we call Sorrow, this wailing crippled thing that to-day drags its maimed limbs over our hearts. The expressions of this happy state of mind prevailing during the Renaissance could not be other than serene and measured, fashioned with rhythm and balance—expressions in what was called the *graceful manner*.

Toward 1560, however, the European soul begins to feel an uneasiness and discontent, a doubt as to whether life be as perfect and complete as the foregoing age believed. Men begin to observe that the lives they desire are better than the lives they lead, that their aspirations are more lofty and extensive than their achievements, that their desires are forces confined in the prison of matter and that they must waste the greater part of them in overcoming the obstacles put in their way.

As a symbolic expression of this state of mind, we may contrast with Leonardo's lines, these others of Michael Angelo, now become the man of the hour, *La mia allegrez'e la maninconia:*

> "*O Dio, o Dio, o Dio!*
> *Chi m'ha a tolto a me stesso,*
> *Ch'à me fusse piu presso*
> *O piu di me potessi, che poss'io?*
> *O Dio, o Dio, o Dio!*"

A man who thus cries out against life cannot express his emotions—the emotions of an imprisoned hero or a fettered Prometheus—in the tranquil and beautiful forms of Renaissance art. Accordingly, precisely during these years, the norms of the classic style begin to undergo modifications. A mere increase in the size of the graceful forms of the Renaissance constitutes the first of these modifications. In architecture Michael Angelo institutes what is called the *grand manner* in opposition to the *graceful manner*. The colossal, the superlative, the enormous is now to triumph in art. It is Hercules and no longer Apollo that affects the aesthetic sense. The herculean is the beautiful.

This is too suggestive a theme to touch upon now, however slightly. Why is it that man found a delight for a time in excess, in the exclusive use of the superlative? What is the meaning of this predilection for the herculean? But let us hasten on. I wanted merely to point out that when the constellation of Hercules rose on the horizon of moral Europe, Spain, at the zenith of her power, was ruling the world and it was then that King Philip in the heart of his native Guadarrama dedicated this monument in the grand manner to his ideal.

To what ideal, we were asking, was this pretentious sacrifice of effort dedicated?

A turn about the vast façades of Saint Lorenzo means a walk of several kilometers. It has its advantages, therefore, as a hygienic measure and will probably arouse a keen appetite. Alas, there is no further reward. The architecture leaves with the observer no impression transcending the stone. The monastery of the Escorial is an effort without implications, anonymous and aimless—a gigantic effort that reacts only upon itself and scorns all else. Like Satan it worships itself and sings its praises into its proper ear. It is an effort devoted to the cult of effort.

The Erechtheum and the Parthenon do not arouse thoughts of the effort expended by the constructors. The white ruins under the clear blue sky irradiate great auras of an aesthetic, political, metaphysical ideality that never loses its power. Intent on absorbing these manifold exhalations, we are not preoccupied by thoughts of the labour that was required to arrange and polish the stones. It does not interest us.

In this monument of our forefathers, on the contrary, we see in a state of petrifaction a soul all will and effort—with no ideas or sensitiveness. The architecture is all desire, longing, and impetus. Nowhere else can we see so clearly defined the essence of the Spanish character, the hidden spring that has gushed forth the history of the most abnormal nation of Europe. Charles V and Philip II heard the confession of their people and these were the words of the confession, spoken in a delirium of candour: "We do not really understand the things that engross other races and to which they devote their care and protection; we do not desire to be wise, nor to be intimately religious; we do not desire to be just and least of all do our hearts crave moderation. We desire only to be great." A friend of mine who visited Nietzsche's sister in Weimar (she once lived in Paraguay and so speaks Spanish) told me of Nietzsche's having once exclaimed: "The

Spaniards! the Spaniards! These men have desired to be too much."

It has been our desire to set up an ideal, not of virtue or of truth, but of our desire itself. The greatness to which we aspired has never assumed in our minds any particular form; like our Don Juan who was in love with love, but could never love any woman, we have desired desire without ever desiring an object. We represent in history the explosion of blind, diffuse, brutal will. The sullen mass of Saint Lorenzo expresses perhaps our poverty of idea, but expresses at the same time our abundance of impetus. In imitation of the work of Dr Palacios Rubio (an author of the sixteenth century who wrote a Treatise on Martial and Heroic Effort) we might call it a treatise on pure effort.

Plato, as we know, was the first to attempt to separate the human mind into its components, or, as they were afterward called, faculties. Knowing that the individual mind is too elusive and unstable to afford opportunity for analysis, Plato sought to find the elements of consciousness by study of races, as representations of the individual on large scale. "In the nation," he says, "we find the individual written in large characters." He noted in the Greek race an indefatigable curiosity and a native dexterity in the manipulation of ideas. The Greeks were intelligent; in them the intellectual faculty was predominant. He observed, however, in the barbarous peoples of the Caucasus a certain quality that he found wanting in Greece and that seemed to him as important as intellect. "The Scythians," says Socrates in the Republic, "are not intelligent, as we are, but they have Θύ μος." The Latin equivalent is *furor,* that is effort, courage, impetus. With this word as basis, Plato constructed the idea that we now know as will.

This is a genuinely Spanish faculty. Against the vast background of universal history, we Spaniards have represented a gesture of courage. All our grandeur is in this one gesture—and all our misery.

Our energy has been so isolated and undirected by thought that it has been merely an untamed impetus, an ardent but blind desire that continues indefatigably to deliver its furious but aimless assaults. By its very nature it can have no purpose. A purpose is always the product of intelligence, of calculating or planning. For the man of valiant effort, therefore, action holds no interest. Action is energy directed toward an end and the end is the measure of its value. For the man of valiant effort, however, the value of an act is not measured by its end, by its utility, but by its sheer difficulty, by the amount of courage expanded to encompass it. He is not interested in action, but only in feats of heroism.

Allow me at this point to bring up a recollection from my own life. For personal reasons I shall never be able to look upon the Escorial landscape without seeing vaguely before my eyes, like the pattern of a fabric, the image of another little town, far away and as unlike the Escorial as can be imagined. It is a little Gothic town on the banks of a dark and gentle river, hemmed in by round hills entirely covered with deep forests of fir and pine, bright beeches, and splendid box-trees.

In that town I spent the equinox of my youth, it was there that I acquired the half at least of my hopes and practically the whole of my discipline—in Marburg on the banks of the Lahn.

But to return to my story. Several years ago I spent a summer in this Gothic town on the Lahn. Hermann Cohen, one of the greatest philosophers of our time, was then writing his work on aesthetics, Aesthetik des Reinen Gefühls. Like all great creators, Cohen was of a modest disposition and often discussed with me questions of beauty and art. The problem as to what constitutes the genus novel contributed more than any other question to give rise to dispute between us. I spoke to him of Cervantes. Cohen thereupon put aside his work to reread Don Quixote. I shall never forget those nights that filled the steep black heavens with agitated golden stars, trembling like the heart of a child. I would direct my steps to the home of the master and find him bowed over the great book of our race, translated into German by the romanticist Tieck. And almost always the venerable philosopher, raising his noble head, greeted me with these words: "But, my dear fellow, this Sancho is always using the very word that Fichte makes the basis of his philosophic system." True enough, Sancho often uses the word *hazaña;* it is a good mouth-filling word for him, *hazaña* has been translated by Tieck as *Tat-handlung;* that is, an act of will or determination.

Germany had been, for centuries, the intellectual nation of poets and thinkers when, in the works of Kant, the will asserted its right to a position beside that of thought, ethics to an importance equal to that of logic. In Fichte the scale inclines to the side of will; he assigns a greater importance to the deed than to logic and rates the *Tat-handlung,* the act of courage, as above reflection. This is the basis of his philosophy. Behold how the nations change! Is it not patent that Germany took to heart the teachings of Fichte that Cohen saw anticipated by Sancho?

But what can pure effort lead to? To nothing at all; or rather to but one end, melancholia.

Cervantes in Don Quixote wrote the critique of pure effort. Don Quixote like Don Juan is a hero of a low order of intelligence. His ideas are so ingenuous, stagnant, and rhetorical that they are really not ideas at all, but rather paragraphs of stereotyped quotations. Except for a nondescript mass of hackneyed thought, as old and well-known as the songs of sailors, his mind is empty. But Don Quixote is a man of valiant effort. The fact of his courageous energy, untainted by mockery, may easily be disengaged from the comic *débacle* that he made of his life. "The sorcerers," he says, "may rob me of success, but my courage and will they cannot take from me." He is a man of valour; his valour constitutes his sole reality and around it he raises a world of inept phantoms. Everything about him he uses as a pretext to call into play his will-power, kindle his courage, and launch his enthusiasm. But there comes a time when there arise in that incandescent soul, grave doubts concerning the sense of his heroic deeds. And then Cervantes begins to heap up words of sorrow. From chapter fifty-eight to the end of the novel, all is bitterness. "Melancholy overflowed his heart," says the poet. "From sheer heaviness of heart he stopped eating," he continues. "He was all sorrow and melancholy." "Let me die," he says to Sancho, "a prey to my thoughts and my afflictions." For the first time an inn is an inn to him. And finally there is the anguish of this, his confession: "The truth is that I do not know what I achieved by my travails; I do not know what I attained by my efforts."

JOSÉ ORTEGA Y GASSET

[OCTOBER, 1924]

A NOTE ON HAWAIIAN POETRY

By Padraic Colum

HAWAIIAN poetry—and this is probably true of Polynesian poetry generally—comes from a root that is different from the root that our poetry comes from. In our poetry, the primary intention is to communicate some personal emotion; in their poetry the primary intention, I believe, is to make an incantation, to cast a spell. Hear Hawaiian *mele* chanted with all of their prolonged vowel-sounds, and you will be made to feel that what is behind the *mele* is not a poet but a magician. I can think of only one or two poems in English that are in their intention, in their evocative sound, anything like Hawaiian *mele*. One is the incantation that A.E. has put into his Deirdre, the incantation that bespells Naisi and his brothers. In the play as it was first given A.E. himself used to chant the spell with the very intonations of the surviving Hawaiian chanters:

> "Let the Faed Fia fall,
> Mananaun MacLir:
> Take back the day
> Amid days unremembered.
> Over the warring mind
> Let thy Faed Fia fall,
> Mananaun MacLir.
>
> Let thy waves rise,
> Mananaun MacLir,
> Let the earth fail
> Beneath their feet,
> Let thy waves flow over them,
> Mananaun,
> Lord of Ocean!"

The Open Polynesian syllables, with their vowels arbitrarily lingered on, naturally give more of the effect of an incantation than even lines that have sounds as evocative as "Mananaun, Lord of Ocean." Another poem that I can imagine being chanted in the

Hawaiian way, and producing the same effect of incantation, is Blake's:

> "Hear the voice of the Bard!
> Who present, past, and future sees;
> Whose ears have heard
> The Holy Word
> That walked amongst the ancient trees,
>
> Calling the lapsèd soul
> And weeping in the evening dew,
> That might control
> The starry pole,
> And fallen, fallen light renew."

But if Hawaiian poetry had in it only this evocative sound it would be of little interest to us who have been trained to appreciate other qualities in poetry. It has a personal and human appeal too. And the Hawaiian poet has anticipated effects that the cultivated poets of our tradition have been striving for: he is, for instance, more esoteric than Mallarmé and more imagistic than Amy Lowell.

Every Hawaiian poem has at least four meanings: (1) the ostensible meaning of the words; (2) a vulgar double-meaning; (3) a mythological-historical-topographical import; and (4) the *mauna* or deeply-hidden meaning. I have sat gasping while, in a poem of twelve or twenty lines, meaning under meaning was revealed to me by some scholar, Hawaiian or Haole, who knew something of the esoteric Hawaiian tradition.

But the main thing that Hawaiian poetry has to offer an outsider is the clear and flashing images that it is in its power to produce. The languages of the Pacific, it should be noted first, have no abstract terms. If an Hawaiian wants to refer to my ignorance he speaks of me as having the entrails of night; if he wants to speak of someone's blindness he will bring in eyes of night. Abstractions become images in the Polynesian language. The people themselves have an extraordinary sense of the visible things in their world: they have, for instance, a dozen words to tell of the shades of difference in the sea as it spreads between them and the horizon. And their language forces them to an imagistic expression. Their poetry then, when it is at all descriptive, is full of clear and definite images. I open Nathaniel Emerson's Unwritten Literature of Hawaii, a book upon the hula that is also a great anthology of Hawaiian poetry, and I find:

> "Heaven-magic, fetch a Hilo pour from heaven!
> Morn's cloud-buds, look! they swell in the East.
> The rain-cloud parts, Hilo is deluged with rain,
> The Hilo of King Hana-kahi.
>
> Surf breaks, stirs the mire of Pii-lani;
> The bones of Hilo are broken
> By the blows of the rain.
> Ghostly the rain-scud of Hilo in heaven.
>
> The cloud-forms of Pua-lani grow and thicken.
> The rain-priest bestirs him now to go forth,
> Forth to observe the stab and thrust of the rain,
> The rain that clings to the roof of Hilo."

I know one poem in English that in its clear and flashing imagery resembles the passages that we must regard as the best of Hawaiian poetry: that poem is Meredith's Nuptials of Attila. No Hawaiian poet has been able to tell a story, no Hawaiian poet has been able to give an organization to a poem that is at all like Meredith's, but all this is like Hawaiian poetry:

> "Flat as to an eagle's eye
> Earth hung under Attila. . . .
>
> On his people stood a frost.
> Like a charger cut in stone,
> Rearing stiff, the warrior host,
> Which had life from him alone,
> Craved the trumpet's eager note
> As the bridled earth the Spring."

It is in an attempt to reproduce something of this clear and flashing imagery that I have made the three pieces that are in the present issue of THE DIAL, and the piece that was published in a previous issue, The Lehua Trees.

Pigeons on the Beach is an attempt to make a poem in the spirit of the Hawaiian, and The Lehua Trees has the same to be said of it. There are no originals for these. There is an original for the Hawaiian Evening Song, and for the piece that I call The Surf Rider; the first is based on the Hawaiian of John Ie; the original and a translation is given in the Memoirs of the Bernice Pauhi Bishop Museum, Volume 6, Number 2, and the second is given in Nathaniel Emerson's Unwritten Literature of Hawaii, published by the Smithsonian Institute. I have both condensed and expanded the Evening Song, and I have changed the character of the poem that I give the title of The Surf Rider to by changing it from a *mele-inoa,* a name-song, into a descriptive piece.

There are several words in these pieces that have to be explained: "Tapu" is the word that was written "taboo" by the mariners who first came into touch with Polynesian civilization. The word means more than "forbidden"; it means "belonging to the gods," and the Hawaiian poet who describes night as being "tapu" is drawing on the same sort of associations as Homer drew on when he spoke of "the sacred night." I have imagined that some sign has been set up to show that "tapu" has been declared, but that is not in the original. Ku, Lono, and Kane are the great Polynesian divinities. In Pigeons on the Beach, the word "tapa" means the bark-cloth of the Polynesians: white tapa, wrapped around a king's staff was a sign of "tapu." In both The Surf Rider and the Evening Song, I have made "Kahiki" into "Tahiti." "Kahiki" is "Tahiti," but "Kahiki" is also a mythical land in the remote ocean: the tapu that extends to Kahiki extends to the furthest place. The wave that comes from Kahiki comes from the furthest place. And the wave has been coming from the time of Wakea: Wakea is the name that comes first in the Polynesian genealogies; the wave, then, has been coming from the furthest place for the longest time conceivable.

[APRIL, 1924]

THREE HAWAIIAN POEMS

By Padraic Colum

THE PIGEONS ON THE BEACH

White like tapa, like the tapa that goes on the staffs of Kings is the beach beside the two-hued Pacific.

Pigeons come down to the beach; they run along taking grains of the coral sand into their crop. They rise up; they fly, they hang above the reef that the surf foams across.

And beyond is the Ocean. They sway a little way above it. Then they come back across the reef that takes the foam. They run along the beach taking sands into their crops, pigeons that have come down from the dove-cotes behind the orchards.

A wave-break startles them where they run. They rise up. And now they see the dove-cotes beyond the orchards and they are gathered to them.

But in the dove-cotes all night they will hear the surf breaking, and they will dream of strong mates and craggy breeding-places and powerful flights that will win to them.

And at daybreak they will go to the beach; they will run along taking sands into their crops; they will rise up and they will fly; they will hang above where the reef gathers the foam.

A little while only they will hang above it; a little way only they will sway beyond it; they will come back and take sand into their crops. And as they run along the beach they will not know that the plover and the sand-piper have departed, flying through brightness and through darkness until they find for themselves the atolls and the craggy islets around which ranges the eight-finned shark.

Pigeons that have come down to the beach beside the two-hued Pacific!

THE SURF RIDER

From afar it has come, that long rolling wave; from Tahiti it has come; long has it been coming, that wide-sweeping wave; since the time of Wakea it has been on the way.

Now it plumes, now it ruffles itself. Stand upon your surf-board with the sun to lead you on! Stand! Gird your loin-cloth! The wave rolls and swells higher; the wave that will not break bears you along.

From afar it has come, that long rolling wave; long it has been coming, that wide-sweeping wave. And now it bears you towards us, upright upon your board.

The wave-ridden waves dash upon the island; the deep-sea coral is swept inshore; the long rolling wave, the wide-sweeping wave comes on.

Glossy is your skin and undrenched; the wave-feathers fan the triumphing surf rider; with the speed of the white tropic-bird you come to us.

We have seen the surf at Puna; we have seen a triumphing surf rider: Na-i-he is his name.

MELE AHIAHI

(Hawaiian Evening Song)

The sign is given; mighty the sign: *Tapu!*
All murmurs now, speech, voice
Subdue: inviolable let evening be.

Inviolable and consecrate:
Edgeways and staggering descends
The sun; rain vanishes;
A bonus of bright light comes back.
Hawaii keeps the ordinance: *Tapu!*
Even far Tahiti now is still, perhaps.

The Island's shelter-giving houses stand;
The Chief withdraws, the sacred cup is his;
The mothers call on Kuhe as they give
Their child to sleep. O early slumber
Of the heavenly company thou art indeed!
O Ku, O Lono, O Kane, they are yours
The evening hours (subdue
All murmurs now, speech, voice
Inviolate let evening be).

It is evening; it is hallowed for being that:
Let tumult die within us all: *Tapu!*
The spies of heaven, the stars return: *Tapu!*
And peaceful heaven covers peaceful earth.

[APRIL, 1924]

IN A THICKET

By Glenway Wescott

THE mist thinned and broke like a cobweb in the May sunshine. A young girl opened her eyes; through the window beside her bed they rested on a cloud of plum-trees in flower. The little house where she lived with her grandfather stood in a thicket of trees, blackberries, and vines. She saw the vapours gather as dew upon some cabbages and lettuce in the garden, and the black crooked trunks sustaining a weight of flowers.

She was troubled by a memory of the night in incomprehensible fragments. She had been aroused suddenly by sounds which her mind, confused with sleep, could not estimate. The moon, submerged in mist, had swept the cottage with a whirling and opaque atmosphere. She had lain still, her heart beating fast and loud.

Then, another movement, some footsteps on the porch. Seemingly padded, they were separated from one another by silence. Was it an animal? Too heavy for a cat, too elastic for a dog. Were there wilder beasts in the thicket? The door between her bedroom and the room opening upon the porch stood open. Her speculations died down with her breath. Something pressed upon the wire screen of the window. It brushed against the screen door, and seemed to shake it by the latch. It paced back and forth, a soft persistent prowl.

She trembled with curiosity and fear. An instinct warned her that it was not an ordinary thief. She would have liked to rise, to see, to know; her limbs would not respond. The night, both grey and dense, unnerved her.

Subdued noises and movements persisted irregularly for what must have been an hour. Once she heard them sweep across the grass to the backdoor, also hooked from within, and return. But her vigilance relaxed; waves of unconsciousness blotted out whole sounds and moments of hush; and suddenly she was awake in the tranquil sunshine.

In the kitchen her grandfather was moving in a pleasant odour of eggs and butter. For three years the orphan, now fifteen, had lived with the old man—a schoolmaster whose needs had been so simple that he had saved, from the miserable salaries of many

years, enough to provide for his old age and more. She found him on
the porch, last autumn's wild cucumber vines flecking his face with
shadows, his hands in his lap.

"Good morning, Lily," he said, in his sweet high voice.

"Good morning, gran'pa." She kissed his cheek where it was
cool and like paper above the white beard, and crouched on the
steps.

What little they had to do was as simple and solitary as a movement
brought about by the sunlight, which dropped delicately upon fresh
leaves, vegetables, the strawberry bed, grass, birds, and petals. They
were shut off from the road, from noise and passers-by, from the sight
of other houses, by the grove, which opened on one side only, on a
wheat-field bounded by trees.

For two years Lily had not gone to the district school because
of the age and remote dwelling of her grandfather, who taught
her, easily and informally, at home, where she turned the pages
of his library broodingly, with vague disappointment: books of history,
letters, and particularly of natural history, such as the note-books of
Audubon and Agassiz. Meanwhile he wandered in the grove or on
the lawn, or farther afield. His hands clasped behind his back, he
hummed and whistled. In the early twilight they worked together in
the garden, upon the products of which, with those of the hen-coop
and wild nuts and berries in season, they lived. His existence had
shrunk into the circle of trees, and he was content with their non-
committal beauty, their concentration. But the girl's eyes sometimes
ran darkly upon the horizon.

"Are you ready for breakfast, child?" the old man asked. When
they had eaten, he polished his silver spectacles on a corner of the
blue table-cloth, arose, and took down a Bible from a small shelf
of its own. Slow and firm, he read a chapter of Revelations.

If there had ever been an interruption of this morning worship,
Lily would have dreaded its return. To-day her emotion revealed
itself more clearly, as if a carving in low relief had moved outward
and detached itself from the stone. The tumult of course emotion and
unknown crime which agitated the old text disturbed, even offended
her. She remembered the night and the intruder. Her grandfather
knelt by his chair, she by hers.

"Oh dear heavenly Father," he prayed, "mould us to do thy
will. Let our feet ever walk by the light which thou hast given

us. Do not let them stray into temptation, or be stained by sin. Dear Father, we come to thee humbly, knowing we have been evil—covetous, quick to anger, lusting for power, licentious. Do not punish us according to our deeds, but forgive us according to the sacrifice of thy dearly beloved Son."

The girl's thoughts wandered, excited by the solemn beauty of his voice, by the obscurity of the words. What was it which had wakened her? What did it want? Where was it now? Should she ever see it, ever know?

"And bring us at last into thy heavenly house, to abide with thee for ever. Amen."

As Lily washed the few dishes and placed them on the lace-papered shelves, she heard voices on the piazza; and found her grandfather talking to Mrs Biggs, a woman who sometimes came to do their cleaning.

"And what had the man done?" he said.

With a cunning look at the girl, the woman ignored his question. Having stopped on her way to another farm-house to bring a piece of news, she felt obliged by the presence of this young sober creature to omit its details. She squinted at the sun, red hands upon her hips, and outlined the exciting but commonplace story.

A negro had escaped from the penitentiary. The state prison brooded over this countryside, a hideous fortress of red brick made more hideous by a row of trees planted against the walls. From tower to tower upon these walls guards walked, night and day; separated from the building by a bare courtyard in which every shadow was immediately visible. At night one of the towers upheld like a lighthouse a gigantic lamp, which twinkled into many bedroom windows, a reminder of something mysterious and submerged, over the forests, marshes, farms, and melancholy black dense hemp-fields.

Lily blanched and withdrew cautiously through the door.

The negro, imprisoned some years ago for a crime of violence, had seemed, in the prison, so subdued, so contented, that he had promptly become a privileged trusty. He drove the superintendent's car, and sometimes went about the town alone upon errands. From time to time he displayed an internal excitement taken to be religious or even penitential, since it was indicated by a greater degree of gentle sadness and by low fitful singing of spirituals. It had been thought best to restrict his movement during these emotional fits; but the warden had sent him carelessly to the post office the day before. He had left the car less than a mile from the prison and disappeared.

Almost immediately the bewildered authorities swarmed over the country, expecting to take him by nightfall. But they were disappointed; the felon was still at large. He had been wandering around all night. He was loose now.

Lily was in a storm of excitement. It made nothing more clear; the relation of the news to her experience seemed insubstantial and incomplete; but she felt that the obscurities which had troubled her, the unknown, the difficult, the hypnotic, were to be revealed in a flash of light, emanating from Mrs Biggs. She shrank into a chair.

Mrs Biggs repeated each fact several times, panting with eagerness. She lowered her voice and rolled her eyes. But at last she reached the end of her information, and paused, discouraged.

The silent moments prolonged themselves in a twitter of birds and fowls. The old man sighed and stroked his beard. "Well, poor man," he said, "I suppose they'll catch him."

Mrs Biggs asked loudly, "Aren't you at all afraid?" For the second time the girl felt a surreptitious glance upon her.

"Oh, no," he returned mildly. "We are simple people, poor people. We have no money. We haven't anything he'd want."

Then, with something like timidity, she asked, "Do you like to live here in the thicket, so far back from the road? I've always wondered why you did it."

"Well, I don't know," was his absent reply. "I'm used to it. I've been here a long time. We don't get any noise and dust from automobiles, and the birds come here."

He descended slowly the verandah steps. Mrs Biggs hurried off with her burden of alarm; her shawl caught upon weeds and bushes. In the sunlight his beard glimmered beneath the honey locusts.

In the silence of the house Lily went about her interrupted tasks.

At dinner her grandfather was silent and aloof. He had his days of a preoccupation which the girl called "growing old." It arose within him, pure, unannounced, and unearthly, like the radiance which a candle-flame shoots through the wax beneath. She wondered if the negro's sad spells were like his. She knew that he had forgotten the morning's news, that he brooded upon nothing known to her.

As the afternoon passed by, a globe of light and fragrance, his mood deepened and darkened. For a year she had struggled to understand it, with only vague weak conclusions. Was it sadness at the expenditure of his life? Loneliness for those whose knowledge was simultaneous with his? Was it memory which troubled that mind like a pool, as if sunken things arose and floated on the surface?

His eyes seemed to turn away from the trees, clouds, birds, shadows, garden, away from her, to look within. He worked only a few minutes, but paced around the garden and sat in a wicker chair, shading his eyes with one hand.

Under the trees beside him the girl mended some clothes. Her courage sank low and lower, but persisted. The sun declined in the plum-trees. Acute rays came between the trunks of the thicket; those of the poplar became silver, the birch pink, the ironwood black. In silence the voices of some geese, trembling through the air, set up there a vibration like themselves.

She arose and kissed her grandfather; his face was smooth, cold, and frail to her lips. "A good girl," he murmured. Should she tell him about the night? For she was sure the negro would return. What was to keep him from coming in? Nothing, nothing at all.

As she thought of the situation she found resources in herself which she did not name. Her ignorance provided no concrete images to feed fear; and something within her implored the indefinite to break apart, to take shape. In her courage there was curiosity; in her curiosity, a challenge.

Night appeared in little flecks on the under-sides of leaves. Lily watched her grandfather. As twilight thickened, a similar shadow seemed to gather within him, behind his eyes. He was unnaturally pallid—a mere shell separating two shadows. One day it would crumble; she would be alone, always alone, bodily alone, as she seemed then.

Suddenly she thought of the stranger with security. What harm could he do her? How could she be harmed? She saw him quite distinctly, not in person, but as a separate outline as small as her hand, singing to itself, and an embodiment of sadness.

It pleased her now to add reasons to her instinctive decision not to share the secret. Her grandfather was old and not strong; he would not understand; it would only frighten him and remind him of his deafness. Now it was too dark to sew, she folded the white cloths and laid them on the grass.

In the night she awoke and knew that the negro had come. As before, her body was already rigid, her heart accelerated. On the floor the moonlight fell in crisp rectangles. Some trees rose in columns from the lawn, seamless and abrupt. Between them the light clinked like a castanet.

The footsteps on the porch were undisguised and reckless. He fumbled at the screen door, at the windows. He scratched the wire tentatively with another metal, and ceased as if afraid of the noise. She arose in the bed upon her elbows. A deep sigh, sibilant against the teeth.

Her arms ached with tension. A great silence arose as a growing plant arises. Her imagination fixed upon it, half in terror, half in hope. It spread and shook out its leaves.

In the garden a tree toad tinkled to itself.

She slipped out of bed. Her night-gown swung about her ankles. As she crossed the moonlight her legs glimmered in the sheer cloth. A braid caught and slipped over the back of a chair. Her progress was slow and irregular, as if she wavered or floated. Not a board protested under her bare feet, upraised at the instep. Her eyes spread to admit something not yet apparent, and she was guided between chairs and tables by instinct.

The porch door thrust into the dark room a broad short blade of light. Lily skirted it, and saw the black man.

He was on the steps, his legs spread, his bare head bent enough to fix his gaze in the grey grass. He wore tennis-shoes, trousers, and a battered coat. Between its buttonless edges, the moonbeams rested on the close hard folds of his belly, like furrows turned by a chisel.

She had never seen a negro; separated from her by ten feet and a thin fabric of wire, he was not so black as her imagination of him. In the dead brilliance his cheeks glimmered softly, pallid not in themselves, but as a surface burnished. Only a film of colour clung to his lips. He rested his chin within hands almost white across the palms, and turned his great white eyes toward her. The damp curled upward around her bare body.

Midnight passed. The two poised there side by side. Consciousness was suspended in the air; but it did not establish the contact which would have altered their relation. The moon slipped through the sky. Sometimes his sighs were clear; he seemed to breathe forth a single mysterious vowel.

She brushed against a pillow, which fell and settled heavily on the floor. Surely he would hear and come. The blood rushed to her head in a loud flood.

But he did not. His desires, the tentacles thrust outward toward something in that house, had been withdrawn; and gathered, in a knot almost visible, about some inner crisis. He rose abruptly, stretched himself, and strode away, over the grass. The dew plashed on his canvas shoes.

Before her grandfather came down stairs, she arose into a day lurid and insecure. Some robins worked upon the flagrant bright green sod. Everywhere were clots of colour and vortices of movement she had never seen. A superb thunderhead palpitated in the sky like a tree with black blossoms.

As she regarded it, a smaller sight arrested her: upon the screen door a gash three inches long, made by a wedge or chisel before she woke. She stared at the opening, from which the soft wire bent back neatly.

The old man, whistling like a boy, found her there. He did not see the trace upon the door.

[JUNE, 1924]

DR FREUD ON ART

By Clive Bell

SUPPOSE an aesthete, armed with an hypothesis—the hypothesis, say, that Significant Form is the one thing common and peculiar to works of art—were to imagine that this hypothesis of his would explain every human activity: suppose, for instance, he were to tell you that what a poker-player really aims at is to hold a hand in which reds and blacks, court cards and plain, achieve a perfectly harmonious and aesthetically satisfying rhythm, to which end he (the player) discards and draws; suppose he were to add that those persons who hopelessly lack aesthetic sensibility, who can never establish an aesthetically significant sequence, are the irremediably bad players: what would you think of him? Certainly, you would have to tell him that he was barking up the wrong tree; but whether you would be justified in considering that this mania for forcing all nature to submit to a theory disabled his judgement on all questions is less clear. I beseech you to think twice or thrice before making up your mind; for on your decision depends the reputation of no less a person than Dr Sigmund Freud.

Hark to him:

"He (the artist) is one who is urged on by instinctive needs which are too clamorous; he longs to attain to honour, power, riches, fame, and the love of women; but he lacks the means of achieving these gratifications. So, like any other with an unsatisfied longing, he turns away from reality and transfers all his interest, and all his Libido too, on to the creation of his wishes in the life of phantasy. . . . He understands how to elaborate his day-dreams." [1]

The artist, in fact, is one who has set his heart on driving expensive women from expensive restaurants in expensive motorcars, on getting a title and becoming "a celebrity," and generally living

[1] Introductory Lectures on Psycho-Analysis.

sumptuously. This, unluckily, he cannot afford to do. But he dreams; and he dreams so intensely that he can communicate his dreams to others, who share them, but cannot dream so vividly. For, in Dr Freud's words, "to those who are not artists the gratification that can be drawn from the springs of phantasy is very limited; their inexorable repressions prevent the enjoyment of all but the meagre day-dreams which can become conscious." But through "the artist's" "art" the public obtains, in the world of make-believe, satisfaction for its clamorous needs, and pays the artist so handsomely for the benefit that he soon obtains satisfaction for his in the world of reality. Art is, to stick to the Freudian jargon, "wish fulfilment"; the artist "realizes" his own dreams of being a great man and having a good time, and in so doing gratifies a public which vaguely and feebly dreams the same dreams, but cannot dream them efficiently.

Now this, I dare say, is a pretty good account of what housemaids, and Dr Freud presumably, take for art. Indeed, the novelette is the perfect example of "wish fulfilment in the world of phantasy." The housemaid dreams of becoming a great actress and being loved by a handsome earl; Dr Freud dreams of having been born a handsome earl and loving a great actress. And for fifteen delirious minutes, while the story lasts, the dream comes true. But this has nothing to do with art. Any artist or any poker-player may, or may not, have a taste for expensive pleasures, but *qua* artist or poker-player he has other ends in view. The artist is not concerned with even the "sublimations" of his normal lusts, because he is concerned with a problem which is quite outside normal experience. His object is to create a form which shall match an aesthetic conception, not to create a form which shall satisfy Dr Freud's unappeased longings. Neither Dr Freud's day-dreams of fame, women, and power, nor yet his own, are what the artist is striving to express; though they are what Dr Freud and his like wish him to express. The artist's problem is aesthetic; hence the endless quarrel about happy endings between a popular novelist who is ever so little an artist and his public. The public wants to have its wishes fulfilled; the artist wants to create a form which shall be aesthetically right. It is disagreeable for the young lady who has been dreaming of herself as Cordelia to be hanged in the last act. Shakespeare, however, was not considering the young lady's dreams nor even his own of what would be a nice sort of world: he was concerned with an artistic problem. Of that problem Dr Freud, unluckily, knows nothing. He knows nothing about art, or about the feelings of people who can appreciate art. There is no reason why he should know anything about either; only, being ignorant, he ought to have held his tongue.

Art has nothing to do with dreams. The artist is not one who dreams more vividly, but who is a good deal wider awake, than most people. His grand and absorbing problem is to create a form that shall match a conception, whatever that conception may be. He is a creator, not a dreamer. And we, who care for art, go to it, not for the fulfilment of our dreams of desirable life, but for something that life can never give—for that peculiar and quite disinterested state of mind which philosophers call aesthetic ecstasy. We ask the artist, not to make our dreams come true, but to give us a new thing, which comes out of his own experience.

I once heard Mr Roger Fry trying to explain this to a roomful of psychoanalysts; and, following in his footsteps, I have attempted the same task myself. I have begged them—the psychologists—to believe that the emotion provoked in me by St Paul's Cathedral has nothing to do with my notion of having a good time. I have said that it was comparable rather with the emotion provoked in a mathematician by the perfect and perfectly economical solution of a problem, than with that provoked in me by the prospect of going to Monte Carlo in particularly favourable circumstances. But they knew all about St Paul's Cathedral and all about quadratic equations and all about me apparently. So I told them that if Cézanne was for ever painting apples, that had nothing to do with an insatiable appetite for those handsome, but to me unpalatable, fruit. At the word "apples," however, my psychologists broke into titters. Apparently, they knew all about apples, too. And they knew that Cézanne painted them for precisely the same reason that poker-players desire to be dealt a pair of aces.

As a matter of fact, Cézanne would very likely have preferred flowers, the forms and colours of which are said by many to be even more inspiring than those of fruit; only flowers fade, and Cézanne was extraordinarily slow. It was not till late in life he discovered that artificial flowers would serve his purpose just as well as real ones. Apples are comparatively durable; and apples can be depended upon to behave themselves. It was the steadiness as much as the comparative immarcescibility of apples which endeared them to Cézanne—a secret which once, by accident, he betrayed. He was painting a portrait of M Ambroise Vollard, for which I have heard he demanded not less than fifty sittings. Now, in the warm Provençal afternoons, M Vollard used to grow sleepy, and used sometimes to doze. But when the model dozes inevitably the pose changes. To counteract this danger Cézanne so arranged the chair on the model's throne that the slightest movement on the sitter's part would bring him crashing to the ground. M Vollard's spirit was all right, but the flesh was weak; lunch was over, the afternoon warm, off nodded the sitter, and down came the chair. Slightly stunned—the throne was a high one—M Vollard was picking himself up when he saw and heard the artist advancing furiously upon him: *"Tu ne peux pas te tenir tranquil, donc? Pourquoi bouges-tu? Les pommes ne bougent pas."* Unhappily, as the only language known to English psychologists is German, my story, like its subject, fell miserably flat.

Dr Sigmund Freud has made himself slightly ridiculous by talking about things of which he knows nothing, by imagining that the books and pictures he likes are works of art, and that the people who react to works of art feel what he feels for the books and pictures he likes. Are we, on this account, to conclude that Dr Freud is not to be trusted on any subject? "Yes," says Dr Johnson.

"A physician being mentioned who had lost his practice, because his whimsically changing his religion had made people distrustful of him, I maintained that this was unreasonable, as religion is unconnected with medical skill. *Johnson.*—Sir, it is not unreasonable; for when people see a man absurd in what they understand, they may conclude the same of him in what they do not understand."

But I doubt the great doctor was a little hasty and, like Dr Freud himself, something given to generalizing on insufficient data. To me it seems that Dr Freud may be an excellent psychoanalyst; but I am sure he had better leave art alone. [APRIL, 1925]

STORM CENTRE

By Genevieve Taggard

Past noon, past the strong
Hour for full song,
—However late—
Mere silence holds me.

              Here are met
Furious winds, and the great
Silence is desperate.

Utterly still they stand locked.
Once only the earth rocked
With the weakening of one.

This is battle, forehead-on.
Barbarous singing follows when
One triumphs. Now the centre
Tightens again,
Closes. None enter—

It is silent where
Wrestles the air.

[APRIL, 1925]

MARIANNE MOORE

By William Carlos Williams

THE best work is always neglected and there is no critic among the older men who has cared to champion the newer names from outside the battle. The established critic will not read. So it is that the present writers must turn interpreters of their own work. Even those who enjoy modern work are not always intelligent, but often seem at a loss to know the white marks from the black. But modernism is distressing to many who would at least tolerate it if they knew how. These individuals who cannot bear the necessary appearance of disorder in all immediacy, could be led to appreciation through critical study.

If one come with Miss Moore's work to some wary friend and say, "Everything is worthless but the best and this is the best," adding, "—only with difficulty discerned," will he see anything, if he be at all well read, but destruction? From my experience he will be shocked and bewildered. He will perceive absolutely nothing except that his whole preconceived scheme of values has been ruined. And this is exactly what he should see, a break *through* all preconceptions of poetic form and mood and pace, a flaw, a crack in the bowl. It is this that one means when he says destruction and creation are simultaneous. But this is not easy to accept. Miss Moore, using the same material as all others before her, comes at it so effectively at a new angle as to throw out of fashion the classical-conventional poetry to which one is used and puts her own and that about her in its place. The old stops are discarded. This must antagonize many. Furthermore there is a multiplication, a quickening, a burrowing through, a blasting aside, a dynamization, a flight over—it is modern, but the critic must show that this is only to reveal an essential poetry through the mass, as always, and with superlative effect in this case.

A course in mathematics would not be wasted on a poet, or a reader of poetry, if he remembered no more from it than the

NOTE: Observations. By Marianne Moore. 12mo. 120 pages. Lincoln MacVeagh. The Dial Press. $2.

geometric principle of the intersection of loci: from all angles lines converging and crossing establish points. He might carry it further and say in his imagination, that apprehension perforates, at places, through to understanding—as white is at the intersection of blue and green and yellow and red. It is this white light that is the background of all good work. Aware of this one may read the Greeks or the Elizabethans or Sidney Lanier, even Robert Bridges, and preserve interest, poise, and enjoyment. He may visit Virginia or China, and when friends, eager to please, playfully lead him about for pockets of local colour—he may go. Local colour is not, as the parodists, the localists believe, an object of art. It is merely a variant serving to locate some point of white penetration. The intensification of desire toward this purity is the modern variant. It is that which interests me most and seems most solid among the qualities I witness in my contemporaries; it is a quality present in much or even all that Miss Moore does.

Poems, like paintings, can be interesting because of the subject with which they deal. The baby glove of a Pharaoh can be so presented as to bring tears to the eyes. And it need not be bad work because it has to do with a favourite cat dead. Poetry, rare and never willingly recognized, only its accidental colours make it tolerable to most. If it be of a red colouration those who like red will follow and be led restfully astray. So it is with hymns, battle songs, love ditties, elegies. Humanity sees itself in them, sees with delight this, that, and the other quality with which it is familiar, the good placed attractively and the bad thrown into a counter light. This is inevitable. But in any anthology it will be found that men have been hard put to it at all times to tell which is poetry and which the impost. This is hard. The difficult thing to realize is that the thrust must go through to the white, at least somewhere.

Good modern work, far from being the fragmentary, neurotic thing its disunderstanders think it, is nothing more than work compelled by these conditions. It is a multiplication of impulses that by their several flights, crossing at all eccentric angles, *might* enlighten. As a phase, in its slightest beginning, it is not yet nearly complete. And it is not rising as an arc; it is more a disc pierced here and there by light; it is really distressingly broken up. But so does any attack seem at the moment of engagement, multiple units crazy except when viewed as a whole.

Surely there is no poetry so active as that of to-day, so unbound, so dangerous to the mass of mediocrity, if one should understand it, so fleet, hard to capture, so delightful to pursue. It is clarifying in its movements as a wild animal whose walk corrects that of men. Who shall separate the good Whitman from the bad, the dreadful New England maunderers from the others, put air under and around the living and leave the dead to fall dead? Who? None but poems, such as Miss Moore's, their cleanliness, lack of cement, clarity, gentleness. It grows impossible for the eye to rest long upon the object of the drawing. Here is an escape from the old dilemma. The unessential is put rapidly aside as the eye searches between for illumination. Miss Moore undertakes in her work to separate the poetry from the subject entirely—like all the moderns. In this she has been rarely successful and this is important.

Unlike the painters the poet has not resorted to distortions or the abstract in form. Miss Moore accomplishes a like result by rapidity of movement. A poem such as Marriage is an anthology of transit. It is a pleasure that can be held firm only by moving rapidly from one thing to the next. It gives the impression of a passage *through*. There is a distaste for lingering, as in Emily Dickinson. As in Emily Dickinson there is too a fastidious precision of thought where unrhymes fill the purpose better than rhymes. There is a swiftness impaling beauty, but no impatience as in so much present-day trouble with verse. It is a rapidity too swift for touch, a seraphic quality, one might have said yesterday. There is, however, no breast that warms the bars of heaven; it is at most a swiftness that passes without repugnance from thing to thing.

The only help I ever got from Miss Moore toward the understanding of her verse was that she despised connectives. Any other assistance would have been an impoliteness, since she has always been sure of herself if not of others. The complete poem is there waiting: all the wit, the colour, the constructive ability (not a particularly strong point that however). And the quality of satisfaction gathered from reading her is that one may seek long in those exciting mazes sure of coming out at the right door in the end. There is nothing missing but the connectives.

The thought is compact, accurate, and accurately planted. In fact the garden, since it is a garden more than a statue, is found to be curiously of porcelain. It is the mythical, indestructible garden of pleasure, perhaps greatly pressed for space to-day, but there and intact, nevertheless.

I don't know where, except in modern poetry, this quality of the brittle, highly set off porcelain garden exists and nowhere in modern work better than with Miss Moore. It is this chief beauty of to-day, this hard crest to nature, that makes the best present work with its "unnatural" appearance seem so thoroughly gratuitous, so difficult to explain, and so doubly a treasure of seclusion. It is the white of a clarity beyond the facts.

There is in the newer work a perfectly definite handling of the materials with a given intention to relate them in a certain way— a handling that is intensely, intentionally selective. There is a definite place where the matters of the day may meet if they choose or not, but if they assemble it must be there. There is no compromise. Miss Moore never falls from the place inhabited by poems. It is hard to give an illustration of this from her work because it is everywhere. One must be careful, though, not to understand this as a mystical support, a danger we are skirting safely, I hope, in our time.

Poe in his most read first essay quotes Nathaniel Willis' poem, The Two Women, admiringly and in full and one senses at once the reason: there is a quality to the *feeling* there that affected Poe tremendously. This mystical quality that endeared Poe to Father Tabb the poet-priest, still seems to many the essence of poetry itself. It would be idle to name many who have been happily mystical and remained good poets: Poe, Blake, Francis Thompson, et cetera.

But what I wish to point is that there need be no stilled and archaic heaven, no ducking under religiosities to have poetry and to have it stand in its place beyond "nature." Poems have a separate existence uncompelled by nature or the supernatural. There is a "special" place which poems, as all works of art, must occupy, but it is quite definitely the same as that where bricks or coloured threads are handled.

In painting, Ingres realized the essentiality of drawing and each perfect part seemed to float free from his work, by itself. There is much in this that applies beautifully to Miss Moore. It is a perfect drawing that attains to a separate existence which might, if it please, be called mystical, but is in fact no more than the practicability of design.

To Miss Moore an apple remains an apple whether it be in Eden or the fruit bowl where it curls. But that would be hard to prove—

"dazzled by the apple."

The apple is left there, suspended. One is not made to feel that as an apple it has anything particularly to do with poetry or that as such it needs special treatment; one goes on. Because of this the direct object does seem unaffected. It seems as free from the smears of mystery, as pliant, as "natural" as Venus on the wave. Because of this her work is never indecorous as where nature is itself concerned. These are great virtues.

Without effort Miss Moore encounters the affairs which concern her as one would naturally in reading or upon a walk outdoors. She is not a Swinburne stumbling to music, but one always finds her moving forward ably, in thought, unimpeded by a rhythm. Her own rhythm is particularly revealing. It does not interfere with her progress; it is the movement of the animal, it does not put itself first and ask the other to follow.

Nor is "thought" the thing that she contends with. Miss Moore uses the thought most interestingly and wonderfully to my mind. I don't know but that this technical excellence is one of the greatest pleasures I get from her. She occupies the thought to its end, and goes on—without connectives. To me this is thrilling. The essence is not broken, nothing is injured. It is a kind hand to a merciless mind at home in the thought as in the cruder image. In the best modern verse room has been made for the best of modern thought and Miss Moore thinks straight.

Only the most modern work has attempted to do without *ex machina* props of all sorts, without rhyme, assonance, the feudal master beat, the excuse of "nature," of the spirit, mysticism, religiosity, "love," "humour," "death." Work such as Miss Moore's holds its bloom to-day not by using slang, not by its moral abandon or puritanical steadfastness, but by the aesthetic pleasure engendered where pure craftsmanship joins hard surfaces skilfully.

Poetry has taken many disguises which by cross reading or intense penetration it is possible to go through to the core. Through intersection of loci their multiplicity may become revelatory. The significance of much reading being that this "thing" grow clearer, remain fresh, be more present to the mind. To read more thoroughly than this is idleness: a common classroom absurdity.

One may agree tentatively with Glenway Wescott, that there is a division taking place in America between a proletarian art, full of sincerities, on the one side and an aristocratic and ritualistic art on the other. One may agree, but it is necessary to scrutinize such a statement carefully.

There cannot be two arts of poetry really. There is weight and there is disencumberedness. There can be no schism, except that which has always existed between art and its approaches. There cannot be a proletarian art—even among savages. There is a proletarian taste. To have achieved an organization even of that is to have escaped it.

And to organize into a pattern is also, true enough, to "approach the conditions of ritual." But here I would again go slow. I see only escape from the conditions of ritual in Miss Moore's work: a rush through wind if not toward some patent "end" at least away from pursuit, a pursuit perhaps by ritual. If from such a flight a ritual results it is more the care of those who follow than of the one who leads. "Ritual," too often to suit my ear, connotes a stereotyped mode of procedure from which pleasure has passed, whereas the poetry, to which my attention clings, if it ever knew those conditions, is distinguished only as it leaves them behind.

It is at least amusing, in this connexion, to quote from Others, Volume 1, Number 5, November 1915—quoted in turn from J. B. Kerfoot in Life: "Perhaps you are unfamiliar with this 'new poetry' that is called 'revolutionary.' . . . It is the expression of a democracy of feeling rebelling against an aristocracy of form."

> "As if a death mask ever could replace
> Life's faulty excellence!"

There are two elements essential to Miss Moore's scheme of composition: the hard and unaffected concept of the apple itself as an idea, then its edge to edge contact with the things which surround it—the coil of a snake, leaves at various depths, or as it may be; and without connectives unless it be poetry, the inevitable connective, if you will.

Marriage, through which thought does not penetrate, appeared to Miss Moore a legitimate object for art, an art that would not halt from using thought about it, however, as it might want to. Against marriage, "this institution, perhaps one should say enterprise—" Miss Moore launched her thought not to have it appear arsenaled as in a text book on psychology, but to stay among apples and giraffes in a poem. The interstices for the light and not the interstitial web of the thought concerned her, or so it seems to me. Thus the material is as the handling: the thought, the word, the rhythm—all in the style. The effect is in the penetration of the light itself, how much, how little; the appearance of the luminous background.

Of marriage there is no solution in the poem and no attempt at a solution; nor is there an attempt to shirk thought about it, to make marriage beautiful or otherwise by "poetic" treatment. There is beauty and it is thoughtless, as marriage or a cave inhabited by the sounds and colours of waves, as in the time of prismatic colour, as England with its baby rivers, as G. B. Shaw, or chanticleer, or a fish, or an elephant with its strictly practical appendages. All these things are inescapably caught in the beauty of Miss Moore's passage through them; they all have at least edges. This too is a quality that greatly pleases me: definite objects which give a clear contour to her force. Is it a flight, a symphony, a ghost, a mathematic? The usual evasion is to call them poems.

Miss Moore gets great pleasure from wiping soiled words or cutting them clean out, removing the aureoles that have been pasted about them or taking them bodily from greasy contexts. For the compositions which Miss Moore intends, each word should first stand crystal clear with no attachments; not even an aroma. As a cross light upon this Miss Moore's personal dislike for flowers that have both a satisfying appearance *and* an odour of perfume is worth noticing.

With Miss Moore a word is a word most when it is separated out by science, treated with acid to remove the smudges, washed, dried, and placed right side up on a clean surface. Now one may say that this is a word. Now it may be used, and how?

It may be used not to smear it again with thinking (the attachments of thought) but in such a way that it will remain scrupulously itself, clean, perfect, unnicked beside other words in parade. There must be edges. This casts some light I think on the simplicity of design in much of Miss Moore's work. There must be recognizable edges against the ground which cannot, as she might desire it, be left entirely white. Prose would be all black, a complete block, painted or etched over, but solid.

There is almost no overlaying at all. The effect is of every object sufficiently uncovered to be easily recognizable. This simplicity, with the light coming through from between the perfectly plain masses, is however extremely bewildering to one who has been accustomed to look at the usual "poem," the commonplace opaque board covered with vain curlicues. They forget, those who would read Miss Moore aright, that white circular discs grouped closely edge to edge upon a dark table make black six-pointed stars.

The "useful result" is an accuracy to which this simplicity of design greatly adds. The effect is for the effect to remain "true"; nothing loses its identity because of the composition, but the parts in their assembly remain quite as "natural" as before they were gathered. There is no "sentiment"; the softening effect of word upon word is nil; everything is in the style. To make this ten times evident is Miss Moore's constant care. There seems to be almost too great a wish to be transparent and it is here if anywhere that Miss Moore's later work will show a change, I think.

The general effect is of a rise through the humanities, the sciences, without evading "thought," through anything (if not everything) of the best of modern life; taking whatever there is as it comes, using it and leaving it drained of its pleasure, but otherwise undamaged. Miss Moore does not compromise science with poetry. In this again she is ably modern.

And from this clarity, this acid cleansing, this unblinking willingness, her poems result, a true modern crystallization, the fine essence of to-day which I have spoken of as the porcelain garden.

Or one will think a little of primitive masonry, the units unglued and as in the greatest early constructions unstandardized.

In such work as Critics and Connoisseurs, and Poetry, Miss Moore succeeds in having the "thing" which is her concern move freely, unencumbered by the images or the difficulties of thought. In such work there is no "suggestiveness," no tiresome "subtlety" of trend to be heavily followed, no painstaking refinement of sentiment. There is surely a choice evident in all her work, a very definite quality of choice in her material, a thinness perhaps, but a very welcome and no little surprising absence of moral tone. The choice being entirely natural and completely arbitrary is not in the least offensive, in fact it has been turned curiously to advantage throughout.

From what I have read it was in Critics and Connoisseurs that the successful method used later began first to appear: If a thought presents itself the force moves through it easily and completely: so the thought also has revealed the "thing"—that is all. The thought is used exactly as the apple, it is the same insoluble block. In Miss Moore's work the purely stated idea has an edge exactly like a fruit or a tree or a serpent.

To use anything: rhyme, thought, colour, apple, verb—so as to illumine it, is the modern prerogative; a stintless inclusion. It is Miss Moore's success.

The diction, the phrase construction, is unaffected. To use a "poetic" inversion of language, or even such a special posture of speech, still discernible in Miss Moore's earlier work, is to confess an inability to have penetrated with poetry some crevice of understanding; that special things and special places are reserved for art, that it is unable, that it requires fostering. This is unbearable.

Poetry is not limited in that way. It need not say either

> Bound without.
> Boundless within.

It has as little to do with the soul as with ermine robes or graveyards. It is not noble, sad, funny. It is poetry. It is free. It is escapeless. It goes where it will. It is in danger; escapes if it can.

This is new! The quality is not new, but the freedom is new, the unbridled leap.

The dangers are thereby multiplied—but the clarity is increased. Nothing but the perfect and the clear.   [MAY, 1925]

THE HOLLOW MEN

By T. S. Eliot

A penny for the Old Guy.

I

We are the hollow men
We are the stuffed men
Leaning together
Headpiece filled with straw. Alas!
Our dried voices, when
We whisper together
Are quiet and meaningless
As wind in dry grass
Or rats' feet over broken glass
In our dry cellar

Shape without form, shade without colour,
Paralysed force, gesture without motion;

Those who have crossed
With direct eyes, to death's other kingdom
Remember us—if at all—not as lost
Violent souls, but only
As the hollow men
The stuffed men.

II

Eyes I dare not meet in dreams
In death's dream kingdom
These do not appear:
There, the eyes are
Sunlight on a broken column
There, is a tree swinging
And voices are
In the wind's singing

More distant and more solemn
Than a fading star.

Let me be no nearer
In death's dream kingdom
Let me also wear
Such deliberate disguises
Rat's coat, crowskin, crossed staves
In a field
Behaving as the wind behaves
No nearer—

Not that final meeting
In the twilight kingdom
With eyes I dare not meet in dreams.

III

The eyes are not here
There are no eyes here
In this valley of dying stars
In this hollow valley
This broken jaw of our lost kingdoms

In this last of meeting places
We grope together
And avoid speech
Gathered on this beach of the tumid river

Sightless, unless
The eyes reappear
As the perpetual star
Multifoliate rose
Of death's twilight kingdom

The hope only
Of empty men.

[MARCH, 1925]

A CHRISTMAS STORY

By Feodor Dostoevsky

Translated From the Russian by C. M. Grand

IT was Christmas Day, the second Christmas after I had been brought to the Dead House. The convicts had been granted a holiday in honour of the occasion, and dispensed from work, which after all is not such a great favour, because it is better to work than to think, and what can one do but think when one's hands are not busy, and what can be more dreadful than thinking, when this means the remembrance of other times and other days, and what tormentor has ever been able to evade the agony of thought, when it presses with all its dead weight upon a human creature?

On that Christmas Day, the prison was very still and quiet, while its inmates were whispering to each other in hushed tones, as if afraid to break this silence and this calm otherwise than by the noise of their chains which clinked whenever they made a movement—these chains which were there to remind the poor wretches who wore them that their misery was still going on, and would go on . . . for how long . . . none could tell or remember. But for some, this was certain, until death came to release them from the burden of their doomed existences.

The prisoners had as usual received gifts from kind people in the town who had wanted them to share some of their own Christmas gladness, and they had been taken to Church, and given a better dinner than on other days. And after this meal had been partaken of, there remained nothing more for them to do but come together to cheer each other as well as they could in the big hall which served them when not out of doors, as a sleeping place and spot of reunion. Save for the flickering of a lantern left by one of the guards next to the door leading into the yard, darkness had fallen upon them, a weird unearthly kind of darkness which reminded one of all the evil thoughts kept hidden in the souls of all these men, so many among whom were criminals but in name.

The convicts, free for a few moments from the perpetual watch kept over their movements, were lying or sitting on the large wooden platform on which they slept at night; and while one of them was playing softly on a violin, half of the strings of which were either broken or missing, another was relating Christmas tales to his comrades whose attention was riveted upon his words. This was Timofey, the Thief, as he was called, who declared that he had never been so happy as in prison, because there at least he had food, and clothes, and had a roof over his head, luxuries which at times during the course of his adventurous and criminal life he had often been without. This Timofey was considered as something like a hero in the prison. He had not killed anybody, but he had taken a part in so many hold-ups and robberies that his reputation had preceded his arrival in the penal settlement, where he had immediately assumed a preponderant position by virtue of his past misdeeds. He was always jovial and pleasant, and ready to oblige others, and he had ever so many amusing stories to relate about his past life, before he had been arrested and sent to prison for several years, the number of which he had already forgotten, so satisfied did he feel with his present lot. The guards all liked him, because he had never been caught in an act of disobedience or insubordination; and yet there was a general feeling all around, among the convicts as well as among the turnkeys, that Timofey had better be left alone, and not be interfered with, because if aroused, he might . . . well he might turn out disagreeable, and we all know what this word means in a prison.

I was looking at all the shaved heads around me, and wondering what I could do next, when a deep sigh aroused my attention. It came from a fellow sitting a little apart from the other prisoners, all by himself, a fellow who was known by the name of Illia the Fool. He was a new-comer, and it was his first Christmas in the prison. His nickname had come to him, because of the complete indifference which he displayed in regard to everything that was going on around him, and of his dumb docility not only before the guards, but also in complying with the many requirements of the other convicts, who tyrannized over him, and used him as a kind of man of all work, saddling upon him those tasks of the prison which no one cared to perform, such as to carry out the pails, and so forth. He was about thirty years old, a short, rather stout fellow, blind in one eye, with a face deeply scarred by smallpox. He had committed murder, and was serving a life sentence, but he had never been heard to complain about it, nor to imply that his sentence had not been a just one, but seemed to have accepted it, as something that was due him, and this was what had earned for him, at least partly, his nickname of "Fool," which Timofey had been the first one to give him. As you know, nicknames are very frequent in penal settlements, liked as a rule by convicts, perhaps because their guards invariably call them by their numbers. Illia was no exception, and always grinned when he heard them call out, "Fool, where are you?"

But on this Christmas afternoon, Illia the Fool, appeared to me to be different from what he was on other days. For one thing he had sighed, and this I had never heard him do before. There was such bitter sorrow in the sound of that sigh, moreover, that it struck a soft cord in my heart, and made it ache as it had not done for a long while. I drew nearer to the man and ventured to ask him of what he had been thinking, that made him so particularly sad.

"Oh, my little Pigeon, you could not understand it," he replied, "I was only thinking of my small Wassia, of my little goat. What has happened to Wassia, where is Wassia? This is the only thing I would like to know. Oh, if anybody could just tell me where is Wassia and whether Wassia is happy and well cared for, I would ask nothing further from God, or from His Saints!"

"Who is Wassia, will you not tell me?" I enquired, expecting that he would mention the name of a brother or of a sweetheart.

He looked at me, replying with an accent of surprise, "Why, I have just told you, Wassia was my little goat."

I still did not understand, but not wishing to grieve the poor fellow, who was in real misery, I asked him if he would not relate to me the history of Wassia.

"It is Christmas Day, and perhaps it would soothe your grief if you told your story to someone who could sympathize with you," I added.

He sighed again.

"Ah! Little Pigeon, how could you understand it? But you are right all the same; perhaps it will do me good to tell you!"

And as he spoke, I saw a tear drop from his one eye and roll down his cheek.

"I will tell you, Little Pigeon," he said at last, "I will tell you, although I have never yet told it to any one before; there are days when one must speak or one will die. You see, Little Pigeon, I never had a mother. I was found lying in a basket—a baby just a few days old—by the grave-digger of our village in the church-yard, when he went to dig a grave for a woman who had died that morning. The grave-digger was a good man and he took me to his home. The same afternoon, the priest baptized me and they gave me the name of Illia because it had been on the day of Illia the Prophet that I had been found. Since no one knew who were my parents, of course people thought that my mother had never been married, and had abandoned me out of shame. As I grew up, the other boys laughed at me and taunted me with my dis-grace, until I used to think sometimes I hated them all. But still I was not unhappy; you must not think that I was unhappy, Little Pigeon, because it would not be true. The grave-digger was a good man, his wife, also, was a good woman who cared for me, gave me food, made me some clothes, and did not beat me too much or too often. Then when I was about ten years old, God sent them a little daughter. I loved that child so much, so much. Anisia she was called, and I used to watch over Anisia while her mother was out in the fields working. I rocked her in my arms, drove the flies away from her face, and led her by the hand when she began to walk. Then one day when a big dog wanted to bite her because she had teased it, I threw myself before her; you can see here, Little Pigeon, where that dog bit me instead of her," and as he spoke, he raised the sleeve of his shirt, and made me look at a deep scar on his arm. "Anisia was all the world to me; when I was twenty years old and she was ten, I used to take her on my knee, and to tell her that when she was grown up, I would marry her. A neighbour heard me one day, and told my foster mother, who scolded me and said that I must not say such things to Anisia because it was putting wrong ideas into her head, because she could never become my wife. But still I went on say-ing them to her, only I took care that no one should hear me. I really thought then that Anisia loved me and would always care for me.

"Well, Little Pigeon, one day after I had worked hard in the fields and got very wet from the rain that surprised us on our way home, I became ill, and the *feldscher* who was called to see me said that I had caught smallpox. He took me away to the hospital in the district town. After I had recovered, my face was what you see it to-day, and I had lost the sight of my right eye. I was not an object for any girl to like to look upon, and was wise enough to know it. So when I returned home, I did not say any more to Anisia that I wanted to marry her; I only tried to please her, and to make myself useful to her. After I had scraped a little money together, I bought her a present for Christmas—a little goat she had admired one morning when she had seen it in the village. It was such a pretty little white thing, we called it Wassia. I used to take care of it and to feed it, so that Anisia had no trouble whatever with it, but only played with it when she liked."

He stopped for a moment, the tears gathering in his one eye, then asked me, "Are you sure I do not bore you, Little Pigeon?"

"No, no, go on," I replied, because by that time I had become intensely interested.

"Well, time went on; at last Anisia was grown up; the boys began to hang around her, and the women to say that she would soon be married. She was the beauty of the place, and Foma, the innkeeper, who was reputed to be the richest man in the whole village, was constantly seen with her and danced with her at all the harvest festivals to which she was bidden. This did not please me, because I knew that Foma was a good-for-nothing fellow who had been in many scrapes with girls, always coming out of them by some trick or other. I tried to warn Anisia, but she refused to listen to me, and at last became very angry with me, saying that she would never speak to me again unless I stopped talking about Foma. I could see that she was quite changed. She did not care any more for Wassia and ceased to caress or play with it. So that poor Wassia, who by this time was quite an old goat, seemed to feel it, looking so sad when unable to attract her attention that I had to take it in my arms to comfort it. Then we would weep together, and I thought that at least there remained one being in the world who cared for me, to whom I could be useful.

"It is dreadful, Little Pigeon, to feel quite alone in the world. This was my case; and when one day, Anisia came to tell me that she was going to marry Foma after lent, I felt that if Wassia had not been there, I would just have gone down to the river and thrown myself in it.

"Well, time passed, the summer was over, and the harvest had all been taken in. Then Anisia and Foma were married. Anisia came to show herself to me in all her bridal finery, with quantities of red beads around her neck, and a nice red handkerchief tied around her throat. Foma had a new pair of boots bought for the occasion, and a new pink shirt; and everybody said that they were a comely pair. Before she went away to her husband's *isba,* Anisia came to me again, and told me that she would leave me Wassia to take care of; and in saying so, seemed to imply that she was conferring a great favour upon me. Perhaps she was. Who knows!

"Well, Little Pigeon, I hardly ever saw her afterwards, and Wassia was all that was left to me. My little goat! It did not mind my one eye and scarred face. We used to sleep together on the straw in the barn; it would put its head upon my shoulder, and lick my face with its tongue. I was happy then, Little Pigeon, because I could imagine that it was Anisia who was kissing me.

"Well, this did not last long," he went on, his voice trembling a little, "there came a day when Anisia returned, and told me that she wanted to have Wassia back, to take it to her own cottage to play with as she used to do when she was a little girl. By that time I knew that she was not as happy as she had expected to be with Foma, but this was not a reason why she should want to take Wassia away from me, who had nothing else but this little animal to make me happy. I begged her to leave me the goat, I said that she would not know how to take care of it, that Wassia was an old goat requiring more attention than she would have the time or the patience to give. I said everything I could think of to induce her to leave me the animal, but she refused to listen to me. She laughed when I told her that Wassia was all I had left in the world to remind me of her. She laughed and said that her husband wanted Wassia, and that she was going to take it away with her and give it to her husband!

"Then, Little Pigeon, something went over me I had never felt before. I happened to have an axe in my hand with which I had been chopping wood and—and I killed Anisia!"

And a deep sob shook his strong frame.

"Fool, oh, you Fool, where are you?" called a voice from the other end of the room, where the convicts were all talking as loud as they could now that their attention had been diverted from the sadness of their own lot by the stories Timofey had been telling them.

"Fool, Fool, where are you?" one of the prisoners cried out again. "Come over here, you are wanted to empty the *parascha.*"

"I am coming, I am coming," responded Illia as he rushed to obey, murmuring between his teeth, "Wassia—who can tell me what has become of her! Where is Wassia!"

[SEPTEMBER, 1925]

COMMENT

THE DIAL is an intellectual sewer.
John Christen Johansen.

AMONG the industrial centres of the State of Massachusetts there is one well-known as Worcester. In this wholesome and brimming receptacle of legitimate activity a morning newspaper, entitled The Worcester Telegram, remains [since the death of the late G. Stanley Hall] the outstanding intellectual effort.

Myself having had the fortune to be born in the City of Worcester, I am naturally sensitive to the good opinion of her townsmen. I was therefore appreciably let down at reading in The Worcester Telegram:

"THE DIAL is an intellectual sewer."

Mr John Christen Johansen, to whom the generously-typed heading of the six-column illustrated interview alludes as

FAMOUS AMERICAN ARTIST

and of whom his interviewer writes:

"He studied with Vanderpoel, Duveneck, Whistler, Freer, Lawrens [sic]—but why mention his masters? He is Johansen!"

this distinguished gentleman has been painting a portrait of the President of what in Worcester, Massachusetts, is alluded to as "An Institution of the Higher Learning"; to wit, Clark University. It was therefore wholly natural that he should be interviewed at length by The Worcester Telegram, and wholly natural he should express himself in a straightforward fashion upon the present state of that art which he practises. And there is no reason under heaven why he should not say his word upon those workers, contemporary with himself, whom he regards as at once misled and misleading. And I wholly agree with Mr Johansen (and with Pablo Picasso as well [1]) that, as Mr Johansen briefly puts it,

[1] Cf. the interview with Picasso printed in The Arts for May, 1921: "Cubism is no different from any other school of painting. The same principles and the same elements are common to all." And *passim*.

"There is no such thing as 'the modern,' or 'the new' in art. There is good, or bad."

I regret only that Mr Johansen is so misinformed as to believe:

"They ['modern' artists] are not willing to spend any time on craft, in learning how to do things well."

Failing personal acquaintance with any serious 'modern' artist, a reading of THE DIAL (did Mr Johansen not take his moral exception to it) as, for example, of the article by Hans Purrmann on Henri Matisse,[1] might have disabused Mr Johansen of this wholly ungrounded if, among the vulgar, wide-spread illusion.

But why narrate this anecdote?

"Several years later I saw that 'modern' painter again, with some other pictures he had recently made to hang in his own home. They were nothing at all like the horrors we had seen before. They were real art.

" 'What has become of your enthusiasm over the futuristic school?' I asked.

" 'Oh,' he replied, 'I am painting for my own pleasure and not for the public.' "

Surely Mr Johansen is not unaware that the canvases of Picasso, when he was yet painting in a relatively realistic manner, were quite regularly bringing decent figures? And that his public pretty generally[2] refused to stomach and to buy his cubistic work? And that there are scores of such 'modern' artists now working throughout Europe and America, men who must carry on their daily industry in the teeth of the matter-of-fact knowledge that there exists

---

[1] Purrmann, writing as a student in Matisse's "workshop," reports: "Matisse's efforts were directed to the establishment of a rigid discipline in his studio. He proclaimed the value of caution, he led painters back to the solid foundation of study, to a long and patient observation." And he quotes Matisse as follows: " 'You are not committing suicide if you lean more on nature and strive for an exact reproduction. You must first subject yourself to nature, recapture it, then motivate it and perhaps even heighten its beauty! But you must be able to walk well on the ground before you get on the tight-rope.' "

[2] Certain German buyers were an exception.

in this world no market for their product? And that these men might, if they would but paint as they learned to paint in the schools, and as they there demonstrated they well can paint,—that these men might then earn what is vulgarly called 'a gentlemanly living'? And that, after all, it is Mr J. C. Johansen and not either Pablo Picasso or Miss Georgia O'Keeffe who is in the anyhow financially enviable habit of being invited to paint a life-sized portrait of President Wallace Walter Atwood of Clark University?

And why in discussing 'Modern Art' pose this question?

"Why try to force the beliefs and ideas of Eastern Europe on us? We are not the type of people for it. It is our ambition to be clean, wholesome, decent."

Is not Mr Johansen aware that the tendency in art against which he inveighs originated in France? And that its leaders, with the exception of Picasso, who is a Spaniard, have been Frenchmen? Is France (or is Spain, for that matter) in Eastern Europe? Is it the ambition of the French "type of people" to be unclean, unwholesome, indecent?

And surely one who, like Mr Johansen, would appear to prefer that artists should paint for their "own pleasure and not for the public" [1] cannot be correctly reported as having said:

"I remember that a woman who had no taste asked my advice about buying pictures. Any academic mind can discover what is really best in paintings or pictures. I told her to buy a $5 one, and live with it a while, then to buy a $10 picture, and live with it, and when she felt like it to buy another, a $15 picture, and when she had three, she would begin to have a basis for comparison of values, and would begin to learn!"

Not only, one guesses, must his word have been '*un*academic' but also this counsel to buy pictures at different prices must be an emanation of a less idealistic mind [2] than that of Mr J. C. Johansen. Buy three pictures; live with them; compare their values as pictures,—by all means! But what has their *commercial* value, their value for the picture-buying *public*, to do with this affair at all?

[1] See the previous page.
[2] The interview with Mr. Johansen was obtained by Margaret Brandenburg, the wife of the Professor of Economics at Clark University.

The intelligence that Mr Johansen already "has painted Hague [sic], Joffre, Diaz, and many military heroes whose portraits are hung in the National Museum of Art, Washington, D. C." and that "his next portrait will be that of President Coolidge" (also, one gathers, for the same august asylum) brings, at this juncture, to the American Citizenry very general relief. Citizens have read how their Chief Executive, as also his good wife, the First Lady of Our Land, have recently been rendered upon canvas (and with natural *éclat*) by Mr Howard Chandler Christy; and of how these two in many ways very considerable canvases now enliven the interior of Washington's Historic Whited House. Some of us have indeed been so privileged as to glimpse, in the elegant photogravure reproductions, these domestic Van Dykes. It is therefore, just now, particularly reassuring to know that despite this recent aesthetic enrichment of the Executive Mansion the balance of aesthetic power, at our seat of government, need not be disturbed. The National Museum of Art, Washington, D. C. can, THE DIAL is now confident, continue to keep up its august end.

From this illuminating interview I further quote two consecutive paragraphs, these latter merely for their documentary value as bearing upon Contemporary American Civilization:

"And it is because Mr Johansen is intellectual, and critical, that he likes to paint college professors and presidents, men identified with science, literature, economic and educational questions.

"Few women have been included among his portraits. Perhaps one reason is that he paints people as they are upon the stage. If they are too refined, the effect is lost."

We herefrom may deduce:—*Primum*, that, as in that England from which the original American settlers emigrated, so in America to-day, women are not "upon the stage." *Secundum*, that refinement is in America, by and large, an appurtenance of the female sex. *Tertium*, that in America "college professors and presidents" are not "too refined." . . . Upon this third point we had indeed, from the same Worcesterian source, been adequately *documentés*.

One recalls that a nationally known American economist was invited, with the consent of the President, to address a group of students in Clark University; and that because this guest's economic opinions, despite signally measured utterance, did none the less occasion in the learned President of that University an acute disorder, this guest was not permitted to complete his address,— that the learned President in person mounted the platform and commanded the janitor to put out the lights. . . .

One recalls that The Worcester Telegram then published this pertinent paragraph:

"Preston E. James of Dr. Atwood's geography department said yesterday that Harvard University, by retaining Dr. Laski, a so-called Liberal professor, had lost $1,000,000 in endowments. He said that if such speakers as Nearing were allowed, Clark would suffer similar consequences."

And that the same esteemed contemporary journal, after regretting, upon the part of the student body of Clark University, misplaced interest in Freedom of Speech, adventured the following pertinent editorial observation:

"Perhaps it is unfortunate Clark college boys do not indulge themselves more extensively in baseball, football and other matters of such critical importance in the lives of ordinary collegians."

That the natural interest of young manhood in athletic games and competition should in America be so hypertrophied as quite to expunge all moral, political, and intellectual interests from American university undergraduate life would appear to be not wholly insusceptible of explanation.

[MAY, 1925]

SPRING FLIGHT

THE GREAT GATSBY. *By F. Scott Fitzgerald. 12mo.*
218 pages. Charles Scribner's Sons. $2.

THERE has never been any question of the talents of F. Scott Fitzgerald; there has been, justifiably until the publication of The Great Gatsby, a grave question as to what he was going to do with his gifts. The question has been answered in one of the finest of contemporary novels. Fitzgerald has more than matured; he has mastered his talents and gone soaring in a beautiful flight, leaving behind him everything dubious and tricky in his earler work, and leaving even farther behind all the men of his own generation and most of his elders.

In all justice, let it be said that the talents are still his. The book is even more interesting, superficially, than his others; it has an intense life, it must be read, the first time, breathlessly; it is vivid and glittering and entertaining. Scenes of incredible difficulty are rendered with what seems an effortless precision, crowds and conversation and action and retrospects—everything comes naturally and persuasively. The minor people and events are threads of colour and strength, holding the principal things together. The technical virtuosity is extraordinary.

All this was true of Fitzgerald's first two novels, and even of those deplorable short stories which one feared were going to ruin him. The Great Gatsby adds many things, and two above all: the novel is composed as an artistic structure, and it exposes, again for the first time, an interesting temperament. "The vast juvenile intrigue" of This Side of Paradise is just as good subject-matter as the intensely private intrigue of The Great Gatsby; but Fitzgerald racing over the country, jotting down whatever was current in college circles, is not nearly as significant as Fitzgerald regarding a tiny section of life and reporting it with irony and pity and a consuming passion. The Great Gatsby is passionate as Some Do Not is passionate, with such an abundance of feeling for the characters (feeling their integral reality, not hating or loving them objectively) that the most trivial of the actors in the drama are endowed with vitality. The concentration of the book is so intense that the principal characters exist almost as essences, as biting acids that find themselves in the same golden cup and have no choice but to act upon each other. And the *milieux* which are brought into such violent contact with each other are as full of character, and as immitigably compelled to struggle and to debase one another.

The book is written as a series of scenes, the method which Fitzgerald derived from Henry James through Mrs Wharton, and these scenes are reported by a narrator who was obviously intended to be much more significant than he is. The author's appetite for life is so violent that he found the personality of the narrator an obstacle, and simply ignored it once his actual people were in motion, but the narrator helps to give the feeling of an intense unit which the various characters around Gatsby form. Gatsby himself remains a mystery; you know him, but not by knowing about him, and even at the end you can guess, if you like, that he was a forger or a dealer in stolen bonds, or a rather mean type of bootlegger. He had dedicated himself to the accomplishment of a supreme object, to restore to himself an illusion he had lost; he set about it, in a pathetic American way, by becoming incredibly rich and spending his wealth in incredible ways, so that he might win back the girl he loved; and a "foul dust floated in the wake of his dreams." Adultery and drunkenness and thievery and murder make up this dust, but Gatsby's story remains poignant and beautiful.

This means that Fitzgerald has ceased to content himself with a satiric report on the outside of American life and has with considerable irony attacked the spirit underneath, and so has begun to report on life in its most general terms. His tactile apprehension remains so fine that his people and his settings are specifically of Long Island; but now he meditates upon their fate, and they become universal also. He has now something of extreme importance to say; and it is good fortune for us that he knows how to say it.

The scenes are austere in their composition. There is one, the tawdry afternoon of the satyr, Tom Buchanan, and his cheap and "vital" mistress, which is alive by the strength of the lapses of time; another, the meeting between Gatsby and his love, takes place literally behind closed doors, the narrator telling us only the beginning and the end. The variety of treatment, the intermingling of dialogue and narrative, the use of a snatch of significant detail instead of a big scene, make the whole a superb impressionistic painting, vivid in colour, and sparkling with meaning. And the major composition is as just as the treatment of detail. There is a brief curve before Gatsby himself enters; a longer one in which he begins his movement toward Daisy; then a succession of carefully spaced shorter and longer movements until the climax is reached. The plot works out not like a puzzle with odd bits falling into place, but like a tragedy, with every part functioning in the completed organism.

Even now, with The Great Gatsby before me, I cannot find in the earlier Fitzgerald the artistic integrity and the passionate feeling which this book possesses. And perhaps analysing the one and praising the other, both fail to convey the sense of elation which one has in reading his new novel. Would it be better to say that even The Great Gatsby is full of faults, and that that doesn't matter in the slightest degree? The cadences borrowed from Conrad, the occasional smartness, the frequently startling, but ineffective adjective—at last they do not signify. Because for the most part you know that Fitzgerald has consciously put these bad and half-bad things behind him, that he trusts them no more to make him the white-headed boy of The Saturday Evening Post, and that he has recognized both his capacities and his obligations as a novelist.

GILBERT SELDES

[AUGUST, 1925]

BRIEFER MENTION

SPECULATIONS, by T. E. Hulme (8vo, 271 pages; Harcourt, Brace: $3.75) is a book of stimulating suggestion rather than a treatise of accumulative logical power. Mr Hulme thinks at the sword's point. His opinions resolve themselves into a positively ferocious statement of two opposed sets of antipodal ideals; the first to be denounced in terms of opprobrium, such as "sloppy," "messy," "sticky," "slushy"; the second to be commended in terms of emphatic praise, such as "Byzantine," "applied Egyptian," "cubistic," "non-vital." The two sets of ideals are applied to art, ethics, religion, and politics, and may be summed up thus. What is reprobated is described as romantic, democratic, humanistic, naturalistic. What is eulogized is described as classical, geometrical, traditional, hard, dry, and cheerfully tragic. The "new Weltanschauung" he advocates has something in common with that of Heraclitus; but more with that of L'Action Française.

[FEBRUARY, 1925]

CHILLS AND FEVER, by John Crowe Ransom (12mo, 95 pages; Knopf: $1.50). Unrewarding dissonances, mountebank persiflage, mock mediaeval minstrelsy, and shreds of elegance disturbingly suggestive of now this, now that contemporary bard, deprive one of the faculty to diagnose this "dangerous" phenomenon to which one has exposed oneself. [APRIL, 1925]

PRINCIPLES OF LITERARY CRITICISM, by I. A. Richards (12mo, 290 pages; Harcourt, Brace: $3.75). The author here undertakes to study art values in accordance with his contention that there is no "aesthetic emotion," no experience in art different from experience outside of art "as, say, envy is from remembering, or as mathematical calculation is from eating cherries." By his analysis of the nature of communication he shows how any simple divorce between art and life is purely verbal, while the conception of beauty as a quality attached to objects is merely the result of a linguistic convenience being mistaken for some external denotable attribute. Mr Richards' doctrines are eclectic; they are arranged and applied with much deftness, his equipment including not only a keen sense of artistic values, but also a grasp of allied problems, a knowledge of the psychology laboratory, and a gratifying skill at definition.

[JULY, 1925]

IN THE AMERICAN GRAIN, by William Carlos Williams (10mo, 235 pages; A. & C. Boni: $3). Appraising in the name of beauty, Montezuma, Christopher Columbus, Ponce de Leon, Benjamin Franklin, Abraham Lincoln, Edgar Allan Poe, Aaron Burr, and others, Dr Williams finds in these separate studies, interrelated proof of American aesthetic deprivedness, or is it depravity? "Morals are deformed in the name of PURITY;" he says, "till, in the confusion, almost nothing remains of the great American New World but a memory of the Indian." Unsubmissive to his pessimism and sometimes shocked by the short work which he makes of decorum, verbal and other, we wisely salute the here assembled phosphorescent findings of a search prosecuted "with antennae extended." In The Discovery of the West Indies and in The Destruction of Tenochtitlan, in the giltheads, parrots, lizards, and wandlike naked people of the one, as in the eloquent minutiae of the other, we recognize a superbly poetic *orificeria* of meaning and of material—in the idols, the jasper, the birds of prey, the "lions and other animals of the cat kind," the wrought stone and wrought leather, the silver, the gold, and the courtyard "paved with handsome flags in the style of a chessboard." [MARCH, 1926]

THE VATICAN SWINDLE, by Andre Gide, translated from the French by Dorothy Bussy (12mo, 278 pages; Knopf: $2.50). An impostor was thundering from the Vatican; meanwhile the true Pope Leo XIII had been confined in a dungeon under the Castle of San Angelo, from which he could be rescued only by an enormous bribe. Such was the lie at the basis of the Vatican swindle. The adventures of the swindlers and their victims form a rapid and fascinating, in many respects a great novel; its significance goes far beyond the theme. It may or may not be M Gide's best work. Probably it is "the last from the standpoint of his development as a novelist," as M Lalou said; and certainly it is the novel which has exerted the most powerful influence on the development of French literature since the war. [MAY, 1926]

THE PLUMED SERPENT, by D. H. Lawrence (10mo, 445 pages; Knopf: $3). Like the theme of a symphony which recurs again and again in the midst of shifting harmonies Mr Lawrence's *idée fixe* shows itself in each of his succeeding books. Here is the same love motif, the dark "sex-alive" male, savage yet childish, and the disillusioned, sophisticated woman craving sex domination. Together, as usual, they "flash" in "strange reciprocity." The background of the present novel is that of modern Mexico, and we are initiated, with Mr Lawrence's customary imaginative insight and versatility, into the various activities of this sensational country. If one is interested in the revival of ancient religious cults, in bullfights, and in revolutions, there is much that is instructive and entertaining in this volume, but if one's chief interest is Mr Lawrence there is nothing new to learn. [JUNE, 1926]

THOSE OF LUCIFER

By Malcolm Cowley

Out of an empty sky the dust of hours
a word was spoken and a folk obeyed
an island uttered incandescent towers
like frozen simultaneous hymns to trade

Here, in their lonely multitude of powers
thrones, virtues, archangelic cavalcade
they rise
   proclaiming Sea and sky are ours
and yours O man the shadow of our shade

Or did a poet crazed with dignity
rear them upon an island to prolong
his furious contempt for sky and sea

To what emaciated hands belong
these index fingers of infinity

O towers of intolerable song

[July, 1925]

261

PARIS LETTER

April, 1926

PAUL VALERY has written: "It was my idiosyncrasy to love . . . in art only the creative process." [1] This saying might well be inscribed as epigraph upon the last page of André Gide's new novel, Les Faux Monnayeurs, in which Edward who is Gide himself observes similarly: "I make notes day by day of the progress made by my novel in my mind, keeping as it were a sort of diary. Imagine the interest which such a note-book from the pen of Balzac or Dickens would have for us! An account of the prenatal origins of the novel would be more absorbing perhaps than the novel itself." Although Les Faux Monnayeurs is long—it contains nearly five hundred pages and this is long for a French novel—it is never tiresome. Possibly piqued by recent attacks upon him, it would seem that Gide has, while retaining his more familiar characteristics, made a point in this book of appearing suave and even amusing. The book comprises five or six interrelated plots which far from confusing and tiring the reader are cleverly developed and maintained, thanks to the central character, Gide himself, who with extreme clarity and self-awareness follows step by step the progress of his book, ridiculing its faults— none of which escapes him—and disarming all possible criticism. In the first plot, a young man finds that he is an illegitimate child, and leaves home. His subsequent travels, diversified by many dangers, form a theme upon which have been embroidered the philanderings of a vain, unscrupulous adventurer. By comparison with other portraits in an excellent gallery of contemporaries, the portrait of Lady Griffith, the English *inamorata,* seems lifeless and artificial. To compensate for this disappointment, we have in each of the other situations, one unforgettable caricature: Count de Passavant whose artistic tastes and snobbish respect for so-called "advanced" talent, not to mention morals, have placed beyond the pale of society—a composite photograph of two well-known Parisians, recognizable to everyone and whom as a matter of fact everyone has recognized; and the old music-teacher, La Pérouse, a touching figure, over whom hovers the genius of Dostoevsky.

[1] Cf. Entretiens avec Paul Valéry, by Frédéric Lefèvre.

Starting from the same point, Valéry and Gide advance toward diametrically opposed solutions of the literary problem. Valéry posits as his goal pure, gratuitous intellectual energy, the gratuitous activity of disinterested mind, indifferent to the very content of its thought and reduced to "the supreme poverty of purposeless power." His theory is explicit in Une Soirée avec Monsieur Teste [1] and in Introduction à la Méthode de Léonard da Vinci.[2] This ideal activity is in sharp contrast to the ideal passivity with which Gide meets the external world—a world envisaged as a neutral ground where causes are generated and effects derived while the work of art matures as indifferently as a plant. Gide even denies having selected special characters. "I did not seek them," he asserts ruefully; "They happened to be ahead of me in my path, and I followed them." Rather, he followed himself through the labyrinths of his curiosity, a curiosity that has grown stronger each year until it has become identical with human sympathy; though when we consider his refusal to summon a doctor on the occasion of Olivier's suicide, we must admit that this sympathy is tempered by a fair share of prudence. Perhaps it is after all only a kind of scepticism, intelligent, uncourageous, keeping him always, in spite of everything, on the edge of life. Because he has desired above all else plasticity, he has ceased to exist. Once again in Les Faux Monnayeurs there is that Gidesque mingling of protestantism and paganism which permeates all his work from L'Immoraliste to L'Enfant Prodigue. After all we must continue to take Gide as we find him. Even people who appear to themselves extremely unstable never really change. They never rid themselves of their failings— and that is excellent; for when we seek to improve ourselves, we succeed merely in substituting for natural vices artificial virtues. And only what is natural matters.

In Les Faux Monnayeurs we have a definition of the ideal novel, which begins: "A novel which would be at once as true and as remote from reality, as human and as fictitious as Athalie . . ." What Gide describes thus, and what he will himself never create, for he lacks that true sympathy for human beings which is the first requisite of a novelist, has been achieved by Proust, whose sudden

[1] Published in THE DIAL, February 1922, under the title, An Evening with M Teste.
[2] Cf. Note and Digression, appended to Introduction to the Method of Leonardo da Vinci, and published in this issue of THE DIAL, pages 447–457.

fame so disquieted Gide. La Prisonnière, the two volumes of M
Proust's new book, concludes the long series of A La Recherche
du Temps Perdu, which began in 1913 with Du Côté de Chez
Swann. There still remains to be published Le Temps Retrouvé.
The first volume of La Prisonnière, in which we learn of the sudden
death of Albertine, is a long analysis of the suffering caused by
the death of a dearly loved person, especially of the forgetting that
ensues. In 1916 I left for Rome. "I am very sorry," Proust
said to me, "first because you are leaving, but especially because I
know I am going to forget you." The whole of La Prisonnière is
contained in this ironic sally. In the second volume we again encounter Gilberte, Swann's daughter, whose love-affair with the
author, one recalls, fills a large part of the first book. She is now a
Gilberte grown worldly, and avid for social position, which she obtains and transcends by marrying Saint Loup; the marriage turns
out badly. Reading these last volumes, in which the brilliant
aristocrats of the early books have become adventurers, perverts,
feeble puppets in the hands of their secretaries and their servants,
has a curious effect on one. Certainly we recognize here Proust's
appreciation of the aesthetic value of social contrasts, the obligation
laid upon the novelist to show how society evolves, how the great
are brought low and the humble raised up. But the lesson of
Proust's world derives from something more personal than the
exigencies of art. Implicit in his conclusions is a lust for sacrilege,
a compulsion to defile and degrade that aristocratic society which
was once worshipped by him to excess, and to be thus washed clean
of the taint of servility. His passionate interest in servants can
be explained perhaps as a form of the spirit of revolt inherited from
Jewish ancestors. In short his preoccupations can be traced to
mysterious, deep-rooted emotional trends which would justify ex-
haustive study. The essay on death with which the first volume
opens is a prolonged lament in which the very depths of grief
are plumbed. These pages, the essay on the jealousy of Swann, and
the chapters devoted to the inconstancies of the heart, must surely
place Proust with Montaigne and Meredith. Even in the unfinished,
tentative condition of a posthumous work (for we all know how
carefully Proust revised his proofs) we recognize in reading this
book the exaltation of the great immortals. Proust employs no pretentious literary devices: he describes, he indulges in reminiscences,
he initiates chains of association, he makes us forget Albertine

by tempting us to meditations upon universal themes—then ends
each paragraph with the simple words: But Albertine was dead—
words which explain everything, and efface everything. It is impossible to describe the solemn grandeur of this veritable *Dies
Irae*. It recalls the liturgical chants of the Jews before the Wall
of Lamentations, in which unconsoled by the hope implicit in other
religions we seem to touch the profoundest depths of human woe.
The darkest, the most desperate annihilation has for Proust this
same irresistible attraction.

To these two books of supreme importance to French letters
there has recently been added a third, Bella by Giraudoux. A
novel which has firmly established the reputation of its talented
young author, it has provoked a storm of controversy in France
and created a sensation abroad, particularly in Central Europe.
Giraudoux has beyond doubt been successful in this first attempt
of his to treat a subject of wide implications and of such immediate
contemporary interest that it is, as it were, still hot to the touch.
The book is a Romeo and Juliet of modern life. We have a
poetic simplification of the Capulets and Montagues in the families
of two French statesmen, the din of whose quarrels has re-echoed
throughout France during the past ten years—the Poincaré and
the Berthelot. The son of the latter (called by Giraudoux the
Durandeau) has fallen in love with Bella, the beautiful daughter
of the Poincaré-Rebendart, and Bella, like Juliet, by dying con-
trives the *dénouement*. This novel is a welcome innovation in
Giraudoux's work, for with Juliette au Pays des Hommes, his
next-to-the-last book, he had exhausted the possibilities of his
early method; we had grown weary of his exquisite but ghostly
creatures, beyond words aerial and unearthly. In Bella the author
abruptly breaks with the tradition to which his readers had become habituated and creates figures of substance and weight, in-
controvertibly flesh and blood. Employing qualities of social
satirist and political cartoonist which few of us had suspected, he
has given us not only a remarkable political pamphlet but a great
work of art.

André Maurois has published this week a collection of three short
stories, Meïpe ou la Délivrance.[1] The curious word Meïpe which

[1] Mape: The World of Illusion. By André Maurois. Translated by Eric Sutton.
16mo. 247 pages. D. Appleton and Company. $2.50.

has no meaning in any language, and is neither the name of a place nor of a person, is used by him to designate an imaginary planet, an unknown land, and is an invention of the author's little daughter. Thither she retreats when our unromantic life becomes too tiresome. "In Meïpe it never rains, everyone has a good time, fathers do not read all day long, and never say when they are asked to play Old Maid, I have to work. Children in that country go to a shop and choose their own parents." Maurois himself draws the conclusion: "Only artists who are truly great can create a world as unpredictable as the real one." The three stories are like three trains travelling at different rates of speed, all bound for Meïpe. In one railway-carriage Goethe is our fellow-traveller. He tells us of his youth and recounts in a series of sentimental adventures, in which he was both actor and spectator, the conception and growth of Werther. In the second tale, we have a young man who models his behaviour upon Balzac and patterns his love-affairs after those of an imaginary hero of the great novelist (for other books also serve to transport us to Meïpe). The last—and best—story depicts the life of the beautiful Mrs Siddons, so daring, so virtuous, and, as one said in those days, so *"sensible."* In that kind of vivid, animated, poetic biography, whose secret was first captured by Strachey, the author recreates the past and its vanished personages. The English-speaking public of whom Maurois is so fond and who reciprocates his affection, will be sure to read his new book with a satisfaction equal to our own.

Pierre Benoit, world's champion of one hundred and one dramatic situations, alternates purely fictitious so-called "novels of adventure" with novels of psychological adventure where rapid, highly-simplified emotions are generated, brought into contact, and in the end reciprocally destroyed. Such feminized emotions are less simple and more perverse than the majority of the unsophisticated readers of this popular novelist would believe. Lacking the psychological dexterity of Mademoiselle de la Ferte, which is Benoit's finest book, Alberte is nevertheless a very engaging younger sister.

Turning to works of literary criticism, I should like to note Figures Etrangères by Edmond Jaloux: studies of Cervantes, Walpole, Shelley, Jane Austen, Whitman, Meredith, Chekov, et cetera. Jaloux who has read everything written in French and has also gained much from association with foreign authors (in any case more than most of his compatriots) appears in this book what he really is—the most impartial, the most intelligent, and the most thoroughly-informed critic that we have.

The book on Péguy by the Tharaud brothers is not only the pious discharging of a debt to friendship but also the best biography of Péguy that has been published. Péguy exercised a notable influence upon the group of young intelligences which was before the war united under the aegis of the Cahiers de la Quinzaine. This review was discontinued in 1914—upon the rim of disaster. (Is it not upon the edge of precipices that geologists study to best advantage the strata of the earth?)

Jean Cocteau, in Le Retour à L'Ordre, has assembled in one book a number of articles published since 1920: Le Coq et L'Arlequin,[1] Carte Blanche, Le Secret Professional, Picasso, et cetera—a series of illuminating and witty commentaries on the modern battle of the arts. These essays date from yesterday; the title which suggests a reaction on the part of the temerarious writer is of to-day. There is not perhaps between the two so intimate a connexion as the author would like to think and the curve of progress is more sinuous than consistent; but the book remains none the less a very useful contribution to the history of the years since 1920, years so vital for France and so chaotic for us all.

I noted recently the important work of Monsieur L. Duchâtre entitled La Comédie Italienne. The same author, in collaboration with Monsieur R. Saulnier, has just had published by La Librairie de France a book, beautifully illustrated, entitled L'Imagerie Populaire. It will, I hope, be followed by other books on the printing of broadsheets, particularly on this art of the people as practised in Spain, England, and Italy.

American bibliophiles should lose no time in securing French fine-paper editions if they wish to take advantage of the present low prices. In France we shall soon have a state of affairs like that which prevailed in Germany immediately after the War, for the increased cost of raw materials and of manual labor throughout the world is now being felt here and will eventually affect the production of choice editions.

As for the theatre, M Bernard Zimmer has given us Le Veau

[1] Published in THE DIAL, January 1921, under the title, Cock and Harlequin.

Gras and Les Zouaves, two plays which La Nouvelle Revue Française has published in one volume—virulent satires on contemporary society written with a ferocity which places the author in
the direct tradition of Mirbeau. M Bourdet's play, La Prisonnière,
bears not altogether inappropriately the title of Proust's book, for
it presents a similar problem of jealousy, a man's jealousy of a
woman who eludes him to return to previous *amours* in which he,
as a man, can have no part. M Bourdet has had the courage to
present for the first time upon the stage a subject which has hitherto
been treated only in the discreet and shadowy confessional of the
novel.

PAUL MORAND

[JUNE, 1926]

NOCTURNE

By Archibald MacLeish

The earth: still heavy and warm with afternoon,
Dazed by the moon

The earth, tormented with the moon's light,
Wandering in the night

Full moon, moon-rise, the old old pain
Of brightness in dilated eyes

The ache of still
Elbows leaning on the narrow sill

Of motionless cold hands upon the wet
Marble of the parapet

Of open eyelids of a child behind
The crooked glimmer of the window-blind

Of sliding, faint, remindful squares
Across the lamplight on the rocking-chairs

Why do we stand so late,
Stiff fingers on the moonlit gate?

Why do we stand
To watch so long the fall of moonlight on the sand?

What is it we cannot recall?

[July, 1926]

269

MODERN ART

I F my notes this winter have been more than ever concerned with detailing the arrivals of foreign art in this country it is simply that these importations have been more significant than our exports. I am, in the limited DIAL space at my command, to touch upon the high-lights in the New York season and to give my readers an echo of the talk and opinions that generate when individuals who have access behind the scenes meet. These individuals, or those I have met at least, have talked of the Maillols of the Goodyear Collection, of the French Moderns in the Quinn Collection and in the Tri-National Exhibition and quite lately there have been agitations in regard to the Brancusi carvings in the Wildenstein Galleries and the sensational "theatre arts" that Miss Jane Heap saw in the Decorative Arts Show last summer in Paris and has been sponsoring here. But there has not been a single excitement of native origin. To date, not a soul has plucked me by the sleeve to tell me of a sensational little Bowery boy who has been rescued from the slums to exhibit in So-and-So's Gallery. The little Bowery boys have been rescued—plenty of them —and So-and-So has been energetically sounding the trumpets for them—but without attracting general attention. Nevertheless, I, who rejoice more over the new genius that is saved from oblivion than over the ninety-and-nine just Academicians that we have always with us, am not discouraged. Far from it. On the contrary, I consider that we have had, we Americans, the healthiest and most prosperous year since the war; have, in fact, finally got over the war.

If there be no new talents to mention, the familiar ones, on the other hand, have been doing very well. Mr Alfred Stieglitz ensconced himself in a little room and proceeded to give a series of Intimate Exhibitions of work by his protégés. Chief of these John Marin, led off with his usual success and possibly more so. When an artist has reached the heights there is nothing to do but stay there and that Mr Marin certainly does. The variations he achieves on the heights are not to be instantly measured—a little distance is necessary for that—but the new little room was undoubtedly a more helpful background to his art than the bigger galleries where it was exposed last year. My own opinion is that nobody anywhere in water-colour makes such profound and passionate tributes to nature as John Marin. Technically his drawings are superb. The commonplaces of water-colour he has disdained long since and in the fury of composition, it must be allowed that he permits roughnesses that act as stumbling-blocks to all save those, like myself, who are willing to pay any price for elevation of spirit. At the same time, since Marin practically grew up in this medium, it is never possible for him, however rough, not to be in it. He is always the worker in water-colour, and nine times out of ten, there are breath-taking passages of elegant *bravura,* thrown in by way of good measure—but never thrown in, you may be sure, for their own sakes.

Of Georgia O'Keefe, the second candidate for fame in the Intimate Gallery, I cannot say so much; though the women do. I begin to think that in order to be quite fair to Miss O'Keefe I must listen to what the women say of her—and take notes. I like her stuff quite well. Very well. I like her colour, her imagination, her decorative sense. Her things wear well with me, and I soon accept those that I see constantly in the same way that I accept, say a satisfactory tower in the landscape; but I do not feel the occult element in them that all the ladies insist is there. There were more feminine shrieks and screams in the vicinity of O'Keefe's works this year than ever before; so I take it that she too is getting on.

Another gallery that bears watching, and this year more than ever, is the Whitney Studio Club Gallery. The last thing I did last spring was to expatiate upon the merits of this organization as made manifest in its members' exhibition. I hesitated to fix the burden of genius upon any of the young Whitneyites who were shouldering themselves into notice but felt quite sure, all the same, that Fame's only hesitation lay in the embarrassment of choosing among so many. The members' exhibition this year has already occurred and is not quite so striking as the one that bowled me over last year—but that may be only because I am no longer surprised by merit but expect it. Also, alas, some of these young men and women are beginning to foresake the parent institution for the more precarious delights of uptown recognition. Niles Spencer, Alexander Brook, Yasuo Kuniyoshi, Peggy Bacon, and Henry Schnakenberg have had one-man exhibitions—all of them with professional approbation and some of them with pecuniary recompense. Niles Spencer begins to be regarded as a fixed luminary having greatly pleased everybody two years running and Alexander Brook for the first time revealed in paint the lively interest in the world's spectacle his friends know to be his. Two others of the Whitney Studio Club must be mentioned in any account of the winter's activities—Leon Hartl and Glenn Coleman. Mr Hartl had the great good sense to do what I wish all the young painters with reputations to make would do; he put modest prices upon his work. He was so modest about it that Greenwich Village in shocked surprise was stampeded into buying almost all of his things. A selling success does not always include the other kind of success but this time it did. Critical opinion also was upon the side of Mr Hartl. As a painter he has abandoned the sophisticated methods and aims to spare the public the necessity of learning technical tricks. Henri Rousseau, no doubt, is the god of his particular school but Mr Hartl is by no means submerged in an admiration for this master and manages to make a distinct contribution of his own. As for Glenn Coleman he is a most witty and pleasant painter and it is odd, to say the least, that he is so slow in gaining a vogue. He paints a great deal in Mexico and Cuba and his slightly mocking comments on scenes that look to sober northern eyes like rather reckless opera settings ought to find ready acceptance.

Quite a few of those connected with the Whitney Studio Club figured in the sale at Anderson's, of Mr Albert Rothbart's collection. Mr Rothbart, as a collector, is quite fearless and never hesitates at a picture that pleases him even though signed with an unfamiliar name. He crowded his house with productions by the men we now call "modern," so much so that in order to continue collecting, which is very much his wish, he felt obliged to "clean house" and start anew. Besides, he said he thought an auction of work by the newer men, would help in establishing values. . . . It was, undoubtedly, a fine gesture. . . . Also, it was expensive, as fine gestures often are, and the auction was a chilly, disastrous affair, speaking financially, and none of the artists rose to added distinction through it. The two participants most to be congratulated, I thought, were Charles Sheeler and Alexander Brook. The sums obtained for their works were not formidable but the excited bids that both extracted from all corners of the room were distinctly flattering.   HENRY McBRIDE   [MAY, 1926]

MINA LOY

By Yvor Winters

Mr. Sacheverell Sitwell once wrote a very long poem, two lines of which stay in my memory:

> "My natural clumsiness was my only bar to progress
> Until I conquered it by calculation."

As I go through such of Miss Loy's poems as I possess, this seems to describe her. If she has not actually conquered the clumsiness which one can scarcely help feeling in her writings, she has, from time to time, overcome it; and these occasional advantages have resulted in momentous poems. Or perhaps it is not clumsiness, but the inherently unyielding quality of her material that causes this embarrassment. She moves like one walking through granite instead of air, and when she achieves a moment of beauty it strikes one cold.

More intent on the gutter and its horrors than any of the group with which she was allied, and more intensely cerebral, perhaps, than any save one of them, her work ordinarily presents that broken, unemotional, and occasionally witty observation of undeniable facts that one came to regard as the rather uninviting norm of Others poetry. (Let me hasten to explain that I do not wish to appear to disparage Others, but norms, which are useful only as definite places from which to escape. Others seems to me the most interesting single group manifestation that has yet occurred in American verse.) Her unsuccessful work is easier to imitate than that of any of the three other outstanding members of her set—Miss Moore, Dr Williams, and Mr Stevens—and beyond a doubt has been more imitated. Rhythmically, it is elementary, whereas the metres of Miss Moore and Dr Williams are infinitely varied and difficult, and those of Mr Stevens are at least infinitely subtle. Emotionally, Dr Williams is no farther from what one might regard as some sort of common denominator than Miss Loy, and he has covered—and opened to poetry—vastly more territory, so that the likelihood of his becoming the chief prophet of my own

273

or some future generation is probably greater. Already, in fact, he is something of this nature, as the Dada movement has added to the principles that he has at one time or another stated, indicated, or practised, nothing save a few minor vices. Of all contemporary poets, he is, I should say, the closest in spirit to Miss Loy. Miss Moore, on the other hand, as a point of departure, is unthinkable—like Henry James, she is not a point of departure at all, but a terminus. Her work suggests nothing that she herself has not carried to its logical and utmost bounds. And Mr Stevens, with his ethereal perversity, inhabits a region upon which one feels it would be a pity to encroach.

And yet I think that few poets of my own generation would deny that these writers as a group are more sympathetic, as well as more encouraging, than either the Vorticists or the Mid-Americans. Their advantage over the professional backwoodsmen consists in part, perhaps, in superior intellectual equipment, but mainly, I suspect, in a larger portion of simple common-sense—they have refused from the very beginning to consider themselves in any way related to Shawnee Indians or potato-beetles, and have passed unscathed through a period of unlimited sentimentality. Their advantage over the Vorticists consists not so much in their having superior brains, but in their having used their own brains exclusively. Had their own brains been unequal to the task, this would have been but little advantage, as Mr Pound, Mr Eliot, and H.D. are formidable rivals, and, it seems to me, genuinely great poets, but the courage of the Others group appears, by this time, to have been pretty thoroughly justified. It was a hard-headed courage, and little repaid by adulation, and is nearly as admirable as its poetic outcome. One can find little in contemporary poetry of a similar sturdiness except in the work of Messrs Hardy and Robinson.

Of the four Mr Stevens and Miss Moore deserve the least compassion for their struggle, if compassion is to be meted out—one suspects that they always knew they could do it; and Dr Williams, hurling himself at the whole world with the passion of the former bantam-weight champion who bore his name, has achieved a blinding technique and magnificent prose and poetry by sheer excess of nervous power. And indeed compassion is scarcely the proper offering to bring Miss Loy—one feels timorous in bringing anything.

She attacked the dirty commonplace with the doggedness of a weight-lifter. Nearly any one might have written her worst poems, and innumerable small fry have written poems as good. Her success, if the least dazzling of the four, is not the least impressive, and is by all odds the most astounding. Using an unexciting method, and writing of the drabbest of material, she has written seven or eight of the most brilliant and unshakably solid satirical poems of our time, and at least two non-satirical pieces that possess for me a beauty that is unspeakably moving and profound. Satires like The Black Virginity and the piece on D'Annunzio need give little if any ground before the best of Pope or Dryden, and poems like Der Blinde Junge and the Apology of Genius need, in my judgement, yield ground to no one. And then there is the host of half-achieved but fascinating poems like Lunar Baedecker. One cons them—with the author's pardon—as one might a rosary, and is thankful if the string doesn't break, but most of the beads are at the very least spectacular:

> "Delirious Avenues
>   lit
>   with the chandelier souls
>   of infusoria
>
> .   .   .   .   .
>
> Onyx-eyed Odalisques
>   and ornithologists
>   observe
>   the flight
>   of Eros obsolete"

They are images that have frozen into epigrams. It is this movement from deadly stasis to stasis, slow and heavy, that, when unified and organized, gives to her poetry its ominous grandeur, like that of a stone idol become animate and horribly aware:

> "Lepers of the moon . . .
>   unknowing
>   How perturbing lights
>   our spirit

on the passion of Man
until you turn on us your smooth fool's faces
like buttocks bared in aboriginal mockeries

.   .   .   .

In the raw caverns of the Increate
we forge the dusk of Chaos
to that imperious jewelry of the Universe
—the Beautiful . . ."

Such an apology is in itself a proof of genius—and of a genius that rises from a level of emotion and attitude which is as nearly common human territory as one can ever expect to find in a poet. Mr Rodker once said that she wrote of the SOUL (in four capital letters, unless my memory betrays me) but the word doesn't mean much, no matter how one spells it. One might substitute the *subconscious* (which Mr Rodker doubtless meant) but this word is nearly as frayed. Whatever tag one fastens to it, and regardless of what happens to her emotion in passing through her brain (which, being a good brain, is responsible for her being a good poet) one can scarcely help sensing at bottom a strange feeling for the most subterranean of human reactions, of a padding animal resentment, and of a laughter that is curiously physical. This habitation of some variety of common ground, although it may have no intrinsic aesthetic virtue, yet places her beside Dr Williams as one of the two living poets who have the most, perhaps, to offer the younger American writers—they present us with a solid foundation in place of Whitman's badly aligned corner-stones, a foundation which is likely to be employed, I suspect, for a generation or two, by the more talented writers of this country, or by a rather large part of them. This suggested development is not a call to salvation, nor even a dogmatic prediction, but simply a speculation. If it materializes, Emily Dickinson will have been its only forerunner.

[JUNE, 1926]

THE MEANING OF MEANING

By Bertrand Russell

THE book by Messrs Ogden and Richards [1] which bears the above title is one of considerable importance—I will not say "philosophical" importance for fear of being asked what I "mean" by that word. The importance of their book lies, first, in the importance of their problem, which has been strangely neglected in traditional philosophy. (I know what I mean by the word this time: I mean the writings of those labelled "philosophers" in catalogues, or whatever is not theology in the section "theology and philosophy" in a bookseller's list. To this meaning, which is precise and clear, I propose to adhere in what follows.) A second and no less weighty reason for welcoming this book is that its methods and theories are scientific, not mythical. A third reason is that quite possibly some of those theories may be true. I think myself that the authors suffer slightly from a form of optimism, namely the belief that most problems are simple at bottom—which affects me much like the theory that there is good in everybody, to which I have a wholly irrational aversion. My own form of optimism is different: it consists in thinking that most problems need mathematical logic for their solution. I recognize, however, that this is a less kindly optimism than the other; I shall not attempt, therefore, to enlist the reader's sympathy on this count.

To begin with a little autobiography. When, in youth, I learned what was called "philosophy" (and was philosophy, by the above definition), no one ever mentioned to me the question of "meaning." Later, I became acquainted with Lady Welby's work on the subject, but failed to take it seriously. I imagined that logic could be pursued by taking it for granted that symbols were always, so to speak, transparent, and in no way distorted the objects they were supposed to "mean." Purely logical problems have gradually

[1] The Meaning of Meaning. A Study of the Influence of Language upon Thought and of the Science of Symbolism. By C. K. Ogden and I. A. Richards. With an Introduction by J. P. Postgate and Supplementary Essays by B. Malinowski and F. G. Crookshank. 8vo. 544 pages. Harcourt, Brace and Company. $3.75.

led me further and further from this point of view. Beginning with
the question whether the class of all those classes which are not
members of themselves is, or is not, a member of itself; continuing
with the problem whether the man who says "I am lying" is lying
or speaking the truth; passing through the riddle "is the present
King of France bald or not bald, or is the law of excluded middle
false?" I have now come to believe that the order of words in time
or space is an ineradicable part of much of their significance—in
fact, that the reason they can express space-time occurrences is
that they are space-time occurrences, so that a logic independent
of the accidental nature of space-time becomes an idle dream. These
conclusions are unpleasant to my vanity, but pleasant to my love
of philosophical activity: until vitality fails, there is no reason to
be wedded to one's past theories. So here goes.

Let us begin by enumerating a set of truisms about words, which
it seems desirable to fix in our minds (or larynxes, as Dr J. B. Watson
would say) before attempting any elaborate theory.

1. *Words are social.* They are, that is to say, like laws and governments and parliaments, part of the mechanism by means of which
people manage to live in communities. The natural function of words
is to have effects upon hearers which the speaker desires. (For simplicity I shall ignore written words, and confine myself to such as
are spoken.)

2. *Words are bodily movements.* Strictly speaking, a word is
a class of bodily movements. There are as many instances of the
word "dog" as there are occasions when the word is spoken; the
word "dog" is a class, just as Dog is a class. But each instance of
the word is a bodily movement. Only convenience has led to the
choice of movements in the mouth and throat; any bodily movement may serve as a word, e.g. a shrug of the shoulders, or a long
nose.

3. *Words are means of producing effects on others.* I once can-
vassed a retired Colonel in the Liberal interest during an election,
and he said: "Get out, or I'll set the dogs upon you." These words
had, and were intended to have, the same effect as the dogs would
have had.

4. *Words, like other bodily movements, are caused by stimuli.*
The stimulus need not, of course, be external to the body; it may
be a toothache, for example. When we know that the stimulus is

not external to the body, but cannot localize it accurately, we attribute the words to "thought." Thus the more physiology we know, the less we shall think we think.

5. *Heard words are stimuli,* and are in general intended as such by the speaker, except when overheard by accident. Thus in analysing language as a factor in behaviour, we must consider not only the causes of spoken words, but the effects of heard words. Neither alone suffices, since both are equally essential.

6. *It is not of the essence of words to express "ideas."* Whether there are such things as "ideas" or not, I propose to leave an open question. What I am saying is that, whether there are "ideas" or not, they are not implied in the ordinary use of language. People used to speak of "association of *ideas,*" but now-a-days association is rather between bodily movements. The essential phenomenon is what Dr Watson calls a "learned reaction." Two stimuli A and B occur together, and B causes a bodily movement C. Later on, A may cause C, though it previously had no tendency to do so. All words are "learned reactions" in this sense. There is no need to postulate a "mental" intermediary between the stimulus and the reaction.

7. *The distinction between the emotional and the logical use of words is illusory.* Since all words are intended to have effects on hearers (except when we talk to ourselves), the question of the way in which these effects are brought about is subsidiary. Sometimes the viscera (especially the ductless glands) play a large part in the causation, sometimes not. When they do, speech is emotional, when not, logical. But the distinction is only one of degree, since there is always both a logical and an emotional aspect to our words.

8. *In the individual, heard language is earlier than spoken language.* That is to say, an infant hears words and is affected by them as the speaker intends, before it can itself utter words with intention. I think this is of some importance, since it suggests that perhaps our account of language should begin by heard words rather than spoken words. Of course it may be urged that the first spoken word must have preceded by a fraction of a second the first heard word. But this would be a fallacy, both because there cannot have been a first word in any definite sense, and because a sound may serve as a word to a hearer without being

so intended by the speaker—e.g. an infant's cry heard by a mother, and interpreted as signifying hunger. The infant soon learns to use the cry as a means of conveying information, but at first it is a pure reflex. This illustrates the fact that a noise may be a word to the hearer, though not to the speaker. The converse occurs whenever two people attempt to converse without knowing each other's languages.

Let us now proceed to frame a theory of "meaning" in accordance with the above truisms; and especially let us see how far the theory of Messrs Ogden and Richards is satisfactory.

These authors urge—rightly, as I now think—that "images" should not be introduced in explaining "meaning." They do not, like Dr Watson, maintain that there are no such things as images, but they hold that "meaning" can be adequately defined without reference to them. It is always well to avoid one problem when dealing with another, if this is in any way possible. Let us, therefore, leave on one side the question whether there are images, and construct, if we can, a theory of "meaning" which makes no reference to them.

"Direct apprehending" is another notion which is criticized by Messrs Ogden and Richards; and in the same connexion they show the ambiguities and confusions lurking in the notion of a "datum." One expects, during their discussion, to find "direct apprehending" rejected altogether, but their conclusion is as follows: "To be directly apprehended is to cause certain happenings in the nerves, as to which at present neurologists go no further than to assert that they occur. Thus what is directly apprehended is a modification of a sense organ, and its apprehension is a further modification of the nervous system." I think myself that "direct apprehension" is not a very useful notion; but if it is to be retained, I should say that it consists, not in a modification of the nervous system, but in the use of words, either out loud or *sotto voce*. I shall return to this point later, in connexion with verification.

I come now to the central doctrine of Messrs Ogden and Richards as to what is meant by "meaning." In explaining what we mean by saying that when we strike a match we expect a flame, they say:

"A thought is directed to flame when it is similar in certain respects to thoughts which have been caused by flame. As has been pointed out above we must not allow the defects of causal language either to mislead us here or alternatively to make us abandon the method of approach so indicated. We shall find, if we improve this language, both that this kind of substitute for 'directed to' loses its strangeness, and also that the same kind of substitution will meet the case of 'direction to the future' and will in fact explain the 'direction' or *reference* of thinking processes in general. . . . The suggestion that to say 'I am thinking of A' is the same thing as to say 'My thought is being caused by A' will shock every right-minded person; and yet when for 'caused' we substitute an expanded account this strange suggestion will be found to be the solution."

They add in a foot-note: "The difference between the theory here developed and that advanced in The Analysis of Mind may be brought out by the rough statement that this is a 'causal' theory and Mr Russell's an 'effect' theory."

Before proceeding further, I will say a few words on this question of "causal" theories and "effect" theories. It is obvious that the causal theory applies to the speaking of words, and the effect theory to the hearing of them. These are different things. As I have said in The Analysis of Mind,[1] "We may say that a person understands a word when (a) suitable circumstances make him use it; (b) the hearing of it causes suitable behaviour in him. We may call these two active and passive understanding respectively." I advocated, in that book, an effect theory of passive understanding, and a causal theory of active understanding. Messrs Ogden and Richards do not seem to have considered passive understanding, or to have noticed the parts of my discussion which deal with active understanding. After discussing passive understanding I continue: "To understand the function that words perform in what is called 'thinking,' we must understand both the causes and the effects of their occurrence." The conclusion as to their causes is as follows:

"We may lay it down generally that, whenever we use a word, either aloud or in inner speech, there is some sensation or image (either of which may be itself a word) which has frequently occurred at about the same time as the word, and now, through habit, causes the word. It follows that the law of habit is adequate to account for

[1] The Analysis of Mind. By Bertrand Russell. 8vo. 310 pages. The Macmillan Company. $4.

the use of words in the absence of their objects; moreover, it would be adequate even without introducing images. Although, therefore, images seem undeniable, we cannot derive an additional argument in their favour from the use of words, which could, theoretically, be explained without introducing images."

I cannot therefore admit the justice of the criticism offered by Messrs Ogden and Richards. To explain the causes of speaking, we need a causal theory; to explain the effects of hearing, we need an effect theory. I provided both, whereas they provide only the former.

However, they will reply that they are considering the meaning of a "thought," not of a word. A "thought" is not a social phenomenon, like speech, and therefore does not have the two sides, active and passive, which can be distinguished in speech. I should urge, however, that all the reasons which led our authors to avoid introducing images in explaining meaning should have also led them to avoid introducing "thoughts." If a theory of meaning is to be fitted into natural science as they desire, it is necessary to define the meaning of *words* without introducing anything "mental" in the sense in which what is "mental" is not subject to the laws of physics. Therefore, for the same reasons for which I now hold that the meaning of words should be explained without introducing images—which I argued to be possible in the above-quoted passage—I also hold that meaning in general should be treated without introducing "thoughts," and should be regarded as a property of words considered as physical phenomena. Let us therefore amend their theory. They say: " 'I am thinking of A' is the same thing as 'My thought is being caused by A.' " Let us substitute: " 'I am speaking of A' is the same thing as 'My speech is being caused by A.' " Can this theory be true?

Of course it cannot be true quite crudely. When you see Jones, you say not only "How are you?" but "How is Mrs Jones?" If the theory were strictly and exactly true, you could not mention Mrs Jones in her absence. But the word "Jones" is associated with the word "Mrs Jones," so that the sensible stimulus of Jones causes first the word "Jones" and then the word "Mrs Jones." There are two possible routes from the spectacle of Jones to the word "Mrs Jones." One is the above, from the spectacle to the word "Jones," and thence to the word "Mrs Jones"; the other is from Jones to Mrs Jones, and

thence to the word "Mrs Jones." If you have frequently seen Mr
and Mrs Jones together, Mr Jones will tend to have certain of the
effects which Mrs Jones would have, and among these is the occurrence
of the word "Mrs Jones"; thus either of our two roads may actually be
taken. We say that the word "Jones" means Jones rather than his
wife, because the associative train to the word from the man is
shorter than from the woman. And we say that "Jones" is the name of
the man rather than "Mrs Jones," because the associative train
from the man to the word "Jones" is shorter than to the word
"Mrs Jones." Thus we may say that the name of a phenomenon
is the word most closely associated with it, while the meaning of
a word is the phenomena most closely associated with it. I say "phenomena," not "phenomenon," because in general a word applies to
many phenomena—e.g. "Jones," as used by you, applies to all the
appearances which Jones makes in your life. So much for the "meaning" of spoken words.

The "meaning" of heard words is explained in a closely similar
way. A word and an object having been frequently experienced
together, the word, when spoken in your hearing, tends to produce
certain of the effects which the object would produce. The effects
which it thus tends to acquire are those called "mnemic," which
are more or less peculiar to living matter. They are those which
are subject to the law of association, i.e. that they tend to be
produced by any stimulus frequently associated with the stimulus
which originally produced them. A car coming may cause you to
jump aside, or, failing that, may break your bones; the words
"car coming" may cause you to jump aside, but cannot break your
bones. Similarly the word "Jones" can cause the word "Mrs Jones,"
but cannot cause the presence of Mrs Jones herself, which Jones
(perhaps) can cause.

So much for the meaning of words. It remains to say a word
or two about truth and falsehood. This is a large subject, and I
shall only touch on one aspect of it, namely the aspect in which
it is concerned with words as the behaviourist treats them. We
are continually uttering sentences, and it is generally recognized
that these sentences may be either true or false. Of course a
sentence may be true to the speaker and false to the hearer, or
vice versa, if they do not attach the same meanings to its com-
ponent words; but we will ignore this complication, and assume
that they talk exactly the same language. Our statements are

interconnected by all sorts of laws of inference, logical and psychological; but there is in science and daily life a process called "verification," which, when applicable, is supposed to show that a statement is true. What is this process? That is the only question I propose to discuss.

Let us take a simple instance. Suppose that, in the course of a long walk with a friend on a hot day, you both become very thirsty. You say to your friend: "When we get to the next village we shall find an inn where we can get a drink." Your friend says: "I think not; I believe the inn has been shut up." Presently you come in sight of the village and shout: "There's the inn." This is verification. A statement is verified when its repetition is caused by the sensible presence of the objects meant by its substantive words. When a statement can be verified, it is "true." Obviously there are many kinds of statement which are incapable of verification in this simple sense; for them, we shall need more elaborate definitions of truth and falsehood. But at least the above theory has the merit of including what we should naturally regard as most indubitable among matters of fact. We may, in fact, define a proposition as a "datum" when it has been verified in the sense which we have just defined. The theory has another merit, that it is purely behaviouristic, and does not assume that we have "minds"—an assumption which, I am sure, a Martian would regard as unplausible.[1]

I have not space to deal with the many topics occurring in other parts of The Meaning of Meaning. There are discussions of beauty, of the folly of philosophers, of the wisdom of savages, and of a host of subjects more or less cognate to the main theme. Nor have I space to discuss the authors' taste in puns, as exemplified in the precept: "Consider the Mountain Top—it Hums not neither does it Spin." These are matters too grave for my pen; I have confined myself to the lighter aspects of this remarkable volume. To the hardy reader I commend the other aspects as worthy of his serious study.

[AUGUST, 1926]

---

[1] Mr S. E. Hooper, Secretary of the British Institute of Philosophical Studies, has suggested to me that the above should be called the "explosive" theory of truth, a name which I am inclined to adopt. It is not to be inferred that he approves of the theory. It will be seen that the above remarks are strongly influenced by Dr Watson, whose latest book, Behaviorism, I consider massively impressive.

UNDER THE ROOF

By Seán O'Faoláin

HE was seated in the reading-room of the public library, before him
a brown-covered French quarterly, a newly-borrowed book beside
him, a halfpenny in his pocket, his eyes wandering from the clock
to the readers all around. Outside it was drizzling steadily. He had
not worked for a whole week, and between his weary body and the
wet night, between the hunger and his vitals was the solitary coin:
before him was the prospect of a roofless night. He was weary of saying that it didn't matter. He only sat waiting for the clock to reach
nine when he must rise and walk out into the rain, his borrowed volume
sheltered like a baby under his liningless coat.

It didn't matter greatly if a man was out of work: that was to be
expected now and again: Barlow on the quays never refused
a man the shelter of his box and the heat of his fire. But here was
Barlow in the Union with a splintered leg, and no timber on the
jetties anyway; in short there was nowhere to turn for the night.
He had been thinking about it all day and could think of no
solution. Now if it were a warm Summer night! Blarney Street
is the longest street in Cork, and from its summit where the
thatched houses begin and the city ends, you can look down on
the hole of a city underneath, can see the river and its bridges,
can see the mud flats at Lough Mahon and the limestone of
Blackrock Castle with its podgy turret like a white fist with thumb
erect: can see the hills breasting the harbour and the hills breasting the sea: can count the lights of Cork and fall asleep with
them all mixing before your eyes. But it wasn't a Summer night!
He felt the slim coin against his thigh and scratched himself
wearily with its rim. Barlow probably got three shillings a night
on the jetties: three shillings a night: good enough for a dotan-
carryone. Young Foxer would get that much or lose it gambling
away his stock of papers between the tail-end of the morning sales
and the coming of the evening-buffs. What in the name of God
were all those other fellows thinking about? He didn't know a
sinner of them. To stand in a doorway watching the rain pelt-
ing down on the shining flags, that was a nice prospect for the

night: to stand looking at the arc-lamps down the street, dozing, starting, sleepless, and shivering the whole night long, that would be intolerable. He glanced without purpose at the notices on the walls: borrowers are requested to protect books from the weather: and again, to his right, borrowers are requested to protect: silence is requested: and again, to his left, borrowers are requested—to hell with them and their requesting! With their pounds, shillings, and bloody-well pence rattling in their, and he with his solitary make. It wasn't fair: the fellow with the red moustache on the jetties was right: fellow-workers, we the prolesomething must annihilate. The boy in front of him was watching him: achh, it didn't matter anyway. Five to nine. Where was the use in waiting to be turned out. The boy was smiling at a joke in a comic journal: a fool of a man was peering at the advertisement columns of a newspaper: a young man was devouring a final column of Gaelic beside him. The coal-heaver looked at his brown-backed French quarterly, edged back his chair, took his book, and rose. On the steps of the library he halted to turn up his coat-collar, and then walked away through the drizzle. He looked quite a normal man: only his comrades—his acquaintances—would have known that the figure wandering from street to street in the rain had a philosophy—was a philosopher.

The streets were empty now, and the drizzle fell shimmering around the arc-lights, and the calves of his legs became wet. His face was wet, his shoulders were wet, his coat was sodden through, and at last he retired to a doorway to think.

A girl ran past followed by another, the one screaming to the other to hurry, the other screaming to wait. Erect oblongs of light moved from the bottom of the black masses that were houses up nearer to the roofs. Sitting-rooms became bedrooms, and red eyes of light showed bedroom walls when he could no longer see bedroom windows. A moving candle-flare showed the turn of a stairs, a landing, a high, high window, bare boards under bare feet unheeding the silver of hammered nails in the white wood, long, white, neck-frilled nightdresses bending over the balustrades to call to a tiled hallway for surety of locked doors. A blind sank down, squares walking up its yellow ground. A pair of gold parallelograms disappeared, and then began to reappear and vanish, faint or defined, but never steady for a second, and a woman curved over the flames; gentle fingers slipped shoes from feet, silk stockings after. A jingle rattled by, the jehu flogging a shining horse.

The coal-heaver stepped out because the door was giving him little shelter. The rain lashed the shining pavement now, and the spouts poured their overflow across the cement flags. The river flowed in curling pools under the arch, red lights always motionless in the topmost windows, the city falling into the quiet of a dark sleep. Now he felt the rain stab his calves and stab his face, but he could only walk aimlessly ahead. Suddenly a white door stood facing the river, and he halted to look at it. He shoved at it and it swung in; he passed in out of the rain. He had not seen this door ever in his life before.

Now, who lives in this house? But the dark was blackness unbroken, and he had to hold his two hands out, one clasping the book, a crucified coal-heaver walking in the dark of a hallway. His feet struck against the first knee of the stairway and he began to climb. A window-sill and an empty pot: he passed it by. A lead-covered sink, and a dripping tap—tip, tap: tip, tap: he moved on upward. A door! A man, or a family, or a lone girl? This was damn dangerous, to come into an empty house like this: he could stay in the hall: or would it be better to clear out altogether? But the door opened suddenly as if somebody had been standing behind it on the alert, and a girl confronted him, a cigarette hanging from her lips, a newspaper in her hand.

—What do you want?

—Ah?

—Who are you? What do you want?

—I'm a . . . a man.

—A man? What do you want?

—I don't want anything.

She closed the door in his face, and he heard two bolts being shoved into their places. Good job she didn't kick up a row anyway. Clear out, clear out, boy. No! He moved up another flight, feeling with his right hand, slowly, quietly. A sudden clamour broke out above, a man's voice and then another man's voice more incoherent: a cursing voice, a stuttering voice. Looking up diagonally he saw a man in shirt and pants—bare-foot—crouch forward to another man and crash his fists into his opponent's face. He did it again while the other cowered against the wall incapable of defence but the pants and shirt struck him again and again and again. He shouted to him to go away, away, to go away to hell's blazes for a dirty cur: he pushed him down the stairs and the coal-heaver saw a blood-covered cheek and nose and a pair of sodden eyes. Then light appeared as if a door opened and then the light vanished and the drunkard stumbled down past him cursing and whining with pain and anger until he reached the sink. Water ran and gurgled through the plug-hole and then stopped and the uncertain footsteps went from knee to knee of the stairs until they reached the door. It opened and crashed to, and then there was silence but for the rain on a tin roof outside.

He went up higher still and now the ceiling was closing down upon him and he heard the rain on the slates directly above his head. He reached the last landing, the last door, moved to it, and noticed the streak of yellow light at its base. He knocked softly hardly knowing what he was doing. A sweeping-brush stood in a corner; two trunks one above the other; a hat-box; indecipherable pictures on the walls: no answer to his knock. He knocked again, and waited peering down the stairs. Then for a gesture he picked out his halfpenny with his left hand, exchanged it for the book in his right, and sent it flying through the dark to the well of the stairs. It rattled against a wall where the paper was thick and loose-hanging, and rang on the timber, rolling finally to rest. At last he pushed the door inwards and halted—silent.

Seated in an arm-chair before the fire was a very old woman, her corrugated hands clasping a beads, her eyes closed in sleep. For a long while he stood looking at her, moved, hoping he still had a piece of rosary in his pocket: without knowing it he was moved by the peace of this room above the river, warm after the rain. How cosy she was, no, not cosy, but how calm, and yes, how holy: how holy! He looked at her more closely, and then entered, closing the door softly behind him. He placed his hand on her shoulder: on her face: lastly on her left breast. She was dead.

Slowly he looked around, and slowly sat before the fire.

[SEPTEMBER, 1926]

A "LOGIC" OF HISTORY

THE DECLINE OF THE WEST. *By Oswald Spengler.*
Translation with Notes by Charles Francis Atkinson.
8vo. 443 pages. Alfred A. Knopf. $6.

OVER against the H. G. Wells concept of history as a straight
line progressing from savagery to modernity, Spengler opposes the
concept of numberless cultural systems, each of which has followed
through a cycle of its own, growing, flourishing, and decaying in a
fixed order or "periodicity." These cultural cycles, by Spengler's
doctrine, evolve in an irreversible sequence through "spring, summer,
autumn, and winter" aspects, any "season" of one culture being
comparable with the corresponding season of any other culture. These
analogous stages of different cultural systems are called "contemporaneous"; and by aligning the stages of our own cultural cycle
(that of Europe and European America, which Spengler dates from
about 1000 A. D.) with the contemporaneous stages of other cultural
cycles, Spengler claims to produce a series of co-ordinates for de-
termining which of the cultural seasons is now upon us.

Homer, in the Graeco-Roman cycle, would be contemporaneous
with the northern sagas in our own, this era always being "rural and
intuitive," and marked by the "birth of a myth of the grand
style, expressing a new God-feeling." This spring gradually met-
amorphoses into summer, a period of "ripening consciousness" and
of the "earliest urban and critical stirrings"—the pre-Socratics of
the sixth and fifth centuries being analogous to Galileo, Bacon,
and Descartes. In autumn the city assumes a leading position in
the life of the culture. This is the age of "enlightenment" (Socrates
and Rousseau) in which the traditional code is now subjected to a
rigorous questioning, although it is still powerful as a religious and
creative force. The mathematics characteristic of the culture is now
definitely formulated, and the "great conclusive" metaphysical systems are constructed (Plato and Aristotle having their contemporaneous parallel in Goethe and Kant).

But each culture, while exemplifying the laws of growth and
decay common to all cultures, is a self-contained unit, talking in
a language addressed to itself alone. When it has passed, it leaves
us its monuments and its scripts, but the experience which these

works symbolized has vanished, so that subsequent cultures inherit a body of rigid symbols to which they are psychically alien— much the way one of Jung's typical extraverts would be alien to a typical introvert. In this sense, ancient Greek is as undecipherable a language as Etruscan, since there is no word in the Greek vocabulary which corresponds, in its cultural background, to the word which we select as its equivalent in any one of our modern languages. Consider, for instance, the difference in content between "man" as one of a race who stole the fire from heaven and "man" as a link in the evolutionary chain. It is not hard to imagine how a work of art arising out of the one attitude could be "alien" to a reader in whom the other attitude was ingrained.

Spengler lays great emphasis upon this cultural subjectivism, and even insists upon the subjective element in natural science. For even though science deals with empirically provable facts, a specific kind of mentality is required to meditate upon these facts rather than others. The possible modes of natural investigation are dependent upon the interests of the investigators. Spengler characterizes the science of any given culture as the conversion of its religion into an irreligious field—such concepts as "force" and "energy," for instance, merely being an altered aspect of the omnipotent and omnipresent God conceived at an earlier stage in the same culture.

The growth of science is also the evidence of a radical change in a culture's evolution. At this stage, the intellectualistic, critical, and irreligious elements of the culture gradually rise to the ascendancy. The emotional certainty of the earlier epochs, when religious, metaphysical, and aesthetic systems were built up spontaneously, is now past. The culture becomes a civilization. "In the one period life *reveals* itself, the other has life as its *object*." In place of the city we have the metropolis, and the "ethical-practical tendencies of an irreligious and unmetaphysical cosmopolitanism." Winter, thereby, is upon us. Hellenistic-Roman Stoicism after 200—returning to our concept of the contemporaneous—is paralleled by ethical socialism after 1900. The theatricality of Pergamene art is matched by Liszt, Berlioz, and Wagner—and Hellenistic painting finds its equivalent in impressionism. The American skyscraper, instead of being looked upon as the evidence of a new "dawn," is interpreted by Spengler as the symptom of decay corresponding to the "architectural display in the cities of the Diadochi."

Spengler thus finds that the high point of our culture has been passed, while we go deeper into the closing period, the era of civilization. With intellectualistic elements predominant, we are no longer fitted for the production of great works of art, but for technical exploits, for economic, commercial, political, and imperialistic activities. We are, like Rome, which was the civilization of Greek culture, ordained to be superior as road-builders and inferior as artists. And by his doctrine of cultural subjectivism, even those great works of art which our culture in its more youthful and vigorous stages produced as the symbolization of Western-European experience will become alien as this experience itself recedes before the rise of other cultures having other modes of experience to symbolize. In conclusion, then: (a) Even the greatest works of art are couched, not in the language of "mankind," but in the language of a specific cultural tradition, and the loss of the tradition is like the loss of the dictionary; and (b) since art is inevitably inferior in an era of civilization, we are invited to abandon all hope of further artistic excellence in our cultural cycle.

Let us consider first Spengler's subjectivist argument. In discussing each cultural cycle, he finds some dominant trait which characterizes the entire mode of experience peculiar to the culture. Arabic culture, for instance, is "magian," our own is "Faustian," and the Graeco-Roman is "Apollinian." He then shows how these dominant traits manifest themselves in all the various aspects of a culture's "behaviour." The Apollinian trait can be expanded as a sense of the "pure present," a concrete "thisness and hereness," which is to be found equally in the repose of the Greek temple, the "corporeality" of Greek mathematics, and the Greek indifference to time (the Greeks had no system of chronological reckoning comparable to our method of dating from the birth of Christ). This same attitude naturally resulted in the development of sculpture into a major art. In contrast to this, the Faustian culture has a pronounced historic sense, a mathematics of function and time, an "aspiring" architecture; and it has developed music into a major art. In painting, the "corporeal" mentality of the Greeks led to the exclusion of sky-blue as a colour, and the disinterest in perspective; while the Faustian culture, with its feeling for distance, showed a marked preference for this very blue, and developed perspective exhaustively. Spengler considers this as evidence of totally different subjective states; yet could it not, as well, be used to indicate a very fundamental kind of similarity? If blue and perspective are employed by the Faustian for the same reason that they are rejected by the Apollinian, does not this argue a common basis of choice? It is to grant, categorically, that blue and perspective symbolize for both cultures a sense of distance. A genuinely subjective difference between cultures would be undetectable, for it would involve a situation in which the symbols could be employed with directly opposite content. Blue and perspective would then, for the Greek, mean pure present; and we could have formed the Greek temple, rather than the Gothic cathedral, as our symbol of aspiration. The aesthetic symbols of an alien culture could give us no clue as to the mode of experience behind them.

Furthermore, it seems arbitrary that Spengler should stop at cultural subjectivism. Why not epochal subjectivism? If a difference in the traits of a culture involves a difference in the content of its expressionistic symbols, does not his division of a culture into seasons indicate that each season symbolizes a mode of experience peculiar to itself? If a culture speaks a language of its own, then each season has its own dialect of that language.

Why, then, does Spengler not go on to this further stage? What "vested interests" could be endangered for this savant who would so willingly sacrifice an entire culture? The fact is that epochal subjectivism would interfere with his two major conclusions: cultural subjectivism and aesthetic defeatism.

Spengler's division into spring, summer, autumn, and winter is at bottom the formulation of four subjective types, four typical modes of experience which recur in each cultural cycle. Thus, subjectivity is seen to produce its alliances as well as its estrangements. And contemporaneous epochs of different cultural cycles might even be considered to have more in common than different epochs of the same culture—our "irreligious and cosmopolitan" winter, for instance, being nearer to the same mode of experience in the Graeco-Roman cycle than to its own "rural and intuitive" spring. At least, there is more of Apuleius than of Beowulf in the modern *Weltanschauung*. Epochal subjectivity, looked upon in this way, would tend to counteract the estrangements of cultural subjectivity. Cultural subjectivity would not be an *absolute* condition, but an *approximate* one—and the modes of experience in different eras of the world's history would be capable of an approach towards identity. Epochal subjectivity, furthermore, would constitute a sanction of the modern artist. It would force us to recognize that winter, purely by being a different mode of experience from spring, summer, or autumn, is categorically entitled to symbolize this mode of experience in art.

In any case, how can Spengler call modern art inferior? By what subtlety does this absolute judgement manage to creep into a relativistic theory? There is no criterion of excellence inherent in the analysis of a genetic process. His logical machinery provides for no step beyond the observation that in spring we must have the symbolizations of spring and in winter the symbolizations of winter. To emerge with a judgement in such a case would be like concluding, after an explanation of the earth's seasons as being caused by the planet's revolution about the sun, "therefore autumn is better than winter."

The pessimistic connotation which he puts upon the civilization aspect of the culture-civilization dichotomy is purely arbitrary. We might, with as much authority, use a different analogy from that of the seasons, perhaps considering all the earlier stages of a cultural cycle as periods of upbuilding, of pioneering, of grim, hardworking zealotry. Culture, we could say, struggles and wrestles with its environment to amass an inheritance which civilization, coming after it, has the leisure to enjoy. For when a culture is in full swing, it is not only politically and religiously intolerant, but aesthetically intolerant as well. And in any case, the people of Bach's time did not have Beethoven, and those of Beethoven's time did not have Wagner—while in the course of a New York winter we have them all.

Yet, however much one may snipe at Spengler's book, it remains a stupendous piece of work, formidable, lugubrious, and passionate. His historical perspectives are often brilliant and fertile; his methodology [1] unquestionably has a future. And European culture does

---

[1] His treatment of cultural factors differs refreshingly from that of the usual genetic or causalist critic. The sociologist, for instance, will explain aesthetic values as the result of the economic conditions under which they arise. He finds certain aesthetic values paralleled by certain economic conditions; and after observing that any variation in the one entails a concomitant variation in the other, he con-

seem to be undergoing some weakening of the pure cultural strain: whatever interpretation we may put upon the fact, we must recognize that our culture is no longer thorough-bred. We now question, where we once asserted—and even art is trammelled by considerations which prey upon it much the way epistemology has preyed upon metaphysics. Such phenomena are given an elaborate orientation in Spengler's system.

But if our own art cannot suffice for us, if appreciation is as powerful an influence with us as creation, we should be renouncing the half of our inheritance by our almost pathological demand for creativeness as the criterion of self-respect. We must not confuse impoverishment with embarrassment of riches. Aesthetic defeatism is made more plausible by our modern tendency to consider the great works of the past as hostile forces rather than as amenities. For my own part, I can imagine but one really drastic kind of aesthetic desolation: if, by some great futurist upheaval, the traditional monuments of European art were to be eradicated now, so that not one trace of them remained except the *feel* of them in our memory. I imagine us trying to restore, with the bungling of a nightmare, the specific equivalents for these vague qualities which we recalled, trying to find again the actual notes for that suavity which we remember as Mozart, or that severity which we remember as Bach, or that straining Prometheus which we remember as Beethoven. Piecing together, from a line someone half remembers in Australia, and another restored by a traveller in Tibet, the godless rollick of Candide. Consulting THE DIAL of a recent month to recover, with the help of Mr Rosenfeld's word pictures, the inert leap of an El Greco. And so on. But in the meantime, since all these works are still with us, I insist that it is not our *fate,* but our *privilege,* to receive more than we

siders this as evidence that the economic conditions produce the aesthetic values. Spengler, arriving at this point, would merely observe that the two vary concomitantly, and that every other aspect of the same era in history varies concomitantly with them. In place of a causal principle, he would utilize a principle of analogy. He would specify that quality or character of an era which was manifest in any cultural activity of the era (architecture, music, inventions, politics, marriage customs, attitude towards property, and so on) just as we might consider a poet's facial expressions, his method of walking, and his style of writing to be analogous aspects—each in different terms—of his behavior. This method broadens the horizons of such investigations enormously.

give. And though holy texts fail to assure us that we are, in so doing, blessed, they do not, on the other hand, acclaim such status as accursed.

KENNETH BURKE

[SEPTEMBER, 1926]

GERARD HOPKINS

By I. A. Richards

Modern verse is perhaps more often too lucid than too obscure. It passes through the mind (or the mind passes over it) with too little friction and too swiftly for the development of the response. Poets who can compel slow reading have thus an initial advantage. The effort, the heightened attention, may brace the reader, and that peculiar intellectual thrill which celebrates the step-by-step conquest of understanding may irradiate and awaken other mental activities more essential to poetry. It is a good thing to make the light-footed reader work for what he gets. It may make him both more wary and more appreciative of his reward if the "critical point" of value is passed.

These are arguments for some slight obscurity in its own right. No one would pretend that the obscurity may not be excessive. It may be distracting, for example. But what is a distraction in a first reading may be non-existent in a second. We should be clear (both as readers and writers) whether a given poem is to be judged at its first reading or at its nth. The state of intellectual enquiry, the construing, interpretative, frame of mind, so much condemned by some critics (through failure perhaps to construe the phrase "simple, sensuous, and passionate") passes away once its task is completed, and the reader is likely to be left with a far securer grasp of the whole poem, including its passional structure, than if no resistance had been encountered.

Few poets illustrate this thesis better than Gerard Hopkins, who may be described, without opposition, as the most obscure of English verse writers. Born in 1844, he became a Jesuit priest in 1868, a more probable fate for him then—he was at Oxford—than now. Before joining the Order he burnt what verses he had already written and "resolved to write no more, as not belonging to my profession, unless it were by the wish of my superiors." For seven years he wrote nothing. Then by good fortune this wish was expressed and Hopkins set to work. "I had long had haunting my ear the echo of a new rhythm which now I realized on paper. . . . However I had to mark the stresses . . . and a great many more oddnesses could not but dismay an editor's eye, so that when I offered it to our magazine . . . they dared not print it." Thenceforward he wrote a good deal, sending his poems in manuscript to Robert Bridges and to Canon Dixon. He died in 1889 leaving a bundle of papers among which were several of his best sonnets. In 1918 the Poet Laureate edited a volume of poems with an introduction and notes of great interest. From this volume comes all our knowledge of his work.

Possibly their obscurity may explain the fact that these poems are not yet widely known. But their originality and the audacity of their experimentation have much to do with the delay. Even their editor found himself compelled to apologize at length for what he termed "blemishes in the poet's style." "It is well to be clear that there is no pretence to reverse the condemnation of these faults, for which the poet has duly suffered. The extravagances are and will remain what they were . . . it may be assumed that they were not a part of his intention." But too many other experiments have been made recently, especially in the last eight years, for this lofty tone and confident assumption to be maintained. The more the poems are studied, the clearer it becomes that their oddities are always deliberate. They may be aberrations, they are not blemishes. It is easier to see this to-day since some of his most daring innovations have been, in part, attempted independently by later poets.

I propose to examine a few of his best poems from this angle, choosing those which are both most suggestive technically and most indicative of his temper and mould as a poet. It is an important fact that he is so often most himself when he is most experimental. I will begin with a poem in which the shocks to convention are local and concern only word order.

PEACE

When will you ever, Peace, wild wood dove, shy wings shut,
Your round me roaming end, and under be my boughs?
When, when, Peace, will you, Peace? I'll not play hypocrite
To own my heart: I yield you do come sometimes; but
That piecemeal peace is poor peace. What pure peace allows
Alarms of wars, the daunting wars, the death of it?

O surely, reaving Peace, my Lord should leave in lieu
Some good! And so he does leave Patience exquisite,
That plumes to Peace thereafter. And when Peace here does house
He comes with work to do, he does not come to coo,
       He comes to brood and sit.

Hopkins was always ready to disturb the usual word order of prose to gain an improvement in rhythm or an increased emotional poignancy. *To own my heart* = to my own heart; *reaving* = taking away. He uses words always as tools, an attitude towards them which the purist and grammarian can never understand. He was clear, too, that his poetry was for the ear, not for the eye, a point that should be noted before we proceed to The Windhover, which, unless we begin by listening to it, may *only* bewilder us. To quote from a letter: "Indeed, when, on somebody's returning me the Eurydice, I opened and read some lines, as one commonly reads, whether prose or verse, with the eyes, so to say, only, it struck me aghast with a kind of raw nakedness and unmitigated violence I was unprepared for: but take breath and read it with the ears, as I always wish to be read, and my verse becomes all right." I have to confess that The Windhover only became all right for me, in the sense of perfectly clear and explicit, intellectually satisfying as well as emotionally moving, after many readings and several days of reflection.

THE WINDHOVER

To Christ our Lord

I caught this morning morning's minion, king-
   dom of daylight's dauphin, dapple-dawn-drawn Fal-
     con, in his riding
  Of the rolling level underneath him steady air, and
     striding
High there, how he rung upon the rein of a wimpling wing
In his ecstasy! then off, off forth on swing,
  As a skate's heel sweeps smooth on a bow-bend: the hurl
    and gliding

Rebuffed the big wind. My heart in hiding
Stirred for a bird,—the achieve of, the mastery of the
    thing!

Brute beauty and valour and act, oh, air, pride, plume, here
    Buckle! AND the fire that breaks from thee then, a
    billion
Times told lovelier, more dangerous, O my chevalier!

No wonder of it: shéer plód makes plough down
    sillion
Shine, and blue-bleak embers, ah my dear,
    Fall, gall themselves, and gash gold-vermillion.

The dedication at first sight is puzzling. Hopkins said of this
poem that it was the best thing he ever wrote, which is to me in
part the explanation. It sounds like an echo of the offering made
eleven years ago when his early poems were burnt. For a while I
thought that the apostrophe, "O my chevalier!" (it is perhaps superfluous to mention that this word rhymes strictly with "here" and
has only three syllables) had reference to Christ. I take it now to
refer only to the poet, though the moral ideal, embodied of course for
Hopkins in Christ, is before the mind.

Some further suggestions towards elucidation may save the reader
trouble. If he does not need them I crave his forgiveness. *Kingdom of daylight's dauphin*—I see (unnecessarily) the falcon as a
miniature sun, flashing so high up. *Rung upon the rein*—a term
from the *manège*, ringing a horse = causing it to circle round one
on a long rein. *My heart in hiding*—as with other good poets I
have come to expect that when Hopkins leaves something which
looks at first glance as though it were a concession to rhyme or a
mere pleasing jingle of words, some really important point is
involved. Why in hiding? Hiding from what? Does this link up
with "a billion times told lovelier, more dangerous, O my chevalier!"?
What is the greater danger and what the less? I should say the
poet's heart is in hiding from Life, has chosen a safer way, and
that the greater danger is the greater exposure to temptation and
error than a more adventurous, less sheltered course (sheltered

by Faith?) brings with it. Another, equally plausible reading would be this: Renouncing the glamour of the outer life of adventure the poet transfers its qualities of audacity to the inner life. (*Here is the bosom, the inner consciousness.*) The greater danger is that to which the moral hero is exposed. Both readings may be combined, but pages of prose would be required for a paraphrase of the result. The last three lines carry the thought of the achievement possible through renunciation further, and explain, with the image of the ash-covered fire, why the dangers of the inner life are greater. So much for the sense; but the close has a strange, weary, almost exhausted, rhythm, and the word "gall" has an extraordinary force, bringing out painfully the shock with which the sight of the soaring bird has jarred the poet into an unappeased discontent.

If we compare those poems and passages of poems which were conceived definitely within the circle of Hopkins' theology with those which transcend it, we shall find difficulty in resisting the conclusion that the poet in him was often oppressed and stifled by the priest. In this case the conflict which seems to lie behind and prompt all Hopkins' better poems is temporarily resolved through a stoic acceptance of sacrifice. An asceticism which fails to reach ecstasy and accepts the failure. All Hopkins' poems are in this sense poems of defeat. This will perhaps become clearer if we turn to

SPELT FROM SIBYL LEAVES

Earnest, earthless, equal, attunable, vaulty, voluminous, . .
    stupendous
Evening strains to be tíme's vást, womb-of-all, home-of-all,
    hearse-of-all night.
Her fond yellow hornlight wound to the west, her wild hollow
    hoarlight hung to the height
Waste; her earliest stars, earl-stars, stárs principal, over-
    bend us,
Fíre-féaturing heaven. For earth her being has unbound, her
    dapple is at an end, as-

tray or aswarm, all throughther, in throngs; self ín self
  steepèd and páshed—quite
Disremembering, dísmémbering áll now. Heart, you round me
  right
With: Our évening is over us; óur night whélms, whélms, ánd
  will end us.
Only the beak-leaved boughs dragonish damask the tool-smooth
  bleak light; black,
Ever so black on it. Our tale, O óur oracle! Lét life, wáned,
  ah lét life wind
Off hér once skéined stained véined varíety upon, áll on twó
  spools; párt, pén, páck
Now her áll in twó flocks, twó folds—black, white; right
  wrong; reckon but, reck but, mind
But thése two; wáre of a wórld where bút those twó tell, each
  off the óther; of a rack
Where, selfwrung, selfstrung, sheathe- and shelterless, thóughts
  agáinst thoughts ín groans grínd.

Elucidations are perhaps less needed. The heart speaks after
"Heart you round me right" to the end, applying in the moral
sphere the parable of the passing away of all the delights, accidents,
nuances, the "dapple" of existence, to give place to the awful
dichotomy of right and wrong. It is characteristic of this poet that
there is no repose for him in the night of traditional morality. As
the terrible last line shows, the renunciation of all the myriad temptations of life brought no gain. It was all loss. The present order
of "black, white; right, wrong" was an afterthought and an intentional rearrangement; the original order was more orthodox. *Let
life, waned*—the imperative mood carries through to the end; let
life part, pen, pack, let life be aware of. *All throughther* = each
through the other.

I cannot refrain from pointing to the marvellous third and fourth
lines. They seem to me to anticipate the descriptions we hope our
younger contemporary poets will soon write. Such synaesthesis has
tempted several of them, but this is, I believe, the supreme example. Hopkins' technical innovations reach out, however, into many
fields. As a means of rendering self-consciousness, for example, consider this:

> Only what word
> Wisest my heart breeds dark heaven's baffling ban
> Bars or hell's spell thwarts. This to hoard unheard,
> Heard unheeded, leaves me a lonely began.

Or this:

> Soul, self; come poor Jackself, I do advise
> You, jaded, let be; call off thoughts awhile
> Elsewhere; leave comfort root-room; let joy size
> At God knows when to God knows what; whose smile
> 's not wrung, see you; unforeseen times rather—as skies
> Betweenpie mountains—lights a lovely mile.

My last quotations must be the sonnets which most I think, represent the poet's inner conflict.

> Not, I'll not, carrion comfort, Despair, not feast on thee;
> Not untwist—slack they may be—these last strands of man
> In me ór, most weary, cry *I can no more.* I can;
> Can something, hope, wish day come, not choose not to be.
> But ah, but O thou terrible, why wouldst thou rude on me
> Thy wring-world right foot rock? lay a lionlimb against
>   me? scan
> With darksome devouring eyes my bruisèd bones? and fan,
> O in turns of tempest, me heaped there; me frantic to
>   avoid thee and flee?

>   Why? That my chaff might fly; my grain lie, sheer and clear.
> Nay in all that toil, that coil, since (seems) I kissed the
>   rod,
>   Hand rather, my heart lo! lapped strength, stole joy,
>   would laugh, chéer.
>   Cheer whom though? the hero whose heaven-handling
>   flung me, fóot tród
>   Me? or me that fought him? O which one? is it each
>   one? That night, that year
> Of now done darkness I wretch lay wrestling with (my
>   God!) my God.

No worst, there is none. Pitched past pitch of grief,
More pangs will, schooled at forepangs, wilder wring.
Comforter, where, where is your comforting?
Mary, mother of us, where is your relief?
My cries heave, herds-long; huddle in a main, a chief
Woe, world-sorrow; on an age-old anvil wince and sing—
Then lull, then leave off. Fury had shrieked "No ling-
ering! Let me be fell: force I must be brief."

O the mind, mind has mountains; cliffs of fall
Frightful, sheer, no-man-fathomed. Hold them cheap
May who ne'er hung there. Nor does long our small
Durance deal with that steep or deep. Here! creep,
Wretch, under a comfort serves in a whirlwind: all
Life death does end and each day dies with sleep.

Few writers have dealt more directly with their experience or been more candid. Perhaps to do this must invite the charge of oddity, of playfulness, of whimsical eccentricity and wantonness. To some of his slighter pieces these charges do apply. Like other writers he had to practise and perfect his craft. The little that has been written about him has already said too much about this aspect. His work as a pioneer has not been equally insisted upon. It is true that Gerard Hopkins did not fully realize what he was doing to the technique of poetry. For example, while retaining rhyme, he gave himself complete rhythmical freedom, but disguised this freedom as a system of what he called Sprung Rhythm, employing four sorts of feet ($-$,$-\breve{}$,$-\breve{}\breve{}$,$-\breve{}\breve{}\breve{}$). Since what he called *hangers* or *outrides* (one, two, or three slack syllables added to a foot and not counting in the nominal scanning) were also permitted, it will be plain that he had nothing to fear from the absurdities of prosodists. A curious way, however, of eluding a mischievous tradition and a spurious question, to give them a mock observance and an equally unreal answer! When will prosodists seriously ask themselves what it is that they are investigating? But to raise this question is to lose all interest in prosody.

Meanwhile the lamentable fact must be admitted that many people just ripe to read Hopkins have been and will be too busy asking "does he scan?" to notice that he has anything to say to them.

And of those that escape this trap that our teachers so assiduously set, many will be still too troubled by beliefs and disbeliefs to understand him. His is a poetry of divided and equal passions— which very nearly makes a new thing out of a new fusion of them both. But Hopkins' intelligence, though its subtlety with details was extraordinary, failed to remould its materials sufficiently in attacking his central problem. He solved it emotionally, at a cost which amounted to martyrdom; intellectually he was too stiff, too "cogged and cumbered" with beliefs, those bundles of invested emotional capital, to escape except through appalling tension. The analysis of his poetry is hardly possible, however, without the use of technical language; the terms "intellectual" and "emotional" are too loose. His stature as a poet will not be recognized until the importance of the Belief problem from which his poetry sprang has been noticed. He did not need other beliefs than those he held. Like the rest of us, whatever our beliefs, he needed a change in belief, the mental attitude, itself.

[SEPTEMBER, 1926]

LITERATURE, SCIENCE, AND DOGMA

SCIENCE AND POETRY. *By I. A. Richards. 16mo.*
96 pages. W. W. Norton and Company. $1.

MR I. A. RICHARDS is both a psychologist and a student of literature; he is not a psychologist who has chosen to exercise his accomplishments at the expense of literature, nor is he a man of letters
who has dabbled in psychology. One might expect, in our time,
to come across numerous individuals of his species; but the double
gift, rarer than the double training, is rarely given; and Mr Richards is almost alone. The Foundations of Aesthetics and The Meaning of Meaning (works of collaboration) are books which will certainly gain in importance and estimation. His first wholly original
book, The Principles of Literary Criticism, is a milestone, though
not an altogether satisfactory one. Mr Richards had difficult things
to say, and he had not wholly mastered the art of saying them;
it is probable that what he has there said with much difficulty, he
will be able to say better. The present little book marks a distinct
advance in Mr Richards' power of expression and arrangement. It
is very readable; but it is also a book which everyone interested in
poetry ought to read.

The book is notable not because of providing the answer to any
question. Such questions as Mr Richards raises are usually not
answered; usually they are merely superseded. But it will be a
long time before the questions of Mr Richards will be obsolete:
in fact, Mr Richards has a peculiar gift for anticipating the questions which the next generations will be putting to themselves.
And the question which he asks here is one of the greatest moment;
to realize this and kindred questions is almost to be unable thence-
forth to keep one's mind on any others. Exactly what these questions are will cause us some trouble to explain. This book of
ninety-six small pages is, first of all, an enquiry into a new and un-
explored aspect of the Theory of Knowledge: into the relation between *truth* and *belief,* between rational and emotional assent. It
is an essay in The Grammar of Belief; the first intimation that I
have met with that there is a problem of different types of belief.
It touches on the immense problem of the relation of Belief to
Ritual. It sketches a psychological account of what happens in the

mind in the process of appreciation of a poem. It outlines a theory
of value. Incidentally, it contains much just observation on the difference between true poetry and false. One cannot swallow all these
concentrated intoxicants in ninety-six small pages without becoming
a little dizzy.

Mr Richards' importance—and I have suggested that he is indeed important—is not in his solutions but in his perception of
problems. There is a certain discrepancy between the size of his
problems and the size of his solutions. That is natural: when
one perceives a great problem, one is the size of one's vision; but
when one supplies a solution, one is the size of one's training.
There is something almost comic about the way in which Mr
Richards can ask an unanswerable question which no one has ever
asked before, and answer it with a ventriloqual voice from a psychological laboratory situated in Cambridge. Some of his faiths seem
to be knocking each other on the head. ". . . Our thoughts are
the servants of our interests," he says on page 22: it is the up-to-
date psychologist speaking. But as we read on we find our thoughts
turning out to be very poor servants indeed. For it appears to
be to our interest (what *is* to our interest, we ask) to hold some
kind of belief: i.e. a belief in objective values issuing from objective reality. One would expect Mr Richards to maintain—and he
does maintain in part—that "science" is purely a knowledge of how
things work, and that it tells us nothing of what they ultimately
are. "Science," he says (p. 63), "can tell us nothing about the
nature of things in any *ultimate* sense." In that case, we should
expect that science would leave "the nature of things in their ultimate sense" quite alone, and leave us free to "believe," in the
"ultimate" sense, whatever we like. Yet science *does* interfere with
the "ultimate," or Mr Richards would not have had to write this
book; for his view is just that science (restricted though it be)
has squashed the religious, ritual, or magical view of nature upon
which poetry has always depended. I think that Mr Richards
will have to reperpend this matter: the objection is not so petty
and frivolous as it looks. If one is going to consider philosophically
the nature of Belief, it is as dangerous to be a scientist as to be
a theologian; the scientist, still more—in our time—than the theologian, will be prejudiced as to the nature of Truth. Mr Rich-

ards is apt to ask a supra-scientific question, and to give merely a scientific answer.

In his theory of value, again, Mr Richards asks the supra-scientific question, and gives merely the scientific answer. His theory of value appears to be the same as it was in his Principles of Literary Criticism. Value is organization (p. 38): "For if the mind is a system of interests, and if an experience is their play (*what does "play" mean?*) the worth of any experience is a matter of the degree to which the mind, through this experience, attains a complete equilibrium." "Interests," for Mr Richards, tend to be atomic units; a difference of strength between interests tends to be merely quantitative. The difference between Good and Evil becomes therefore only the "difference between free and wasteful organization": Good is Efficiency, a perfectly working mental Roneo Steel Cabinet System. The best life (p. 42) for "our friend" (whom we wish well) is one "in which as much as possible of himself is engaged (as many of his impulses as possible)." St Francis (to take a figure in the public eye at the moment) might have chosen a life in which *more* of his impulses were engaged, than in the life which he did choose; he might have chosen a life in which his impulse toward fine clothes (not in itself a bad impulse) might have been included. The goal is the avoidance of "conflict" and the attainment of "equilibrium." The Buddhists have a different name for "equilibrium."

I am not so unsophisticated as to assert that Mr Richards' theory is *false*. It is probably quite true. Nevertheless it is only one aspect; it is a psychological theory of value, but we must also have a moral theory of value. The two are incompatible, but both must be held, and that is just the problem. If I believe, as I do believe, that the chief distinction of man is to glorify God and enjoy him for ever, Mr Richards' theory of value is inadequate: my advantage is that I can believe my own and his too, whereas he is limited to his own. Mr Richards' faculty for belief, in fact, suffers, like that of most scientists, from too specialized exercise; it is all muscle in one limb, and quite paralysed in another. When I peruse Mr Russell's little book, What I Believe, I am amazed at Mr Russell's capacity for believing—within limits. St Augustine did not believe more. Mr Russell believes that when he is dead he will rot; I cannot subscribe with that conviction to *any* belief. Nevertheless, I cannot "believe"—and this is the capital point—that I, any more than Mr Russell and others of the more credulous brethren, get on for one moment without believing *anything* except the "hows" of science.

Mr Richards seems to me to be the dupe of his own scepticism, first in his insistance on the relation of poetry to belief in the past, and second in his belief that poetry will have to shift without any belief in the future. He admits that "even the most important among our attitudes can be aroused and maintained without any belief entering in at all" (p. 72) and goes on to say that "we need no beliefs, and indeed we must have none, if we are to read King Lear." King Lear is after all a pretty huge exception; but the statement is very questionable. I do not know whether Mr. Richards meant to imply that Shakespeare must have had no beliefs in writing it; but I cannot for the life of me see that I need any more belief to read Paradise Lost than to read King Lear: and if yielding onself to works of art fostered beliefs, I should say that I was more inclined to a belief of *some* kind after reading the play of Shakespeare than after the poem of Milton. I wish, in any case, that Mr Richards had given an example of a work of art which could not have been produced without belief. Throughout this chapter (Poetry and Beliefs) Mr Richards seems to me to be using the word "belief" very hazily, usually with the intimation of *religious* belief, though I do not see why he should limit himself to that. I do not suppose that he imagines that Homer believed in the "historicity" of all the monkey-shines of the Olympian troupe; and Ovid, who rather specialized in anecdotes of divinities, could hardly be cited as an example of Roman fundamentalism. Of the Roman poets, the one with the most "belief" was (I venture to suggest) Lucretius, whose beliefs were precisely of a scientific kind, and whose belief in his phantom Venus is very attenuated indeed. But even if we take the poet who might seem the aptest for Mr Richards' purpose—Dante: what right have we to assert what Dante actually believed, or *how* he believed it? Did he believe in the Summa as St Thomas believed in it, and did even St Thomas believe in it as M Maritain does? And how dependent is Dante upon the "magical view of nature"?

The whole problem turns on the question whether emotional

values can be maintained in a scientific universe. Mr Richards is very well aware—as I know from conversations with him—and I know no one who is more aware—that emotions and sentiments appear and disappear in the course of human history, and rapidly too; that certain sentiments of the late Middle Ages, which we should be glad to have if we could, have completely disappeared, like the secrets of the best stained glass or Byzantine enamel-work. It seems quite possible, as Mr Richards suggests, that a future increase in scientific knowledge may be accompanied by a steady deterioration in "spirituality" (the word is mine, not Mr Richards'). Mr Richards thinks that the only thing that can save us from "mental chaos" is poetry, a poetry of the future detached from all belief. What this poetry will be I cannot conceive. If his description of the "poetry of belief" were clearer, we should also have a clearer idea of what he means by the poetry of unbelief. If there is such a distinction as he draws, between the poetry of all the past and the poetry of all the future, then I do not think that he is justified in making exceptions of such poems as King Lear. If he is right, then I think that the chances for the future are not so bright as he hopes. Poetry "is capable of saving us," he says; it is like saying that the wall-paper will save us when the walls have crumbled. It is a revised version of Literature and Dogma.

The chief fault of the book is that it is too small; the subject is immense. In the ninety-six pages Mr Richards covers so much ground that I have had to leave some of his most interesting theses, and all of his penetrating and highly valuable criticism of contemporary poetry, untouched. He has worried and tantalized us, and we demand a bigger book.

It is a pity, by the way, that the seventh line of Wordsworth's sonnet (p. 19) by which Mr Richards illustrates his theory of the process of appreciation of poetry, should have been printed with one syllable omitted (for *to* read *unto*).

T. S. Eliot

[March, 1927]

MUSICAL CHRONICLE

A CAPACITY for the creative combination of popular material with the classical idiom was common to most late-romantic composers. Wagner in Die Meistersinger and Moussorgsky in Boris Goudonow and Khovantschina; Strauss in Aus Italien, Til Eulenspiegel, and Feuersnot, Chabrier in his España Rhapsody, and Debussy in numerous piano compositions, incorporated demotic norms in the substance of imaginative works. In Satie's "realistic" ballet Parade, this capacity found a new exploitable material. Previously, it had been Russian and German, French and Spanish folk-tunes that had been incorporated into their pieces by the masters, or used as models of style. Of American materials, only those associated with the negro and the Indian had been placed under contribution; and while Dvorak had suggested to the Americans themselves the ores buried in the negro tunes, the attitude of Charles Martin Loeffler, quoting with elegant irony the Dies Irae in La Villanelle du Diable and the famous Lorraine marching song in Music for Four Stringed Instruments, symbolized the general attitude of this country toward its own opportunity. But in Parade, Satie incorporated a section strongly imitative of ragtime; and with it there commenced the recent efforts to mint values for art from the polyrhythms and colourations of commercial jazz which Strawinsky, Milhaud, Hindemith, and other Europeans have been showing us. None the less only in the piano concerto of Aaron Copland, played by the composer with the Boston Symphony in New York, February third, has the new situation borne music. If it was necessary for a European to point out the opportunity in America, it has been an American who has been able to profit by it.

There was no imaginative utilization of the popular American idiom in the experiments of Satie and his group, with their fox-trots "Adieu New York," their "Shimmies et Rag-caprices," their ragtimes, bostons, sliding trombones, and syncopations. Because jazz sounded exotic to staid European ears, they were content to transpose the synthetic American (half negro and half Jewish) idiom bodily into their compositions. The Ragtime passage of Parade is a cross-section of most rags, rather more than an abstraction of their characteristic elements; and the authenticity of most of the experiments is well below that of the commercial American

musical product. The constructive attempts of Gershwin are without style or homogeneity, hash derivative elements together, and
never long transcend the plane of things made to please a public
incapable of discrimination. Less compromising and more respectable experimentations with jazz idiom for imaginative purposes
have been made by Still, a pupil of Varèse's. But Copland in his
piano concerto has daringly utilized jazz polyrhythms and colourations in an interest entirely transcending that of the commercial
jazz composers; and it is this usage that really concerns the musical,
and makes the production of the composition displaying it a red-
letter day.

As Copland has pointed out in an extremely significant technical
article recently published by him, the best of the popular composers
make only a timid use of the characteristic jazz polyrhythms. To
make them palatable to the great public, always averse to rhythm,
they sandwich them between worn-out conventional ones. It is
not, however, necessary for us to analyse what is known as "jazz"
to ascertain its tendency. One has but to scrutinize its appeal and
feel its effect to recognize that it tends to bring into play the most
undifferentiated strata of the human being in its animal and mechanical manifestations. Born out of the American's desire to escape
individuation and the choice, values, and responsibilities of the
individual existence, it periodically permits him to become the
blind integer of a crowd, or the will-lessly twitching piece of a
machine he needs to be. Copland's concerto, on the contrary, liber-
ates the characteristic jazz rhythms, letting them develop fully in
their own spirit. Part of his first movement is based on the fox-trot
rhythm—slow 3/8 plus 5/8; and part of the second on the Charleston rhythm—the same 3/8 plus 5/8 considerably speeded up; but
in each instance the rhythms are freely permitted to develop. The
polyrhythms are daring. In one passage 3/4 are beaten against
4/4; and in another 3/4 go against a Charleston. Both the orchestral rhythms and those of the short piano cadenza are passages of
invention comparable to the rhythmically most daring pages of
Strawinsky. The spirit is burlesque in the grandiose, Rabelaisian
sense. The "I don't give a damn" of jazz remains, releasing feeling
instead of confining it on the undifferentiated, automatic plane.
The trombone slides; the saxophone whines and chuckles; but all
the machinery of vulgarization sounds forth wild tremendous laugh-

ter that lets spirit free above the massed vulgarities of life. As in certain writings by contemporary Americans, the demotic idiom is so combined with the traditional means of communication that it sustains ultimate values.

His concerto is Copland's strongest work, an expression of formative power beyond Music For the Theatre, the Serenade for violin and piano, and the choral setting of Pound's An Immorality which justified the poem of its title. (Though rose-leaves die of grieving!) The new work's outline is bold and decided, edged with threefold brass. The music is filled with teeth. Copland's two personal veins, his plaintiveness, hitherto given form in the first movement of his symphony and the third of his suite, and his motor-rhythmic style, apparent in the scherzo of the symphony and the dance-movements of the suite, have acquitted themselves of clangorous pages. The first has contributed the nostalgic music of the commencement and the recapitulation of the concerto, with its almost painful brassy climaxes; and the second is responsible for the dizzy Rabelaisian scandal and burlesque of the body of the work. One got the communication of a great, almost painful struggle for feeling and a release in Rabelaisian laughter; perhaps the contrast and inevitable suite of the opposing inertia and frantic activity of American life. And while Copland's gift remains a little spotty and still in pieces, or like a colt unsteady on its stilts, it has at twenty-seven placed him among the important figures of the country.

Concerts of new music revealed 1. that the two last acts of Les Malheurs d'Orphée by Milhaud are moving through music really felt; 2. that the prelude and second movement of a symphony for orchestra and pianos by Charles E. Ives besides being literary are badly orchestrated as though Schumann had done the instrumentation, doubling all the parts; 3. that Ernst Krenek's Symphonische Musik is clearly constructed and at times original in its sombre colouring; and 4. that Hindemith in both Der Dämon and the Concerto for Wind Instruments is a composer with an extraordinary grasp of rhythmic flow and sequence. They also revealed 5. that there is an unnecessary extremeness in the character of Alfredo Casella. For here he was with an Adieu à la Vie, whereas all that any one would think of demanding of him would merely be his Adieu à la Musique.   PAUL ROSENFELD   [APRIL, 1927]

TO
BROOKLYN BRIDGE

By Hart Crane

How many dawns, chill from his rippling rest
The sea gull's wings shall dip and pivot him
Shedding white rings of tumult, building high
Over the chained bay waters Liberty—

Then, with inviolate curve, forsake our eyes
As apparitional as sails that cross
Some page of figures to be filed away;
—And elevators heave us to our day . . .

I think of cinemas, panoramic sleights
With multitudes bent toward some flashing scene
Never disclosed, but hastened to again,
Foretold to other eyes on the same screen;

And Thee, across the harbour, silver-paced
As though the sun took step of thee, yet left
Some motion ever unspent in thy stride—
Implicitly thy freedom staying thee!

Out of some subway scuttle, cell, or loft
A bedlamite speeds to thy parapets:
Tilting there momently, shrill shirt ballooning,
A jest falls from the speechless caravan.

Down Wall, from girder into street noon leaks,
A rip-tooth of the sky's acetylene.
All afternoon the cloud-flown derricks burn,
—Thy cables breathe the North Atlantic still.

And obscure as that heaven of the Jews,
Thy guerdon . . . Accolade thou dost bestow
Of anonymity time cannot raise:
Vibrant reprieve and pardon thou dost show.

O harp and altar of the fury fused,
(How could mere toil align the choiring strings!)
Terrific threshold of the prophet's pledge,
Prayer of pariah, and the lover's cry—

Again the traffic lights that skim thy swift
Unfractioned idiom, immaculate sigh of stars,
Beading thy path—condense eternity:
And we have seen night lifted in thine arms.

Under thy shadow by the piers I waited;
Only in darkness is thy shadow clear.
The City's fiery parcels all undone,
Already snow submerges an iron year. . . .

O Sleepless as the river under thee,
Vaulting the sea, the prairies' dreaming sod,
Unto us lowliest sometime sweep, descend
And of the curveship lend a myth to God.

[JUNE, 1927]

APPARITION IN EARLY AUTUMN

By Robert Hillyer

MARCEL walked slowly homeward, driving his geese before him. The great beech-trees which lined the way like the aisle of a forest, were already beginning to turn gold. He enjoyed loitering through the September dusk. The smell of wood-smoke was pleasant and the slight chill made his clothes, which all summer had clung to him damply, seem very comfortable. And some time, he thought, a miracle might befall him. Was it not always to young people that the Blessed Virgin Mary had appeared, and the saints who in grottoes or glades of the forest suddenly gladden the eyes of the believer? What better place than this lonely road, what better lad than he, to entertain a shining visitant?

The geese were restive this evening. It was always so in early autumn when their kin were flying south. A call from the high air set them craning their necks upward, honking, and beating their wings. And how they would hiss at him when he waved his arms and mimicked their strain toward the sky! He must clip them to-morrow; the big gander had flown over the barn; he would be off for the south if he had the smallest chance. Marcel was always clipping them to-morrow. It was amazing how time on its casters of dream rolled so quickly and silently away. When had the green ebbed out of the beeches? When had the leaves turned yellow? Already they held the pale light of sunset after the first star had risen. Soon they would be flakes of silver, hissing drily in the winter wind. Yet he had never caught them at their change. It seemed to him that everything was done behind his back, and of a sudden the season had changed, or people were saying to him, "You are quite a man now." Indeed time slips away, but even so one has to wait a long while for a miracle.

Marcel lifted his eyes and watched the geese waddling along unhappily on their webbed feet. He looked beyond them, and under one of the beeches saw a glimmering form taking shape. There was no footfall among the leaves on the ground; the figure had not been there a moment ago. The more he looked at it the clearer it became, and, so it seemed to him, taller and slenderer. His heart pounded. He stopped in his tracks. Certainly this was his miracle—but immediately he wished it had not come so soon. He was not prepared for it; he was afraid. Was it an angel? Was it a saint? Suppose it should be the Blessed Virgin herself and he should not recognize her? In all his day-dreams of the miracle, that possibility had never occurred to him. Yet he should have foreseen it, for something quite as embarrassing had already happened to him. Once a man in dirty corduroy had stopped him in the road and asked directions, and Marcel, because of the man's poor clothes, had talked to him quite naturally. Then in a minute his mother had run out, curtsying and puffing, and bleating, "Yes, Sir! If you please, Sir. Oh I'm glad to be of service, Sir." All the time the shabby traveller had been the rich man from the big house on the hill. Now Marcel was hoping that his apparition would not be the Blessed Virgin. And perhaps life without miracles was really preferable. There would be fewer chances of making some frightful mistake.

Then suddenly the figure came toward him, and if it wasn't only Mary, the cobbler's daughter, in a clean linen frock and a chain of coral beads.

"What's the matter, Marcel? Did you think I was a ghost?"

She came up to him and looked at him very hard out of her dark eyes. Even plain Mary, whom he had known all his life, looked strange this evening. Marcel, without answering, decided with some disappointment that a miracle would have been better after all. He had an obscure feeling that he had spoiled his chances of seeing a miracle by being afraid.

Mary put her hand on his shoulder. "What is it, Marcel?" she said in a strained, breathless voice, as if she were planting her words between heart-beats. "Did I scare you? did you think I was a ghost?" The arm on his shoulder tightened as if she were going to hug him. "I wouldn't frighten little Marcel. . . . No, but big Marcel! He's almost a man, now."

Marcel drew away a little and shuffled his feet uneasily in the dust

"I thought you were an angel," he said.

The words sounded so foolish he hardly dared look at her for fear she would be laughing at him. Instead, she flung her arm off his shoulder, clenched her fists, and regarded him angrily.

"An angel! an angel!" Her voice was fierce and bitter. "Are angels all you're looking for at your age! You, almost a grown

man now, looking for angels! I'd be ashamed of myself! Almost
a grown man and looking for angels!" She laughed abruptly. "Any
one might as well be an angel in this village, the nearest thing to a
man being yourself. O my God!"

"I must drive my geese along," Marcel answered primly, and
rather puzzled.

He started after the white procession, making a clucking sound
to gather in the stragglers.

"Marcel!" Mary had seized his arm now, and swung him round
in her vehemence. "Marcel!"

He noticed how pale she was and how her hair clung in damp
ringlets over her eyes. She looked so silly. But he felt too ill at
ease to laugh at her. Besides, he was almost afraid that she would
hit him.

"What is it?" he asked sullenly.

Then she leaned over him, sighing, and kissed him on the mouth.
She took him in both her arms, pulled him toward her; but he took
no step forward, and, losing their balance, they reeled apart, half
falling against a tree. She laughed queerly. "Don't you like being
kissed, Marcel? Don't you like me? Are you afraid of me?" She
grabbed at him and he ducked.

This was better. It was only one of Mary's foolish tricks after
all. She was always inventing some new game, and you never
could tell when she was just in fun.

"Ho! scared of you! I think not."

Marcel lunged at her in his turn, made as if to kiss her, then
with a great laugh smacked his lips together.

"Well, well; it's time to be going along now. I have my geese
to look after, you know."

The joke had been fairly capped and there was no need of pro-
longing it. Anyway, Mary's pranks were never very amusing except
to herself. Calling "Good-night" over his shoulder, he went on.

As he turned into his own lane, he was shocked to hear Mary
shouting after him. He knew she was only pretending, but suppose someone should hear? Her language was horrid and any one
would think to hear her that she was really in a temper.

"Be careful of your geese, little swine. Don't let the angels
frighten you! Don't run off with the little boy, goosie gander! Little
swine, little angel . . ."

Of course Marcel knew that she was laughing at her own silly joke, but anyone hearing her would think that she were sobbing and that he had been bullying her. She was a fool! He was quite angry with her now, and very lonely.

The geese hurried before him toward the sedges which grew along the little stream. They were home now, he and his geese, and he did not care how chill the autumn night became. They were all home, so safe, so comfortable. He remembered his thought of miracles with distaste.

Far aloft from an unseen flier, fell a soft honking, a call to the south. The big gander stopped, rose up on his webbed feet. He gurgled strangely as if the sound travelled up and down his long neck. He flapped his wings furiously; he was up in the air. He was off! One by one, like white petals fluttering upward on a breeze, the rest of the geese, timorously at first but with each beat of their wings more confidently, followed him into the high night on their way to the south. In a moment they had disappeared. Marcel, watching them, made no effort to stay their flight. He watched them and thought that all this must be a dream.

[FEBRUARY, 1928]

AMONG SCHOOLCHILDREN

By William Butler Yeats

I

I walk through the long schoolroom questioning
A kind old nun in a white hood replies
The children learn to cipher and to sing
To study reading books and history
To cut and sew, be neat in everything
In the best modern way—the children's eyes
In momentary wonder stare upon
A sixty year old smiling public man.

II

I dream of a Ledean body, bent
Above a sinking fire, some tale that she
Told of a harsh reproof, or trivial event
That changed some childish day to tragedy—
Told, and it seemed that our two natures blent
Into a sphere from youthful sympathy,
Or else, to alter Plato's parabell
Into the yolk and white of the one shell.

III

And thinking of that fit of grief or rage
I look upon one child or t'other there
And wonder if she stood so at that age—
For even daughters of the swan can share
Something of every paddler's heritage—
And had that colour upon cheek or hair
And thereupon my heart is driven wild:
She stands before me as a living child.

IV

Her present image floats in to the mind
What quinto-cento finger fashioned it,

Hollow of cheek as though it drank the wine
And took a mass of shadows for its meat,
And I though never of Ledean kind
Have wrong to brood upon—enough of that,
Better to smile on all that smile, and show
There is a comfortable kind of old scarecrow.

V

What youthful mother, a shape upon her lap
Honey of generation had betrayed,
And that must sleep, shriek, struggle to escape
As recollection or the drug decide,
Would think her son, did she but see that shape
With sixty or more winters on its head,
A compensation for the pang of his birth,
Or the uncertainty of his setting forth.

VI

Plato thought nature but a spume that plays
Upon the ghostly images of things
Solider Aristotle played the taws
Upon the bottom of a king of kings.
World-famous golden thighed Pythagoras
Fingered upon a fiddle stick or string
What a star sang and careless Muses heard:
Old clothes upon old sticks to scare a bird.

VII

Both nuns and mothers worship images
But those the candles light are not as those
That animate a mother's reveries
But keep a marble or a bronze repose.
And yet they too break hearts—O Presences
That passion, piety, or affection knows,
And that all heavenly glory symbolise
O self-born mockers of man's enterprise.

VIII

Labour is blossoming or dancing where
The body is not bruised to pleasure soul
Nor beauty born out of its own despair
Nor blear-eyed wisdom out of midnight oil.
O chestnut tree, great rooted blossomer,
Are you the leaf, the blossom, or the bole?
O body swayed to music brightening glance
How can we know the dancer from the dance?

[AUGUST, 1927]

THE THEATRE

IF I were a strict moralist about the theatre, I might take it, or myself, to account, because the plays of the past month have given me exceptional pleasure, and yet I am critically certain that I have not encountered great passions or perfection of form. It is, I must assume, within the capacity of the theatre to give a certain satisfaction without being great.

Paul Sifton's play, THE BELT, was presented by The New Playwrights' Theatre, the same organization which last year, rather self-consciously, put on LOUD SPEAKER and some other experimental works in such a way that the lover of experiments in the theatre began to suspect that the Shuberts were probably right after all. THE BELT is a better play than some of last season's offerings, but not immeasurably better; the production is. It is, in fact, so good that it almost conceals the central fault of the play.

This fault is the author's allowing his interest to shift when the play was half finished. The first act deals with men and women enslaved by the vast processes of large-scale manufacture symbolized by the moving belt—as it is used in the Ford factory and in the packing industry. We see the weary, spiritless faithful worker on the tenth anniversary of his serfdom, demoted from being a foreman because he has been unable to drive his team ahead in a competition with another factory; we see his wife, relishing the comparatively high wages, clinging to the slight dissipations of urban life, and being a little unfaithful to her husband because he is too tired and brighter men, with easier hours, retain a prowess she demands. We see a daughter, stenographer in the big plant; and her "boy-friend," a fiery youth who hates the process by which men are made adjuncts of machinery. Into a sharply drawn picture of dreary lives, satirical relief is introduced: the head of the factory, accompanied by an imported fiddler, heralded by secretaries, arrives, pins a medal on the lapel of the man whose very name he cannot remember, and brings hired dancers to restore the steps of long ago. When all are gone the girl and the boy stir their own passion by dancing to jazz and, broken and weary, fall asleep in each other's arms. In this "compromising" situation they are discovered by the father. Denial of guilt does not satisfy him; but the youth swings the dispute into a tirade against the belt, and suddenly, with the sounding of gongs and the rattle of cog-

322

wheels, the belt comes into view towering above the little human beings, manned by sweating slaves, supremely powerful and deadly. With that something tremendous took place on the stage.

It could only have occurred if the emotions already invoked were profound, and they were. It could only have a sequel if the play of emotions continued, and they did not. From that moment the play went communist: the second act was argumentative, brought in the Ku Klux Klan to avenge the girl's honour, turned into a riot, and ended with the diversion of the crowd's desire to destroy—the threatened seducer turns into a labour leader, announces, with the help of the girl, that the factory is going to be closed down, and leads the mob to destroy the belt. As usual in experimental plays, the destruction, in the third act, is introduced by some fancy jazz dancing, extremely effective while the merciless drag of the belt continues; the president of the factory makes a sentimental speech instead of a financial one, the belt is smashed, and the boy is arrested, reminding the men and women that when they are old they will still recall that once, at least, in their lives, they defied the belt and stood on their hind legs.

The play, in short, turned from a moving study of human beings into an attack upon a system of production; after the first act the belt's effect on human lives was forgotten, and wages and rights and further abstractions, not realized, took their place. It was the first act that made me feel Mr Sifton's power; he has it, and some wit, and a gift for the theatre. After the first act, it was Mr Edward Massey who made the play interesting, who wove groups of people together, who singled out and emphasized the moments when individuals held their own against an idea. I am far from being impartial in Mr Massey's regard, so it pleases me to note that his direction was applauded by most of the critics. In the commercial theatre, one thing would be held against him. It was his idea to bring the belt on the scene at the end of the first act —dramatically he was right. But since the rest of the play could not live up to it, he should have kept the belt for the end—or persuaded Mr Sifton to re-write the play a little.

My programmes for this month's plays have all been lost, so I cannot name the names of some of the players; the two young people were extraordinarily good, playing with simplicity and a surcharge of emotion.

One other play of the month possessed, and created, emotion: Coquette, produced by Jed Harris, who produced Broadway, written by George Abbott, who collaborated on that piece, and by Ann Preston Bridger—a new name. The star is Helen Hayes. For a long time Miss Hayes has used the stage as a platform from which her points of attractiveness could be admired by those who found them attractive; and suddenly, in this play, she acts, with passion and authority; all her tricks and mannerisms have been, as a fellow-critic remarked, subdued to the part. She is a credit to Mr Abbott who directed, and to herself.

The play has certain elements of goodness; some are to be found in Romeo and Juliet and the rest in any melodrama of southern chivalry. These are the best parts of the play, and in indicating their sources I do not mean to belittle them in any way. The weakness of the play is in the meagre creation of character. The coquette is a congeries of characteristics; she is flirtatious, she wheedles, she gets around people, but there is nothing in her words or actions to make her distinctly a person. The roughneck with whom she falls in love is a little better—he has a sort of violence which might pass for power; but he too is close to caricature. Almost all the other characters are stock; the exception is an adolescent, well conceived and well played.

This is a first play re-worked by an old hand. It has fine points, some freshness, and delicacy.

Two melodramas: deft, quiet imported goods in Interference; harsh, slick violence in Nightstick. The end of the second act of the latter is so good that the slow beginning and the trick ending are not at all resented. Interference is more of a piece and has been directed in a languorous, easy-going manner which pleases me by drawing out the intensity of its suspense. It manages, oddly for melodrama, to create a character; with the slightest turn of interest the play could become a straight tragicomedy built around the conception of a rotter who, having once experienced beauty, kills whatever threatens that beauty.

In John, Philip Barry demonstrates again the possession of a considerable talent which is either not for the theatre, or has not yet made terms with the theatre. This demonstration has gone on for some years, and once in a while Mr Barry seems to have learned something. The present play is built around the figure of John the Baptist; toward the end of the first act John is expecting the people of the town to come to hear him preach; he learns that his young disciple, Jesus, is also preaching in the neighbourhood and sends some of his men down to meet the approaching crowd, so that a number of them may be diverted to the younger preacher. And he stands at the door of his tent, watching the multitude, and then, before his messengers have reached them, he sees the entire crowd turn to the place where Jesus is preaching.

This was excellently dramatic, it was beautifully conveyed, silently, to the audience. The rest of the play was swept away in words. Everything was analysed; but the simple things that might have been simply told, the suggestion of political intrigue in which Herod was involved, the background of Messianic hysteria, were smothered; and the crucial thing: that John was not sure of the mission of Jesus, and could only be sure when his own death came, was not used dramatically at all.

Mr Ben-Ami was superb. I am not a foregone admirer of his methods; he seems, at times, to sacrifice a character to his own urgent feeling that everything must be intense and emotional. In this case he seemed to have created on the stage the figure that was in the author's mind; he was hampered by endless speeches —and he is not the actor to whom speech is essential, nor the one who manipulates English with the greatest ease. Yet he lifted himself over every obstacle, and I hope that he will not now return to the tents of Israel.

JOHN was produced by The Actors' Theatre, under the direction of Mr Guthrie McClintic. When Mr McClintic took over the management of this body, after the unsuccessful opening of last season, and instantly produced SATURDAY'S CHILDREN, laurels were placed on his brow. They have withered. Neither in his choice of play nor in his direction did Mr McClintic display any special gift.

Another organization, The Garrick Players, began their season with THE TAMING OF THE SHREW in modern clothes. Basil Sydney played Petruchio and Mary Ellis, Katherina. Far better than HAMLET, the SHREW undergoes the fresh treatment. Especially I liked the introduction of vaudeville and burlesque technique in certain scenes. Merely to see a motor-car or an electric stove while listening to

Shakespearean phrases is a small pleasure—the pleasure one always feels in the presence of a discovered anachronism or incongruity. But to see Shakespeare adapted to our native stage is to recognize an identity—which is a higher pleasure. His comedies are direct descendants of the Venetian *commedia*—and so is our comedy. The current production let us see this, and made the SHREW vastly entertaining. It seemed strange to me that the induction scene and the interruptions from the drunken guest counted for so little. In Gémier's production, seen here a few years ago, much was made of this, and it fitted perfectly.

It must have been a pleasure to Leslie Howard to find himself with a play which allowed him to act, which required of him, for success, something more than walking agreeably through a few salons and bedrooms. It is a pity that ESCAPE, John Galsworthy's new play, should not be more interesting. It has nine scenes; to carry the plot, three or four would be enough. The others are added either to make a night's entertainment (in which case they fail) or to allow Mr Galsworthy to make another cross-section of contemporary British life. There are six scenes in which an escaping convict meets various people and is variously aided or persecuted by them; some of these are as thin and bloodless as anything Mr Galsworthy has written; only two have any real gait and drive. To one of the latter Miss Frieda Inescort contributes a hard and polished gem of acting; to all of them Mr Howard brings precision, sympathy, an engaging reality. But nine *genre* scenes are six too many.

WEATHER CLEAR—TRACK FAST is a romance of the race track in which the hero neither rides nor wins his bet; it has some excellent wisecracks of this year's vintage and is pretty consistently amusing.

An ungrateful city has allowed Miss Mae West's WICKED AGE to disappear after a run of two or three weeks. If this is a rebuke to Miss West because her activities last year brought on the censorship, it may be justified; I fear it is nothing of the sort. Clean and dull though her new play was, Miss West deserved better for a display of technical virtuosity which is—in all seriousness—unparalleled. I do not mean by this that Miss West is a great actress; I mean only that her technique, superbly developed, comes out of our most uncorrupted theatre—the theatre of revue, burlesque, and vaudeville. It is slick, and sly. It is amazingly economical—a look of the eye serving Miss West where the complete battery of close-up expressions are used by much more respected players. Miss West has little range—a few gestures, a few intonations—but she makes them serve. To me she was, in a wretchedly cast and vilely staged play, incredibly fascinating.

Her play—she is also the author—achieved a meaninglessness almost sublime. Two minutes before the curtain fell I was puzzled to see how on earth she could possibly end it—and was baffled because she simply didn't end it at all, merely walked off the stage and let the curtain come down on a stage strewn with loose ends. The best scene, intellectually, was a burlesque in which a newly chosen Miss America writes testimonials; there were also scenes of colossal unintentional humour, and some so broadly absurd that they were obviously put on merely to see how far in silliness one could go. Miss West is neither a portent nor a promise; but I will not of my own accord ever miss a show in which she appears.

Too late for review: SPELLBOUND, with Pauline Lord—mingled interest and distaste; Reinhardt's A MIDSUMMER NIGHT'S DREAM —Reinhardt and his talented companies, including Moissi; THE DOCTOR'S DILEMMA, by The Guild—the best production of Shaw The Guild has done since HEARTBREAK HOUSE, Dudley Digges directing; FUNNY FACE—Gershwin score, in case you have forgotten That Certain Feeling the composer has remembered it; the prodigious Astaires dance and clown in it and Victor Moore is very funny. All these and whatever the gods provide, will be reviewed next month.

GILBERT SELDES

[JANUARY, 1928]

LONDON LETTER

"A SMALL group of friends who were undergraduates at Cambridge at the beginning of the century came to have an influence on their time which can still hardly be gauged. Among these were the sons of Sir Leslie Stephen, the eminent Victorian biographer and agnostic. The Misses Vanessa and Virginia Stephen, their sisters, lived in London; and their house became the nucleus of the group, when the two brothers and their friends left Cambridge." I am quoting from the seventh volume of Sir Raymond Mortimer's trustworthy if academic Studies in Twentieth-Century Culture (Hogarth Press 1960). "The young ladies, who were as remarkable for their beauty as for their intellect, married two of their brothers' friends, Clive Bell and Leonard Woolf, who were to become celebrated, the one as an apostle of contemporary art, a vigorous pamphleteer, a poet, a historian of civilization, and a psychological biographer; the other as an editor, a publisher, and a politician. An important figure in this group was Edward Morgan Forster, novelist, critic, and historian. Perhaps the most influential was Giles Lytton Strachey, who later revolutionized the art of history: he is said to have shown from the first the almost fanatical intransigence in conduct and opinion which marks the leaders of important movements. But the group was always an oligarchy—fierce mutual criticism was the breath of its existence. Another dominating figure was John Maynard Keynes, the economist and politician, who by his marriage years later with Mme Lopokova, the first dancer of her day, brought leadership in yet another of the arts into this astonishing circle. Duncan Grant, though not a member of the University, was an early intimate of the group, and so was Roger Fry, though of an older generation of Cambridge men. It thus appears that from one small band of friends have come the subtlest novelists, the most famous economist, the most influential painters, the most distinguished historian, and the liveliest critics of the post-war period in England."

I have preferred to quote from the veteran critic, because my relations with the persons concerned are too close for me to be able to speak of them easily without impertinence. But the name of Bloomsbury is becoming familiar in Berlin, Paris, and, I presume, New York as well as in London, and I think the time has come when a study of the genesis of the group and the character of those who compose it should be made public. I am certainly not the person to do this; but since I am writing a letter I may perhaps take a letter-writer's privileges and put down a few casual comments on what I see around me.

It is impossible to say where Bloomsbury begins, and where it ends. Are the painters, scholars, and journalists of a younger generation to be included? Arthur Waley? Francis Birrell? George Rylands? Douglas Davidson? Are old and intimate friends who have never become entirely imbued with the Bloomsbury spirit? And in fact what exactly is this spirit? I do not dare a definition. But I would place first a belief in Reason, and a conviction that the pursuit of Truth and a contemplation of Beauty are the most important of human activities. Obviously many of Bloomsbury's fiercest enemies might subscribe to this creed. The distinction of the leaders of the group is that they have acted upon it to an extraordinary extent. No subject of conversation has been taboo, no tradition accepted without examination, and no conclusion evaded. In a hypocritical society, they have been indecent; in a conservative society, curious; in a gentlemanly society, ruthless; and in a fighting society, pacifist. They have been passionate in their devotion to what they thought good, brutal in their rejection of what they thought: second rate; resolute in their refusal to compromise. "Narrow in their tastes, loose in their view of morals, irreverent, unpatriotic, remote, and superior," their enemies say. And, I think, truly. For will not relentless reasoning and delicate discrimination make a man all these things?

Such vivid personalities as the leaders of the group could never of course commit themselves to any corporate doctrine of taste. But they have tended to exalt the classical in all the Arts: Racine, Milton, Poussin, Cézanne, Mozart, and Jane Austen have been their more cherished artists. Already the signs of a romantic revival are everywhere perceptible. The next generation is likely to react vigorously against the intellectualism of Bloomsbury. The younger French care as little for Voltaire as they do for Anatole France.

Keyserling and Maurras, Chesterton and Lawrence, are united in their hatred of intellectualism. Indeed Monsieur Julien Benda seems almost the only important figure on the Continent whose views are akin to Bloomsbury's. But here anti-intellectualism has not yet found a champion adequately armed.

Obviously there is a romantic poet in Mrs Woolf, a mystic in Mr E. M. Forster, whereas Mr Strachey, for all his appreciation of Blake and Beddoes, remains in his outlook almost a contemporary of Voltaire. But compare these three writers with any outside the group, great Edwardians like Wells and Bennett, for instance, and a certain consonance in the Bloomsbury artists becomes, I think, apparent. For one thing they remain singularly unspotted by the world; too disillusioned to expect that their scale of values can ever command general assent. (Perhaps the fact that they almost all possessed small independent incomes gave them an initial advantage over many of their rivals.) The east wind of Cambridge philosophy braces their nerves. Pragmatism, Bergsonism, Oxford idealism, wither beneath it. And the historian of Bloomsbury will have to discuss the enormous influence on the group of George Moore, the author not of The Book Kerith but of Principia Ethica.

Why Bloomsbury? someone who does not know London may ask. It was Mrs Desmond MacCarthy, the author of A Nineteenth Century Childhood (she and her husband have always been intimate with the group) who, I believe, first gave it this name from the quarter of London where most of its members lived. It is a quarter honeycombed with spacious squares, where houses built for the gentry in the eighteenth century declined later into boarding-houses for impoverished foreigners and students at the University of London. The houses are for the most part still too big to be inhabited by single families, but the quarter is replacing Chelsea as the home of painters and writers. On summer evenings there is tennis on the lawns, and the Vicar's daughters can be seen playing with the bigwigs, ignorant of the dangerous company they keep. Around are figures reading and talking, and as night falls, the mourning veils in which London soot has dressed the Georgian façades become unnoticeable, and in these gardens you may fancy yourself in the precincts of a college. The passing of a quarter of a century is forgotten, the quick exchanges and curious conjectures, the vehement arguments, remake the past; and the commercial traveller arriving late at St Pancras' from the north, catches a glimpse as he passes of an unfamiliar and unhurrying London, of

> groups under the dreaming garden-trees,
> And the full moon, and the white evening star.

RAYMOND MORTIMER

[MARCH, 1928]

FOUR POEMS

By Louis Zukofsky

I

tam cari capitis

Unlovely you called yourself
And at once I felt I was never lovely:
I, who had few truths to go to,
Found you doubting what I loved.

Now I make you lovely my own way,
Unmentioned were we certain
Of a greater, in small assurances
Others may find trivial!

   .   .   .   .   .

II

SONG THEME

to the last movement of Beethoven's Quartet in
C-sharp Minor

All my days—
And all my ways—
Met by hands—
And ringed with feet—
Into laurel-branch the hands
Are gone, into fertile soil the feet;

So these praised ones that are fallen off
Are a signal in the trees,
Are a beacon in the sun,—

Sun and death and stir, and death's unlit love,—

All their days,
And all their ways.

III

Someone said, 'earth, bowed with her death, we mourn
Ourselves, our own earth selves,'—yet for me crept
Rattling a small wind bitter, and I wept
But your own little form that might be torn.
And suddenly I could see your face borne
Like the moon on my sight, it had not slept
But looked, as once, at rest though waking, stepped
To the grave peace of death and not yet worn.

'Look at the moon,' you said: 'Those are no tears
Falling, unclasped through space, for what appears
Dead crater sheds no tears.' And your face from
Where it came vanished, so I was too soon
Oblivious among the wind, the moon
Clouding then, her high dissolution come.

IV

The silence of the good that you were wrought of,
Do I find it transformed by some strange leaven
From you to earth only my earth knows aught of,
And know it silent mound outlined on heaven,
Till all the life of you in our still room
Returns to me—your presence past the wall
Of death, the confines of your dark? So fall
Death's guerdon to me neither sun nor gloom;

But quiet—your silence, when you would stir
With me—its being, what you are and were.
It cannot change though it must change the mode—
Not with you living, but with you dead to darkle—
Yet is no less obliged to corrode
In earth with you—earth, shadow of your sparkle.

[DECEMBER, 1928]

A GLANCE AT THE SOUL OF JAPAN

By Paul Claudel

Translated From the French by Lillian Chamberlain

WHEN I was asked by my friend, Goraï, collaborator with Professor Michel Revon in the compilation of that admirable Anthologie de la Littérature Japonaise (which never leaves my work-table) to discuss the subject of French tradition, I said that I was not quite equal to the task. It is almost as difficult to speak of one's country as of one's self. Between the impression which we have of ourselves and that which we make upon sincere and unbiassed persons who have come expressly to study us, there is a difference which the books of travellers permit us to savour in all its piquancy. And while it is easy to accuse them of naïveté of malice, is it quite certain that they are always in the wrong, and that we only are irrefutable witnesses of ourselves? For the most part, to tell the truth, people act without being really conscious of what they are doing, they are not actuated by reasonable and definite motives which they could instantly explain, but by habit, by instinctive, extemporized response to the impulsions of circumstance, duty, necessity—by an empirical application of instruction accepted without question and acted upon without reflection. We inhabit a certain corner of nature and society as we inhabit our bodies—in the same naïve, comfortable, ignorant, animal way—and when we are invited by a direct question or false inference to explain this or that action, are subject to confusion or offence much as if we had been asked to justify our eyes or nose. It has to be so because it *is* so, and we cannot visualize the pictorial, pristine effect that we have on strangers. They alone can distinguish what is characteristic, special, and at times unique in an act or mode of behaviour, a mental attitude which seems to us natural and inevitable. A native, however, again has the advantage when he attempts to understand reasons for the often bizarre and disconcerting effect which he makes upon visitors. As throwing light on it he has in his possession a rich store of archives, of incidents, and of data, which afford him in relation to himself, somewhat the outside disinterested position of critic, and at the same time, a sort of intuitiveness and

NOTE: An address before the students of the University of Nikko.

sympathy which enable him retroactively to prolong for his consideration the experiences of his forefathers and ancestors, very
much as if their life were his own. It is this experience, short, long,
conscious or unconscious—that we call national tradition. You have
more direct access to it than is afforded in the briefs of our country
or in a few arbitrarily selected illustrations. Entrance to this most
intimate tribunal of our national mind, to this sort of continual parlia-
ment where all litigation is carried on, where all cases are heard and
all judgements are rendered, this supreme record which enters into
all our legal proceedings, all our intellectual customs, is our language.
The French language is at once the most perfect product and most
incontrovertible certificate of our national tradition. It has been the
chief means of building up a people comprising twenty distinct races,
from the residue of I know not how many invasions and migrations
following one upon the other. Arrived at this land's end, brought up
short against the European jetty, these peoples found themselves compelled to establish between their distinctive strata and cross-sections,
a solidarity, an accord which the land also imposed upon them.
Though ethnologically diverse, France is one and indivisible geographically, and counsels to disruption are less puissant by far than
are the necessities for concentration. There could be among the French
none but spiritual controversies, and to the intellect alone could the
task of reconciliation be confided. Every citizen of this chance vari-
form assemblage which had emerged from the ruins of the Roman
Empire and the moraines of Barbary thus found himself inclined to
become an orator, a diplomat, a jurist. He was led to seek in general
and enduring forces underlying special fortuities, an explanation of
the existence of the nation. Add that geographically France is not
the slave of fixed conditions, is not committed indefinitely to a repetition of the same course of action, but is so situated that nothing of
general import can take place in the occident without involving her.
And she must continually arrange her affairs in such a way as to
balance conditions, modifying them at times by inducing, at times by
arresting action, always counter-balancing some element in the general situation. To solve the new problems with which he was constantly
being confronted the Frenchman had need not so much of empiricism
as of a general principle for forming judgements. Our longest war, the
Hundred Years' War, was but a juridic debate punctuated with ap-
peals to arms. That France should have been placed by providence

at the intersection of all continental interests precludes the possibility of rigidly prescribing her destiny or of arbitrarily setting limits for her. Law must intervene. The treaties of Westphalia and Utrecht and the acts of Vienna and Versailles were not mere redistributions of territory, they were above all, formulated principles of which the new map divisions were but a consequence. And what is true of our foreign policies is equally true of our domestic ones. Each Frenchman, . . . heir of twenty miscellaneous races, has always constituted—to himself—a little sovereignty carrying on a continual diplomatic and judicial interchange of thought and feeling with neighbouring sovereignties, under the authority of a sort of scattered but all-powerful tribunal called Opinion. From this fact arises not only the importance we attach to literature and to language, but also that thing so characteristically essential to both—whether it be prose or poetry, whether concerned with psychology or description—the passionate desire for accuracy. We are always explaining, and explaining ourselves. The desire with us to perfect the language and make it efficient has been not merely the ambition of a few highly cultured persons, but a matter of great practical importance; we could not too highly esteem and cherish the chief instrument of our national unity which, in the course of a continually open debate, has permitted us to take cognizance of our permanent mission and successive obligations. Thus was established little by little, this habitual attitude of the Frenchman to life, having for its main characteristic, inclination for discussion. He is by nature a jurist, in every instance his instinct is to seek causes and, if I may be permitted to play on words, also to plead them (since the same term with us is used to designate the explanation of a thing's existence and the legal process by which is established one's right to it). In France literature has not been the expression of a few exceptional minds; it has been rather the necessity of an entire race, the uninterrupted means of communication between its different geographical divisions, conducive to mastering every new problem brought forward. Every Frenchman has always had the sense of speaking before a tribunal of experts, any one of whom was qualified to ask him to explain every word.

It is one of these Frenchmen whose mental attitude I have been trying to give an idea of, who would bring his still naïve testimony, before reflection and habit have had time to distort and blunt it. . . . Pilgrim of many journeys, it was but yesterday that he disembarked on this shore which for so many years had enriched his mental horizon. And having once passed the utilitarian zone in which the everyday needs of humanity are supplied in Japan as elsewhere by the same apparatus of machinery and buildings, he immediately finds himself face to face with a country which is not, like so many countries in Europe or America, a simple agricultural or industrial enterprise, the inn of a day or a night, patronized without special intention or thought—but an hereditary domain the significance of which is less the practical convenience of its immediate occupants than the composing of a solemn and instructive spectacle. Everything Japanese from the outline of a mountain to that of a hairpin or a *saké* bowl is in conformity with a single style. In order to discover Japanese tradition it is not necessary, as in the case of the French, to penetrate to that intimate tribunal in which ideas arise and mental attitudes make trial of their strength; there is nothing to do but open eyes and ears to this irresistible concert about us to which each generation must in turn tune its instruments and voice.

Let us listen, but in order to hear we must first create silence. Music begins only where noise ceases. Let this confused tumult of velleity and words subside in us. If I were one of your mystic pilgrims, I should induce this by having an ancient ritual prayer recited over me and should surrender myself to the benediction of the little brush which confers purity and contemplativeness. Here I am, one of the followers in the train of a certain personage in your literature, the poetess Murasaki, or the bonze Kennko, who persuades me to tread silently in the path of mysteries. It seems to me I hear the rustle of noble silk or the click of the chaplet against the alms-bowl. I follow an endless alley of enormous cedars with coloured trunks which lose themselves in black velvet; a fierce ray of sunlight sears with lightning stroke an indecipherable inscription on a stone pillar. The windings of the strange road serve to evade demons and to separate me for ever from a profane world. Over a coral arch I cross a jade pool (is it this pool which by a fugitive gleam of light between the motionless pads of the lotus, will discover to me my invisible companions?). Shadowed by the centuries I pour upon my hands from a sebilla, water so piercing, so cold, that I am born again. Behind the closed door I listen for the bell tolling slowly as though meditating; a waxlight burns, and below in the chaos of leaves I hear the voice of the cuckoo answering the liturgy of the cascade.

And it is here I perceive the distinctively Japanese attitude to life to be that which for lack of better equivalent—French does not offer great resources for expressing this sentiment—I shall call reverence, respect, free acceptance of an exaltation too great for the intellect, the sinking of personality in circumambient mystery, the sense of an enveloping presence which makes incumbent upon one a measured decorum. It is not for nothing that Japan has been called the land of Kami, and this traditional characterization . . . seems to me the most perfect that has been achieved. Japan is like a dense bank of clouds on the bosom of a boundless ocean. Its jagged shores, its inner harbours, its mysterious openings are to the sailor a continual surprise. Its mountainous framework constitutes not only one of the most complex formations in the world, but one disturbed by mysterious convulsions, the precarious nature of which is attested by the tremors which still agitate the unstable soil. It is like a stage-setting which the mechanics have just left, the back-drop and wings still shaking a little. The plains of Japan are among the most populous parts of the world, but certain mountainous districts, vast tracts of veritable jungle recalling the tropics, are still as uninhabited as at the day of Creation. On every side, nothing but valleys, folded and refolded; forests blacker than night, inextricable tangles of reeds, ferns, and bamboos. Over it all, and at some seasons almost continuously, descends a curtain of rain; here wander those strange vapours of which ancient and modern Japanese painters have with such sovereign result availed themselves, vapours which by turns hide and disclose as though on purpose corners of the landscape, as if someone wished to call them to our attention and expose for a moment their occult significance. And above the whole country, dominating plain and mountain, sea and island, the most majestic altar as it were, that Nature ever raised to her Creator—a landmark thousands of years old, worthy to commemorate the spot where the Sun after speeding far over watery wastes, prepares to engage in the human phase of its activity —rises the heroic form of Fuji.[1]

Thus to whichever side one directs his glance, he finds himself surrounded with veils which open only to close again, with silent

[1] In Japan a man need not pray; the very soil is divine. Hitamara.

awe-inspiring retreats to which there are long winding paths like those of an initiation ceremony, with funereal shades, with strange objects—an old tree-trunk, a stone worn by water, like indecipherable sacred documents—with perspectives which discover themselves to him only through rock porticoes or colonnades of trees. All nature is a temple prepared for worship. In Japan there are none of those great rivers, none of those vast plains with gradually ascending sky-lines, which entice the dreamer and invite the spirit to endless voyaging. At each step the imagination is arrested as it were by the fold of a screen and an arranged perspective, the hidden meaning of which bespeaks the homage of his attention. The artist or hermit need only mark it by a Shinto gate-way or a lantern, or a splendid temple, or by erecting a simple stone. But it is never the edifice, however gilded, which seems to me to be as in Europe, its soul. It is a casket, a censer placed obscurely to induce a consciousness of the great solemnity of nature, and so to speak objectify it. Like these few characters or brush-strokes, with a vermilion seal added, which the poet or artist disposes on a sheet of white paper.

While the European of to-day sees in his environment a realm merely calculated to contribute to his comfort or profit, without doubt to the traditional Japanese, Creation is first of all the work of God, still permeated with divine influences; and since in Japan one does not enter the home of the humblest peasant without removing one's shoes, with what reverence ought not mortals to comport themselves in approaching the parvis before the abode of Higher Powers, privileged by them to use it in common with them? Repeating what I said a moment ago, just as temples here seem not to have been built with a deliberate purpose but rather in answer to the latent prayer of the landscape, thickening by art the dense forest shade, as here in sacred Nikko; guiding the voices of these ever-flowing waters; rendering permanent on the black of the foliage the gold and scarlet of a ray of sun; imprisoning the thunder under a bronze bell; repeating and making more solemn by the upward flight of porticoes and stairways, an ascending earth; reiterating by their avenues of giant witnesses the reticent appeal of the sanctuary; so in the same way, what else do their crowds of pilgrims venerate—those pilgrims who with an affecting zeal, do not cease to throng these temples?—what do they worship behind the ever lowered curtains? A mirror as it were reflecting heaven, a drop of the primordial Waters, the name of saint or ancestor carved on a tablet, something confounded with night—above all, night itself, that mystery upon which the naïve heart piously meditates.

I have been struck forcibly by the fact that as expressions of Buddhism during the primitive period in Japan, at Nara for example, one sees numbers of very beautiful statues. Later, and in proportion as Japan had time to impose her own character on the imported religion, these set representations became more and more rare. They withdrew into denser and denser shade until finally, in modern times, they have neither form nor voice.

It is something quite invisible in the sacred cave that they are trying to reach—this humble woman who claps her hands two or three times, this group of mystics who cast a handful of pennies into the box, this little girl who climbs the temple steps uncertainly and wakens the bronze frog at the end of the thrice-twisted cotton rope.

The supernatural in Japan is then nothing but nature, is literally supernature, that region of superior reality in which brute fact is metamorphosed into meaning. It does not contradict law but rather emphasizes the mysteriousness of it. The whole purport of religion is to induce humility and silence in the presence of that which is everlasting. The patriotism of the Japanese accordingly seems to me above all, unbroken communion with his country—that is to say, poignant contemplation of the face of nature. Among the crowds of voluntary pilgrims at all the noted scenic spots, nothing could be more striking than the long file of school-children whom their masters are conducting to a special point that they in turn may receive the impression by which so many generations have been influenced. This attitude of reverence and ceremony has here become a habit of the soul, not only upon visiting spots signalized as privileged seats of divine influence but in the presence of all created beings who are, like us, the work of one father and the revelation of his will. The relationship expresses itself in gesture and ceremonial. I recall how, upon an early visit to Kyoto, as I walked in one of the beautiful gardens which are the charm of that incomparable city, a great pine that I saw stirred me, penetrating my consciousness; it was almost ready to fall, but was supported by a sort of enormous crutch that someone had piously fitted to it. This tree seemed to me not merely what it would be to an American or European—a mine of boards, a mute thing in the landscape— but a live being, a sort of vegetable grandfather to whom someone had lent filial assistance. Nothing is commoner than to see a tree of unusual proportions or a distinctively shaped rock encircled with a strand of sacred rice straw and thus placed among things Kami, testifying to the attention visitors have bestowed on it and to their gratitude for its existence. When a household pet has died, it is carried to the temple where the *nembutsu* is recited over it by the bonze; no life however humble is, in disappearing, too valueless for religious commitment. A merchant, a seller of rat-poison, will commemorate by a service, rodents his product has destroyed; and a stationer, old brushes which are past usefulness. Finally and prettiest of all—I read the other day in a newspaper that the wood-engravers' association of Tokyo had engaged in a ceremony to honour the cherry-trees whose substance they had used in their art.

It is this reverent, worshipful feeling—a kindly, tender fellow-ship with the world of creatures—in which the secret of Japan's art consists. It is striking that in appreciating the products of it, our taste has long been at variance with that of Japan. We prefer the engravings and paintings of the Ukigoye school, looked upon in Japan as of a rather decadent period, but one for which I may be pardoned for having, personally, kept my first enthusiasm: it admits of a strong, stately, dramatic, brilliant, witty, picturesque infinitely varied and animated rendering of familiar sights, man in his customary setting and employments being given chief place in it. Whereas the trend of Japanese taste is toward antiquity— pictures from which man is absent for the most part or is present only in monastic equivalent, as immobile nearly as the trees and stones. A carp, a monkey hanging from a branch, a few flowers, a landscape with level superimposed above level, which a master brush has painted with strokes as definite as handwriting—such are the things presented for the most part on these priceless kakemonos recovered from the depths of the past by their happy possessors and unrolled before us with infinite care. And sometimes just at first, we barbarians, who feel that we must be surprised and entertained, have a sense of disappointment. We lack the humility which would permit the soul to be affectionately united to this tender shoot be-

ginning to quicken, to this potent stroke of the tail of the fish rising
from the dusky slime into regions of aquatic light. It is but gradually we perceive that life itself is before us in this delightful sup-
pleness, this exactitude, this exquisite suspension of movement which,
for instance, directs and informs this monkey from the points of
his claws to the tip of his tail (it is not a monkey in motion, but
motion become monkey), this savant, naïve choice of treatment,
this patient contemplation joined to lightning rapidity of hand,
this rigidly austere suppressing of unnecessary alien elements; it
is no longer art but life itself, in action, which is disclosed to you,
more divine by reason of its anonymity. Observe this trivial fraction
of life which, thanks to the devout unselfative artist, has become
alive for all time. And even as the grand seigneurs of former days
preferred to gold and crystal vases a simple earthen bowl to which
the potter had imparted the resilience of flesh and the brightness
of dew, so in striving to express the eternal, these great artists,
often priests, have painted not only gods and symbols but things
the most fragile and ephemeral, the most pristine stirring of the
ineffable source, a bird, a butterfly, less: an opening flower, a falling leaf. By the magic point of a brush this has been so ordained.
The very thing is here before us, alive and immortal, its transitoriness
henceforth indestructible.

So evident is this to me that I shall not labour the manner in
which a reverence so deep in the heart of the Japanese, has come
to determine the modalities of their ordinary life. The nature of the
tie between the nation and their sovereign is well known; it is not
exaggeration, moreover, to say that in ancient Japanese society,
all human relationships of family, clan, and corporation, were
obedient to the dictates of an all but sacred ritual. In no country
has the Confucian principle of seemly behaviour been more generally or more nobly exemplified. If indeed something of mystery
and divinity be attributed to inanimate objects, how much more
appropriately would it pertain to man. Japanese grammar yields
itself to variations of time and circumstance, and to degrees of
respect and formality required by the dignity of the speaker and
of the persons addressed, and of the occasion in question. It is
marked by an hereditary politeness which I truly hope the Japanese
will never lose despite the bad examples set them.[1] It is always

[1] The profound, oft repeated reverences, set off by words and glances, with
which Loti diverts himself in Madame Chrysanthemum, testify to the satisfaction

a surprise to us occidentals to see one coachman salute another pleasantly in passing as though to apologize, instead of reviling him as would be the case in London or Paris. Can you imagine a chauffeur who, like the chauffeur of one of my Tokyo colleagues, goes weekly to burn incense at the tomb of the forty-seven Ronins? It is moreover the personal consciousness in each man, of something sacred and inviolable which explains the extreme nature of Japan's ancient code of honour. When the inmost sanctuary of his personality had suffered insult, a man had to disappear or cause his insulter to disappear. Finally, I detect this mystic instinct, this sanctity even in the sensibility which informs profound feelings and emotions, in the very care even, with which objects that you hold dear are concealed—even in the complicated art of boxes and multiple envelopes in which presents, purchases, and small domestic treasures are cunningly clothed and dissembled. Regarding this little thesis as no more than a surface enquiry into psychology, as but a tentative summing-up, I shall close with what illustrates as it seems to me the way in which Japanese religious feeling has something in common with that of humanity as a whole. I am reading with much admiration and benefit, the reminiscences of a man who has devoted his life to serving the poor, who lives among beggars and prostitutes in one of the most wretched quarters of Kobe, and I borrow from him to make myself clear to you. He writes, after having been converted to Christianity, that what made the strongest impression on him in the teachings of the gospel was the commandment not merely to love one's neighbour but also to honour him. Not only ought we to love creatures the most degraded spiritually and materially, but also to value and honour them as being, like us, the creatures, the living temples of Divinity. They, even more than we, bear the special mark of his hand (like this pine twisted into the supplicating attitude of a paralytic!). Nothing is more Christian than this sublime sentiment, and I rejoice to believe, more characteristically and profoundly Japanese.

There remains for me but to glance back with you over the landscape we have been regarding, and to conclude with a consideration of certain prospects which the future holds out to us.

It seems to me that at the foundation of the traditional Japanese

we experience in penetrating further and further the identity of those we meet. They give time for preparation, for the adjusting of our hearts, *siaosin* in the Chinese proverb.

soul is respect—a subordinating of personality to the object considered, deferent recognition of the life and of the things which
surround one. Religion in Japan has not thus far been the worship
of a transcendant Being, but is specifically associated with nature
and with that society in which it exists; and although it resembles
the religions of India and China in that it is without belief in a
precise revelation from the other world, it differs profoundly from
both. The Indian is essentially a contemplative, meditating continually on the same thing—a verdure eternally non-existent, ever
hiding and ever hidden. The Chinese, distributed over the greatest
fertile tract of land on the face of the earth has been preoccupied for
the most part with regulating the individual's relations to his
fellow-man, with the formulating of moral and practical laws en-
abling brothers to divide an inheritance of land and water without violence or recourse to law. The Japanese belongs to an isolated unit that has shown throughout centuries its ability to forgo
contact with the rest of the world. His country is a kind of
sanctuary built and adorned, in which he watches a brilliant, significant ceremonial, progress throughout successive rites, from one
year's end to the next, from January snows till the shoots make
their way up out of the earth under the warm rain of the *nynbai,*
from April's exhalations of the rose to autumn's conflagration. Life
for him is participation in this august calendar as the child of an
ancient family takes part in the traditional anniversaries of the
household. He allies himself with nature rather than subjugates
it, adjusts his life to her ceremonial, observes her, follows her,
renders her speech and her detail more perfect; their lives inter-
mingle. In no country is there more acute understanding between
man and nature, or a more evident reciprocal imprint. For two
centuries they have but contemplated each other. May one not
hope that this communion shall endure and that its teaching to the
rest of humanity shall not fail, that alien buildings, commonplace
and unrelated to the ground on which they stand, shall not—like the
howls of slaves and of the damned—drown with discord the music
of these enchanted isles? As often as I return to France I note
with chagrin the growth of a vile invention, a scourge worse than
phylloxera, which is destroying the beauty of our landscape: I
refer to the machine-made tile, a thing of artificial and rigid aspect
like the soul of a serf, whose strident red is replacing the beautiful

tapestry of faded purple like Bokhara wool, the honourable old roofing of Champagne and Provence. Introduced into the most harmonious landscape, a single touch of this insolent, inexpugnable carmine is enough to ruin every other effect like an imbecile's laugh shattering orchestral harmony. So, in Japan also, unless means are found to check these pernicious materials, I fear that re-enforced concrete and zinc may work like havoc. According to an old Chinese superstition, the *fong shui*, natural harmony cannot be impaired with impunity, and should nature be travestied or its form and meaning effaced, human beings in that dishonoured region will be exposed to every malign influence. I hope there may never be such a day for Japan, and that peaceful union of man and earth will endure through the ages, as in the words of your national hymn, "like the moss on the rock."

[NOVEMBER, 1928]

ON THE SHORE

By Albert Halper

HE and I checked in together and worked side by side, tossing letters hour after hour into the small squares. It was a stormy winter but we did not see much snow; the drifts in the streets were shovelled away immediately by laborers; and though the sun came out nearly every day we caught only flickers of it. We were going to school, working nights at the post-office, and managing to sleep a few hours. It was a grind; the days passed like slides thrown on a screen. No fun, no dates, no time to read. School, study, sorting letters addressed to people we should never see and were not interested in.

We wore short aprons when we stood at the mail-cases so that contact with the ledge for our mail-trays as we bent forward, reading the addresses and moving our arms, would not make our vests shiny or wear them out. We had tucked our sleeves up, our arms kept going; white, brown, tan arms. Every few minutes, in the same tone of voice, the dispatcher would call out trains, bags were locked, piled on trucks and rolled away by big negroes humming a tune, their bodies shifting a bit in turning down the aisle to the platform. The night went slowly. The many clocks against the walls were controlled by current and every minute the thick black hands would jerk forward with a clicking sound.

We became accustomed to the rows of moving arms, the one tone of voice, the rumble of belts, and rattle of cancelling machines as they testified that letters had been received on a certain day, at a certain hour.

At first we had not much to say as we worked, but in a few weeks knew the separations of the case and did not bother to glance at the labels above the states. We had the feel now. Our arms were mechanical arms but our minds were freed. As we worked we began to think.

In the mailing section there were perhaps a thousand men—whites, negroes, Filipinos—young and middle-aged, but we all felt old. There was a deadness, a dulness overhead. Many of us were students, some from small towns and farms, working for tuition, board, and rent. We were paid by the hour; no loafing here. Though some of us were attending universities, we did not look like college men; there was a plodding air about us—about our very clothing. We looked like scrub-women hired by the management of loop buildings to clean up at night—but for ever thinking of their children, husbands, and homes.

I had a friend, a tall well-built negro of about twenty-two, with light brown skin. He was intelligent, and the slow easy grace of his moving arms as I watched them out of the corner of my eye, fascinated me. He had one defect—physical. When he smiled you could see his teeth were beginning to decay.

He had come from Pontiac, Michigan, to study law and was having a hard time. Although comparatively young, his parents were forced to accept charity. He himself was in a sense old.

When we had been working on the same shift for a week or so, I had said a few words, casually. In a few days we were talking together and from that time on when we checked in at the desk, he was always behind me.

A group of whites, Pontiac business men, had paid his fare to Chicago, given him a hundred dollars, and told him to come back a lawyer. Pretty fine of them, he thought. I learned from him that negroes were multiplying in Pontiac, that some had money, owned homes—that generous men had sent him to school with a purpose, and that a job was promised him, a position with a real estate firm; that he was to handle the coloured trade for the white man, that he was well liked by his people.

After the holiday rush the mail work slackened. One night we were through in about three hours and a half and I suggested to Bart that we take a walk.

The night air was clean and cold, Jackson Boulevard was lighted, and people were just beginning to come out of shows. We walked toward the lake and as the wind blew against us, some papers that stuck out of the books Bart was carrying, kept flapping in the wind.

Michigan Avenue was quiet. We headed for the outer drive by the lake and slowly crossed the old wooden bridge at Randolph Street. The wind was stronger there and we began to feel chilled, we were so used to being inside.

We kept on walking. As they approached the shore the waves

shattered themselves to a fine spray; and lakeward, in the darkness, it was active mist against the dark blue distances. We grasped our books tighter.

We stopped and faced the lake. The sounds of the water, the hurrying of the winds, the darkness, were things great and deep to us—alone in the night—two boys who did not know anything. We could only realize that we knew nothing at all as we sat there on some pieces of slab a few yards from the shore, hunched up, looking at the lake. Behind us was the Avenue, flanked by lights. I felt warmer and did not mind the wind.

Bart told me of his boyhood, his folks, a girl that he knew. He talked. He was not bitter, did not bemoan the fate of the negro or become excited, and to-day I cannot remember the words, but what he said went deep into me, as something warm and genuine.

A big wave struck the shore; the wind carried the spray into our faces, and we got up and crossed the old bridge again, above the railroad tracks leading everywhere. We could see a brakeman's red light wavering as he walked, and from the distance it looked as if a fellow were trying to light a cigarette in the wind. We were on Michigan Avenue again. Toward the north on a large illuminated clock-tower it showed past midnight. At Wabash Avenue we separated, Bart taking the elevated south; I, walking to State Street for a car west.

The next evening, at the mail-cases, neither of us had much to say. Bart's brown arms were going fast and threw a great quantity of mail. I did not feel quite at ease. The night before we had walked out near the lake, talked a bit, felt the spell of space and water. Had I said something, done something? Did Bart feel that he had said too much?

Our arms kept going, white, brown, tan. Train numbers were called by the dispatcher and the monotone drifted away. Bodies leaned forward, letters were tossed, the supervisors walked slowly down the aisles and the hours went by—short hours again that night. As soon as our set was checked out, Bart disappeared and I was alone outside on the steps. The lights in Nick's Lunchroom across the way were being put out. Too late for a cup of hot coffee. I took a car to my rooming house, studied for more than an hour, and crawled into bed.

In a week or so we began to be at ease again, only there was a little something, an indescribable shred between us.

The days moved on. It was now spring. We were studying, working, plugging away. Then the warm days of May, and in June school was over for the year. I was going home for the summer, but Bart would work all through the hot months in the mailing section. He needed money more than I did.

I had obtained leave of absence and was on my way out of the building, would take a train that very night. I was going home. On the stairs I met Bart and told him I was going. He smiled and I noticed his teeth for the thousandth time. He had a fine face. It was late afternoon and the street was filled with traffic. Buses ground by, close to the curb. There was a jam at Clark Street and automobiles were honking; it got on one's nerves but Bart smiled. He said he envied me.

Loneliness enveloped us, each separately. I caught it in his eye and knew that he saw it in mine. What was it?

"I hope you'll have a good rest," Bart said. I noticed his faded cap, and a weary look about his eyes.

We shook hands. There was no barrier between us. We felt through our gripping fingers a sensation difficult to put on paper. We now knew we could be fit interpreters of the word brotherhood. We looked at the traffic and heard the sound of the city. After exchanging a few words I descended the stairs and Bart went in to work. Men, women, young girls in a hurry; the late sun covering sides of buildings, street-cars going carefully, impatiently, the warm wind. Slowly I began to think of other things.

[MARCH, 1929]

DEATH IN MOONLIGHT

By Stanley J. Kunitz

A leopard no more secret
Is than she who goes
By night alone, observing
Moon-foam upon the rose;

A doe is not more gentle
Than she who palely treads
Through peonies' white clusters,
Brushing small rabbit-heads.

Her steps are light as dewdrops
Among imagined sheep,
Timid that she may startle
A herd of rocks from sleep;

She tarries for a moment
Beside a sky-deep pond
To watch a floating turtle;
Enchanted, moves beyond

To greet a glittering forest,
A tall and starry town.
Supple, her proud sweet body
Crying plunges down.

[February, 1929]

PARIS LETTER

March, 1929

ONE of the most interesting literary phenomena of the past few years, and one unannounced by sign or symptom, has been the discovery by the French public of contemporary American writers. The symbolist and Parnassian generation of thirty years back knew Poe through the lyric interpretations of Baudelaire and Mallarmé; Whistler had introduced to a very limited circle of artists in Paris a few writer compatriots now forgotten. Thanks to his translators, Whitman was known in France some time before the war, but his case was the unique exception. The wit of Mark Twain was wholly lost upon us here. Although a few literary connoisseurs knew and lauded Hawthorne, he had no established following. Henry James and after him Mrs Wharton owed their repute in France rather more to advantageous personal relationships here and throughout the continent than to being widely read, and were thus more celebrated, than actually known, although readers of Bourget and De Maupassant, et cetera, could feel at home in their pages. Just before the war the Nouvelle Revue Française had attempted without much success to introduce to the French public Thoreau and Waldo Frank. In short we can say that until about 1926, American novelists were not known to the French public. Since that time, however, the frequent, almost annual, visits of American writers, Dreiser, Sinclair Lewis, and even members of the younger group, Glenway Wescott, Seldes, Cummings, their interviews printed in our literary journals, formal receptions to them by various associations of French colleagues, like the French branch of the Pen Club, have directed attention to American writers and to their works. Régis Michaud, professor in the University of California, published two years ago The American Novel To-day; Bernard Faÿ who for a part of each year is a member of the faculty at Columbia, returned to Paris each winter full of admiration for American literature. And then, there were a few of us, very few, who ourselves crossed the Atlantic to become better acquainted with our American confrères. If I may speak of myself, I visited New York three times within three years, simply to satisfy my own curiosity and for the pleasure of experiencing at first hand the real America; Durtain, Maurois followed me two years afterwards. The effects of this *rapprochement* were soon evident: French interest in American writing began to grow.

Of course there are many other influences which I cannot take up here in detail. English literature from which many French literary people had in the XIXth century drawn either emotional inspiration (the Romantic movement), or a larger understanding of the world beyond our own borders (Kipling, Wells, et cetera) suffered an eclipse in the post-war years. With the exception of D. H. Lawrence and Virginia Woolf, who, moreover, were still unknown in France, English writers available in translation here were Garnett, Gerhardi, Clemence Dane, Aldous Huxley, all of great talent but influenced by the continent and none of them really an innovator. In its eager search for the new, Paris turned from England to America.

Then, too, the cost of the American novel at 80 francs had long been prohibitive to our public—the translation rights equally so to our publishers. When the franc rose and we could buy American novels for two dollars and a half, the situation began to be more possible. For all these reasons we are now witnessing here an influx of American letters. From Winesburg, Ohio to Fifty Thousand Dollars, from Dreiser to Anita Loos, the American novel is little by little invading Paris. Right now, Manhattan Transfer is enjoying a great vogue. Nigger Heaven has been translated (I myself had the pleasure of presenting it to the French public); Carl Van Vechten has followed his book and is himself at present among us. And, speaking of Harlem, we might add that McKay, now in Marseilles, and Walter White (whose work has also been translated) round out our education in American negrophilie. Just a while ago Marcus Garvey in a public appearance essayed to win us over.

The Association de Coopération Intellectuelle, under the auspices of the League of Nations at Geneva, is doing its part to systematically encourage the mutual understanding of the peoples. Under the direction of Bergson, of Valéry, the French Section attempts to influence the choice of works to be translated, hitherto pretty much left to chance, often betraying such a lack of understanding on one or both sides that more harm than good has come to the authors of the original work (read Ernest Boyd's excellent discussion of this subject). If the League's activities in this direction turn out well, American writers will gain thereby. American and French universities have very successfully organized international exchanges. Why could novelists not do likewise?—and of course this need not be limited to novelists. Would not some such Institute as the Carnegie do well to subsidize, for example, a good French translation of Edgar Lee Masters?

J. E. Blanche gave us last summer a very amusing book of art criticism: De Gauguin à la Revue Nègre. Blanche is well known in addition to his being a painter of repute, as an observer and critic of what is going on in the studios and literary circles of our epoch. Friend of George Moore, Blanche has worked with Monet: he was the interpreter of Sickert to England: remaining younger than any of us, he loves and appreciates Picasso and Segonzac, approves of Cocteau and Bérard; entirely independent, he has no hesitation in talking snobbery to snobs, exposes combinations of paid critics and dealers; and when a Matisse or a Cézanne is mediocre, has no embarrassment in saying so, giving his reasons which are excellent and supported by convincing analysis.

In the next letter I shall write of two works—just out—which will not fail to have a run this winter: one is the life of Louis II of Bavaria, in novel form, by Guy de Pourtalès, entitled Hamlet-Roi; the other is a novel by Maurois, called Climats. I want now, however, to call attention to an extremely interesting novel by a young French writer who may very well be the recipient of the Goncourt ward: Les Conquérants, by André Malraux. This is the story of Canton in 1925; and, recounted from the other side, of Shameen, the European concession of Canton, as seen from the point of view of the bureaux of Bolshevist propaganda and of Kuomintang. Malraux at the time had access to the bureau which Borodine directed there in the service of Moscow. He actually lived the decisive hours when a few European adventurers held England powerless, boycotted Hong-Kong, and continuing the work of Sun Yat Sen to the profit of Lenin, struggled to give consciousness to that immense informity—China. A few American newspaper correspondents apart, I doubt whether any other white man was so favourably situated to study the rising new world, South China. Conflicts of ideas,

colourful depiction of the leading Bolshevists, the presidents of the
Chinese unions, mass movements, panoramas of the countryside
in the upheaval of civil war—everything is to be found in this book,
admirably put together, of an even and continuous emotional curve,
well written and profoundly thought out: these scenes experienced
by the author himself, and novelized with unmistakable artistic com-
petence, class this newcomer (to whom we already owed a philosophical essay of two years ago on the inter-relations of East and
West, Tentation de l'Occident) among the leading French writers
under thirty.

PAUL MORAND

[APRIL, 1929]

RETREAT

For Lancelot Andrewes, Essays on Style and Order. *By T. S. Eliot. 10mo. 159 pages. Double-day, Doran and Company. $2.*

If it is impossible to read Mr T. S. Eliot's criticism without respect, it is also becoming increasingly impossible to read it without misgivings. In The Sacred Wood, and again in Homage to John Dryden, Mr Eliot provided his immediate generation with a group of literary essays which were an admirable corrective for many of the intellectual and aesthetic disorders of the time. They were compact, precise, astringent; they brought the past to bear on the present, the present into a visible relation with the past; in short, they helped materially to restore, for a literary generation which had lost its bearings, a sense of tradition as a living and fruitful thing. If one had any complaint to make, with regard to these essays, it was not of their main tendency, which was wholesome; nor had one any fault to find with Mr Eliot's intelligence and aesthetic tact, which were acute; it was rather with regard to the plane on which Mr Eliot chose to conduct his analysis—and the tone which he adopted—that one might have cavilled. In the matter of plane, one had to note that Mr Eliot tended to be somewhat abstract, not to say academic. His analysis was more often analysis of the document itself than of the psychological dynamics of which the document was the sign; he seemed to regard literary forms as absolute and autonomous; and correspondingly, he seemed to minimize the merely functional, or social and psychological, elements in the creation of literature.

These restrictions made for simplicity and weight; but they also gave one an uncomfortable feeling that a great deal was being left out. In his very preoccupation with what was past and fixed, Mr Eliot was perhaps already beginning to define himself, and his limitations, more candidly than he was quite aware. It was as if the immediate, the fluidly immediate, the here and now— whether it were to be seen in terms of personality, and the relation of personality to the work of art, or in terms of the relation of the work of art to its social "moment"—were positively frightening to him. Again and again he took elaborate pains to evade or

355

minimize the problem of personality: even going so far as to maintain that the work of art is an *escape* from personality; a very revelatory view. It may here be pertinently questioned whether it is not precisely in this curious *doctrine* that Mr Eliot is seeking an "escape from personality." From the psychological chaos of the "I" and the "now," let us seek refuge in a world of canons, forms, and rituals.

But if one felt, now and then, a shiver from this quarter in The Sacred Wood, one is exposed to a merciless blast of it in Mr Eliot's new book, For Lancelot Andrewes. In this, Mr Eliot seems to be definitely and defeatedly in retreat from the present and all that it implies. A thin and vinegarish hostility towards the modern world is breathed from these pages. Seeking certainties, or at least a hope of certainties, Mr Eliot sounds a quavering recall, and attempts to lead us back to classicism in literature, to royalism in politics, and to the Anglo-Catholic church in religion. Humanism he condemns as merely a "sporadic" ancillary of religion, a kind of parasite, unable to exist fruitfully in its own right. Reason is bankrupt. Of the human race, the less said the better. Of Machiavelli, he remarks in this new book: "He was no fanatic; he merely told the truth about humanity. The world of human motives which he depicts is true—that is to say, it is humanity without the addition of superhuman Grace. It is therefore tolerable only to persons who have also a definite religious belief; to the effort of the last three centuries to supply religious belief by belief in Humanity the creed of Machiavelli is insupportable. . . . What Machiavelli did not see about human nature is the myth of human goodness which for liberal thought replaces the belief in Divine Grace."

It is hard to describe this as anything but a complete abdication of intelligence. And *pari passu* with this abdication goes a striking change in Mr Eliot's whole outlook and style. A note of withered dogmatism sounds repeatedly in these pages; the circle of Mr Eliot's sympathies has narrowed and hardened; in his essays on Andrewes and Bramhall, he is even led, by his propagandist zeal, to write dully of dull subjects. Throughout the entire book —unless we except some excellent pages on Middleton and Baudelaire—we feel the presence of a spirit which is inimical to everything new or bold or generous. Cautiously, jejunely, with an air of puritan acerbity, it seeks a refuge from humanity in Grace, from personality in dogma, and from the present in the past. Turning its back on the living word, it retreats into a monastic chill; and denies the miracle and abundance of life. But can the miracle and abundance be denied in this fashion? Not, one suspects, so simply or so summarily. The moment is still with us, it is a world to be explored, and there are still intrepid explorers. Mr Eliot might have been one of these—as indeed in his verse at times he *has* been—and, but for the Grace of God, he might be yet. It is to be hoped that he will not continue to prefer a narrower and safer path.

CONRAD AIKEN

[JULY, 1929]

NOTES ON CONTRIBUTORS*

[JAMES OPPENHEIM (1882–1932) one of the first settlers in Greenwich Village, was a zealous spokesman for a resurgent American literature. His chief passions were centered in the Bible, Whitman, and Freud, and his poetry and prose manifest an effort to fuse all three. As founding editor of *The Seven Arts,* he acquired considerable authority for a very short time.—Ed.]

[CARL SANDBURG (b. 1878) at the time of his appearance in *The Dial* was admired as a major new voice in a resurgent American poetry. Since that time, as is generally known, he has become a scholar and biographer of Lincoln, folk balladeer, Civil War buff, and TV sage.—Ed.]

[JOHN GOULD FLETCHER (1886–1950) was one of the first official Imagist poets in the circle surrounding Ezra Pound in London before the First World War. Pound's influence included politics as well as poetry: Fletcher, an expatriate until 1933, returned to the United States as a propagandist for fascism. In his instance, however, there is no question of disloyalty. Indeed, in 1936 he was commissioned to write an epic poem on Arkansas, his native state, and this led indirectly in 1939 to a Pulitzer Prize. But Fletcher lived a tumultuous inner life and in 1950 was found dead, drowned in a pool near his home in Little Rock, presumably a suicide.—Ed.]

[EDNA ST. VINCENT MILLAY (1892–1950) is often described as the creator of her own legend. And the legend persists though the reputation—despite a Pulitzer Prize in 1923—and influence are modest.—Ed.]

ALBERT C. BARNES, a student of modern painting, has the largest collection of Renoirs outside of France. [Barnes (1872–1951) was trained in science and managed to make a fortune in the manufacture of Argyrol. He began collecting paintings in the early 1900's, chiefly Monet, Cézanne, Degas, Renoir, Matisse, Picasso. In 1922 he established the Barnes

* *The Dial's* note, where one was supplied, has been reprinted here to recall the contributor's situation at the time of his appearance in the magazine. I have included more recent information, and added my own judgments, in brackets.

359

Foundation at Merion, Pennsylvania, a center of study which was until
1961 closed to those scholars whose credentials did not suit Barnes or his
staff. His views were derived mainly from John Dewey, whose *Art as
Experience* was dedicated to Barnes; indeed, Barnes conceived his
Foundation as a monument to Dewey's aesthetic system, to the idea of
deep interconnection between art and life. Barnes spent most of his later
years battling with art critics, art journals, art editors—including *The
Dial*'s editors, Scofield Thayer and J. S. Watson, Jr., to whom he once
offered $2,000 on the condition that the money be awarded as a prize
in art criticism to a man of his choice.—Ed.]

[JOHN DEWEY (1859–1952), an editor of the fortnightly *Dial,* at the
time of his appearance here was completing work on a major book,
Human Nature and Conduct. As president of the American Psychological
Association, president of the American Philosophical Society, founder
and first president of the American Association of University Professors,
"father" of progressive schooling, Dewey "more than any other thinker,"
said Jan Christian Smuts, "wedded philosophy to life" and strove to
make philosophy a compelling force "not only in the thought but also
in the practice of his day."—Ed.]

[JAMES JOYCE (1882–1941) appeared in *The Dial* only once. Thayer, who
championed *Ulysses,* was unsympathetic to *Finnegan's Wake*—the novel
which preoccupied Joyce throughout the 20's. Watson, however, hoped
to publish Joyce, was eager to print "Anna Livia Plurabelle" when *The
Dial* received this famed piece during the time Marianne Moore served
as editor. But when Joyce refused to accept certain of Miss Moore's
changes, the manuscript was returned.—Ed.]

The verse and fiction of KENNETH BURKE, formerly a student at Columbia University, have recently begun to be published in American
magazines. [Burke (b. 1897), who has written literary and music and
social criticism, is best known as a literary theorist of wide influence.
During his *Dial* days, translating Mann and others whose work was un-
available in English, he was responsible for *The Dial*'s introduction of
major European writers to American audiences. Today Burke continues
to publish at regular intervals books that represent his continuing effort
to formulate an all-encompassing theory of art and action.—Ed.]

MARIANNE MOORE was graduated from Bryn Mawr in 1919. She has contributed to *The Egoist* and to *Others,* and lives in New York. [Miss Moore (b. 1887), editor of *The Dial* from 1925 to 1929, is one of few women, and one of a very small group of poets, who have acquired both general celebrity and critical acclaim in America. In 1924 when The Dial Publishing Company printed *Observations*—and *The Dial* itself gave her its Award—she achieved her first fame. "To Miss Harriet Weaver, H. D., Mrs. Kenneth Macpherson, Richard Aldington, T. S. Eliot, Ezra Pound, Alfred Kreymborg," Miss Moore said in 1942, "Scofield Thayer and Dr. J. S. Watson, and *The Dial,* to Morton D. Zabel, of *Poetry,* I am under lasting debt." She celebrated her seventy-fifth birthday recently in Brooklyn, N.Y.—Ed.]

A review of JEAN COCTEAU's poetry appears in this issue. . . . *Le Coq,* of which he was an editor, was commented on in the August *Dial.* [Cocteau (1891–1963), in his later years elected to the French Academy, experimented with classic literary genres, invented some new techniques of art, and expanded the range of existing forms—ballet, circus, film, surrealist painting, jazz. For a time the Church absorbed and stirred his energies, but he remained "the only person for whom the Myth opens its gates," Rilke said, and permits a return "bronze as from the seaside."—Ed.]

Although EZRA POUND has not previously been a contributor to *The Dial,* his name has appeared frequently in its pages. [Pound (b. 1885) began as a college teacher at Wabash in 1907. Today he lives in exile, a victim of character and circumstance, in Italy, where he returned after release from a mental hospital in Washington, D.C. His praise for *The Dial,* the first journal to distribute his views to a wide national and international public, has always been grudging. Perhaps the reason is, as one of his friends has said, that Pound never admired anything he couldn't control. Despite these difficulties of character and career, he is indisputably one of the most striking modern poets and one of the most devoted if erratic servants of modern American art.—Ed.]

T. S. ELIOT, after studying in Harvard, in Paris, and at Oxford, took up residence in London. Perhaps the most distinguished of the younger poets, in England he is even better known as a critic. [Eliot (b. 1888),

Nobel Laureate in literature, poet, critic, dramatist, editor, publisher, prophet, has clearly lived one of the most remarkable literary lives of all time. In 1922 *The Dial,* publishing "The Waste Land" and presenting him with its Award, lifted him up when, according to Pound, he was down and out.—Ed.]

MR. HENRY McBRIDE will write each month a brief note on contemporary movements in art, displaying their qualities and suggesting their place and value in the history of artistic creation. [McBride (1867–1962), trained as a painter, began his career as an assistant to John Ward Stimson, Van Wyck Brooks' father-in-law, at Stimson's Artist-Artisan Institute. Successor to James G. Huneker as art critic on the *New York Sun,* McBride brought to *The Dial* a light touch and sharp eye. "Whether listening to café gossip in Paris or writing a first-rate report of the famous Brancusi case," says Daniel Catton Rich, McBride managed to inject serious criticism into amiable comment on the social scene.—Ed.]

LOUIS ARAGON is the author of *Anicet,* recently published and highly regarded by French critics. He . . . was one of the principals at the seances Dada of a year or so ago. [Aragon (b. 1897) turned from Dada to surrealism, a movement which he helped to found and lead. Then, deciding for socialist realism in art and communism in politics, he became an editor of *L'Humanité* and *Ce Soir.* During the Vichy regime he edited a clandestine paper which printed poems that made him a kind of folk poet to the Maquis. This experience determined the design of a career which until the 40's had gone in fits and starts.—Ed.]

[PAUL ROSENFELD (1890–1946), original member of *The Seven Arts* group, staff member on *The Dial* until 1927, disciple of Alfred Stieglitz, wrote nine books and hundreds of magazine pieces on literature, painting, music, photography, popular culture. A learned critic and an appreciative student of all modern forms in art, he was admired by almost everyone—from Allen Tate to Kenneth Patchen.—Ed.]

D. H. LAWRENCE is now visiting America, and living on a ranch in New Mexico. [LAWRENCE (1885–1930) had come to New Mexico from Australia. During his few remaining years of life, he supplied *The Dial* with abundancies of prose and verse, grateful to find a journal which opened its pages to all his work. This was, incidentally, the period of his most ambitious labors and led to *The Plumed Serpent, Lady Chatterley's Lover,* and *The Man Who Died.*—Ed.]

[MAXWELL BODENHEIM (1883–1954), until his murder lived disreputably in Greenwich Village and the Bowery, a legendary bad boy of modern writing. His fiction and verse, grotesque, brilliant, recall a leading practitioner in the age of experiment.—Ed.]

[AMY LOWELL (1874–1925) is presented here in her best light. For it is not as a clever poet or as the dowager lady of literature, sister of the President of Harvard, nor as a power politician of art, is her name worth preserving. Rather it is her effort in behalf of other writers, alive and dead, that recall her to us now.—Ed.]

ALFRED A. KROEBER . . . studied and first taught at Columbia University. He is now professor of anthropology and curator of the Anthropological Museum at the University of California. He is the founder of the American Anthropological Association and has written *The Arapaho, The Yokuts Language,* and *Luni Kin* and *Clan* [Kroeber (1876–1960) was a pioneer scholar in a field of study which his own work helped to establish as a major enterprise of modern thought. A man much admired by later generations of students in linguistics and ethnology, he was honored first by the Royal Anthropological Institute, then by Yale, California, Harvard, and Columbia.—Ed.]

WALLACE STEVENS is a lawyer. He lives in Hartford, Connecticut. [Stevens (1879–1955), in response to the editor's request for information, offered only what was repeated here. He remains the man of mystery in American verse: no one has managed to square his work as a vice-president of the Hartford Accident and Indemnity Company with his career as a maker of the most intricate, elegant, learned and philosophic poetry written in America. Stevens, whom everyone on *The Dial* admired, contributed many items but not nearly so many as the management sought. Had he been more responsive to their request for additional material, he would have received The Dial Award. As it is he did receive the Bollingen Prize, The National Book Award, and the Pulitzer Prize.—Ed.]

MINA LOY (Mme. Arthur Craven), a member of the Paris Salon, was born in England and has lived and travelled in both Europe and South America. She now resides in New York.

Since his service with the Norton-Harjes Ambulance and the American Army in France, JOHN DOS PASSOS has lived abroad, chiefly in Spain. [Dos Passos (b. 1896) began as a novelist of the Left and has become today a dogmatist of the Right. After the great novel *U.S.A.*, he began to intrude private opinions, Malcolm Cowley says, "as if he thought they were more important than the characters, and finally it was the opinions we had to review." Forty years ago it was the ceaseless foe of the top dog, the inventor of new forms in fiction, that everyone admired in this gifted man.—Ed.]

[BABETTE DEUTSCH (b. 1895) has long helped to shape literary life in New York. Early acquaintance with Randolph Bourne led her to create a fictional portrait, in her novel *A Brittle Heaven* (1925), of the man under whose influence Thayer originally conceived *The Dial*.—Ed.]

JOHN EGLINTON was the editor of the Irish magazine, *Dana,* and more recently a regular contributor to the *Irish Statesman.* . . . There is a detailed study of Mr. Eglinton's work in *Appreciations and Depreciations* by Ernest Boyd, whom John Eglinton succeeds as *The Dial's* Dublin correspondent.

E. E. CUMMINGS, now living in New York, has not previously published in any of the regular periodicals. [Cummings (1894–1962), whom Pound once called *The Dial's* fair-haired boy, was represented here by drama, drawing, verse, and prose. Undergraduate friend of Thayer and Watson, he was indeed the one modern figure whom they sponsored without reserve.—Ed.]

EDMUND WILSON, JR., was graduated from Princeton in 1916. Since the war he has been an assistant editor of *Vanity Fair.* [Wilson (b. 1895), a student of virtually every trend of mind in twentieth century thought, has become a specialist in mediation between advanced ideas and general culture. He is surely the most cultivated and one of the most brilliant men of our age.—Ed.]

[DJUNA BARNES, a founder of the Theatre Guild, in 1936 published the novel *Nightwood* which was praised by the best critics everywhere. Thereafter it lost its audience and only now begins once again to engage serious attention. Her last major work, *The Antiphon* (1958), Edwin Muir called "one of the greatest things that have been written in our time."—Ed.]

RAFFAELLO PICCOLI . . . who this month begins his correspondence for *The Dial,* was born in Naples in 1886. He has the degree of Doctor of Letters from Padua, and has studied in Florence and at Oxford. In 1913 he lectured on Italian Literature at Cambridge University; in 1919 he returned to Italy to lecture on English letters at Pisa. From 1919 to 1921 he was exchange professor, at various American universities for the International Institute of Education.

LUIGI PIRANDELLO . . . studied at Palermo, and at Rome, and later went to complete his studies at the University of Bonn. Here he received his doctorate in letters and philosophy. He returned to Italy in 1901 and settled in Rome where, since 1907, he has been an instructor in rhetoric at the Istituto Superiore di Magistero Femminile. Although he is best known in America as a playwright, Signor Pirandello has also published several volumes of verse, stories, novels, and criticism. [Pirandello (1867–1936) was at this time engaged both in writing plays and in creating an Italian national theatre. The latter effort failed but his writing acquired ever-enlarged audiences and in 1934 he received the Nobel Prize—despite Mussolini's displeasure.—Ed.]

The work of THOMAS MANN, who is held to be the greatest of the German naturalistic novelists, is virtually unknown in English. His massive novel, *Buddenbrooks,* portrays the decay of a family through four generations and compares in method with *Madame Bovary*. He is, says the translator of [his fiction, Kenneth Burke], "a disciple of Schopenhauer and Nietzsche writing in the technique of Flaubert." [Mann (1875–1955) was represented in these pages more often and to better advantage than in any other English or American journal. His Nobel Prize, 1929, would have meant very little to English-speaking readers had they not come to know him in *The Dial*. Arriving in the United States during the Hitler era, he first lived in Princeton and lectured at the University and then, after adopting American citizenship, moved to the Pacific Palisades.

After World War II he lectured in both East and West Germany. He died in Switzerland.—Ed.]

GEORGE SANTAYANA . . . graduated from Harvard in 1886 and there taught the history of philosophy and kindred subjects from 1889 to 1911, since when he has lived abroad. His first published work was a volume of poems, in 1894; a discussion of aesthetic theory appeared under the title of *The Sense of Beauty* in 1896, and *The Life of Reason,* in five volumes, in 1905 and 1906. *Three Philosophical Poets, Winds of Doctrine,* and *Character and Opinion in the United States,* are among Mr Santayana's more recent works. [Santayana (1863–1951), born in Madrid, lived there until 1872 when he and his father came to Boston to join his mother, a woman not American by birth but reared in Virginia. This confusion of origins pervaded Santayana's life and in 1912 he went to Rome, where he lived until his death. His influence on *The Dial* is measureless: Thayer, his disciple, was an assistant at Harvard in the famous course that had resulted in *The Sense of Beauty.* Both Thayer and Watson were also at different times editors of *The Harvard Monthly,* the undergraduate magazine Santayana had helped to found. And it is thought that Thayer served as one of the models after whom Santayana shaped the life of his hero in *The Last Puritan.* Thayer printed great batches of his teacher's work in *The Dial,* most notably the *Dialogues in Limbo.*—Ed.]

MIGUEL DE UNAMUNO . . . has taught Greek, the language and the literature, at the University of Salamanca. Author of novels, poetry, and philosophical works, he is generally considered the leading man of letters in Spain. *The Tragic Sense of Life in Men and Peoples* is the only one of his books that has been translated in English. [Unamuno (1864–1936), very little known in the United States during the early 20's, wrote philosophy and fiction based in paradox and himself lived a life of paradox. Professor and Rector at the University of Salamanca, he was forced to resign these posts and forced into exile. In 1936 Unamuno, a major public figure in Spain, a man who had very early fought for land reform, gave his support to Franco. Then shortly before his death he renounced fascism. Today these events are forgotten and it is as a philosopher of the tragic vision, an early student of Kierkegaard, and a fictionist that he is remembered.—Ed.]

WILLIAM CARLOS WILLIAMS is a physician, aged thirty-six, a resident of Rutherford, New Jersey. His father was a British subject; his mother was

born in the French West Indies of French and Spanish stock. As a follower of the new school of poetry, he has published his work in various
current magazines. He is the author of *Al Que Quiere* (*Four Seas*), one
of the most remarkable books of poetry of the last few years. [Williams
(1883–1963) was unique among the jobless wandering minstrels of the
1920's: he stayed put in Rutherford and practiced medicine. "Too much
dynamite inside me to want to go . . . about wasting time traveling.
What the hell is there to see, anyway, compared with what's on the inside?" A lyric and epic poet, he long conducted experiments with what
he called the American Idiom—experiments which received special notice only when the Beat writers proclaimed his authority among them.
Kenneth Burke, in *The New York Review of Books* (Summer, 1963),
remarks in eulogy: "Williams' lyric utterance is essentially a flash of
drama, a fragment of narrative, a bit of personal history mirrored as well
in talk of a thing as in talk of a person." Treating things and persons,
Burke says, the lifelong aim of Williams' lyricism was "contact."—Ed.]

ALEXANDER ELIASBERG was born in Minsk, Russia, in 1878, and studied
there and in the Department of Physics and Mathematics of the Moscow
University. He has translated numerous works on Russian art and literature into German. [Eliasberg, who published a well-known book on
Russian church architecture, died in 1924.—Ed.]

LOLA RIDGE was born in Dublin, Ireland, but spent her childhood in Sydney, Australia, and in New Zealand. . . . She is the author of two books
of verse, *The Ghetto and Other Poems,* published in 1918, and *Sun-Up
and Other Poems,* published in 1920. She was an associate editor of *Others,*
American editor of *Broom,* and has contributed prose and verse to various modern magazines. [Miss Ridge (1883–1941), despite the life of a
semi-invalid, was a poet and painter, selfless in behalf of causes in
art.—Ed.]

JOSÉ ORTEGA Y GASSET occupies the Chair of Metaphysics at the University of Madrid. He is the director of *La Revista de Occidente,* Spain's
leading cultural magazine. His work is versatile; it includes a study of
the failure of Spanish national life, which he calls *Espana Invertebrada,*
aesthetic criticism of Spanish art and literature, which he has collected
under the titles *Meditaciones del Quijote,* and *Personas Obras Cosas,*
and cultural and literary studies of the European field in general, in-

cluded under the titles *El Espectador* and *El Tempa de Nuestro Tiempo.* [Ortega (1883–1955), the best known and most influential modern Spanish writer, was introduced in America by *The Dial.* And he in turn sought permission to reprint Spanish translations of *The Dial*'s material. Not until he published *Revolt of the Masses* (1930, English translation 1932) did he acquire international fame.—Ed.]

[PADRAIC COLUM (b. 1881) arrived in the United States in 1914 after having participated as a dramatist in the Celtic Revival. Interest in Hawaiian materials occurred as a result of an invitation from the Hawaiian legislature to survey Polynesian folklore. And the invitation was issued to Colum because of stories written after his arrival here, children's stories based on Irish legend. The Hawaiian items are of course timely today but Colum's first volume treating this material, *The Bright Islands,* appeared in 1925. In 1952 he received the Award of the American Academy of Poets, and in 1953, the Gregory Medal of the Irish Academy of Letters.—Ed.]

GLENWAY WESCOTT was born within the present century in the hill-marsh country near Kewaskum, Wisconsin. He has lived in New Mexico and is now in England. *One minute book of lyrics* constitutes his previous publication. [Wescott (b. 1901) made a quick reputation with *The Grandmothers* in 1927, while he lived abroad. Returning to the United States in 1939, he wrote his second important book, *Apartment in Athens,* which portrayed the rise of fascism in Europe. In 1952, summarizing his modest accomplishment, he decided that he should call himself a man of letters not a novelist. Ten years later his collection of essays seemed to justify this decision.—Ed.]

[CLIVE BELL (b. 1881) married Virginia Woolf's sister Vanessa Stephen and joined the distinguished Bloomsbury Group in London. From 1914 until 1934 he published works of art history and criticism which established him, along with his mentor Roger Fry, as a central figure in matters of taste. Since that time Bell has written very little.—Ed.]

GENEVIEVE TAGGARD was born in Waitsburg, Washington, in 1894. When she was two years old, she was taken to the Hawaiian Islands, where she lived until the age of eighteen. In 1919 she graduated from the University of California. She is the author of *For Eager Lovers* and of

Hawaiian Hilltop. [Miss Taggard (d. 1948) is little-read today but in the 20's and 30's she was a lyric poet of considerable note. A substantial number of her poems were set to music by Aaron Copland and Roy Harris.—Ed.]

FEODOR DOSTOEVSKY was a political exile in Siberia during the years 1849–1855. Originally part of his reminiscences of those years, *A Christmas Story,* which is published in this issue of *The Dial,* was to have been included in his *House of the Dead,* but was excised by the Russian Censor. The story then came into the possession of [C. M. Grand's] family, and appears now for the first time.

[GILBERT SELDES (b. 1893), an early student of popular culture, resigned his duties as managing editor of *The Dial* and began the work which resulted in his famed book, *The Seven Lively Arts* (1924). From that time until now he has devoted his life to opening new ground, and this effort continues today at the University of Pennsylvania where he is Director of the new School of Communications.—Ed.]

[MALCOLM COWLEY (b. 1898), a noted editor, critic, historian of literary affairs, began his career as a serious and respected poet. In *The Dial* he is responsible for large numbers of expert short reviews in the section called "Briefer Mention."—Ed.]

ARCHIBALD MACLEISH was graduated from Yale in 1915, and later from The Harvard Law School. A contributor to various magazines among which are *The Atlantic Monthly, The Yale Review,* and *The New Republic,* he is the author of a book of poems, entitled *The Happy Marriage,* which appeared in 1924, and of *The Pot of Earth,* which appeared in 1925. [MacLeish (b. 1892), according to his own comment, began writing poetry under the influence of Pound and Eliot and Miss Moore. As a poet, as "an expatriate in the Twenties, a political liberal rediscovering America in the Thirties, a government official in the Forties, a college professor in the Fifties," MacLeish's public life has mirrored general traits among American intellectuals in our time.—Ed.]

YVOR WINTERS is a native of Chicago, and has spent most of his early years in the foothills of southern California and in Seattle. For the last four years he has been living in New Mexico, where he is teaching school in a mining camp. [Winters (b. 1900), now at the end of a vigorous career, was for thirty years a leading editor, critic, poet, teacher. Chiefly because of his presence, Stanford has long served as a main source of new ideas and new writing.—Ed.]

BERTRAND RUSSELL . . . writes from London: "Your letter of October 6 [1921] reached me in Peking, and before I had time to answer it I began to die. I have now finished with this occupation, although the Japanese journalists first announced my death and then tried to make the announcement true by mobbing me as I passed through Japan when I was convalescent." [The Third Earl Russell, Viscount Amberly (b. 1872), Nobel Laureate, is today a leader of pacifist movements in England. Philosopher, mathematician, social critic and historian, fictionist, Russell recently celebrated his ninetieth birthday.—Ed.]

SEÁN O'FAOLÁIN was born in Cork, Ireland, in 1900. His work has been for the most part written in Irish, *Under the Roof*, being a translation by him of his Irish version. He has contributed to *The Irish Tribune*, Cork, and to *The Irish Statesman*, Dublin. A student of English and of Irish mediaeval literature, he will this autumn come to America to continue his studies. [Charter member of the Irish Academy of Letters, short-story writer par excellence, O'Faoláin is best known today as an unsympathetic critic of Ireland and its people.—Ed.]

I. A. RICHARDS is a Fellow of Magdalene College, Cambridge, and a lecturer in English at Cambridge, his special subject being modern fiction and poetry. He is the author of *Principles of Literary Criticism* published in 1925, and is with Mr C. K. Ogden, joint author of *The Meaning of Meaning*. He has contributed to *The New Criterion*, to *The Forum*, and to other journals in England and America. [Richards (b. 1893) has been for many years at Harvard where, in addition to his work as a psychologist of literature, he remains an active student of and propagandist for Basic English. Having acquired, too, some note as a poet, he now possesses new credentials as a critic: no longer can his views be dismissed, as Eliot once maintained, because he is a theorist unskilled in the art.—Ed.]

HART CRANE is a young man engaged in business in Cleveland, Ohio. Poems of his have appeared in *The Little Review* and various magazines of verse. [Crane (1883–1932) was ambitious to embody in epic poetry the experience of industrial America. A tormented man, Crane now and then managed to bring his ambitions and his genius into harmony. His relations with *The Dial,* however, and with Miss Moore, were discordant even though the journal published much of his best verse.—Ed.]

[ROBERT HILLYER (1895–1961), a "conservative and religious poet in a radical and blasphemous age," for many years Boylston Professor at Harvard, received the Pulitzer Prize in 1934. In recent years his chief fame resulted from an essay in the *Saturday Review,* 1948, which began the controversy over Ezra Pound's receipt of the Bollingen Prize for *The Pisan Cantos.*—Ed.]

[WILLIAM BUTLER YEATS (1865–1939) was a figure of glamor and mystery in his own day and is now generally regarded as the most distinguished modern poet. *The Dial's* happiest coup, at a time when Yeats had only a small national following, was its acquisition of exclusive magazine rights to his poetry in America.—Ed.]

RAYMOND MORTIMER is a young English writer who has not previously published in America. [Mortimer, writer and critic, appears now in the London *Sunday Times.*—Ed.]

LOUIS ZUKOFSKY was born in 1904, in New York City where he is now living. He has studied at Columbia University from which he received the degree of Master of Arts in 1924. He has contributed to *Poetry, The Forum,* Ezra Pound's *Exile,* and to other magazines.

PAUL CLAUDEL (His Excellency the French Ambassador to Washington) . . . is a member of the Institute of France, and has been an official representative of his country at Pekin, Tien-Tsin, Prague, Frankfort, Hamburg, Rio Janeiro, Copenhagen, and Tokio. He has given to literature many wise and highly imaginative writings—poems, essays, plays, and translations. [Claudel's life (1868–1955) was distinguished less by diplomacy or poetry than by his passion for his Church. Religion absorbed his mind and led to a regular correspondence, during twenty-five years, with André Gide. Their letters were published in a volume which somehow acquired greater note than any of Claudel's earlier work.—Ed.]

[ALBERT HALPER (b. 1904) in 1928 came from Chicago to New York, an unpublished writer. Printing his fiction (about people who "earn their daily bread in factories, stores and offices"), *The Dial* thus supported a writer and a subject that were to assume major importance in the 30's.— Ed.]

STANLEY J. KUNITZ was born in 1905 in Worcester, Massachusetts. After undergraduate and graduate work at Harvard University, he came to New York where he now lives. He received while at Harvard the Lloyd McKim Garrison Prize; he has done newspaper work and has contributed verse and criticism to *The Nation, The Saturday Review of Literature,* and to *The New York Herald-Tribune.* [Kunitz, who received his first serious attention in *The Dial,* was awarded the Pulitzer Prize in 1959. During the last thirty years, however, he has become best known as a teacher, anthologist, bibliographer, and editor.—Ed.]

[CONRAD AIKEN (b. 1889), another member of that extraordinary class at Harvard (John Reed, Walter Lippmann, Robert Benchley, Heywood Broun, T. S. Eliot), was the first of Eliot's friends to enlist himself in Eliot's causes. But another friendship with George B. Wilbur, editor of *The American Imago,* led very early to psychoanalysis. This system of thought became a chief source of inspiration for Aiken's remarkable fiction, criticism, and verse. Recently there has been a revival of critical interest.—Ed.]